Oliver Goldsmith, Christopher Smart, Samuel Johnson

The World Displayed

A curious collection of voyages and travels - Vol. 6

Oliver Goldsmith, Christopher Smart, Samuel Johnson

The World Displayed
A curious collection of voyages and travels - Vol. 6

ISBN/EAN: 9783337348106

Printed in Europe, USA, Canada, Australia, Japan

Cover: Foto ©Andreas Hilbeck / pixelio.de

More available books at **www.hansebooks.com**

The WORLD DISPLAYED;

OR, A

Curious Collection

OF

Voyages AND Travels.

Selected and compiled from the

WRITERS of all NATIONS:

BY

Smart, Goldsmith, & Johnson.

FIRST AMERICAN EDITION,

Corrected & Enlarged.

IN EIGHT VOLUMES.

VOL VI

Philadelphia.

Publish'd by Dobelbower, Key, and Simplon. 1796.

W. Harrison fen. Sculps.

THE

TRAVELS

OF

Sir JOHN CHARDIN,

THROUGH

MINGRELIA AND *GEORGIA* INTO *PERSIA.*

Containing an account of his setting out from Paris in the service of the French king; a description of the different places he touched at; of the manners, customs, and religion of the inhabitants; together with an account of the various adventures that took place till his return to Europe.

I LEFT Paris on the 17th of August 1671, to return to Persia, where the late king had by letters patent made me his merchant, and ordered me to procure many jewels of value, his majesty having drawn with his own hand, the models by which he would have them set. Mr. Raisin, a gentleman of great integrity, who had been my companion in my former travels, engaged again in this trade. We spent fourteen months in the richest countries of Europe, in search of the largest stones, and the finest wrought corals. We caused to be made the richest goldsmith's work, watches and curious clocks, and besides, took with us twelve thousand ducats in gold.

We travelled by the way of Milan, Venice and Florence, and arriving at Leghorn, embarked in a ship under a Dutch convoy; and sailed to Smyrna,

which we reached on the fecond of March 1672, and
twelve days after arrived at Conftantinople.   In
this city we remained four months ; but in the
mean while there happening a quarrel between the
grand vizier and the French ambaffador, a report
was fpread, that the former intended to arreft, not
only the ambaffador, but all of the French nation
in that city, when being afraid that our goods,
which were very rich, would be feized, we endeavoured by all poffible means to leave Conftantinople,
and to proceed on our journey to Perfia.   The
caravans in thofe hot months did not travel ; but
the Porte being about to fend a new commander with
foldiers, and the annual fupply of money to the
fort of Azoph on the lake Mœotis, we obtained a
paffage in a Turkifh faick belonging to the fleet,
and on the 27th of July embarked at a port in the
Thracian Bofphorus.

This ftreight which is about fifteen miles in length,
and in moft parts about two in breadth, though in
others it is lefs, is fo called, from its being fuppofed
that an ox may fwim over it.   It is certainly one of
the moft delightful channels in the world ; for the
rifing fhores are covered with pleafure-houfes, gardens, woods, parks, and wilderneffes, watered with
a multitude of fprings and fountains. In fair weather
the paffage through it is rendered exceeding diverting, from the great number of barks that are continually failing backwards and forwards ; and the
profpect of Conftantinople from the top of it at
about two miles diftance, is more charming than
can be imagined.   There are four caftles well fortified with great guns, two of them oppofite each other,
eight miles from the Black Sea, and two at the
mouth of the channel.

On the third of Auguft in the morning, we arrived
at Caffa, a port in the Tauricus Cherfonefus, a
peninfula fo called, from its being firft inhabited by
the Scythians of Mount Taurus.   It is thirty-five

leagues from north to fouth, and 55 from eaft to welt. But the ifthmus that joins it to the continent is not above a league in breadth. It is inhabited by the Crim Tartars, who dwell in cities and towns, while their neighbours the Nogays and Calmucs, dwell in tents, as the reft do on the continent.

Caffa is a large town in Crim Tartary, built at the bottom of a hill, on the bank of the fea, extending in length nearly from north to fouth. It is furrounded with ftrong walls, and has a caftle at each of the two ends, which advance into the fea, whence the town on being viewed from a veffel in the harbour, appears to built in the form of an half-moon. The caftie to the fouth is on an eminence, which commands all the parts about it. it is very large, and the refidence of the baffa : the other is fmaller, but is well provided with artillery. The houfes in the town are computed at about 4000, of which about 3200 belong to the Turks and Tartars, and the reft to the Greeks and Armenians : they are fmall, and built of earth, as are alfo the mofques, bazars, and bath ; for it has not any edifice of ftone, if we except eight ancient ruinous churches erected by the Genoefe: the foil about it is dry and fandy, bearing little fruit, and the water is bad ; but the air is very pure and wholefome. All provifions are very cheap and good, mutton being not above a farthing a pound, and other things in proportion. There is a great trade carried on here in falt-fifh and caviare, which being taken out of the lake Mœotis, at twenty fix miles diftance, in great quantities, are tranfported into Europe. The inhabitants alfo furnifh Conftantinople and feveral other places, with corn, butter, and falt; for the Caffa butter is the beft in all Turky.

On the 30th of Auguft we left Caffa, in a fhip bound for Mingrelia, and the next day arrived at Donflow, or the falt-pits, which are fituated on the fhore fifty miles from Caffa. Here are great quanti-

ties of falt made by letting in the fea water, and
fuffering it to congeal by the heat of the fun. The
people fay, that two hundred veffels are annually
laden with this falt, paying only two fhillings a day
to thofe who load it. About a mile from the fhore
is a village of the Tartars, where there is not above
ten or twelve houfes with a little mofque, and round
about is a great number of tents with feveral waggons clofe covered, which ferve them inftead of
houfes. Some of thefe tents are handfome enough,
being made of round poles with others croffing
them, covered on the outfide with large felts drawn
tight over them. They have a door of the fame,
and above a little window, to admit the light, and
let out the fmoke. The infide is hung with tapeftry,
and the floor alfo covered with it. Every family
has not only one of thefe tents, but two others,
covered with a large coarfe woollen cloth, one for
the fervants and kitchen, in which is a pit five
feet deep to make a fire in for dreffing their meat,
the other tent is for their horfes and cattle. Their
corn and forage they ftore in magazines under
ground, which they cover fo exactly that none can
find them but themfelves. They can remove their
tents with little trouble, and in a very fhort time ;
on which occafion they carry them away in carts
drawn by horfes and oxen, of which they breed a
great number : they profefs the Mahometan religion,
but intermix it with ridiculous opinions of divination.

   From Donflow we failed along the channel to
Cape Cuodos, the Corocondama of Ptolemy, where
the coafts that bound the lake Mœotis, which are
very mountainous, are feen at thirty miles diftance.
From Caffa to the ftreights that open into this lake
is 120 miles. The country on both fides is fubject
to the Turks, and thinly inhabited by the Tartars,
almoft all the coaft being defert. From the ftreight
to Mingrelia is reckoned 600 miles along the fhore,
which confifts of pleafant woods, thinly inhabited

by the Circaffian Tartars, who are neither fubject nor tributary to the Porte. The veffels that come from Conftantinople to Mingrelia trade with this people, but do it with their arms in their hands, and by hoftages; for they are remarkable for their infidelity and perfidioufnefs, and feldom fail to fteal wherever they find an opportunity. The trade with them is carried on by exchange; the Circaffians bringing down flaves of all ages and fexes, honey, wax, leather, jackals, and the fkins of fome beafts, for fuch commodities as they want.

Circaffia is a pleafant and fertile country that produces great plenty of all forts of fruit without labour, as apples, pears, cherries, and walnuts; but the chief wealth of the inhabitants confifts in cattle, as fheep, whofe wool is as fine as that of Spain, deer, goats, and well fhaped horfes, fo fwift and ftrong, that they will tire wild beafts, and overtake them in the chafe. They fow no grain but millet for their bread, and barley for their horfes, and their women till and manure the ground. Their drink is water and boza, which is a liquor made of millet, as intoxicating as wine. They l.ve in wooden huts, and go almoft naked : their beds are made of fheep-fkins fewed together, and ftuffed with millet leaves beaten in the thrafhing as fmall as oat chaff. They were formerly Chriftians; but now of no religion, except obferving fome fuperftitious ceremonies borrowed from the Chriftians and Mahometans; and they are all fworn enemies to thofe who live in the provinces round about them.

The Abcas border upon the Circaffians, and poffefs about a hundred miles on the coaft between Mingrelia and Circaffia. They are not fo favage as the Circaffians; but are as much inclined to robbery; fo that the merchants are obliged to take the fame precautions in trading with them. They, like their neighbours, are in want of all the conveniences of life, and have nothing to exchange for them but human creatures, furs, the ſkins of deers and tygers, box-wood, wax and honey.

On the 10th of September we arrived at Iſgaour a port in Mingrelia, where all the veſſels lie that trade thither. It is a deſert place without any houſes; the traders therefore build themſelves huts and booths of boughs for the time of their ſtay, which is uſually as long as they find themſelves ſafe from the Abcas.

Colchis or Mingrelia, is ſituated at the end of the Black Sea. It is bounded on the eaſt by the little kingdom of Imeretta, on the ſouth by the Black Sea, and on the north by Mount Caucaſus. The rivers Codours and Rione part it, the firſt from Abcas, and the other from Imeretta. Its length is about 110 miles, and its breadth ſixty. It was once fortified againſt the Abcas by a wall of ſixty miles in length, which has been long ſince demoliſhed.

The inhabitants of Caucaſus who border upon Colchis are the Alanas, Suanes, Gigues, Caracioles or Cara-cherks, that is, black Circaſſians, ſo called by the Turks, not from their complexion, for they are eſteemed the faireſt people upon earth : but from their country, which is always darkened with clouds and fogs. They were anciently Chriſtians, but now live by robbery and rapine, and profeſs no religion, having little beſides ſpeech that can intitle them to humanity. They are very tall and portly, and their very looks and ſpeech ſhew their ſavage diſpoſitions, they being the moſt reſolute aſſaſſins, and daring robbers in the world.

The ancient kingdom of Colchis was much larger than Mingrelia is at preſent, it extending on one ſide to the lake Mœotis, and to Iberia on the other. Its capital city named Colchos, was at the mouth of the Phaſis, a river to the weſt. The country is uneven, full of hills and mountains, valleys and plains : it is almoſt covered with woods, except the manured lands which are but few, and thoſe preſerved by grubbing up the roots that are continually fpreading into them. The air is temperate with refpect to heat and cold, but as it rains almoft continually, the wetnefs and warmth of the climate breed in fummer the peftilence, and feveral other difeafes It abounds with rivers which defcend from Mount Caucafus, and fall into the Black Sea. The foil is very bad, and produces little corn or pulfe, and the fruits are without tafte and unwholefome, except their vines, which thrive well, and produce moft excellent wine. Did the inhabitants know how to prepare it in a proper manner, it would be the beft wine in the world. The vines encompafs the trunks of the trees, and rife to their very tops. In feed-time the earth is fo moift, that they fow their wheat and barley without plowing ; for they fay, that fhould they plow it, the land would be fo foft as not to be able to fupport the ftalk. For their other corn they plow their land with plough-fhares of wood, which in this moift foil, make as good furrows as iron. Their common grain is gomm, which is as fmall as coriander feed, and refembles millet. Of this they make a pafte, which they ufe for bread, and prefer it to wheat: this is not to be wondered at, for it is very agreeable to the palate, and conducive to health, it being cooling and laxative. They have alfo great plenty of millet, fome rice, with wheat and barley, which are very fcarce. The people of quality eat wheaten bread as a rarity, but the meaner fort feldom or never tafte it.

The ordinary food of the country is beef and pork, of which laft they have great plenty and the beft in the world. They have alfo goats flefh, but it is lean and ill tafted. Their venifon is the hart, ftag, and fallow deer. They have alfo wild boars and hares, all which are excellent food. They have partridges, pheafants, and quails in abundance, with fome river fowl, and wild pigeons, which are good meat, and as big as crammed chickens; thefe pigeons they take in nets, and thus catch great numbers in summer.

Their nobility spend their whole time in the field, using hobbies, goshawks, &c. for their sports, to catch water fowl and pheasants ; but the pastime in which they most delight is flying the falcon at the heron, which they catch only for the sake of the tuft upon his crown, in order to put it upon their bonnets, for they let him go again, when they have cut it off, that it may grow up afresh.

Mount Caucasus produces a great number of wild beasts, as lions, tygers, leopards, jackals and wolves ; which last make great havock among their cattle and horses, and frequently disturb the inhabitants in their houses with their dreadful howlings. They have great numbers of very good horses, almost every man keeping several of them ; for they cost little or nothing, as they neither shoe them nor feed them with corn. They have no cities nor towns, except two by the sea side ; but their houses are so scattered up the country, that you can hardly travel a mile, without seeing three or four of them. There are nine or ten castles in the country, the chief of which where the prince keeps his court, is called Rues This castle has a stone wall; but it is so small, and so ill built that it might be battered down by the smallest piece of artillery ; it has, however, some cannon, which the other castles have not. They are made in the following manner : in the midst of a thick wood the people build a stone tower thirty or forty feet high, capable of containing fifty or sixty persons. This tower is the place of strength, where they shut up all the riches of the lord, and of those who put themselves under his protection. Near this tower are five or six others of wood, which serve for magazines of provisions, and as places of retreat for their wives and children, in case of an attack. There are also several huts made of wood, others of branches of trees, and others of canes and reeds.

The area in which they are inclofed is furrounded by a clofe hedge, and by a wood which is every where fo thick, that it is impoffible to find thefe retreats but by the way cut to them, which is ftopped up by trees, whenever they apprehend the approach of an enemy.

The houfes of the Mingrelians are built with timber, which they have in great plenty ; but the poorer fort never raife them above one ftory, nor the rich above two. The lower rooms are always furnifhed with beds and couches, to lie down or fit upon, on account of the moifture of the earth ; but they are inconvenient, from their having neither windows nor chimnies, and their having but one room for the whole family, fo that they all lie together, and at night have alfo their cattle with them.

The men are well fhaped, and the women fo handfome, that they feem born to infpire love ; yet they all paint their faces, and particularly their eyebrows. They drefs themfelves in as ornamental a manner as they can, wearing a Perfian habit, and curling the hair. They are witty, civil, and full of compliments ; but, on the other hand, are proud, deceitful, cruel and libidinous. The men have alfo many mifcheivous qualities ; but that which they moft practife is theft, and this they make their employment and glory. They juftify the lawfulnefs of having many wives, by faying that they bring them many children, which they can fell for ready money, or exchange for neceffary conveniences ; yet when they have not the means of fupporting them, they hold it a piece of charity to murder new-born infants, and fuch perfons as are fick and paft recovery, becaufe by this means they free them from mifery. Adultery and inceft is fcarce confidered as crimes in Mingrelia : when a man catches another enjoying the embraces of his wife, he has a right to oblige

him to pay a hog; he feldom takes any other method
of revenge, and they all three commonly fit down
to feaft upon it. It is common for them to have two
or three wives at a time.

As the gentlemen have full power over the lives
and eftates of their tenants, they fell or difpofe of
their wives and children as they think fit; befides
every hufbandman is bound to furnifh his lord with
as much corn, wine, cattle and other provifions as
is in his power. Thus his riches confift in the
number of his peafants. The lords decides the
quarrels of their vaffals; but when they themfelves
are at variance, they determine the difpute by arms,
and therefore all go armed with a lance, bow and
fword.

Their drefs is very fingular. All the men, except
the ecclefiaftics, fuffer but little of their beard to
grow. They fhave the top of the head, leaving only
a little hair over the forehead, and down to their
ears; and even that is clipped fhort. They wear a
bonnet of fine felt, which in winter is lined with
fur; but they are in general fo poor, that to prevent its being fpoiled, they put it in their pocket
when it rains, and go barcheaded   Thofe in mean
circumftances go almoft naked, and have in general
only a covering of a triangular form, at one end of
which is a hole, through which they put the head;
this covering, which is of ftrong felt, they turn to
the fide whence comes the wind or the rain. Over
their bodies they wear fhirts which reach to their
knees, and tuck into a ftreight pair of breeches;
but they never have above one fhirt and one pair of
breeches, which laft them a year, and in all that
time they never wafh the fhirt above thrice; however
once or twice a week they fhake it for a certain
purpofe over the fire. Their fhoes, or rather fandals,
are made of the raw fkin of a buffalo untanned,
tied round the foot, and faftened with thongs of
the fame fkins; but when the fnow lies thick on

the earth, they wear a kind of fnow-fhoes, which fpreading much farther than the feet, prevent their finking into it.

The whole family, both males and females, eat together without diftinction : The king with all his train to his very grooms, and the queen with her maids and fervants. In fair weather they dine in open court, and if it be cold, make a large fire, for wood cofts them nothing. Upon working days the fervants have nothing but gomm, and the mafters pulfe, dried fifh, or flefh; but on holydays, or when they make entertainments, if they have no venifon they kill an ox, a cow, or a hog. Both the men and women are very great drinkers, and at their feafts, make their friends drink as much as they can. Their wine is drank unmixed, and beginning with pints they proceed to much greater quantities. The men at their merry meetings difcourfe about their wars and robberies, and the women tell ob- fcene tales of their amours.

Mingrelia is but thinly peopled, which is occafion- ed by their wars, and the vaft numbers fold by the nobility to the Perfians and the Turks. All their trade is carried on by the way of barter ; for their money has no fettled value. The current fpecie are piaftres, Dutch crowns, and abaflis, which are made in Georgia, and bear the Perfian ftamp. The reve- nues of the prince of Mingrelia do not exceed 20,000 crowns, which are raifed by cuftoms on goods export- ed and imported, by felling of flaves, and by im- pofitions and fines. But this he lays up, for his flaves ferve him for nothing, and his crown lands furnifh his court with more provifions than he can fpend. He is not able to raife above 4000 men fit to bear arms, and thefe are moftly cavalry, for he has not above three hundred foot. Thefe foldiers are not diftributed into regiments, or companies. Each lord and each gentleman leads his men to battle without order, and without officers ; they follow him as well in flying, as in charging the enemy. The prince's court upon folemn feftivals confifts of two hundred gentlemen, but upon other days of about 120.

The religion of the Mingrelians or Colchians was formerly the fame with the Greeks, they being converted, according to ecclefiaftical hiftorians, by a flave in the reign of Confiantine the Great. But the Mingrelians fay, that St. Andrew. preached among them in a place called Pigaitas, where a church now ftands,. whither the catholicos, or chief bifhop, goes once in his lifetime to make the holy oil ; but yet I was unable to find a Mingrelian who knew what is meant by religion, by fin, the facrament or divine worfhip : for they are now fallen into fuch a profound abyfs of ignorance, that they look upon the life eternal, the day of judgment, and the refurrection of the dead, as mere fables : their clergy perform fcarcely any ecclefiaftical duties ; for there is hardly one of them that can either write or read, and they have in a manner loft the method of performing divine worfhip. They make a public profeffion of fortelling things to come, and perfuade the people to believe that future events are revealed in their books. The Mingrelians are indeed fo infatuated with this opinion, that as foon as any one is fick, they call in the prieft not to pray for the patient; they have not the leaft notion of that, but for him to look in his book, to fee whether the fick will die of that difeafe, and for him to declare all its confequences. The prieft then opens the book, which he has brought with him, and having with great attention turned over all the leaves, pronounces with the voice of an oracle, that the cati, for thus they call their images, is enraged againft him, and has ftruck him with a difeafe ; that he will be appeafed by a prefent ; but if a good one is not immediately given the patient will die. This prefent confifts in a goat, a hog, a cow, or the like, which the poor man, under the apprehenfion of death, immediately gives the prieft, to offer to the image.

The catholicos of Mingrelia, is not only the head of all the clergy of that country, but alfo of Abca, Guriel, Imeretta, and Mount Caucalus; yet the prince appoints or depofes him at his pleafure. He has a very great revenue; for he has 400 vaffals under him, who furnifh his houfe not only with the neceffaries, but with many of the fuperfluities of life. He fells their children to the Turks, and when he vifits the dioceffes under his jurifdiction, it is not to reform the clergy or to inftruct the people, but to fpoil them of their goods, and rake together great fums. He will not confecrate a bifhop for lefs than 600 crowns, nor fay a mafs for the dead under 800; nor any other mafs under 100. His fanctity confifts in abftinence from flefh and wine in lent, and in long prayers day and night; but he is fo ignorant, that he can hardly read his breviary and miffal. He has fix bifhops under him, who generally take no care of the fouls of the people, nor ever vifit their churches and dioceffes; but fuffer the priefts to live in ignorance, and the people to commit the groffeft crimes. They are chiefly employed in feafting and banquetting, and are drunk almoft every day. They are rich, but their principal revenues arife from the oppreffion of their vaffals, and their felling their wives and children. They, however, like the Greek bifhops, abftain from flefh: for they place the whole Chriftian religion in fafting, and think that almoft the only duty they are obliged to perform. Their cathedral is pretty neatly kept, and well adorned with images, which they embellifh with gold and jewels, believing that by this means they fatisfy the divine juftice, and atone for their fins. They are clothed in fcarlet and velvet, and alfo differ from the feculars in wearing their beards long, and their bonnets black, high, and round.

The Mingrelian priefts are very numerous, but are a miferable fort of creatures. They till their own grounds, and thofe of their lords, and are no lefs flaves than the feculars, nor have they any refpect fhewn them, except when they blefs the food at meals, or fay mafs. Their parifh churches have no bells, inftead of which they call the people to. gether by knocking with a great ftick upon a board ; they are kept as nafty as ftables, and the images are foul, broken, and covered with duft ; yet the worfhip they pay to them is in the higheft degree idolatrous, for they do not pay them a relative adoration, but pay their devotions to the material fubftance. They worfhip fuch moft as are fineft adorned, or famed for their cruelty, and if they fwear by any of thefe, they will never break the oath. St. Giobas is one of the moft formidable images, and him they will not approach nearer than where they can juft fee him, and leave their prefents at that diftance ; for they pretend that he kills all who approach him.

They have no value for any of the Romifh Saints except St. George, to whom they pay the higheft reverence, as do the Georgians. Their mafs is after the Greek manner. Their cup or chalice is a goblet of wood ; the cover is of the fame materials, and their patten is a wooden difh. They never fay mafs in lent, but on Saturdays and Sundays ; for they hold that the communion fpoils their fafting. They confecrate either leven or unlevened bread, without any difference, and mix no water with the wine, except it is very ftrong. They anoint the foreheads of their children as foon as they are born with their holy oil, and baptize them by immerfion ; but this is never performed till they are able to make a feaft for the prieft, godfathers and guefts. Their marriages are a contract by way of bargain and fale ; for the parents agree upon the price with the perfon who defires her ; and here the price of a woman who has been divorced is the loweft ; for a widow more is demanded ; but for a maid moſt of all. When the bargain is once made, the young man may keep company with the woman till the money is paid, and it is no ſcandal if ſhe is with child by him. If any one has married a barren woman, or one of an ill diſpoſition, they hold it not only lawful but requiſite to divorce her. They obſerve almoſt the ſame faſts as the Greeks, for they keep the four great lents : the firſt beſore Eaſter, which is 48 days ; that before Chriſtmas, which is 40 days ; St. Peter's faſt, which is near a month, and the laſt obſerved by the eaſtern Chriſtians in honour of the Virgin Mary, which continues 15 days. They make the ſign of the croſs when they drink wine and eat pork ; but not as any mark of Chriſtianity. Their prayers are all addreſſed to their idols for their temporal benefits, as their own proſperity, and the ruin of their enemies. They offer ſacrifices, obſerve no Sabbath, and abſtain from work only at the feſtivals of Chriſtmas and Eaſter, which they celebrate no otherwiſe than by eating and drinking in their houſes to exceſs. Their great feſtivals are when the image of a ſaint is carried through their country, upon which occaſion they put on their beſt clothes, make a great feaſt, and provide a preſent for their idol.

In mourning for the dead, the women gnaſh their teeth, rend their garments, tear their hair and fleſh, beat their breaſts, and make dreadful lamentations. The men tear their clothes, ſhave their heads and faces, and likewiſe beat their breaſts. The mourning laſts 40 days, on the ten firſt of which it is accompanied with the moſt extravagant ſigns of grief; which then gradually diminiſhes till the fortieth, when the body is interred. A feaſt is then made for all the relations and friends, and for all who come to weep. The biſhop ſays maſs, and afterwards lays claim to every thing that belonged to the deceaſed, his horſes, clothes, arms, money, if he had any, and every thing of the ſame kind. For death is the ruin of the families of the Mingrelians. But when a bifhop dies, the prince fays the mafs for the dead on the fortieth day of mourning, and takes all his moveable goods.

It muft not be omitted that thefe people have certain monks of the order of St. Bafil, who wear the habit, and live after the manner of the Greek monks. They have black bonnets, eat no flelh, and fuffer their hair to grow, but mind nothing of religion, except obferving their fafts with great exactnefs. They have alfo nuns of the fame order, who obferve their fafts, and wear a black veil, but they have no nunneries, nor are under any vows, but quit the habit when ever they pleafe.

The neighbouring nations live and act in almoft all refpects after the fame manner, only thofe who live near Perfia and Turky are more civilized.

On the confines of Mingrelia lie the principality of Guriel and the kingdom of Imeretta, the former is very fmall, it bordering upon Imeretta on the north, upon mount Caucafus on the eaft, upon Mingrelia on the weft, and upon the Black Sea on the fouth. It lies along the fea fhore from the river Rione to the caftle Gonie, which is held by the Turks. The inhabitants are of the fame difpofition and irregularity of manners as the Mingrelians, they having the fame inclinations to lewdnefs, robbery and murder.

The kingdom of Imeretta, the Iberia of the ancients, is fomething bigger than the country of Guriel, and is encompaffed by mount Caucafus, Mingrelia, the Black Sea, the principality of Guriel, and part of Georgia. It is 26 miles long, and 60 in breadth; it is full of woods and mountains like Mingrelia, but the valleys are more pleafant, and the plains more fertile, they producing corn, pulfe, cattle, and a variety of herbs. There are fome iron mines in the country, and fome money current among the people, which is coined in the kingdom. They have alfo feveral towns ; but their manners and cuftoms differ but little from the Mingrelians. The king has three good caftles, the one called Scander, feated on the fide of a valley, and two on mount Caucafus, called Regia and Scorgia, which, from their fituation, are almoft inacceffible. The fortrefs of Cotatis was once in the jurifdiction of this prince ; but is now in pof-feffion of the Turks.

The people of Guriel, Mingrelia, and Abca, were fubject to the king of Imeretta, after they had all four freed themfelves from the power of the emperors, firft of Conftantinople, and then of Trebifond ; but in the laft century fetting up for themfelves, they became involved in continual wars, till calling in the affiftance of the Turks, they were all made tribu-tary to them. The king of Imeretta pays a tribute of 80 boys and girls from 10 to 20 years of age. The prince of Guriel pays 46 children of both fexes, and the prince of Mingrelia 60,000 ells of linen cloth made in that country. The Abcas, however feldom paid any thing at firft, and now pay nothing.

As foon as our veffel had entered the road of Ifga-our, I landed with the Greek merchant who con-ducted me, with the hopes of finding houfes, fome provifions, and affiftance ; but I was much deceived. The Inhabitants had fenced round a place, a hun-dred paces from the fhore, 250 long, and 50 broad ; this was the grand market of Mingrelia. It had a ftreet formed of about a hundred little huts on each fide, built of branches of trees tied together. Each merchant took one, in which he lay, and there fold fuch commodities, as he hoped to difpofe of in two or three days time : thofe they bought, and thofe they had no probability of felling immediately, were kept on board the fhips. No refreshments were to be had in the market, nor was there a peafant's houfe in its neighbourhood. At this I was equally fur-prifed and afflicted, for our provifions were almoft confumed, and nothing was to be fold by the natives, but flaves chained together. There were above a dozen naked wretches, who with their bows and arrows in their hands ftruck every one with terror; thefe were the officers of the cuftoms. But my furprize and affliction were much increafed, on my being informed that the Turks and the prince of Guriei had taken up arms againft the Mingrelians, and begun the war by plundering the houfes of their neighbours, and carrying off them and their cattle, wherever they found them.

On my taking the refolution to go into Mingrelia, I had depended greatly on the Theatine miffionaries, who have a houfe 40 miles by land from Ifgaour, where I was told I might live in fafety, and that they would fpeedily procure me a paffage into Perfia. I therefore fent an exprefs with a letter to the Prefect of the miffion, and returned on board much dejected.

Two days after, a number of peafants who fled from the enemy, paffed by Ifgaour, and raifed a great alarm, by reporting that the Abcas, whom the prince of Mingrelia had called to his affiftance againft the Turks, plundered and burnt every thing before them; and carried off all the men and beafts that fell into their hands. Adding, that they were already near the port. All were now in a hurry to carry their effects on board. Each of the commanders of the fhips landed two pieces of cannon, and the men were under arms all night: but the next day they reimbarked, chufing rather to abandon the wool, filt, earthen ware, and other merchandize, they had not been able to bring on board, than to expofe themfelves to the danger of falling into the hands of the Abcas. About ten at night we faw all the market in a flame, and the next morning, fome men landing, they found nothing but the remains of the conflagration.

I now endeavoured to buy from the mafters of the fhips as much provifions as poffible; but all I could

purchafe from the feveral merchants was fixty pounds
of bifcuit, a little pulfe, eight pounds of butter, and
twelve pounds of rice. This was but little for fix
perfons; but good management maue it laft longer
than I could have imagined. We had, however,
dried fifh in abundance, and fcarce ate any thing
elfe ; I was wonderfully delighted when I had prevailed on my men to make a meal without bread.

At length hearing no news of the the Prefect, and
not being able to guefs the reafon, I informed my
men of the necellity we were under that one of them
fhould go to him ; becaufe none but he could fecure
us from the evils with which we were threathened, or
deliver us from thofe we endured, and that were
encreafing every day. My valet offered to undertake
the journey. I therefore gave him letters and prefents for the Perfect and his brethren, and he fet out
on this expedition.

On the morning of the 4th of October my valet
returned, bringing with him the Prefect, who was
a native of Mantua, called Don Maria Jofeph Zampy. I immediately ran to embrace him, when he
cried, " God forgive thofe who have advifed you,
" Sir, to come hither: you are arrived at the moft
" barbarous country in the world : and the beft ftep
" you can take, is to return to Conftantinople by
" the firft opportunity." The joy we had conceived
at feeing this prieft was damped by this difcourfe.
I took him into my cabin, and there with my comrade
deliberated on what was to be done. He told us
that he was come to ferve us to the utmoft of his
power; that he would take us to his houfe if we defired it: but that he had no bread ; that no provifions
were to be had : that the air of the country was unhealthy, and the people more wicked than it was
poffible to imagine. I told him that I had a letter of
recommendation to the prince of Mingrelia; but
he replied, that he was as great a villain, and as
bafe a robber, as any of his fubjects: and then ad-

ded, that if after this notice I was refolved to venture
he would do all in his power to preferve our perfons
and baggage, and procure us a fafe paffage into
Perfia.

I did not ftay to deliberate on what the father had
reprefented ; the evils with which I was threatened
in Mingrelia were future, and I hoped to avoid
them : but thcfe I fuffered were prefent, they filled
my imagination, and my heart funk under them.
I therefore reprefented to him, that whatever mif-
fortunes might happen to us in Mingrelia, they muft
be iefs than thofe of returning to Caffa, by which we
muft infallibly perifh; and this opinion I ftrengthened
by many reafons.   He was foon convinced by my
arguments, and now only confulted on the manner
in which we fhould travel.   The barque wherein
we had come down the river with my valet, was
proper for our purpofe.   It was freighted for going
and coming : we therefore embarked in it with all
our baggage, and I gave the value of an hundred
crowns in goods to father Zampy, who knew the
price fet upon it, and was to buy it for me.   The
baggage being embarked before noon, we immediately fet fail.   I was filled with joy at leaving the
fhip, where I could not endure the ftink, nor bear
the fight of the infamous commerce carried on in it. .
It was become a prifon for flaves, in which the men
and boys were chained two and two every night,
and ioofened every morning.   The war of Mingrelia
was of advantage to our merchants, who bought the
booty and flaves taken by the Abcas, who were
now continually coming on board, to exchange
them for arms, clothes, and other commodities.
A Greek merchant, whofe cabin was next to mine,
bought a woman and her fucking child for twelve
crowns: the woman was twenty-five years of age;
her face was extremely beautiful ; her fkin had the
whitenefs of the lily ; and I never faw a finer breaft
or a rounder neck.   This lovely woman filled me

at the fame time with fuch envy and compaffion, that giving her a dejected look, I faid to myfelf, unhappy beauty, thou fhouldeft not create thefe un-eafy fenfations was I in another ftate, and did I not find myfelf on the point of falling into greater miferies, if there can be greater, than that of being a flave. What furprized me moft, was to fee that thefe miferable creatures were not dejected, and that they appeared infenfible of the mifery of their con-dition. As foon as they were bought, their rags were taken off; they were dreffed in new linen habits, and fet to work ; the men and boys in doing fome-thing about the fhip, and the women in fewing.

But to proceed : we had a pretty good wind, and our little barque advanced both with fails and oars. During the voyage, I agreed with father Zampy on the means to prevent our falling into the hands of the enemy, and of being neither plundered nor affaffinated by the Mingrelians.

At midnight we arrived at the entrance of the Aftolphus, one of the greateft rivers in Mingrelia, and called by the natives Langur, where ftopping, we fent two of our mariners to Anarghia, to enquire after the enemy, and to fee if the inhabitants had not fled. Anarghia is a village two miles from the fea, and the moft confiderable place in all Mingrelia. It confifts of about a hundred houfes ; but they are fo far diftant from each other, that it is two miles from the firft to the laft. There are always Turks in that village to purchafe flaves, and barques to carry them off. It is faid to be built on the place where anciently ftood the great city of Heraclea.

The next morning before day, the two mariners returned with the news that the Abcas had been no nearer than within fifteen miles of Anarghia, and that every thing there was as ufual. Father Zampy caufed the men to row hard, in order to arrive early at that village, that we might all land without being feen. This happened according to our wifhes. We

went to lodge with a peafant who had the beft ac-
commodations of any in the place ; and as we had
many chefts, the largeft of which was full of books,
father Zampy adviled me to open it as foon as we
were at our lodgings, under the pretence of looking
for fomething, to prevent their imagining that thefe
chefts were filled with treafures ; he at the fame
time propofed my pretending to be a religious,
and that we had brought nothing with us but books.
I followed this advice. The people of the houfe
were aftonifhed at feeing fo large a cheft thus fil ed,
and I believe imagined that the contents of the
others were the fame.

On the ninth of October a lay Theatine, who was
phyfician and furgeon to all Mingrelia, came to
fee us. The accefs which his art gave him to the
houfes of the prince, and of all the great, had raifed
his vanity. I received and treated him in a manner
that flattered his pride, and in return he gave me a
thoufand affurances of his protection and affiftance.
Some days after he came to inform us that the Abcas
had returned home ; and had carried off 1200 perfons, much cattle, and a great booty. He then told
father Zampy that we might all go to their houfe
at Sipias, and that the prince and catholicos had
ordered him to tell me and my comrade, that we
were welcome, and that they would grant us men
and horfes to conduct us into Georgia. Upon receiving this agreeable news, we refolved to fet out the
next day.

While we ftaid at Anarghia we had no fcarcity of
provifions, but had plenty of fowl, hogs, and goats,
which my men exchanged for needles, thread, combs
and knives. We had every thing very cheap, and
this being the time of vintage, we had wine in
plenty, and nothing was fcarce but bread. There
was a widow lady of quality at Anarghia, whofe
hufband had been vizier to the prince. Father Zampy
conducted me to her, and I made her a prefent of

fome trifles. In order to obtain others, fhe fent me every day a cake of bread that weighed about half a pound, with fome other refrefhments : thus one day fhe fent me a hog, another day a cake of wax, another fome honey, another a pheafant, and on fending thefe fhe always begged for fome trifles, as knives fciffars and ribbons ; fhe made me pay double the price of her prefents. One day fhe paid me a vifit, when fhe was extremely obliging, but made many demands.

Father Zampy made me pafs for a capuchin, obferving, that I fhould meet with fome of that order in Georgia. To fupport this character, I dreffed as meanly as poffible, and affected poverty on all occafions. I acted my part well enough, but the conduct of my fervants prevented my impofing on the people : for they broke all my meafures by their cookery, and bought the greateft delicacies, let them coft what they would.

On the 14th we fet out two hours before day for An rglia, and proceeded two leagues up the river Aftolphus, after which we landed our baggage, and with it loaded fix fmall carts ; befides two others filled with the provifions bought by father Zampy. Thefe eight carts made a great noife ; for the Mingrelians were not accuftomed to feé fuch a quantity of goods at a time. In lefs than two days the whole country was informed that fome Europeans were arrived who had eight carts loaded with their baggage. We proceeded four leagues and a half by land, and arrived in the evening at Sipias.

Sipias is the name of two churches, one of them a parifh church of the Mingrelians, and the other belonging to the Theatines, an order of friars who firft came into Mingrelia in 1627, when they were admitted as phyficians, and a piece of land given them, on which they built feveral wooden houfes after the manner of the country, fome with only the ground floor, and others with a room above. Each of the friars have one of thefe houfes to dwell in ; for they are all feparate : the fmalleſt are for their flaves, and two families of peafants who are their tenants ; but though they have good employment as phyficians, none will embrace their religion, the very flaves re-fufing to communicate with them : for they will not allow the Europeans to be Chriſtians, becaufe they have neither fo many faſts as they, nor are afraid of images.

On the 18th the princefs of Mingrelia came to the Theatines. She was on horfeback attended by about ten men and eight women, very badly clothed, and ill mounted, with feveral men on foot who ſtood about her horfe. Father Zampy went imme-diately to receive her, when ſhe told him, that ſhe had heard there was fome Europeans in his houfe, who had brought a great quantity of baggage : that ſhe was glad of it, and defired to fee them, in order to tell them that they were welcome. I was then inſtantly called, and father Zampy told me, that I muſt make her a prefent, fince it was the cuſtom to pay in this manner for the vifits of a prince and princefs. Being told that I fpoke the Turkiſh and Perfian tongues, ſhe called a flave who knew the Turkiſh, and afked me a thoufand queſtions about my rank, and my voyage. I told her that I was a capuchin. She caufed me to be afked, if I was in love ? if I had ever been in love ? how it happen-ed that I had never been in love ? and how I did to live without a woman ? She carried on this con-verfation with great vivacity, and all her retinue were very merry upon it : but for my part, I was much dejeĉted, and would have been glad of the abfence both of the princefs and her train ; whom I every moment feared would pillage our lodgings ; for ſhe afked three times to fee what I had brought ; but father Zampy promifing to bring her the ufual prefent the next day, ſhe departed, feemingly well fatisfied.

The next morning fhe fent to invite me to dinner. She was at a houfe only two miles from ours ; but did not live with the prince, who had a great diflike to her, having been forced to marry her. I found her better dreffed than the day before. She was painted, and feemed to endeavour to appear lovely ; fhe was clothed in gold brocade, and had jewels in her head drefs. She fat on a carpet, with nine or ten women by her fide, and near her were many fhabby fellows half naked, who compofed her court. They afked for my prefent for the princefs, before they fuffered me to enter. It was brought by my fervant, who delivered it to them, and confifted of cafes of knives, fciffars, and other things which coft about twenty fhillings, and was worth about 3*l.* in Mingrelia. The princefs was fatisfied, and fuffered me to enter after having feen them. Near her was a bench, on which the flave who fpoke Turkifh defired me to fit. She firft 'told me that fhe would have me to marry one of her friends, and that I fhould not leave that country ; for fhe would give me houfes, lands, and flaves. But a ftop was put to her difcourfe, by one coming to inform her that dinner was ready.

The houfe in which fhe lived was in the midft of five others, each at a hundred paces diftance. Before one of them was a raifed place built with wood, eighteen inches high, over which was a fmall dome. Here a carpet being fpread, the princefs feated her-felf upon it, as did her women at four paces diftance on other carpets. The fhabby wretches who com-pofed her court, and were about fifty in number, feated themfelves round on the grafs. There were two benches near the place raifed for the princefs, one of which ferved the Theatines and me for a feat, and the other for a table. When the princefs was feated, a long painted cloth was laid before her, and at one end of it were placed two large and two fmall flagons, four plates, and eight cups of different fizes, with a filver bafon, ewer, and fkimmer. Other fervants at the fame time laid boards before thofe who were feated, to ferve as tables; and one was alfo put before the women. This being done two kettles were brought in and placed in the middle, one of them, which was very large,. was carried by four men, and was full of common gomm; the other, which was fmaller, was brought in by two, and was full of white gomm. This gomm was a kind of pafte, of which the Mingrelians make the fame ufe as we do of bread. Two other men brought in upon a kind of bier, a hog boiled whole, and four others entered with a large pitcher of wine. The princefs was ferved firft, then her women, then us, and afterwards her attendants. The princefs was alfo ferved with a wooden bowl of gomm, and fome herbs, and with a filver difh, in which were two fowls, one boiled, and the other roafted; but both of them had a very difagreeable fauce. The princefs fent me a part of the bread and fallad, and caufed me to be told, that I fhould ftay fupper, and that fhe would kill an ox; but this was mere compliment. A little after fhe fent me two pieces of fowl, and afked with a loud voice, why there never came into Mingrelia any of the European artificers, who work fo well in metals, filk, and wool, and why there only came monks who had no bufinefs there, and whom they did not want. It is eafy to guefs at the confufion into which this queftion muft throw the poor Theatines who were prefent. I anfwered, that the artificers of Europe laboured only for gain, and having employment enough there, had no inclination to go father; but that the religious having in view the glory of God, and the falvation of fouls, thefe great concerns induced them to leave their country, and travel fo far.

The repaft lafted about two hours; when it was half ended the princefs fent me a cup of wine, and caufed me to be told that it was the wine fhe herfelf ufed, and the cup out of which fhe drank. Three times fhe did me this honour, and was much fur-prifed to fee me mix water with my wine, faying, fhe had never feen that done before. Indeed, fhe and her women drank it unmixed, in great quanti-ties. Dinner being ended, fhe fent to enquire if I had brought any fpices or china-ware ; fhe alfo afked me for a variety of things, and finding that I had none to give her, fhe at laft grew angry, and faid fhe would fend to examine my goods; but though I was much frighted, I anfwered fhe might do it when ever fhe pleafed ; to which fhe replied, that fhe was only in jeft. However, as foon as we rofe from table, I entreated one of the Theatines who had accompani-ed me, to make all poffible hafte to my comrade, and tell him what the princefs faid, in order that he might prepare for all events. After dinner fhe again fpoke of the marriage, and faid fhe would foon fhew me the woman fhe would give me; but I replied as before, that monks never marry, and was going to take my leave ; when unhappily fhe perceived under the mean frock I wore, that I had whiter and finer linen than what they had in Mingrelia. She came up to me, took me by the hand ; pulled up my fleeve to the elbow, and held me for fome time by the arm, talking all the while in a low voice to her women. I was extremely embarraffed, and what gave me moft pain, was my not knowing what fhe faid, though I could perceive by her geftures, that fhe was talking earneftly about me. I was at a lofs how to behave in public to a woman who had at the fame time the title of fovereign, and the impudence of a proftitute. But fhe foon threw me into greater confternation ; for going up to father Zampy, fhe faid, You both deceive me: you fhall come again on Sunday morning, and this ftranger fhall fay mafs. The father was going to reply; but the princefs turned her back, and bid us go home.

I returned to our lodging very fad and penfive ; the princefs's avarice made me apprehend fhe would do me fome ill turn ; and father Zampy told me that he was infallibly certain of it. I therefore the fame night caufed a deep pit to be dug in his apart- ment, in which I put a cheft that contained a clock, and a box of coral ; this was fo well buried, that there was not left the leaft fign of the ground having been opened. I then went into the church with the fame defign, when father Zampy advifed me to open the grave of a Theatine who had been buried fix years before, and to depofit among his afhes a fmall cafket I was willing to conceal ; but happily I chofe to bury this cafket, in which was 12,000 gold ducats, in a corner of the church behind the door, for which purpofe I made a deep pit like the former. I afterwards concealed in the roof over the chamber where I lodged, a fabre and a poignard fet with precious ftones. My comrade and I kept about us what was of the leaft weight and the greateft value, and fuch things as were not worth a great deal, we gave the Theatines to keep for us.

On the 23d after dinner, a perfon came to in- form father Zampy that there were two gentlemen at the door who afked for him. Thefe gentlemen, who were neighbours, were on horfeback, and had with them thirty men, horfe and foot, well armed. My comrade and I were immediately called. I could not penetrate into their defign ; but I knew it too foon ; for on our coming up to them, they caufed us to be feized and tied by their men ; telling the Prefect, and the other Theatines who came to falute them, that if they ftirred they would kill him. The Prefect being feized with fear, fled ; the others, however, would not leave us, and the lay brother not only made ufe of all his intereft in our behalf ; but though a fword was held up to his neck, he would not abandon us. Our fervants were immediately feized, and one of them making refiftance, and defending himfelf with a knife, was thrown down, and tied to a tree. They then declared they would fee what treafures we had. To which I replied, that they might do as they pleafed ; we were poor capuchins, and all our wealth confifted in books papers, and a few ordinary goods, which, if they would offer us no violence, we would fhew them. This anfwer fuccceded, they untied me, and bid me open my chamber door.

We had kept about us, as I have already obferved, our moft precious jewels ; my comrade had fewed his in the neck of a clofe coat lined with fur ; but I had made mine up into two fmall packets, which I had hid in my cheft among my books ; not daring to carry them about me for fear of being robbed or affaffinated on their account. I therefore defired my comrade and the lay brother to take the two gentlemen afide, and to amufe them by offering a little money, in order to give me time to take the two valuable packets out of my cheft, and to conceal them in another place. They did fo ; I entered my chamber and fhut myfelf in. The gentlemen fufpected my defign, and went to the door which I had faftened on the infide ; when my comrade bid me, in a low voice, be on my guard, as they watched me through the cracks : this made me fnatch the two packets out of the thatch in which I had already concealed them, for fear they had feen me put them there. I then put them in my pocket, and feeing the villains were breaking open the door, I threw myfelf out of the window into the garden. In a lefs preffing neceffity I would not have made that leap on any confideration ; but a mind feized with fear, dreads nothing but the firft object of its apprehenfions : I ran to the bottom of the garden, and threw the two packets into a thicket of briars ; but was in fuch confufion, that I did not with fufficient care obferve the place were I put them.

I immediately returned to my chamber, which I found full of thefe robbers, fome of whom were ftruggling with my companion, while others were beating with their weapons on my chefts to break them open. Knowing there was now nothing in them of great value, I took courage, and bid them take care what they did, as I was fent for by the king of Perfia, and that the prince of Georgia would take a fevere revenge for the violence that was offered me. I then fhewed the king of Perfia's paffport, which one of the gentlemen took, and was going to tear it, faying, he neither feared nor valued any man upon earth; but the other flopped him; for the writing in gold, and the gilt feal infpired him with refpect. He, however, bid me open my chefts, and faid that no harm fhould be done me; but if I made any further refiftance, they would fever my head from my body. I began to reply, inftead of fhewing my obedience; but this had like to have coft me dear; for one of the foldiers drew his fword, and was aiming it at my head, when the lay-brother ftopped his arm. I now immediately opened the chefts; they began to plunder them, and every thing that pleafed thefe gentlemen was taken away.

During the time this pillage lafted, I leaned againft a window, and turning my eyes away from thefe wretches, that I might not encreafe my grief by beholding them, I caft a look into the garden, and there perceived two foldiers removing the brambles, juft where I fuppofed I had concealed my two packets of jewels. I ran in a rage to the place, followed by one of the Theatine fathers; but the foldiers, I knew not why, retired as foon as they faw us coming towards them. I inftantly fought for my two packets, but the confufion I was in prevented my knowing the place where I had put them, and my not finding them, made me certain that they had difcovered and taken them away. The reader may judge from the value of thefe packets, which amounted to 25,000

crowns, of the confternation with which I was feized.
In the mean while my comrade and the lay-brother
calling me as loud as they were able, I left the garden, and ran into the chamber. On my entering it
I was feized by two foldiers, who dragged me into a
corner, and took every thing they found in my
pockets, which was of no great value. They then
feized my hands, and attempted to tie them. I cried
out---I refifted --I made figns that they fhould lead
me to their mafter. I caufed the chief of the villains
to be told, that they need not tie me, either to carry
me away or to kill me ; for I was difpofed to fubmit
to whatever they did with me. They replied, that
fince we were ambaffadors, they would take me to
their prince. I let them know that we would go
without being tied, and that we hoped he would do
us juftice, as we had letters to him, to which he would
certainly fhew refpect. It was late, the night approached, and the prince's caftle was at fifteen miles
diftance, they therefore releafed us, and only took
the fervant who had been tied to a tree, and whofe
liberty I procured a fortnight after for ten piafters.

As foon as I was out of the hands of thefe robbers,
I went into the garden: the prieft who had followed
me when I went to fetch the two packets of jewels I
had concealed, told every body in the houfe of the
misfortune I believed I had fuffered, and nobody
doubted but that thefe foldiers having obferved me,
had followed and taken what I had concealed among
the brambles. Allaverdy, one of our Armenian
valets, followed me, and to my great aftonifhment
threw his arms about my neck, with his face bathed
in tears. Sir, faid he, we are ruined. Fear and the
common misfortune have made us forget what we all
are. I was at firft fo furprized, that I took him for
fome Mingrelian who was going to ftrangle me, and
when I knew him, I was moved by his tendernefs,
Sir, faid he, have you made a thorough fearch ? I
have fearched fo much, cried I, that I am quite fure

of my misfortune.   He was not contented with this;
he would have me fhew him the place, and the manner in which I concealed them.   I did fo merely out
of complaifance for the poor youth who fhewed fuch
affeǎion ; but was fo fully perfuaded that he would
lofe his labour, that I would not affift him.   It was
now night, and I was fo uneafy that I knew not what
I did ; but at length to my great aftonifhment, Allaverdy came again to carefs me, and gave me the two
packets which he pulled out of his bofom.   I could
not help imagining that the finger of heaven was in
this, and believing now that I was the care of the
Almighty, I became confident of the divine affiftance,
and entertained thofe hopes of deliverance, that
have ever fince fupported me under all my diftreffes.

I now went to my chamber, and told my comrade
of my fuccefs.   I found him putting our things in
order.   What they had taken confifted of clothes,
linen, arms, brafs veffels, and other things of fmall
value, which did not amount to 400 crowns ; and
we agreed to conceal the recovery of my two packets
from the Theatines, that they might think we had
little elfe to lofe.

The next morning the Prefeǎ of the Theatines,
and the lay-brother, went with me to the prince,
and the Catholicos, to demand juftice; but neither of
them could give us any fatisfaǎion.   The prince
obferved, that while the war lafted, he had but little
authority over the nobility ; but at another time he
would have done his utmoft to recover what we had
loft.   The Catholicos, to whem we gave a cafe of
filver hafted knives and forks, talked in the fame
manner, and endeavoured to comfort us.   They,
however, each of them appointed a gentleman to go
on their parts to demand what had been taken from
us ; but their endeavours to find the robbers were
ineffeǎual ; from them we learnt that the princefs
was concerned in the robbery, and had a third part
of the fpoils ; and that the Turks had entered Min-

grelia, and were laying wafte all the country through which they paffed with fire and fword.

I was now in fo refigned a difpofition, that this news did not much move me ; the Theatines, however, were filled with terror, and both they and we prepared for flight. At midnight we heard the report of two great guns, fired from the fortrefs of Rucks to give notice of the approach of the enemy. At this fignal every body began to fly ; and at break of day we ourfelves fet out. I left every thing that had been buried, and concealed in the roof and other places, thinking them much fafer than what we took with us. The Theatines had no other carriage but one cart drawn by bullocks, and two horfes. In the cart was carried the baggage, the Lay-brother mounted one of the horfes, and my comrade, who was fick, rode the other, while two Theatine friars and I followed on foot, accompanied by all the flaves and fervants. One of the friars ftaid alone to guard the houfe in which were a thoufand things that we could not take away for want of carriages. I left my books, moft of my papers, and my mathematical inftruments, imagining that neither the Turks nor the Mingrelians would take the trouble to remove them. The wars there confifting chiefly in chafing and plundering, the enemy foon retires. For this reafon they always leave a perfon or two at each houfe, to prevent the neighbours ftealing the corn, wine, and other things that could not be carried away. Thefe men are feldom furprifed by the enemy, becaufe they are always upon the watch, and take care to efcape into the woods, which are not only near, but thick, and proper for concealment.

The place to which we retired was a fortrefs in the woods, like thofe I have already defcribed. The Lord of the place who was called Sabatar, was a Georgian, who had been a Mahometan, and had turned Chriftian. We arrived at his caftle, after having proceeded five leagues through the dirt and mire, in which the cart was continually sticking fast, so that it was obliged to be unloaded and loaded twenty times. Mean while we were in continual danger of being robbed and murdered. We met with a favourable reception, and the Theatines telling the Lord Sabatar that I would repay the obligation he should confer on us, he lodged us in a bakehouse, a little mean hut, in which we were sheltered but little better than if we had been in the open court, for the rain poured in on all sides. Our having it was however a great favour, as it prevented our being mingled with a multitude of miserable objects. The fortress was full of people before we arrived, and contained 800 persons, almost all of whom were women and children.

On the 27th, the prefect of the Theatines left us to go to the house for some vessels and provisions we had left behind. I designed to have accompanied him ; but he set out two hours before day. On entering the house, he found it full of rangers belonging to the bassa, and the prince of Guriel, who beat him with their staves, and insisted on his opening the church, saying he had concealed there all the treasure ; but the prefect had cast the key among the brambles, immediately on his perceiving them, and notwithstanding the ill treatment he received, he refused to tell where it was. At length stripping him of part of his clothes and taking out of the house only such things as were light and of little value, they went away, without touching either my books or my papers. However, on the 29th, a gentleman of Mingrelia with thirty of his men, went thither in the night, and uncovered almost all the roof of my chamber, with the hopes of finding something, I might have concealed. He carried off all the chests that had been left, and my more cumberfome moveables ; in short, every thing which the Turks had left except what was of great value, which he happily did not discover. This rapacious wretch having no light, made a fire with papers and books; tearing off the covers becaufe they were finely guilt; for I had caufed my best books to be curioufly bound before I left Paris, and this villain did not leave me one.

On the 30th in the morning, I with the deepeft concern learnt thefe particulars. We began to be in want of the neceffaries of life; my fervants were reduced to defpair, and we had nothing before our eyes, but the profpect of death or flavery. This made me refolve to hazard every thing in order to leave Mingrelia while I had ftrength to do it. I caufed guides to be every where fought for. I promifed, I entreated, I made prefents, but none would conduct me. They told me that men in arms poffeff-ed all the paffes of Imeretta, between Mingrelia and Georgia, and that it would be the greateft folly to go thither, fince we fhould all be certainly made flaves. I then propofed to make the tour of Mount Caucafus, or to proceed along the fea fhore; but no-body would conduct me: for it can fcarcely be conceived how afraid the Mingrelians are of death; no reward can induce them to undergo the leaft danger.

Sabatar, to whom the fortrefs belonged, had now fubmitted to the Turks, and was not only to enjoy all his lands, but to have a Turkifh guard for the fecurity of his caftle: for which he was to pay 25 flaves, and 800 crowns, which he was refolved to raife among thofe to whom he had granted his pro-tection. From every family that had four children, he took one; and it was the moft dreadful fight in the world, to fee them torn from the arms of their mothers, tied two, and two, and led to the Turks. I was taxed at twenty crowns.

At length I was conftrained to take the refolution to go by fea, that is to take a compafs of feventy leagues; for that purpofe I went to Anarghia, a village and fmall port, already defcribed, and having found there a Turkifh felucca, I freighted her for Gonia, and returned to the houfe of the Theatines to prepare for the voyage.

I left the caftle on the tenth of November early in the morning, having agreed with my comrade on the methods I fhould take, in order to deliver him out of Mingrelia, if it fhould pleafe God to give me a happy voyage. I took with me a hundred thoufand livres in precious ftones, 800 piftoles in gold ; with a part of the baggage that remained. The jewels were concealed in a faddle made in Europe for that purpofe, and in a pillow. I took one of our fervants with me, the fame whom I had redeemed from flavery, who was a wicked drunken fellow, and whom it was not fafe to leave in Mingrelia. Father Zampy accompanied me as he had always done, and the lay-brother alfo went with me to Anarghia. The prefect and I walked, becaufe we could only hire one horfe, on which was placed my baggage and my valet ; but the lay brother rode on horfeback, he having a horfe of his own. I cannot exprefs the fatigue we endured in the two days we were upon the road, for it rained very hard, and we were obliged to wade through the mud, in which I commonly funk above the knees. On the night of the fecond day we arrived at Anarghia, foaked through with rain.

On the 19th, father Zampy received advice that the night before, the church had been broke open, and nothing left but the bare walls ; the tomb had been opened, and every thing taken out, which the poor Theatine who had been left in the houfe, had buried in it. It is eafy to imagine the apprehenfions with which I was feized at receiving this news ; I having left above 7000 piftoles buried in the church. I immediately difpatched a meffenger with a letter to my comrade, who wrote me word that they had not touched our money, and that every thing we had buried was fafe. This news revived my courage, and I went to haften the Turks, of whom I had hired the felucca.

While I ftaid at Anarghia I was invited to two chriftenings which were performed in the following manner : the prieft being fent for about ten o'clock in the morning, went into the buttery where they keep the wine, and fitting down on a bench began to read an half torn octavo volume, running on very faft in a low voice, and in fo carelefs a manner that he did not feem to regard what he was doing. In about a quarter of an hour the father and god-father brought in a boy about five years old ; and the godfather having fixed up a fmall candle againft the cabbin door, fcattered a few grains of incenfe upon a few embers. The prieft ftill continued read-ing in the fame carelefs manner, breaking off to fpeak to every body that came in ; the father and godfather were all the time walking in and out, and the little boy did nothing but eat. In about an hour's time a bucket full of warm water was got ready, and the prieft having poured into it a fpoon-ful of the oil of walnuts, bid the godfather undrefs the child, which being done, he was fet on his feet in the water, and the godfather wafhed the whole body very well. The prieft then took out of a leather purfe, which hung at his girdle a fmall quantity of the oil of unction, and giving it to the godfather, he anointed the child on the crown of the head, the ears, the forehead, the nofe, the cheeks, the chin, the fhoulders, the elbows, the back, the belly, the knees, and the feet, while the prieft continued reading the godfather had dreffed the child ; when the father bringing in boiled pork and wine, they fat down to table, with the family and the guefts, and foon got drunk.

All the other acts of religion are celebrated with the fame irreverence. One day as I was going by a church, the prieft who was faying mafs heard me afk the way of fome people who were standing at the door, and cried out from the altar, Stay and I'll shew you ; a moment after he came to the door, muttering the mafs as he walked; then having afked, whence we came, and whither we were going, he civilly shewed us the way, and returned to the altar.

On the 27th of November I left Anarghia, and after an hour's failing reached the fea ; for the river Langur is very rapid, and we proceeded with great fwiftnefs down the stream.

The Euxine or Black Sea is two hundred leagues in length, nearly from eaft to weft, and its greateft breadth from the Bofphorus to the Borifthenes is about three degrees: but the oppofite end is not half fo broad. The water of this fea appears neither fo clear, fo green, nor fo falt as the ocean, which probably arifes from the great rivers that difcharge themfelves into it. It did not receive its name from the colour of the water, but from the tempefts, which are faid to be there more frequent and more furious than in other feas ; hence the Greeks gave it the name of Axin, which fignifies intractable, and the Turks that of Cara Denguis, or the ftormy fea ; for cara, which properly means black, alfo fignifies ftormy.

On the 19th we reached the river Phafis, and proceeded a mile up it, to fome houfes where the mafter of the felucca landed, and put fome goods afhore. The river Phafis has its fource in mount Caucafus, and is now called by the people of that country the Rione. It is confined within a narrow bed, and runs with great rapidity. I fought for the great city of Sebafta, which geographers have placed at the mouth of the Phafis ; but the ruins of that city, like thofe of Colchis, have no traces of them left. All that I obferved to have any conformity with what the ancients have written of this part of the Black Sea is, that it abounds with pheafants. There are

authors, (and among others, Martial) who fay, that
the Argonauts brought thofe birds from Greece,
where they had never been feen before, and that
they gave them the name of pheafants, from their
being taken on the banks of the Phafis. This river
feparates Mingrelia from the principality of Guriel,
and the little kingdom of Imeretta.

On the 30th in the afternoon we arrived at Gonia,
about 40 miles from the Phafis. This is a large
fquare caftle built of hard rough ftones of an extraordinary fize, fituated on a fandy bottom on the fea
fhore. It has neither ditch nor fortifications, and
only confifts of four fquare walls, fortified with two
pieces of cannon, and defended by a garrifon of a
fmall number of Janizaries. Within it are about
thirty fmall, low, inconvenient wooden houfes, and
near it is a village that contains about the fame
number.

Here is a cuftom-houfe belonging to the Grand
Signior, but the officers pay no refpect either to the
quality of the perfons who land there, or to the fultan's paffports. Thofe who command in this extremity of the empire, think themfelves fo far from
him, that his hand cannot reach them.

Our felucca no fooner came to land than my valet
leaped afhore, kiffed the earth, and fhewed the moft
extravagant and frantic figns of joy ; and then entering the caftle, left me at a time when I moft wanted
him. Soon after the cuftom-houfe officer, and the
lieutenant-governor came to fee my things landed,
and to receive the duty ; they inftantly let me know
that they were informed of my being an European,
and of all the misfortunes that had happened to me
in Mingrelia. This furprized me, for I found I was
betrayed by my rafcal of a valet. The officer of the
cuftoms afked me feveral queftions, and gave orders
for examining my goods ; but they could find nothing I wanted to conceal. My faddle, however,
weighed very heavy, and this rendered it fufpected,

efpecially as the Turkifh faddles are extremely light, It was examined and handled on all fides: but being able to find nothing within it befides hair and wadding, they laid it down.

Of the 800 piftoles I had brought, I carried half of them about me, and the other half in a wallet, faftened with a padlock, with fome things, which though of fmall value, I knew the Turks would feize if they faw them. The cuftom-houfe officer and his Janizaries being told of this wallet, ordered me to open it, on which I told them I would freely do it in the houfe; but not on the fea fhore before fo many men. On which the officer of the cuftoms took me home with him to his houfe, and the lieutenant-governor went with us. The latter made me pay the value of one per cent. on my goods, and the other five. The cuftom houfe officer likewife took 22 piftoles in gold, and every thing he liked that was found in my wallet; among the reft he got from me a pair of piftols, which were the only arms I had; he, however, paid me for them, but gave me no more than half their value. After this rapacious behaviour he invited me to lodge with him; but I could not help exprefling my aftonifhment, that he, who had unjuftly made me pay a duty for the gold and filver I had brought, fhould immediately affume the mafk of friendfhip; but he vindicated what he had done, renewed his invitation, and even promifed to fupply me with a guard to protect my baggage, and conduct me over the mountains. But though he renewed his entreaties, and as I afterwards found, really meant me well, yet I was afraid of accepting his invitations, for fear he fhould take that opportunity of caufing my faddle, and my clothes to be more narrowly examined.

It was almoft night when I left this officer of the cuftoms, who was alfo governor of the territory of Gonia. My valet had carried my baggage to the place where the men who came with us lodged.

This was a wretched cottage which admitted the air on all fides, and was as dirty and ftinking as poffible. I then received many compliments of condolence, if I may ufe the term, for all the men appeared forry for my lofs, and blamed me for not letting them keep the wallet for me : their goods paying no duty. While I was eating a piece of a bifcuit, a Janizary came to tell my valet that the lieutenant-governor wanted him ; my valet went ; and an hour after the fame Janizary came for me. I found the lieutenant and my valet fitting together, both drunk. Having obliged me to eat and drink, the lieutenant demanded 200 ducats, as due to his mafter from all Chriftian church-men who came there, this occafioned a long difpute ; I attempted to retire, but was detained by force, and threatened to be put in irons, and was at laft glad, to efcape by paying an hundred ducats to the lieutenant and four to the Janizaries. But this was not all, the lieutenant obliged me to entreat him to take the money, and to fwear that I would not complain of him. The next morning the officer of the cuftoms fent a party of foldiers to my miferable lodgings to examine again my faddle, and to fearch me ; but though they filled me with the greateft uneafinefs, they could make no difcovery. After this I was allowed two men to carry my baggage, and a Turk to conduct me as far as Acalzika ; he alfo gave me a paffport, and advifed that I and my valet fhould wear a white turban, in order to be treated with the greater refpect. This I did, and fet out at eight in the morning, tranfported with joy, at leaving fo wicked and dangerous a place, and at having nothing more to fear. I then began to feel fome peace of mind. For five months paft I had fuffered the moft dreadful agitations ; infult, flavery, marriage, the lofs of my fubftance and liberty, during all this time diftracted my mind by turns, and a thoufand real evils had kept me under the deepeft dejection. I now afcended mount Caucafus with a lightnefs which furprized my porters ; for the body is literally light when the heart is eafed of a heavy load ; this is true without a figure ; for I feemed to have been delivered from the weight of a mountain. I now proceeded four leagues together among the rocks.

The next day, which was the third of December, I proceeded five leagues on foot, three men carrying my baggage. We went frequently fo near the moft frightful precipices, that it was impoffible to avoid being ftruck with terror. We kept conftantly afcending, and in thofe five leagues had not a level path of two miles in extent. I arrived in the evening at a village inhabited by Turks and Chriftians, where the rain and fnow obliged us to ftay all the next day.

On the 5th and 6th I proceeded eleven leagues ; but I could not ride above five of them, being every moment obliged to difmount on account of difficult paffages, and the roughnefs and fharpnefs of the way, where the horfes could fcarce keep their feet. The two following days I advanced fixteen leagues, and reached the top of mount Caucafus ; for the four following leagues we were continually defcending. At half way of the defcent, we faw the ruins of many caftles and churches deftroyed by the Turks.

Afia is divided by a chain of mountains, one at the end of the other, the three higheft of which have been named Taurus, Imaus, and Caucafus. The firft advances fartheft into Afia, and the whole chain in general is called by the name of mount Taurus. I fay in general, becaufe each part has its particular name, by which it is called by the nation neareft it.

But to return to the defcription of mount Caucafus ; which is the higheft mountain, and the moft difficult to pafs of any I have feen. It has frightful precipices, and in many places the roads are cut out of the folid rock. When I paffed it, it was entirely covered with fnow, which was almoft every where ten feet deep : and my conductors were in many

places obliged to clear it away with ſhovels ; they
wore ſnow ſhoes in the form of rackets without handles, which prevented their ſinking in the ſnow, and
enabled them to run with great ſwiftneſs upon it.
The top of mount Caucaſus, which is eight leagues
over, is indeed perpetually covered with it.   I paſſed
the night of the 7th and 8th in the midſt of the ſnow ;
where I cauſed ſome fir-trees to be cut down, and lay
upon the boughs by the ſide of a great fire.   On our
arrival at the top, my conductors made long prayers
to their images, to do us the favour to prevent a wind ;
and indeed if it had been high, we ſhould doubtleſs
have been buried in the ſnow, for as it is as ſmall as
duſt, a little wind fills the air with it.   The horſes
ſunk ſo often into holes covered by it, that I often
thought we ſhould looſe them.   I almoſt conſtantly
walked on foot, and did not ride above eight leagues
in croſſing this frightful mountain, which is thirty-
fix leagues over.

During the two laſt days, I ſeemed in the clouds,
not being able to ſee twenty paces before me.   It is
true, the firs with which the top of the mountain
is covered, greatly obſtruct the view.   On deſcending it I ſaw the clouds move under my feet.   On
our reaching the bottom, we entered a beautiful and
fertile valley, three miles broad, covered with villages, and watered by the river Kur, which paſſes
through the middle of it.

Mount Caucaſus is fertile almoſt to the top, and
its ſides abound in honey, corn, fruits, hogs and
large cattle.   The vines twine about the trees, and
rife ſo high that the inhabitants cannot gather the
fruit from the upper branches.   There are many
ſtreams of excellent water, and a great number of
villages.   It was the time of vintage, and I found
both the grapes and the new and old wine admirably
good.   The peaſants live in cabins built of wood,
each family having four or five of them, and in the
midſt of the largeſt they make a great fire, which

ferves for all the cottages around it. The women grind the corn as often as they want bread; and bake the dough on round ftones, about a foot in diameter, and hollowed two or three fingers deep. The ftone being well heated, they put the dough into it, and cover it with hot afhes, and burning embers. In fome places they only fweep a part of the hearth, place the dough upon it, and cover it with hot afhes in the fame manner. Yet the cruft is white enough, and the bread very good. I lodged every night at the houfe of a peafant, of whom I hired horfes, and men to carry my baggage. The Turk who had been given me as my conductor, caufed me to be as fpeedily and as well ferved as the place would permit. The natives fupplied us with fowls, eggs, pulfe, and fruit in abundance; for every houfe in the neighbourhood brought a great jug of wine, a bafket of fruit, and another of bread. For all this nothing was demanded, and my conductor hindered me even from making them any prefent in return.

The inhabitants of thefe mountains are for the moft part Chriftians of the Georgian church. They have very fine complexions, and I have feen among them very beautiful women. They are infinitely better accommodated than the Mingrelians.

On the ninth I proceeded five leagues in the fertile plain already mentioned, where the hills with which it is bounded, are covered with a great number of cattle. And at at night I arrived at Acalzika. This is a fortrefs built on Mount Caucafus, in a hollow between near twenty little hills, from which it may be eafily battered down on any fide. It has a double wall and towers, with ancient battlements on the top; but it has very few guns. On thefe eminences are about 400 houfes, all of them new and lately built; the only ancient buildings are two Armenian churches The town is inhabited by Turks, Armenians, Georgians, Greeks and Jews. The Chriftians have churches, and the Jews a fynagogue. There

is alfo a fmall caravanferai built of wood, as are moft
of the houfes in the place. The river Kur or Cyrus
paffes near it; it has its fource in Mount Caucafus;
and at length difcharges itfelf into the Black Sea.
The baffa of Acalzika lodges in the fortrefs, and
the principal officers and militia dwell in the neighbouring villages.

On the 13th at two hours after midnight, I fet
out from Acalzika, proceeding to the eaft, and
having gone three leagues, found the plain of Acalzika contract, and the mountains approach each
other, fo that the plain is not more than half a
league in breadth It has there a ftrong Turkifh
caftle built on a rock, on the fide of the river Kur.
The foot of this rock is encircled by a double wall,
and about it is a little town on the land between the
fortrefs and the oppofite mountain. As there is here
an officer of the cuftoms, I was under great apprehenfion of being ftopped and examined; but they
fuffered me to pafs without oppofition. This town
is named Ufker, and two leagues from thence we
afcended a mountain that feparates Perfia from the
dominions of the Turks, and then proceeded along
the fide of it. Upon this mountain are many villages:
at its foot runs the Kur, and we there fee the ruins
of feveral caftles, fortreffes, and churches, veftiges
of the former grandeur of the Georgians, and of the
conquefts of the Turks and Perfians.

The two following days we paffed through the
delightful plain of Surham, by a large village, with
a fortrefs of the fame name. This plain is covered
with little woods, villages, fmall eminences, the
houfes of pleafure, and the fmall caftles of the Georgian lords. This fine country is entirely cultivated:
We then paffed over a mountain, leaving on the
right a city, which has now no more than about
five hundred inhabited houfes: though it is faid to
have had formerly 12,000, and to have been the fee
of a bifhop.

On my defcending this laft mountain, I approached Gory, but inftead of entering that town, went
directly to the houfe of Capuchins, who are Italian
miffionaries of the congregation de propaganda fide,
to whom I had letters of recommendation. I related
to thofe fathers the misfortunes I had fuffered in
Mingrelia ; and my being obliged to leave there the
things I had brought for the king of Perfia, under
the care of my comrade, and that I was come into
Georgia in fearch of affiftance ; entreating them to
give it me. They were touched with my diftreffes,
with the dangers to which my comrade was ftill expofed, and with the hazard of our lofing our fubftance.
They affured me that they would do every thing in
their power to ferve me, as foon as they received
the orders of their prefect, who was at Teflis, the
capital of Georgia. They gave me fuch reafons for
going thither, that I refolved to fet out immediately,
and having hired a horfe for me, the fuperior directed
a lay-brother named Angelo de Viterbo, to accompany me.

This lay-brother was both an honeft man, and an
able phyfician and furgeon. He had the happinefs
to cure feveral difeafes and fome wounds that were
here thought incurable, on which account he was
much refpected and efteemed. He was well acquainted with the language, and the different parts of
thefe countries, and being alfo endowed with much
good fenfe, courage and patience, I could not have
a better companion.

In two days we arrived at Teflis. The lay-brother
who accompanied me, led me to the convent of the
Capuchins, where having no time to lofe, I immediately told the prefect the caufe of my journey, and
gave him my letters of recommendation. He was
foon fenfible of the neceffity of going at all hazards
to endeavour to recover what I had left there. It
was agreed to fay, I was a Theatine, who had been
fent by thofe of Colchis, to beg affiftance of the

Capuchins, and they were to fend one of their companions with me, in order to bring them away, on account of their being reduced to the greateft diftrefs by the war.

This was no fooner determined, than I prepared for the journey ; I took out of my faddle and my pillow, the jewels I had concealed in them, and putting them in a cafket, committed them to the care of the prefect. We thought we never fhould have been able to hire horfes, for no body would go with us into Mingrelia ; but at laft by the means of money we gained over two men, and gave fecurity for their horfes and clothes in cafe they fhould be robbed of them. I alfo difmiffed my valet, who played me a thoufand villainous pranks, and many times attempted my deftruction ; after I had expoftulated with him on the numerous inftances of treachery of which he had been guilty, I paid him for the whole time he had ferved me, and exhorted him to amendment. But the mildnefs of this treatment had no effect upon him : he was enraged at being difmiffed in a ftrange couutry ; and gave me room to fear fomething fatal from his refentment. I was tempted to lay him in irons, which I could have done for a word fpeaking, the Capuchins having fuch credit at Teflis, as to be able to do it with the greateft eafe : but I pitied him ; and the reader will foon fee the dangerous fnare he laid for me.

On the 20th of December I fet out with brother Angelo and a Georgian belonging to the Capuchins, who had frequently been at Colchis, and all the neighbouring countries, and whom the prefect recommended as a perfon in whom I might place the greateft confidence. We were only five men with four horfes. Brother Angelo and I mounted two, the two others carried provifions, and we every where gave out, that we were going in fearch of the Theatines of Mingrelia. We again paffed mountains covered with fnow, and at length coming to

the banks of a large river, croſſed it in a boat; then
deſcending a mountain, we entered a large valley
that extends into Mingrelia, and is watered by
ſeveral ſtreams. Here we lay in a village named
Seſano, ſituated in the fineſt part of the country of
Imeretta.

Seſano is near a caſtle belonging to an old lady,
aunt to the King of Imeretta, who being now ſick,
and hearing that a Capuchin was arrived at the village,
ſent for him, all the miſſionaries being in theſe countries taken for Phyſicians, and indeed they all prac-
tiſe phyſic. Brother Angelo went to her, and was in
hopes of making this event turn out to our advantage.
Two hours after he left us, to my great ſurprize, a
Capuchin of Gory, arrived on horſeback with a guide
to inform us, that the valet I had diſmiſſed had been
at Gory, where he had diſcovered all he knew of my
enterprize: ſwearing to ruin me, and that he was
gone nobody knew whither. This news greatly
alarmed me, and having given the Capuchin a thouſand thanks, I prevailed on him to accompany us.

The next day we proceeded five leagues through
the above plain, which contains many villages and
woods; leaving on our right the fortreſs of Scander,
ſaid by the natives to have been built by Alexander
the Great. We afterwards paſſed by Chicaris, a
village that contains fifty houſes, and took up our
lodging at the diſtance of a league from it, where
we were obliged to ſtay two days; our carriers refuſ-
ing to proceed any farther. The news of the war
with which they were entertained by every paſſenger,
made their hearts fail them; and they were ſeized
with the dread of being led to death or ſlavery. To
raiſe their courage, we called the carriers and the
Georgian recommended by the prefect, and told
them that they had nothing to fear; that we were
well informed of every thing; that we had our lives
and goods to preſerve as well as they, and that we
would anſwer for the ſafety of their horſes and per-

fons. One of them then fpoke for the reft, and defired me to give them a writing, by which I would engage to buy them, in cafe they fhould be taken for flaves, or 120 crowns to their wives, if they fhould die. This I readily granted, and making them alfo other great promifes, prevailed on them to proceed.

The next day we reached Cotatis, and lodged at the houfe of the bifhop, who was not at home, but his officers knowing brother Angelo, gave us a very kind reception. Cotatis is a town built at the foot of a hill on the banks of the river Phafis, and contains only about 200 houfes. At a little diftance are thofe of the lords and the king's palace. The town has neither fortifications nor walls, and is every where open, except being inclofed in part by the river and a mountain, at the foot of which it is fituated. On a higher mountain on the other fide of the river oppofite the town, is the fortrefs of Cotatis, which has a high double wall, ftrengthened with towers.

I ftayed at the town all the next day, when while I was at dinner with the two Capuchins; the carriers and my guide being alfo according to the cuftom of the country, at table with us; I faw the rogue of a valet, enter with an Armenian and a prieft, who came to fhew him the houfe. I was not much furprifed at feeing him, for my apprehenfions kept him conftantly in my thoughts. I did not, however, difcover the leaft fear: I imagined he was turned Mahometan from his wearing a turbant. The villain entered with fury in his looks, and feated himfelf by my men, without being afked. This infolence offended me ftill more, and I afked, from whence he came? He replied, from Acalzika, whence he had come in two days. I afked, if the way was fo eafy, and the mountains fo little covered with fnow, that he could crofs them in fo fhort a time? The way is the worft in the world, he cried; and the mountains are covered with fnow like thofe we paffed in coming to Gonia. You fhall fee, for you muft come to Acalzika ; I have orders from the baffa to bring you to that town. You muft have more force to carry me thither, faid I, for I have no bufinefs there. You are ill advifed ; you know I paid you at Teflis ; and if you are not fatisfied, you ought to make known your demands ; for without going fo far as Acalzika on fo trifling an affair, there are fufficient numbers at Cotatis capable of deciding it. This I fpoke with the greatéft mildnefs poffible. But the villain turned with a furious air to his companion, and bid him bring in the Turks. He went out immediately ; but this was only an artifice to terrify me : I was indeed extremely frighted, and thought myfelf loft. The prieft of Cotatis was ignorant of what paffed, becaufe we talked in the Turkifh tongue ; but being informed by father Angelo of the nature of the difpute, and the equity of my propofal, he immediately interefted himfelf in the affair, and with feveral Georgians, preffed the fellow to agree to fo reafonable an offer ; but the more they faid, the more infolent and abufive he grew. Till at laft, lofing all patience, I ftruck at him with my fword ; but they ftopped my hand, and the villain fled in a great fright.

It was now refolved that brother Angelo fhould the next morning proceed forward into Mingrelia, while the other Capuchin and I fhould ftay behind ; the principal reafon was our being unable either to buy or hire horfes, and the neceffity of fending one for the ufe of my partner.

The next day, which was the 2d of January, brother Angelo fet out with all the horfes and men I had brought from Teflis, while I returned to Chicaris with the Capuchin, where we propofed to wait till brother Angelo's return.

I had continued there a fortnight, when one morning at break of day, I was agreeably awaked by my comrade. He told me that brother Angelo with the men and horfes arrived at Sippias on the

9th, when to his great joy he heard of my arrival at
Teflis, and that I was then waiting for him near
Cotatis. He inftantly prepared for the journey, dug
up the chefts, and took out of the roof of the houfe
half of what he had concealed there, and having
ftaid till the eleventh, to reft the horfes, fet out,
leaving the remainder of the treafure to the care of
the moft faithful of our valets, not daring to run
the hazard of lofing the whole at once.

Having proceeded thus far, he added: "Don't
" be frighted at what I am going to relate, every
" thing goes well. On Saturday the 14th we happily
" arrived at Cotatis, and brother Angelo took me
" to the bifhop's houfe. I did not know of the
" menaces made you by the valet you had difmiffed,
" till yefterday ; if I had I fhould not have ftopped
" at Cotatis. Brother Angelo and our men, never
" once thinking of him, entreated me on Sunday
" morning to ftay till noon, in order to refrefh our-
" felves a little after our fatigues. I confented ; but
" while we were at dinner, the rogue of a valet
" entered with twenty janizaries. Where is my
" mafter ? he cried with a loud voice : he attempted
" to kill me, and has not paid me ; but I will
" certainly pay him. He then looked about for you ;
" but not finding you he entered another room, with
" the hopes of finding you concealed there. I
" followed him : entreated him not to ruin us, and
" told him that if my comrade had ufed him ill, or
" had not paid him, I was not anfwerable for it :
" but that let his demands be what they would, I'd
" pay him immediately, if he would but fend away
" the Turks. He anfwered, that he agreed to this,
" and when he had difmiffed them, he would come
" to me again.

" He then returned to the hall, and fhewing
" brother Angelo to the janizaries, bid them take
" that man to the governor of the fortrefs. He
" was inftantly feized. The janizaries looked around

" to fee if there was any thing they could fteal,
" and cafting their eyes on our cloaks carried them
" off. Thefe were all they feized ; they took none
" of my arms, nor the bags I carried about me, in
" which were gold and precious ftones to the value
" of 40,000 crowns. The moment I faw the jani-
" zaries out of the houfe, I fent a valet to follow
" brother Angelo, and conjured the carriers to fly
" with us immediately. We faddled and loaded our
" horfes in an inftant, and, thank God, are arrived
" in fafety, with every thing I brought from Min-
" grelia ; having loft nothing but what the janiza-
" ries have taken, which is fcarcely worth two pif-
" toles."

It is impoffible to exprefs the joy I felt on this occafion. The Capuchin went immediately to the bifhop and the queen, to complain to them both, and
to defire them to procure the deliverance of father
Angelo ; and having now obtained more horfes, my
comrade fet out on his return to Mingrelia, with five
men, to take away the reft of the treafure I left there,
while I, with the Capuchin, and three men, took the
way to Teflis. But being arrived at Gory, I fent
the Capuchin with a fum of money to Cotatis, in order to purchafe the releafe of father Angelo.

On the evening of the 6th of February my comrade arrived at Teflis, with the reft of the treafure,
and the valets I had left in Colchis, together with a
Theatine father, and brother Angelo : as foon as I
had embraced them round, the latter drew me afide,
to tell me the fequel of his adventure.

" You have heard, faid he, in what manner your
" perfidious valet had me feized by the Janizaries.
" The governor of the fortrefs of Cotatis had fent
" them, on his reprefenting that you owed him 300
" crowns ; that you were an ambaffador ; that you
" were going into Mingrelia, in fearch of the trea-
" fures you had left there, and that in your perfon
" he would obtain a prize that would enrich him for-

" ever. The villain preffed the Janizaries who con-
" ducted me to the fortrefs, to bind me and ufe me
" ill ; but there was among them a renegado Italian,
" who caufed me to be treated more mildly. I
" walked along as flowly as poffible, and amufed
" them to give your comrade time to fly ; for I did
" not doubt but he would take that ftep. When
" they had brought me before the governor, he afked
" the villain, if I was his mafter ; he replied that I
" was not, and that he could not find him ; but
" that I certainly knew where he was. The go-
" vernor then examined me about you ; I told him,
" I did not know where you were ; but that when
" you left me, you defigned to go to Teflis. He
" then afked me many queftions about your quality,
" and told me, that I fhould pay the 300 crowns it
" was pretended you owed. I replied, that you were
" a poor friar who had taken the trouble to give me
" notice of the miferable ftate to which thofe of your
" order were reduced in Mingrelia ; and upon this
" I was going to vifit them. That this was all I
" knew of you, and that every body at Cotatis, from
" the king to the meaneft of his fubjects, knew that
" I made a profeffion of poverty.
   " Upon this the governor ordered me to be
" fearched, they found the girdle you had given me,
" wherein were feven piftoles ; but the jewels you
" had wrote to your comrade to give me, I had hap-
" pily not received. The governor then cried,
" wretch, where are the riches thou haft promifed
" me ; haft thou brought me this poor man to mock
" me ? thou art a villain, and I will order thee to
" be baftinadoed to death. My lord, replied he,
" trembling, thefe riches are in the hands of my
" mafter's comrade, who is at the bifhop's. Dog
" as thou art, returned the governor, why haft thou
" not brought him then ? go and fetch him. He
" went with the Janizaries. I was dreadfully afraid
" they would find him ; but my fear was turned into

" joy, when returning the Janizaries reported he
" was fled. The governor flew in a rage againſt
" your valet who appeared confounded. I then re-
" lated the ill offices he had done you, and how ge-
" neroully you had paid him his wages.

" At night the governor invited me to ſupper,
" and learning that I was a phyſician, made me vi-
" ſit ſome ſoldiers in the fortreſs, to whom I admi-
" niſtered remedies. The next day the queen and
" biſhop ſent two gentlemen to the governor to de-
" mand my releaſe, and at noon there came two
" others from a great lord of the country, whoſe
" lady being ill, and he hearing that I was confined
" in the fortreſs for debt, paid the governor 25 crowns
" for my diſcharge, and I was releaſed, notwith-
" ſtanding the clamours of the valet, who ſaid that
" you would give a thouſand crowns, rather than
" leave me there. I now went to viſit the lady, and
" a few days after father Juſtin arrived at Chicaris,
" where hearing that I was with this lord, he came
" to me, reſtored the 25 crowns, and we went toge-
" ther to Chicaris. Two days after your comrade ar-
" rived with the remains of what had been left at
" Mingrelia. He told us the way he had taken to
" avoid coming near Cotatis ; and that he had heard
" the rogue of a valet was confined in the fortreſs,
" and probably would not eſcape without due chaf-
" tiſement."

It was late, but my comrade and I could not go
to ſupper till after we had ſome diſcourſe on the happy
ſucceſs of our labours. We could not have hoped
thus to have ſaved every thing, when we were ſurrounded with dangers that made us dread the loſs of
all ; and yet our loſſes in this fatal journey had
amounted to no more than one per cent.

Georgia, by which I would be underſtood to mean
the whole country of that name ſubject to Perſia, is
bounded on the eaſt by Circaſſia and Ruſſia, on the
weſt by Armenia Minor, on the ſouth by Armenia

Major, and on the north by the Black Sea, and that
part of Mingrelia called Imeretta. This is, in my
opinion, the whole country diftinguifhed by the ancients by the name of Iberia. It has many woods
and mountains that enclofe large and beautiful plains;
but the middle part, which is watered by the river
Kur, the ancient Cyrus, is the moft fertile. The
natives call themfelves Carthueli, and it is faid the
Greeks gave them the name of Georgoi, which in
their language fignifies labourer.

The air of Georgia is dry, very cold in winter,
and hot in fummer. The fine weather does not begin
till the month of May ; but then it lafts till the end
of November. The inhabitants are therefore obliged
to water the earth ; by which means it produces all
forts of grain and fruit in the greateft profufion.
The bread is as good as any in the world. The fruits
are excellent, and of all forts. No part of Europe
produces finer, or better tafted pears and apples,
nor any part of Afia, more excellent pomegranates.
The cattle are extremely numerous and very good ;
the wild boars are as common and as delicate as in
Mingrelia ; and the common people live almoft entirely upon fwine, which are feen all over the country,
and their flefh is not only extremely palatable but
very wholefome.. The wild fowl are incomparable,
and of all forts. Befides the Cafpian Sea, which is
near Georgia, and the Kur which runs through it, afford the greateft plenty of fea and frefh-water fifh.

In no other country do the inhabitants drink fo
much, or fuch excellent wine. The vines grow
about the trees as in Mingrelia, and great quantities
of wine are fent from Teflis into Armenia, Media,
and to Ifpahan, where it is ufed at the fhah's table.
An horfe load, which is three hundred weight, fells
for about the value of eight fhillings: this is the
price of the beft fort, for the ordinary wine does
not fell for more than half as much. Georgia alfo

produces great quantities of filk, which is exported to Turky and the neighbouring countries.

The Geogians are the handfomeft people, not only in the eaft, but, I believe, in the whole world; and I never obferved an ordinary perfon of either fex in this country ; but I have feen fome that have been quite angelical. Nature has given moft of the women fuch graces as are no where elfe to be feen ; and it is impoflible to behold, without loving them. They are tall, eafy, not encumbered with fat, and have flender waifts. But they injure their beauty with paint, which they ufe as an ornament, in .the fame manner as among us are worn jewels and rich clothes.

The Georgians have naturally much wit, and had they a proper education might poflible be diftin- guifhed by their learning, and their fkill in the arts and fciences ; but the neglect of all infiruction, and the force of ill example, render them ignorant, dif- honeft, and extremely vicious. They will, with the greateft effrontery, deny what what they have faid and done, and affert and vindicate the moft notorious falfehoods. They are irreconcileable in their hatred, and never forgive ; but then they are not eafily difpleafed, and never conceive a perpetual hatred without juft caufe of anger. They are addicted to drunkennefs and luxury, which are not even efteemed crimes. The churchmen get drunk as well as the laity, and keep beautiful flaves for concubines. No- body is offended at this, becaufe it is the authorifed cuftom. The prefect of the capuchins affured me, that he had heard the catholicos, or patriarch of Georgia fay, that he who at the great feafts at Chrift- mas, and Eafter, does not get drunk, ought not to be efteemed a Chriftian, and deferves to be excom- municated. The women are no lefs vicious than the men ; their defires are warm, and they are even more to blame than the other fex for that torrent of

2

impurity that overflows the country. The Georgians are alfo great ufurers, they feldom lend without
pledges, and the loweft intereft they take is two per
cent. per month. In other refpects, the Georgians
are friendly, civil, and appear with great gravity.
Their manners and cuftoms are a mixture of thofe
of moft of the nations that furround them. This I
believe, proceeds from the commerce they carry on
with many different countries, and from the liberty
every one enjoys in Georgia of living according to
his own religion and cuftoms, and of freely defending them. Here you fee Armenians, Greeks, Turks,
Perfians, Indians, Tartars, and Mofcovites. The
Armenians are even more numerous than the Georgians themfelves; they are alfo more rich, and fill
moft of the inferior pofts and employments of the
ftate; but the Georgians are more powerful, more
vain, and oftentatious. The difference between their
difpofitions, manners, and belief was caufed a reciprocal hatred. They naturally abhor each other,
and never intermarry. The Georgians, in particular,
confider the Armenians in much the fame light as
that in which many Europeans behold the Jews.

The habit of the Georgians is almoft like that
of the Poles: they wear their bonnets like theirs;
their vefts are open at the breaft, and faftened with
buttons and loops; their covering for the legs and
feet refembles that of the Perfians, and the habit of
the women is entirely Perfian.

The houfes of the great, and all the public edifices,
are erected on the fame models as thofe in Perfia.
They build very cheap; for they have wood, ftone,
plafter, and lime in abundance. They alfo imitate
the Perfians in their manner of fitting, lying and
eating.

The nobility excercife the moft tyrannical power
over their vaffals, whom they oblige to work for
them whole moflths together, and as often as they
pleafe without giving them either pay or food. They

think they have a right to their fubftance, liberty, and lives: they take their children and fell them, or keep them as flaves: but they feldom fell any, efpecially women, who are above twenty years of age.

The Georgians are almoft as ignorant with refpeĉt to religion as the Mingrelians. Both countries received the knowledge of Chriftianity in the fourth century, from a women of Iberia, who embraced the Chriftian religion at Conftantinople ; and both have now loft the fpirit of it. There are many bifhops in Georgia befides the Catholicos or Patriarch. The Prince, though of the Mahometan religion, commonly fills the vacant fees, and generally chufes his own relations ; even the Catholicos is his brother. The churches in the towns are kept in decent order ; but in the country they are very dirty. The Georgians, like other Chriftians fituated to the north and the weft of them, have a ftrange cuftom of building moft of their churches on the top of mountains, in diftant, and almoft inacceffible places. They fee and falute them at three or four leagues diftance: but they hardly ever go to them ; and it is certain that moft of them are not opened once in ten years. They build them, and then abandoned them to the injuries of the weather, and to the birds. The reafon of this cuftom I could never difcover.

Moft of the Georgian lords make an outward profeffion of the Mahometan religion, fome to gain employments at court, or penfions from the ftate ; others to obtain the honour of marrying their daughters to the prince, or only to introduce them to the fervice of his women. There are fome of thefe bafe nobility who will themfelves lead their moft beautiful daughters to the prince ; for which they are rewarded by a poft in the government, or a penfion.

While I was at Teflis, a Georgian lord, letting the prince know that he had a niece remarkable for

her uncommon beauty, his majefty ordered that fhe
fhould be brought to him, and he took upon himfelf
the office of bringing her. The villain went to his
fifter, who was a widow, and told her that the prince
would marry her daughter, and that fhe muft prepare
her for that honour. The mother immediately informed the poor girl of the violence that was going
to be offered her : fhe loved a young lord in the
neighbourhood, who had an equal affeftion for her ;
and the mother had encouraged their paffion. In
this diftrefs they took the refolution to condole with
the lover. They fent for him, and he arrived foon
after. He found the mother and the daughter fhut
up by themfelves, mingling their tears, and in the
deepeft diftrefs, lamenting the feverity of their fate.
The lover threw himfelf at their feet, and let them
know that he dreaded nothing fo much as the lofs of
his miftrefs ; and that the prince could infliét nothing
on him fo dreadful as this lofs. That the only way
of preferving him from it, was their being immediately married, and that the next day they might inform their perfidious uncle, that fhe was no longer a
maid. The propofal was accepted, and the mother
leaving the room, the lover wiped away the tears of
diftrefs that fell from the eyes of his miftrefs, by inftantly marrying her. The uncle difcovered the
whole affair, and told it to his majefty, who being
enraged at his difappointment, gave exprefs ordeis
for bringing to court both the mother, the daughter,
and the hufband. But they fled, and for fome months
efcaped from place to place. At length being convinced that they fhould be at laft taken, they got to
Acalzika, where the Turkifh baffa took them under
his proteétion.

The fear of fuch accidents obliges thofe of the
Georgians who have beautiful daughters, to marry
them as foon as poffible, and even in their infancy.
The poor efpecially marry theirs early, and even in
the cradle, that the lords to whom they are fubjeét,

may not take them away in order to fell, or make them their concubines.

Georgia has but four fortified towns, Teflis, Gory, Suram, and Aly; of which the former is the capital of the province. It is fituated at the foot of a mountain, and by it runs the river Kur. The city is furrounded with handfome ftrong walls, except on the river fide, and extends from north to fouth. It has a large fortrefs on the declivity of the mountain, where the garrifon only confifts of native Perfians. Here is a public fquare, an arfenal, and a market. This fortrefs is a place of refuge for criminals and debtors. The prince of Georgia is obliged to pafs through it, when he goes, according to cuftom, without the gates of the city to receive the letters and prefents fent him by the king of Perfia; becaufe the city has no other entrance in the road from Perfia, but through this fortrefs; and the prince never paffes through it, without the apprehenfions that the governor has fecret orders to feize his perfon. Teflis has fourteen churches, which is a great number in a country where there is fo little devotion. Six of thefe belong to the Georgians, and the reft to the Armenians. The cathedral, which is called Sion, is fituated on the bank of the river, and is entirely built of hewn ftones. It is an ancient building, very entire and has four naves. In the middle is a large dome fupported by four maffy pillars. The great altar is in the midft of the nave facing the eaft. The infide is filled with Greek paintings lately executed by fuch wretched hands, that it is extremely difficult to difcover what they are intended to reprefent. To this edifice joins the bifhop's palace, and the principal churches of the Georgians, who had alfo a handfome church at the fouth end of the city; but it is now converted into a magazine for gunpowder.

Though this city belongs to the empire of Perfia, and as well as the whole province, is governed by a

prince who profeſſes the Mahometan religion, it
has not one moſque. The Perſians have indeed
made uſe of their utmoſt endeavours to build them ;
but have never been able to accompliſh it ; for the
people immediately roſe in arms, pulled down the
work, and beat the workmen. The princes of
Georgia were indeed glad of theſe ſeditions, though
they pretended the contrary ; for having abjured the
Chriſtian religion only to obtain the viceroyalty,
they were not willing to conſent to the eſtabliſhment
of Mahometaniſm. The Georgians are naturally mu-
tinous, fickle, and brave ; and being ſituated near
the Turks, the Perſians have not been willing to
come to extremities with them ; hence Teflis, and
all Georgia, are allowed the liberty of preſerving
their religion. They uſe bells in their churches ;
they daily ſell pork in the market, and wine is ſold
at the corners of the ſtreets.

The public buildings at Teflis make a handſome
appearance ; theſe are of ſtone, and kept in good
order; particularly the bazars, and the caravanſerais.
The palace of the prince is one of the principal ornaments of the city. It has grand ſaloons, which
open upon the river, and face very extenſive gardens.
There are aviaries filled with great numbers of
birds of different kinds ; and a very noble falconry.
Before the palace is a ſquare, in which may be drawn
up near a thouſand horſe. It is ſurrounded with
ſhops, and oppoſite the gate of the palace is the
grand bazar, from the upper end of which the
ſquare and the front of the palace appear in a
beautiful perſpective. In the neighbourhood of the
city are many pleaſure houſes and fine gardens.

On the 10th, the prefect of the Capuchins informed the viceroy of my arrival ; which, indeed could
not be concealed from a prince, who knows the moſt
trifling things that happen at Teflis : but I was
deſirous of ſeeing him, and preſenting the paſſports
of the king of Perſia, addreſſed to all the governors

of provinces, to whom I was ftrongly recommended ;
for I made no doubt but at at the fight of thefe orders
he would give me a good reception, and an efcort
to conduct me out of his dominions.   This prince,
who is called Chanavas Khan, told the prefect that
I was welcome, and that I fhould do him a pleafure
to come and fee him as foon as I could ; and on the
12th, he fent a gentleman to inform me, that as he
was entering on a week of rejoicing, during which
he fhould every day give a public entertainment to
his whole court, he defired me to come.   The Capuchins entreated my comrade and I, to drefs as well
as poffible, and on their account to make a very
noble prefent to the prince.   To this I agreed, being
very glad of an opportunity of fhewing my gratitude
for the important fervices I had received from them.

It was near noon when we went to the palace,
accompanied by the prefect, and one of the community, named father Raphael.   The prince was in
a hall about a hundred feet long and forty broad,
built on the bank of the river, with an open front
on that fide.   The ceiling was covered with mofaic
work, and fupported by a number of pillars between
twenty-five and thirty feet in height, painted and
gilt, and the whole room was covered with rich
tapeftry.   The prince and the principal nobility,
were placed near three fires, which with feveral pans
of coals, fufficiently heated the room.   Chanavas
Khan caufes himfelf to be faluted like the king of
Perfia, by kneeling at two or three paces diftance,
and bowing the head three times fuccellively to the
floor.   But this is difpenfed with in regard to the
Europeans, and I faluted him without kneeling.
Two gentlemen in waiting, afterwards led me to my
place ; but I would not fit above the Capuchins ;
for I was glad of an opportunity of doing them
honour.

While I was bowing a gentleman at the door of
the hall took my letters patent from the king of

Perfia, which I held in my hand, and the prefent for the prince, which I had brought, and had ranged in a large filver bowl. The prince opened the patent, put it to his mouth, and his forehead, then gave it to his firft minifter, for him to tell him the contents. Afterwards he looked at the prefent, which was placed at his feet, with much curiofity and pleafure. It confifted of a large watch in a filver cafe, chafed and gilt : a cryftal mirrour mounted in filver : a gold box enamelled, to hold pills of opium, which molt of the Perfians take feveral times a-day : a very neat cafe of furgeons inftruments, and knives with curious handles.

The firft minifter, after having read the patent, in a low voice, told the prince what it contained. All the great men admired the words wrote in gold, and the flowered work in the margin, which was very large. It was one fheet of paper two feet and a half long, and thirteen or fourteen inches broad. Befides the writing in gold, there were words in blue, and others in red, thus the principal words and fentences were diftinguifhed, while the reft were wrote in black.

In bowing to the viceroy, I fpoke not a word, nor did he move. A moment after I was feated, he fent me half a large loaf, which ftood before him, upon a gilt difh, and ordered me to be told that I was welcome. A little after he fent to afk me, how the war went on between the Turks and the Poles.

I fhall not defcribe the order and magnificence of this feaft ; I fhall only fay, that a great deal of wine was drank, and that a prodigious quantity of meat was eaten. We arofe from the table after having fat three hours ; and yet the roaft meat was not yet brought in. We made a low bow to the prince on our retiring, when he fent again to tell us, we were welcome, and ordered us to be conducted home. -

On the 14th the prince fent us two great flagons of wine, two pheafants, and four partridges. The gentleman who brought them told me, that the prince had given him orders to enquire, whether I wanted any thing ; and whether the Capuchins took care to divert us ; and to tell us, that if we liked the wine he fent us, we might fend every day for it to his pantry. I thanked the gentleman, and defired him to affure the prince, that the Capuchins fuffered us to want for nothing, and that we drank together the prince's health, with the wine he fent. Indeed, we could no where drink better.

On the 16th, the prince invited us to the marriage of his niece, which was performed at the palace. I .went there with the prefect and father Raphael, one of the Capuchins ; but the marriage ceremony was almoft over before we arrived. It was performed in the grand faloon where we had dined before, and it being full of ladies, no other men were admitted but the prince and his near relations.

It is only fince the Georgians have been fubjected to Perfia, that they have forbid their women to converfe with men : this, however, takes place only in the town ; for in the country, and in places where there are no Mahometans, they wear no veils, and make no difficulty of feeing and fpeaking to the other fex ; but as the cuftoms of the Mahometans gradually gain ground in Georgia, with their religion, the liberty of the women decreafes in the fame proportion.

The marriage feaft was on a terrace of the palace, furrounded with a fopha two feet high ; and upon it was erected a grand pavilion fupported on fine columns twenty two feet in height, and about five inches in diameter. The lining was of gold and filver brocade, velvet, and painted linen, fo artfully joined, that by the light of the tapers it appeared like a cieling compofed of flowers and morefco work, The floors were covered with fine carpets, and the

2

place lighted with forty large lamps fixed on ftands refembling candlefticks, moft of which were forty pounds weight, and 15 inches in diameter.; the four next the prince were gilt, and the others filvered. The ftand at the height of a foot and a half, bore a cup full of tallow, which fupplied two wicks with light.

The guefts, who amounted to about an hundred, were ranged on fophas, extending round the room : the prince fat on one raifed above the reft, and covered with a canopy made in the form of a dome. His fon and his brothers were on his right, and the bifhops on his left. The prince made us fit with the Capuchins immediately after the bifhops, and the muficians were below. Soon after we were feated the bridegroom entered, led by the Cathlicos, and having taken his feat, the prince's relations went to make him their compliments, and to offer him a prefent ; and this was afterwards done by moft of the other guefts, each in his rank. This formed a kind of proceffion that lafted about half an hour. The prefents confifted of money in gold and filver, and in fmall filver cups : but all of them together did not I believe, amount to above 200 crowns.

In the mean while fupper was ferved up in the following manner : firft, cloths of the length of the fophas were fpread before all the guefts. The bread was then ferved up, and the meat brought in large covered filver difhes, the difh and cover commonly weighing 50 or 60 * marks. Thofe who brought the difhes into the hall, ranged them on a cloth at the entrance; other officers brought them to the carvers, who filled deep plates, which they prefented to the guefts ; bringing them firft to the prince, then to the others. They firft ferved the fame meat round, then another, and fo on. The feaft confifted of three

* Each mark being eight ounces.

fervices, in each of which there were about fixty of thefe large covered dithes. The firft was of all forts of pilaw or pleo; that is, rice dreffed with meat, which was of various colours and taftes ; the yellow was dreffed with faffron, cinnamon and fugar; the red with the juice of the pomegranate ; but the white, which is the beft, was of the natural colour. This pilaw is very delicate food, and extremely wholefome. The fecond fervice was of tarts, fweet and four fricafees, and ragouts. The third was of roaft meat. All the three fervices were mixed with fifh, eggs, and pulfe for the ecclefiaftics. Every thing was brought in and taken away with furprizing filence: for three Europeans at a table would make more noife than all the guefts and fervants in this hall, who were not lefs than an hundred and fifty.

The prodigious number of drinking veffels was alfo very furprizing ; thefe were about 120, and con-fifted of bowls, cups, and horns, fixty flagons, and twelve tankards. The flagons were of gold polifhed or enamelled. The cups and bowls were fome of gold enamelled, fome of polifhed gold, others adorn-ed with precious ftones, and others of filver. The horns were adorned like the richeft cups, and were of feveral fizes ; but moft of them were about eight inches in height, and of a bright black. Some of them were made of the horn of the rhinoceros ; but the moft common were of cows horns.

I do not know how long the feaft lafted ; for I did not ftay till the end of it ; we retiring at midnight, when the roaft meat was not taken away. Nobody drank till the third fervice, and then they began to drink healths in the following manner. They deliver-ed to eight perfons neareft the prince, four on his right hand, and four on his left, eight fmall cups of the fame fize and fafhion full of wine. Thofe on the right hand drank off the wine firft and then thofe on the left. The others next them were then ferved till the health went round. After which they began again with eight larger cups. It is the cuſtom of the country to drink the healths of the great with the largeſt cups; and the gueſts to ſhew their reſpect, continue this till they are quite drunk. In this manner they drank for the two laſt hours of my being there, I afterwards learnt that they did not break off till it was light. The Capuchins and I were exempted from drinking, and indeed had I drank as much as thoſe who ſat near me, I ſhould have died upon the ſpot: but the prince gave orders that we ſhould drink no more than we liked.

When the healths began, the inſtruments and vocal muſic ſtruck up, with which the whole aſſembly ſeemed tranſported, though to me it appeared rude and barbarous.

On the 20th, I deſired the prefect, and father Raphael to return thanks to the prince for the honours he had conferred upon me, and to deſire him to grant me an officer to conduct me as far as Irivan, the capital of Armenia Major; to which the prince readily agreed He proteſſed to entertain an eſteem for the Europeans, and that he ſhould be glad to have a number of them ſettled in Georgia; and added, that if they came thither for the ſake of trade, he would grant them all the advantages they could deſire; and that as his country extended to the Black Sea, they would find their advantage in travelling through it to the Eaſt-Indies.

On the 28th of February we left Teflis, our mehemander riding before to prevent my paying any duties, and to furniſh us with proviſions and lodgings on the road. The next day we proceeded eight leagues through a beautiful plain, to a town named Cuprikent, or the village of the bridge, from its being built near a very fine one that extends over the river Tabadi. The town conſiſts of about 150 houſes, and the bridge, which joins two mountains that are ſeparated by the river, is ſupported by four unequal arches that riſe from two irregular maſſes of rock found in the river. Thofe at the two ends open on each fide, and are hollowed out into fmall chambers and porticoes, for the accommodation of paffengers : an arch near the middle of the river, has an opennig on each fide, with two chambers at the ends, and two large covered balconies, where the people may enjoy the frefh air during the heat of fummer. You here defcend by two pair of ftairs which are cut down from the arch. This bridge joins to a caravanferai now in ruins ; though it has been one of the fineft in all Georgia.

The three following days we paffed over high mountains difficult of accefs, and arrived on the 4th of March at Dilyjan, a town confifting of about 300 houfes, fituated on a river that runs at the foot of a high and frightful mountain, which, as well as the others we had juft paffed, forms a part of mount Taurus. On thefe high mountains we were much incommoded with the fnow and cold ; but there is every where to be found abundance of water, and here and there are fmall fertile plains. The goodnefs of the foil, and the number of the villages are almoft incredible ; fome of thefe are on points of land fo high, that the paffengers below can fcarcely fee them. Moft of them are inhabited by Georgian and Armenian Chriftians ; but they are not intermixed, for they are fuch enemies, that they will not dwell together in the fame village. In all thefe mountains are found neither caravanferais nor any other public houfes ; but we lodged commodioufly enough with the peafants, who fupplied us with plenty of meat and drink ; for our mehemander went before, to provide for our reception, fo that on my arrival I found a houfe and ftable prepared, a great fire lighted, and fupper ready. The firft day I would have given fomething to my landlord ; but my conductor, prevented me, faying, that was not the cuftom, and that I fhould rather give it to him. I therefore afterwards privately hid fomething for the ufe of the people with whom we lodged. Thus we travelled very commodioufly ; and at night my chamber was guarded by the men of the village who ftood centry, as well to execute my orders, as to guard me from danger, though there was nothing to fear.

Moft of the houfes of thefe villages are properly caverns; for they are hollowed out of the earth. The others are built of large beams quite up to the top, which is made flat, and covered with turf, an opening being left in the middle to admit the light, and let out the fmoke ; this hole they ftop when they pleafe. The above caverns have the advantage of being warm in winter, and cool in fummer.

The town of Delyjan, and all the country for fix leagues round, is called the territory of Cafac, and depends on Perfia, in the fame manner as Georgia, it being always governed by its natural princes, in a direct line from father to fon. Abas the great conquered all thefe countries at the fame time that he made himfelf mafter of Georgia.

On the fifth we proceeded five leagues in paffing the frightful mountain already mentioned. I thought I fhould have died with the fatigue of this journey : I was troubled with a dyfentery, which obliged me to difmount every quarter of an hour : two men fupported me, and a third led my horfe. The whole mountain was covered with fnow, and nothing elfe could be feen above us, no not fo much as a tree or plant. The road was a narrow path of fnow hardened by being trampled upon by travellers and their horfes : and as foon as we fet foot out of this path we funk up to the middle. There is no poffibility of paffing this mountain while the fnow is falling, or when the wind blows ; for then the track is loft, and thus many people perifh every year. This fnow never melts, and the mountain is perpetually covered with it.

The next day, though half dead, I continued my journey, and spurred on by the hopes of finding some relief at Irivan, we proceeded five leagues to Bickni, a considerable town, situated at the foot of a mountain on the banks of the Zengui, and lodged at a handsome monastery belonging to the Armenians, built between the town and the mountain. The monks received me with much humanity ; but it being lent, nothing could prevail on them to make me some chicken broth, and my conductor was obliged to make use of all his authority to get me a few eggs.

The next morning at break of day, we departed, after having made a small present to the monastery, and travelled nine leagues over plains covered with snow. The travelling in these snows is attended with great pain and danger from the rays of the sun, which falling upon it, give it an insupportable brightness, that is very prejudicial to the sight, notwith-standing all the precautions we could take, by following the example of the natives in putting a thin black or green silk handkerchief before our eyes, which only serves to lessen the evil. When we met with peasants, it was necessary to dispute who should enter the snow, for the track is so narrow that two horses cannot pass by each other upon it. When the numbers are equal, they usually come to blows, otherwise the weakest yield. They unload their horses, and make them enter the snow, in which they sink up to their bellies, and thus stand to give a pas-sage to the others. To this all whom we met were obliged by my conductor to submit. We passed by several towns and villages, and at night arrived at Irivan.

Irivan is a large dirty city, the greatest part of which is filled with gardens and vineyards. It is situated in a plain surrounded with mountains, and on the banks of two rivers, the Zengui washing it

MINGRELIA INTO PERSIA. 71

to the north weſt, and a river called the Forty Fountains, from the number of its ſources, running to
the ſouth-weſt. The fortreſs, which is at a little
diſtance, might paſs for a ſmall city. It is of an
oval form, four thouſand paces round, and contains
about 800 houſes. None live in it but native Perſians.
The Armenians have ſhops in which they work,
and trade in the day : but at night they ſhut them
up, and return to their houſes. This fortreſs has
three walls of earth, and battlements of white bricks,
flanked with towers, and provided with narrow ram-
parts, extending on the north to a dreadful precipice
above two hundred yards deep, at the bottom of
which flows the river. This inacceſſible part is only
fortified with terraces furniſhed with artillery. The
garriſon conſiſts of 2000 Perſians. It has many
gates and walls, all of them caſed with iron, and
defended by batteries, portculliſes, and fortified
guard houſes. The palace of the governor of the
province is on the brink of the precipice, and makes
a handſome appearance. On an eminence at a
thouſand paces diſtance is a fort, fortified with a
double wall, and artillery, that commands the fortreſs.

There are ſeveral churches in the city, the principal of which is the biſhop's, and another called
Catovike, theſe were erected during the reigns of
the laſt kings of Armenia. The others which have
been ſince built, are ſmall, ſunk in the earth, and
have ſome reſemblance to catacombs.

Near the epiſcopal church is an old tower built
of hewn ſtones; but I could neither learn the time
nor the uſe for which it was built. On the outſide
are inſcriptions in characters like thoſe of the Armenians, but the Armenians cannot read them. This
is an antique work, of a ſingular architecture, and
around it are ſeveral ruins, which ſeem to have belonged to a cloyſter. Near the above ſtructure is a
moſque in ruins, and at ſome diſtance is a large

fquare four hundred paces in diameter, furrounded with trees. This is ufed for caroufals, horfe-races, wreftling matches, and all exercifes either on horfe-back or on foot. There are many baths in the town and fortrefs, and feveral caravanferais ; the fineft of which is within five hundred paces of the caftle. It was built a few years ago by the governor of Armenia. The gate is eighty paces deep, and forms a fine gallery, filled with fhops, where all forts of ftuffs are fold. The body of the edifice is fquare, and contains three great lodging rooms, and fixty fmall ones, with large ftables, and many fpacious warehoufes. Before it is a market furrounded with fhops, in which are fold all forts of provifions, and by the fide of it is a fine mofque, and two coffee-houfes.

Irivan is fituated in 41°. 15 min. north latitude, and enjoys a good air ; but it is thick and very cold. The winter lafts long, and the fnow fometimes falls in April. The country is, however, fertile, and the wine produced in its neighbourhood, is good and cheap. The Armenians have a tradition that Noah planted the vine near Irivan, and point out the very fpot. All forts of provifions are produced in the neighbourhood of the city, and fold at a low price. The two rivers that flow by its fide, and the lake of Irivan, which is at three fmall days journey to the north weft, furnifh the city with fine fifh, particularly trouts and carp that are remarkably good, and famous all over the eaft : fome of them I have feen three feet long.

The Armenians efteem this the moft ancient city of the world, and believe that Noah dwelt there both before and after the deluge, when he defcend-ed from the mountain on which the ark refted. They even fay, that here was the terreftrial para-dife.

At twelve leagues from Irivan, is the celebrated mountain on which almoft all the people of the

country are firmly perfuaded that the ark refted.
This mountain is fo high and large, that when the
air is clear it does not appear above two leagues
diftant. The Armenians even believe that the ark
is ftill on the fummit of this mountain, and fay
that a monk named James being refolved to fee it,
or die in the attempt, went half way up the accli-
vity; but could go no farther, becaufe having afcended thus far every day, he was, while afleep in
the night, carried back to the place from whence he
fet out in the morning. They add that this continued
a long time, till God being willing to fatisfy in part
his defires, fent him a piece of the ark by an angel,
and ordered him to be told, that all accefs to the
top was forbidden to mankind.

At the foot of the mountain is a village of Chriftians, and a monaftery ; for which the Armenians
have great devotion, believing that Noah firft offered
facrifices there after the deluge. This is called the
monaftery of the apoftles ; from its being pretended
that the bodies of St. Andrew and St. Matthew
were found there, and that the fkull of that evan-
gelift is preferved in the church of the monaftery.
The people relate a hundred other abfurd particulars
of this place, and of the country all around, which
they make their Holy Land.

I having fent to inform the governor of Irivan
of my arrival, a meffenger came to tell me that I
was welcome; and that he was very defirous of
feeing me, and a part of the jewels I had brought.
I was then afked how many men I had with me,
and whether I chofe to lodge in the fortrefs, or in
the great caravanferai. I chofe the latter ; becaufe
there can be no place more fecure, and there is no
want of company ; for merchants come there from
all parts of Afia. On this the governor giving
orders for my having one of the beft apartments, I
went thither the next day, with all my baggage,
and about noon an officer belonging to the governor

brought me an order from the intendant to receive daily from the proper officer, bread, wine, flesh, fish, fruit, rice, butter, wood, and .other neceffaries for fix perfons. The quantity of each is regulated ; but the portion allowed for one perfon is fufficient for two.

On the tenth, I went, by the governor's defire, to pay him a vifit, and found him in a large hand-fome light clofet, with feveral lords of the country. He treated me with great complaifance, told me three times that I was welcome, and entertained me with fweetmeats and Ruffian brandy. I fhewed him my patents, after which, he fpent an hour in afking me news of Europe, in relation to the wars in that part of the world ; the prefent difpofition of the Chriftian princes, and the ftate of the fciences, with the new difcoveries that had been made. He fpent another hour in examining the jewels I had brought, of which he talked like one who was well acquainted with them. He fet afide thofe that particularly pleafed him, and fuch as he thought would be agree-able to the princefs his wife. Having kept me to dinner, he honoured me afterwards with his con-verfation for half an hour longer, and then difmiffed me, ordering my mehemander to fuffer me to want for nothing.

This governor was one of the greateft lords of Perfia ; he was beloved by the king, and revered by the court, his two fons were his majefty's chief favourites ; and he was refpected by the people on account of his juftice and integrity. Indeed he well deferved his good fortune ; for befides thefe amiable qualities, he was a man of fenfe, and fond of the arts and fciences.

On the 12th, I difmiffed the officer belonging to the viceroy of Georgia who had conducted me to Irivan, on which occafion I made him a prefent of eight piftoles.

On the fifth of April the governor went to a camp, which he had caufed to be formed a league from the city, in a large and beautiful meadow, always covered with flowers during the fpring. The two rivers that pafs by Irivan, wind in a ferpentine courfe, with a gentle ftream, forming many fmall iflands. The governor's quarter, that of the princefs his wife, and thofe of the moft confiderable perfons who accompanied them, were feparate, and each in an ifland : but they had a communication with each other by means of fmall flying bridges, The governor's tents were extremely magnificent ; they had all the accomodations of a palace, in miniature, even to baths and ftoves. His houfhold confifted of 500 men, without reckoning women and eunuchs. The great are here accuftomed thus to pafs the fpring in the country. They take the diverfions of hunting, fifhing, walking, and exercifes on foot and on horfeback. Thus they tafte the frefhnefs of the air, of which they are extremely fond, and if they have no bufinefs that calls them to the city, they continue to enjoy thefe delights during the fummer, in the moft delicious parts of the neighbouring mountains.

On the 6th I dined with the lieutenant of the fortrefs, who was a native of Daghellan, an extenfive country covered with mountains, on the confines of Ruffia, and I had the pleafure of hearing him relate many fingularities, with refpect to the manners and cuftoms of his country. The next day the treafurer entertained me in the fame manner. I now made thefe gentlemen fmall prefents, in return for the favours I had received from them. They had been of fervice to me at Irivan, without daring to take the dues which one is obliged to pay in Perfia to the officers of the governors, for the money we receive from their treafuries; becaufe their mafter had ftrictly commanded them to make no demands upon me. The careffes and entertainments they now gave me, were therefore defigned to oblige me to make them a proper return ; for they knew that I was two well acquainted with the cuftoms of the country, to believe that this behaviour to a ftranger, proceeded from mere generofity. In the afternoon I went to the camp, to take leave of the governor, who had before appointed me a mehemander ; he now treated me with the utmoft kindnefs, and on retiring, gave me letters of recommendation to his two eldeft fons, who were the king's favourite eunuchs.

I left Irivan on the eighth of April, and on the 12th arrived at Nacchivan, once a vaft city ; but now a prodigious heap of ruins ; but by little and little it has been in part rebuilt and repeopled. In the midft of thefe ruins have arifen bazars; in which are fold all forts of provifions and merchandize. It has five caravanferais, with baths, taverns, and about 2000 houfes : but the Perfian hiftorians maintain, that this city formerly confifted of 40,000. Without the city are the ruins of a large fortrefs, and many forts deftroyed by Abas the Great, at the end of the laft century.

Five leagues to the north of Nacchivan is a large village named Abrener, which fignifies a fertile field. The inhabitants of this, and feven other neighbouring villages, are of the Romifh religion : their bifhop and priefts are Dominicans : but they perform the fervice in the Armenian tongue. A Dominican of Bologna, 350 years ago, brought this part of the country under the authority of the Pope, and above twenty other villages fubmitted to him ; but they have fince returned to their obedience to the Armenian Patriarch, and to their firft religion. The number of thofe who adhere to the church of Rome, diminifh daily, on account of the perfecution of the Patriarch and the governors of Nacchivan.

The next day having paffed the river Nacchivan, over a large bridge, we proceeded through a dry and barren country, to the river Aras, the ancient Araxes, oppofite the ruins of the city of Julfa the old. That city was fituated on the declivity of a mountain, facing the river. The avenues that led to it, which were naturally difficult of accefs, were guarded by forts. The city, according to the Armenians, had 4000 houfes ; but moft of them appear to have been only caverns in the mountains, more fit to afford fhelter to cattle than for the habitations of men. I do not think there is any where in the world a more hideous and barren place ; neither a tree nor a blade of grafs is to be feen, and though there are places of fertility in its neighbourhood, the city could not have been in a more dry and ftony fituation.

It was Abas the Great who ruined Julfa. That great and polite prince, feeing his forces unequal to thofe of his enemies, and reflecting on the means of preventing their returning every year into Perfia, to make and preferve their conquefts there, refolved to render all the country a defert between Erzerum and Tauris, on a line with Irivan and Nacchivan, which was the way by which the Turks commonly came, and where they fortified themfelves, becaufe they found provifions fufficient for the fubfiftence of their army. He therefore removed the inhabitants and cattle, ruined the edifices of every kind, fet fire to all the fields and trees, and even poifoned feveral fountains.

But to return; the Aras has its fource in the moun-tains on which it is pretended, that Noah's ark refted, and after dividing Armenia and Media, falls into the Cafpian Sea. This river is large and rapid : during its courfe it is fwelled by feveral brooks that have no name, and by many torrents. Bridges have been built over it above Julfa, and in other places ; but however mafly and ftrong they were made, they could not refift the force of the current ; for when the fnows melt on the neighbouring mountains, no piers or buttreffes can withftand its force. Indeed the noife of the waters, and the rapidity of their courfe are very aftonifhing. We pafled it in a large boat, made to carry 20 horfes and 30 perfons at a time. I fuffered none to pafs over with me but my men and my baggage. Four men took care of the boat, and proceded 300 paces along the bank, up the river ; by little and little they got into the ftream, and then made ufe of only a long helm, to direct its courfe to the other bank. The boat was then driven by the current with an incredible impetuofity, and proceeded 500 paces in an inftant. The boat-men were above two hours in going and coming, on account of the efforts they were obliged to make in going againft the ftream.

I have obferved that this river feparates Armenia and Media. This laft kingdom which formerly held the Empire of Afia, compofes only a part of a province of Perfia called Azerbeyan or Afurpaican.

We now proceeded to the north-weft, and the next day reached Marant, a good city compofed of 2500 houfes, fituated at the foot of a hill, at the end of a fine fertile plain, watered by a fmall river named Zeloulou. The gardens of Marant take up more room than the town itfelf, and produce great quantities of fruit efteemed the beft in Media. In this country is alfo gathered the cochineal infect.

From hence we proceeded four leagues, conftantly turning between the mountains, which in fome places approach very near each other, but are no where joined : afterwards we pafled through fine fertile plains, that are well cultivated, and on the 17th arrived at Tauris, the fecond city of Perfia, both with refpect to its extent, its commerce, riches, and the number of its inhabitants.

Tauris is fituated in a plain at the foot of a mountain ; it is of an irregular figure, and has neither walls nor fortifications. Through it pafles a little river named Spingtcha, which fometimes fwelling, carries away the houfes on its banks. Another river called the Agi, pafles by the north fide of the city,

and is falt fix months of the year, from the torrents
which fall into it, after they have palled over lands
covered with falt. The city is divided into nine
quarters or wards ; the bazars compofing the heart
of the city, and the dwelling houfes, moft of which
have a garden, are on the outfide. There are here
many magnificent ftructures the bazars juft mentioned make as fine an appearance as in any part of
Afia, from their largenefs and great extent ; from
the beautiful domes with which they are covered ;
from the multitudes of people, and the vaft quantity
of merchandize with which they are filled. The
fineft of thefe, in which the jewels and moft valuable
merchandize are fold, is an octagon, and is called
the Kaiferie, or royal market. As to the other public buildings they are equally noble. There are
faid to be 300 caravanferais, which are fo fpacious
that 300 perfons may lodge in each ; and the mofques
and baths are anfwerable to the grandeur of the
other buildings. There are three hofpitals in the
city, in which nobody is lodged ; but provifions are
given twice a day to all who come. Upon a hill at
the weft end of the city is a pretty hermitage, and
at the eaft end are the ruins of a caftle.

There is the largeft fquare at Tauris I have ever
feen ; it being much more fpacious than that of If-
paham. The Turks when they were in poffeffion of
this city have frequently drawn up within this fquare
30,000 men in order of battle. In the evening the
populace are diverted there with drolls, mountebanks,
wreftling, ram and bull fights ; the repeating of
pieces in profe and verfe, and dancing wolves. The
people of Tauris place their higheft entertainment
in feeing thefe dances: thofe wolves that are moft
expert at them are fold at 50 crowns each ; and on
their account great commotions frequently happen,
and are with difficulty appeafed. This fpacious
fquare is in the day time ufed as a market for all
kinds of provifions.

The number of inhabitants in Tauris, I believe amounts at leaſt to 550,000 people, beſides a multitude of ſtrangers that are conſtantly there from all parts of Aſia. The fineſt Perſian turbans are made in this city, and I have been aſſured by the principal merchants, that the inhabitants annually manufacture 6000 bales of ſilk. The commerce of this city extends not only all over Perſia ; but into Turky, Ruſſia, Tartary, the Indies, and to the Black Sea.

Though Tauris is ſituated only in the 38th deg. of north latitude, the air is cold, dry, and healthful. This proceeds from its being expoſed to the north, and from the tops of the ſurrounding mountains being covered with ſnow nine months in the year ; from whence the wind almoſt conſtantly blows in the evenings and the mornings. The city abounds with all the neceſſaries and luxuries of life ; and theſe are extremely cheap. The Caſpian Sea, which is not above forty leagues diſtant, ſupplies it with fiſh, which are alſo found in the river Agi, already mentioned. In the ſummer they have abundance of deer and wild fowls : in the mountains are eagles, which the people of diſtinction bring down with the hawk. This kind of fowling is very curious and aſtoniſhing. All kinds of fruit are in the greateſt plenty, and there are ſaid to be above ſixty ſorts of grapes in the neighbourhood of the city. In ſhort, there is not any part of Perſia where a perſon may live better, and cheaper than at Tauris.

In the neighbourhood of the city are large quarries of white marble ; one kind of which is tranſparent : and at a ſmall diſtance are two mines, the one of gold, and the other of ſalt : the gold mine has, however, been long neglected ; the quantity found of that valuable metal being ſo ſmall, as to be ſcarcely worth the labour of procuring it.

I ſtayed at Tauris for ſome time, during which I ſold a number of jewels to the governor and the ſon of the receiver general of the province, for which I

2

received a thoufand crowns; but they would not
allow me to get any thing by them; the firft placed
to my account his father's intereft with the Shah,
and the other that of his brother's, and of his uncle
Mirza Sadec, the great Chancellor, forcing me to
take the letters of recommendation they offored me,
as a recompence for giving them the profit I ought
to have made. It is impoffible to conceive the careffes,
the flattery, the engaging and agreeable behaviour
ufed by the great in Perfia to promote their own
intereft, even in affairs of the fmalleft moment, in
which they act with fuch an appearance of fincerity,
that a perfon ought to be perfectly acquainted with
the genius of the country and of the court, to prevent his being deceived by them.

As this was the time when the Curdes, the Turku-
mans, and other nations who dwell in tents, and
are moftly robbers, quit the plains, on account of
the heat of the fun, and remove with their flocks
and habitations into the mountains, in fearch of
fhade and pafture, we were advifed for the greater
fecurity to wait for company; for this purpofe I
ftayed till the 28th of May, and then fet out with
the provoft of the merchants, who had fourteen
horfes and ten valets.

The firft night we lodged at Vafpinge, a town
confifting of 600 houfes. Several fine rivulets run
with a ferpentine ftream on all fides, and it is adorned
with many gardens and plantations of poplar and
linden trees, that are raifed for the ufe of building.
The next day we proceeded through fertile plains
interfperfed with villages; our road then winded
among the mountains, and again opened into plains,
and after croffing feveral rivers, we arrived on the
fifth of June at the city of Zengan, fituated in a
valley between the mountains, where they are not
above half a league diftant from each other.

This city is furrounded with gardens, and a pleafant country, but on the infide it is only remarkable

for the extent of its ruins. It is faid to have been founded feveral centuries before the birth of Chrift, and that it once contained 20,000 houfes. It was entirely deftroyed by Tamerlane on his firft coming to it ; but he afterwards hearing that the fciences had long flourifhed there, and that it had produced many great men, caufed it to be in part rebuilt: fince that time it has been frequently facked and plundered by the Turks.

On the 6th we paffed through the moft delightful country I ever beheld, the way was even and ftraight, through a fine plain, watered by a confiderable number of brooks that rendered it extremely fertile : we faw fo many villages that we could fcarce count them ; with a variety of gardens and groves, through which were beautiful avenues, that afforded the fineft landfcapes. Having proceeded five leagues through thefe pleafing fcenes, we alighted at a large caravanferai within a cannon fhot of Sultania.

This city, which is fituated at the foot of a mountain, makes a fine appearance at a diftance; but on approaching it, the beauties we admire afar off vanifh. There are, however, fome public edifices that are well built, and about 3000 houfes. The inhabitants fay that this city formerly extended half a league farther to the weft, and that the ruined towers, churches, and mofques, which are to be feen at a diftance, were in the heart of the city. This is not improbable, as the Perfian hiftorians fay, that this was once the capital, and the largeft city in the kingdom.

The next day we travelled through plains as beautiful as the former, and on the 8th arrived at Ebher, a confiderable town intermixed with gardens, built on the banks of a fmall river that runs through the midft of it. Its fituation is extremely agreeable ; the air is good, and the foil produces abundance of fruit, and all the neceffaries of life.

Leaving Cafbin or Cafwin to the right, we proceeded on our journey towards Ifpahan. We had for fome time fet out an hour or two before fun-fet, and completed a journey of five or fix leagues by about midnight. People in the eaft generally travel in this manner during the fummer, to fecure themfelves from the heat of the fun which is very fatiguing both to man and beaft. In the night they travel with greater fpeed. The fervants from time to time proceed on foot, and the mafters themfelves are glad to walk a little to prevent their being feized with fleep, and to keep themfelves warm, which eafes the horfes. On their arrival they go to bed, and gain in the day the fleep they loft in the night. Another advantage of travelling in the night is, that the beafts of burthen takes their reft all the time when they would be incommoded by the heat of the fun and the flies. Befides, what is wanted both for man and beaft may be more eafily provided during the day.

On the 13th, two hours before day we arrived at Sava, a city fituated in a fandy and ftony plain, and took up our lodgings in the fuburbs near the highway. The city is two miles round, and encompaffed with a wall; but it is thinly peopled, and the houfes in the fuburbs are ruinous for want of inhabitants: the walls alfo are but ill preferved. However, the remains of fome grand edifices fhew that it was once a place of importance. The hiftories of Perfia agree that the whole plain of Sava was formerly a morafs or falt lake, like that called the Sea of Salt, which lies twenty leagues to the weft of this city, and is croffed by a caufeway extending thirty leagues, in going from Ifpahan into Hyrcania.

Oppofite Sava to the weft, is a tomb rendered famous by the Perfians going in pilgrimage to it, this is called Echmoul, or Samuel; from the opinion that this prophet was interred there. They have built over his tomb a fine maufoleum in the middle of a magnificent mofque.

At the diftance of nine leagues to the eaft of the city, are fome ruins of the ancient city of Rey, once the largeft in all Afia. The Perfian geographers fay, that in the ninth century it was divided into ninety-fix quarters, each of which had forty fix ftreets, 400 houfes, and ten mofques: that the city alfo contained 4600 colleges, 16600 baths, 15000 minarets belonging to mofques, 12000 mills, 1700 canals, and 13,000 caravanferais. The Arabian authors reprefent it as the moft populous city in Afia, and that except Babylon, no city ever exceeded it in wealth, and the number of inhabitants. Hence it obtained the pompous titles given it in hiftory, as the Spoufe of the World; the Gate of the Gates of the earth; and the Market of the Univerfe. This city was fituated in 35°. 35'. north latitude.

On the 13th we proceeded to Kom, a large city fituated along the bank of a river. It has alfo feveral handfome caravanferais, and fine mofques, the moft beautiful of thefe laft, is that in which are interred the princefs Fatima, Mahomet's daughter, and the two laft kings of Perfia. The ftructure of this mofque is beautiful, and its ornaments extremely fumptuous. The accefs is through four large and ftately courts; the firft of which is a handfome garden, and the laft is paved with tranfparent marble, and furrounded with neat lodgings for the priefts. The door to each maufoleum is plated with filver, and the tombs are furrounded with grates of the fame metal. Nothing can be imagined richer, neater and more magnificent than thefe maufolea. To that of Fatima the Perfians give the name of Maffuma, or pure, and hold it in great veneration. There is a revenue of 3200 tomans belonging to the place.

We left Kom, on the fixteenth, and three days after arrived at Cafan, a large town, the houfes of which are built of earth and brick. It has feveral caravanferais, one of which was built by Shah Abas, and is efteemed the fineft in all Perfia. On the infide are four noble fronts furrounding a fquare court, with an arcade both above and below ; that above being fecured by a baluftrade. The entrance is under a high and magnificent portico, which as well as the reft of the building, is adorned with Mofaic work. In the middle of the court is a refervoir of water, raifed about five feet high.

On the 24th we left Cafan, and on the 29th arrived at Ifpahan, the metropolis of Perfia, and one of the largeft cities in the world ; for including the fuburbs, it is not lefs than twenty-four miles in circumference. Some perfons compute the number of the inhabitants at 1,000,000, but thofe who make the moft moderate computation fuppofe they amount to only 600,000, and the number of houfes were at this time faid to amount to about 29,460, without including the palaces, mofques, public baths, bazars, and caravanferais. The city appears as well peopled as London, which is the moft populous city in Europe.* It is built on the banks of the Zenderoud, over which are three fine bridges, one near the middle of the city, and one at each end. The walls of Ifpahan are about 20,000 paces round ; they are only built with earth, and are fo hid by the houfes and gardens, both on the infide and without, that in many places they cannot be feen. The city is alfo defended by a ditch and a caftie.

The beauty of Ifpahan particularly confifts in the great number of its magnificent palaces, handfome houfes, large caravanferais, beautiful bazars, and in its canals, and fpacious ftreets, the fides of which are

* Ifpahan is at prefent thinly peopled. and the greateft part of the houfes in ruins.

adorned with rows of lofty plane-trees: but the other ftreets are generally narrow and crooked. The worft is they are not paved ; but as, on the one hand, the air is very dry, and on the other the people water the ftreet before their houfes morning and evening, they are neither fo dirty nor fo dufty as might be expected, They have three other confiderable inconveniences. One, that the ftreets being over vaults made for the paffage of the canals which run under them, they fometimes fall in and endanger the lives of the paffengers. Another is, there being wells in the ftreets, the fides of which are even with the earth, by which the paffengers are expofed to the fame danger, if they do not take fufficient care. The third inconvenience is a very difagreeable one, which is, that under the walls of the houfes are large holes for receiving all the filth, and fometimes ferving as common hog-houfes. The ftreets, however, do not ftink as might be imagined ; which is in part owing to the drynefs of the air, and alfo to thefe pits being emptied every day by the peafants, who bring fruit and other provifions to the city, and load their cattle with the ordure, which they carry away to manure their gardens.

The city on every fide appears at a diftance like a wood intermixed with large and lofty domes and minarets.

On the 2d of February, 1674, having fold great part of my jewels, I left Ifpahan, and proceeded to Mayar, a village confifting of 300 houfes, fituated between two mountains, and extending from the one to the other, fo that it is impoffible to pafs between them, without going through it. The country about it is however dry and barren, without trees or the leaft verdure, owing to the fcarcity of the water, though the inhabitants have enough to fupply their gardens.

On leaving this place the next day, the valleys extended three leagues together between the mountain.

Then turning to the right, we entered a beautiful plain of vaſt extent, which I have had the pleaſure of croſſing ſeveral times, and have found that from the middle of March to the middle of November it is covered with flowers, flocks, grain, and fruit. We ſtopt at Comicha, or Komminsja, a town three miles round, but full of gardens, and thinly inhabited. The fineſt buildings here are the dove cotes, which repreſent lofty round towers. It is thought that this place is the Orebatis of Ptolemy. Within a cannon-ſhot from the ſide of the town next Iſpahan, is the tomb of a Perſian ſaint, covered with a dome. In a court before it are two reſevoirs of water at twenty paces from each other. They are furniſhed with fiſh, ſome of which have rings of braſs, ſilver or gold in their noſes. The fiſh of one of theſe baſons are held ſo ſacred, that the people imagine that if any one preſumes to touch them, he will immediately drop down dead.

The two following days we proceeded through a fine country, interſperſed with rivulets and villages, and having paſſed through Anamabaet, a large town, which is ſaid to have ſeparated Perſia from Parthia, took up our lodgings at a town named Yes-de-cas, or Jeſdegaes, ſeated on the ſide of a mountain, with a large valley before it. The houſes riſe from this valley one above the other, affording a fine proſpect at a diſtance. On the top of a round eminence in the midſt of a valley is a caſtle built of earth ; and oppoſite to it is a large caravanſerai. The inhabtants of this town eat the beſt bread in all Perſia.

The next day I was twelve hours on horſeback, in proceeding eight leagues, on account of the ſnow, and the ruggedneſs of a mountain over which we were obliged to paſs ; though my baggage was carried by four vigorous mules, and I myſelf was well mounted. I afterwards paſſed through pleaſant plains, and at length arrived on the 13th at the ruins of the ancient Perſepolis.

At a diftance thefe magnificent remains appear as in a kind of amphitheatre, the mountains forming a half moon as if to embrace them. They are feated in a fine plain that extends two leagues in breadth from fouth-weft to north-eaft ; and near forty leagues in length from north-weft to fouth-eaft. This plain is ufually called Mardasjo, and the inhabitants pretend, that it contains 88: villages, and about 1500 within the diftance of twelve leagues around the ruins, including the villages feated among the mountains ; fome of which are adorned with beautiful gardens. The greateft part of this plain is in the winter feafon, floated with water, which is a very advantageous circumftance with refpect to the rice that grows there at that time. The foil of this agreeable plain is moftly converted into arable lands, and watered with a number of ftreams that render it exceeding fertile. It abounds with many forts of birds, and more particularly with cranes, pigeons, quails, fnipes, partridges, hawks, and vaft flights of crows, which are very numerous throughout all Perfia.

The ancient palace of the kings of Perfia, ufually called the houfe of Darius, and by the inhabitants Chel-menar, or Chil-minar, which fignifies the forty pillars, is fituated to the weft at the foot of the mountain of Kulierag-net, or Compaffion, anciently called the royal mountain, which is entirely compofed of freeftone. That fuperb edifice has the walls of three of its fides ftill ftanding. The front extends 600 paces from north to fouth, and 390 from eaft to weft, as far as the mountain, where an afcent is formed between fome fcattered rocks. Beyond which there appears to have been formerly fome other buildings, the rocks appearing in fome places finely fmoothed and polifhed.

The top of this edifice prefents to the view a platform of 400 paces, extending from the middle of the front wall, to the mountain ; and along three fides of this wall is carried on a pavement of two ftones

2

joined together, eight feet broad. With refpect to the height of the wall, it is in fome places 24 feet ; but it is not every where fo high, in fome places the earth about it is raifed, and in others the wall itfelf has funk. On examining the previous remains, we muft proceed as we do in examining thofe celebrated beauties, whom age or ficknefs has brought low, that is, from the traces of beauty we fee, form an idea of what they were. The ftones of the wall are black, harder than marble, fome of them finely polifhed, and many of them of fuch an amazing fize, that it is difficult to conceive how they were able to remove and raife fuch prodigious maffes.

The principal ftaircafe is placed between the middle of the front, and the northern end of the edifice. It confifts of two flights of fteps that wind off from each other to the diftance of 42 feet at the bottom. Thefe fteps are only four inches high and fourteen in breadth. They are the moft commodious (fays M. Le Bruyn) I ever faw, except thofe of the viceroy's palace at Naples : which are, however, in my opinion, fomewhat higher. There are 55 of thefe fteps on the northern fide, and 53 to the fouth ; but thefe laft are not fo entire as the others. I am likewife perfuaded that there are feveral others under ground, that have been covered over by length of time, as well as part of the wall, which rifes 44 feet 11 inches high in the front. At the bottom of thefe two flights of fteps, is a fingle flight, extending 51 feet four inches from one to the other, from thence the two flights are carried off from each other, and return back from the center at an equal diftance from the extreme parts of the top ; and above thefe flights is a pavement of large ftones, and another fingle flight of fteps 75 feet in width, anfwering to that of the bottom, and leading up to the grand entrance of the edifice. This ftaircafe has a very fine and fingular effect, anfwerable to the magnificent remains of the reft of the building.

On afcending the upper fteps, the fpectator fees before him, at the diftance of 42 feet from the front wall of the ftaircafe, two grand portals, and as many columns. Thefe portals are twenty-two feet four inches in depth, and thirteen feet four inches in breadth. On the infide upon a kind of pilafter on each hand is a large figure in baffo relievo, they bear fome refemblance to the fphynx, and are twenty-two feet from the fore to the hinder legs, and fourteen feet and a half high. The faces of thefe animals are broken off, and their bodies much damaged; but what is moft extraordinary, the breaft and fore feet project from the pilafter. Thofe of the firft portal are turned towards the ftaircafe, and thofe of the fecond, each of which has wings, face the mountain.

On the upper part of thefe pilafters are characters, which, from their fmallnefs and elevation, it is impoffible to diftinguifh. The height of the firft portal is 39 feet, and that of the fecond 28; the pilafters ftand on a bafe five feet two inches in height.

The two colonuns that appear between the portals are the leaft damaged of all, particularly with refpect to their capitals, and the other ornaments of the upper paits; but the bafes are entirely covered over with earth. They are 14 feet in circumference, and rife to the height of 54 feet. There were formerly two others between this and the laft portal, feveral pieces of which lie half buried in the ground.

At the diftance of 52 feet fouth of the fame portal is a large bafon for water, cut out of a fingle ftone 20 feet long, and 17 feet five inches in breadth, and raifed three feet and a half above the furface of the floor. From this bafon to the northern wall is an extent of ground comprehending 150 paces in length, in which nothing is to be feen but the fragments of large ftones, and part of the fhaft of a column that is not fluted like the reft, and is twenty feet in circumference. Beyond this tract of ground, and as

far as the mountain, the earth is covered with heaps
of stones.

Proceeding southward from the portals already
described, you fee two other flights of fteps refembling
the former, the one to the eaft, and the other to the
weft. On the upper part the wall is embellifhed with
foliage, and the reprefentation of a lion rending a
bull in baffo relievo, much larger than the life.
There are alfo fmall figures on the middle wall. This
ftaircafe is half buried under the earth.

From hence extends a wall forty-five feet in
length, beyond the lower part of the ftaircafe, and
then is an interval of fixty-feven feet, extending to
the weftern front, which correfponds with the other,
and has three ranges of figures one over the other,
with a lion tearing an afs that has a horn projecting
from the forehead ; and between thefe animals and
rows of figures is a fquare filled with antique characters, the uppermoft of which are defaced. The
figures are lefs damaged in that part of the ftructure,
where the ground is lower : but the wall which extends from the ftaircafe to the weftern front, has
not any figures. On the other fide the ftairs are three
ranges of fmall figures ; but thofe in the upper row
are only vifible from the waift downwards. Thefe
figures are only two feet nine inches high, and the
wall which is five feet three inches in height, has an
extent of ninety-eight feet.

On the top of the fteps laft defcribed, is an entrance
into an open place paved with large ftones, whofe
breadth is equal to the diftance from the ftaircafe to
the firft columns, which comprehends the fpace of
twenty-two feet two inches. Thefe columns are
difpofed into two ranges, each of which confifts of
fix pillars, but none of them are intire ; there are
alfo eight bafes or pedeftals, and the ruins of fome
others. At the diftance of feventy feet eight inches,
were formerly fix rows of other pillars, each row
confifting of fix : thefe thirty-fix pillars were like-

wife twenty two feet two inches diftant from each other ; but only feven of them are now entire ; however, all the bafes of the others are ftanding.

At the diftance of feventy feet eight inches from thefe rows of columns on the weft, towards the front of the ftaircafe, were only twelve other columns in two ranges, each of which contained fix, but only five are now remaining. The ground is there covered with the fragments of columns, and the ornaments that ferved for their capitals ; between which are pieces of fculpture reprefenting camels on their knees. On the top of one of the columns is a compartment reprefenting camels in that pofture.

On advancing towards the eaft, you are prefented with a view of feveral ruins, confifting of portals, paffages and windows. The infide of the portals are adorned with figures in bafs relief. Thefe ruins extend ninety paces from eaft to weft, and 125 from north to fouth, and are fixty paces both from the columns and the mountains. In the middle of thefe ruins the earth is covered with feventy fix broken columns ; nineteen of which ftill fupport their entablature, their fhafts are formed of four pieces, befides the bafe and capital.

At the diftance of 118 feet from thefe columns to the fouth, is an edifice that rifes higher than any other part of the ruins, from its being fituated on a hill. The front wall, which is five feet feven inches high on that fide, is compofed of a fingle range of ftones, fome of which are eight feet deep ; and the wall extends 113 feet from eaft to weft, but has neither figures nor any other ornaments. However, in the middle of the front are the ruins of a double ftaircafe, on the fides of which are feveral figures. The reft of the building was chiefly compofed of large and fmall portals, and is entirely deftroyed. The largeft of thefe portals is five feet wide, and five feet two inches deep. Among the reft, two portals appear to the north, with three niches or windows walled up. Under these portals are the figures of a man, and two women, down to the knees, for their legs are covered with the earth that is raised against them. Under the other gate is the figure of a man holding a lion by the mane. To the south is a portal and four open windows, each of which is five feet nine inches wide, and eleven in height, including the cornice; their depth is equal to that of the grand portals. The two sides of this gate are carved with the figure of a man, with something on his head resembling a tiara. He is accompanied by two women, one of whom holds an umbrella over his head. On the inside, three niches are covered with ancient Persian characters.

There are two other gates to the west that are not covered; within one of these is the figure of a man fighting a bull; with his left hand he grasps a horn in his forehead, while with his right he plunges a dagger into his belly. On the other side the figure, another man clasps the horn with his right hand, and stabs the beast with his left. The second portal has the figure of a man carved in the same manner with a winged deer, that has a horn in his forehead. Horns were anciently the emblems of strength and majesty; they were therefore given to the sun and moon; and Alexander was called by the Orientals, Dhulkarnam, or the horned, because he made himself king of the horns of the sun, that is of the east and the west.

Behind this edifice are the ruins of another, which exceed it in length by thirty-eight feet. It has also niches and windows, the former of which are cut out of single stones. A little to the south is a double flight of steps, separated by walls embellished with small figures and foliage.

Farther to the south, are subterraneous passages, into which none of the natives of the country dare to enter, though they are said to contain great treasures; this is owing to a general persuasion, that all the lights carried into thele places will go out of themfelves. This opinion did not however intimidate either Sir John Chardin or Mr. Le Bruyn ; they both examined them with the utmoft care, and proceeded with lights through thefe pallages, till they ended in a narrow track, which extended a great length, and appeared to have been originally contrived for an aqueduct ; but its ftraitnefs rendered it impoffible to be paffed.

Still farther to the fouth are the remains of another edifice, which extend 160 feet from north to fouth, and 191 from weft to eaft. Ten portals belonging to it are ftill to be feen, together with feven windows and forty enclofures, that were formerly covered rooms In the middle are the bafes of thirty fix columns in fix ranges, and the ground is covered wi h large ftones, under which were aqueducts.

There anciently ftood another ftructure to the weftward of the laft mentioned building. On the ruins of the wall, which ftill rifes near two feet above the pavement, are cut the figures of men in baffo relievo, each reprefented with a lance. The ground enclofed by this wall contains a number of round ftones that were the bafes of columns.

On the eaft fide of thefe laft ruins are the remains of a beautiful ftaircafe, fixty feet in length, refembling that of the front wall ; but though moft of the fteps are deftroyed by time, the wall that feparates the two flights is ftill eight feet in height, and adorned with figures almoft as big as the life. The front contains the reprefentation of a lion encountering a bull : there are alfo lions of the fame workmanfhip on the wings of the ftaircafe ; both of them accompanied with characters and figures almoft as big as the life. Columns were formerly difpofed between this edifice and the other laft mentioned. Among thefe ruins are four portals each adorned on the infide with the figure of a man.

and two women holding an umbrella over his head.

A little to the north of the thefe two laft edifices are two portals with their pilafters, on one of which is a fo the figure of a man and two women, one of whom holds an umbrella over his head. Above thefe women is a fmall figure with wings, which are expanded to the fides of the portico. The lower part of the buft of this figure feems to terminate on the two fides with a fpread of foliage, and a kind of frieze. Over the fecond figure a man is feated in a chair with a ftaff in his hand, and another ftands behind him, with his right hand upon the chair. A fmall figure above holds a circle in its left hand, and points to fomething in his right. Under this portal are three ranges of figures, all of which have their hands lifted up, and over the third pilaf-ter, which ftill remains, two women hold an umbrella over the head of a man. The carth is alfo covered with fragments of columns and other antiquities.

From hence you proceed to the laft ruins of the ftructures on the mountain. On the fouth fide are two portals, under each of which a man is feated in a chair, with a ftaff in his right hand, and in his left a kind of vafe. Behind him is another figure, which holds fomething on his head like the tail of a fea-horfe, and has a linen cloth in his right hand. Below are three rows of figures with lifted hands ; four in the firft and five in each of the other two rows. They are three feet four inches high: but the feated figure is much larger than the life. Above this are feveral ornamental ranges of foliage, the loweft of which is intermixed with fmall lions, and the higheft with oxen. Over thefe ornaments is a little winged figure, which holds in his left hand fomething that refembles a fmall glafs, and makes a fignal with its right. Thefe portals are twelve feet five inches in breadth, and ten feet four inches deep, and the higheft of the pilafters is from twenty-eight to thirty feet. On the two towards the north a man is feated, with a perfon behind him, like the preceding figures, and behind this are two other men holding in their hands fomething that is broken; before the figure reprefented fitting, are two other figures, one with his hands placed on his lips with an air of falutation, and the other holding a fmall veffel. Above thefe figures is a ftone filled with ornaments, and below are five ranges of figures, three feet in height: thefe are a band of foldiers armed in different manners. From the foot of thefe mountains you have a full view of all the ruins, except the walls and ftair cafes that cannot here be feen.

No other difference is obfervable in the columns, except that fome of them have capitals and others have not; with refpect to the elevation of thofe that are perfect, they are all from 70 to 72 feet high, and are 18 feet five inches in circumference, except thofe near the firft portals. The bafes are round, and 24 feet five inches in circumference; thefe are four feet three inches high, and the lower moulding is one foot five inches thick. They have three forts of ornaments, which may be termed capitals.

Befides the baffo relievos already mentioned, there are many others, particularly the reprefentation of a triumph, or a proceffion of people bearing prefents to a king, confifting of a great number of figures, with fome led horfes, an empty chariot, a led camel, &c. The drapery of all the human figures in this edifice is extremely fingular, and has no relation to that of the ancient Greeks and Romans. Their military habits are agreeable to the mode of the Perfians and Medes. The rules of art are not obferved in the figures, fince no mufcles are vifible in the naked parts, and the figures themfelves have a heavy air: nothing has been obferved but the outlines, and this neglect caufes them to appear ftiff and inelegant: the draperies have alfo the fame defects, and the whole has a taftelefs famenefs. However, the proportions have been finely kept, both in the great and fmall figures, which proves that thofe who made them were not entirely deftitute of capacity, but were probably obliged to be too expeditious to finifh them with proper care. The ornaments muft, however, be acknowledged to be exceeding beautiful, as well as the chairs in which fome figures are feated, notwithftanding their being now much impaired. It is therefore probable that there might be formerly fome fine fragments that have been fince deftroyed. Befides, the generality of the ftones are polifhed like a mirrour, particularly thofe within the portals, and that compofe the windows and pavements. Thefe are of different colours, as yellow, white, grey, red, deep blue, and in fome places black ; but the ftones of the greateft part of the edifice are of a clear blue.

Indeed every thing correfponds with the grandeur and magnificence of a great king's palace, to which the images and relievos give a furprifing air of ma-jefty. It is certain there have been very ftately por-tals and grand galleries to afford a communication with all the detached parts of the ftructure ; moft of the columns whofe remains are ftill fo beautiful, were evidently intended to fupport thofe galleries, and there even feem to be ftill fome remains of the royal apartments. In a word, the magnificence of thefe ruins can never be fufficiently admired, and this ftructure muft undoubtedly have coft immenfe treafures. This palace, which was the glory of all the eaft, owed its deftruction to the debauchery and frenzy of Alexander the Great, who after he had preferved it from the ravages of war, above 2000 years ago, reduced it to afhes at the felicitations of Thais, a Grecian courtezan.

There are two ancient tombs of the kings near the mountain, one to the north, and the other to the fouth, both of them are hewn out of the rock, and are noble fragments of antiquity. Their fronts are covered with figures and other ornaments. The form of both is nearly the fame, and therefore a defcription of that to the north will ferve. That part of the tomb on which the figures are carved is forty feet wide : the height is almoft equal to the width below, and the rock extends on each fide to the diftance of fixty paces. Below a range of four columns fupport the entablature on their capitals, each of which is compofed of the heads of two oxen as far as the breaft, with the fore legs bent on the top of each column. The gate, which is furrounded with ornaments, is placed between two of thefe columns in the middle, but is at prefent almoft clofed up. Above the columns is the cornice and entablature, adorned with eighteen fmall lions in bafs relief, nine on each fide advancing towards the middle, where there is a fmall ornament refembling a vafe. Above the lions are two ranges of figures, almoft as large as life, fourteen in each range, armed and lifting up their hands, as if to fupport the building above them ; and on the fide is an ornament fomewhat in the form of a pillar, with the head of fome animal that has only one horn. Above this is another cornice ornamented with leaves. On the left where the wall projects are three rows of niches, one above each other, each of them containing two figures, armed with lances, and three others on the fide armed in the fame manner. There are likewife two on the right fide with their left hands placed on their beards, and the right on their body ; and on the fide of thefe are three others in the fame difpofition as thofe on the other fide. At fome diftance below, and between thefe figures and an ornament that has fome diftant refemblace of a round pillar, there is another figure on each fide, very much impaired. Above on three fteps ftands a figure that has the air of a king, pointing at fomething with his right hand, and holding a kind of bow in his left. Before him is an altar, on which an offering is made, from whence the flames are reprefented afcending. Above this altar appears the moon, and it is faid, that there was once a fun behind the figure ; but nothing of it is now to be feen. In the middle, and above all this appears a fmall myftic figure, that is to be feen in feveral parts of the other buildings.

Two leagues from thefe ruins is a place called Noxi Ruftan, but the traveller is obliged to take a large circuit to go thither ; becaufe a river croffes the country, which can only be paffed over a bridge, that is at a confiderable diftance ; the plain is alfo cut into a variety of fmall canals, that are fo many impediments to travellers in their way thither. In this place are four tombs of perfons of eminence among the ancient Perfians, that much refemble thofe of Perfepolis ; only they are cut much higher in the rock. This place receives its name from one Ruftan, whofe figure is there carved to perpetuate his memory. He is faid to have been a potent prince of an immenfe ftature : for it is pretended that he was forty cubits high ; and according to the fame ridiculous tradition he is faid to have lived 1113 years.

The tombs have their bafes eighteen feet above the furface of the caufeway, and rife about four times that height, and the rock is twice as high as the tombs, which are fixty feet wide in the middle. Under each tomb is a feperate table filled with large figures in low relief ; and on two of thefe tables are fome traces of men fighting on horfeback. Between thefe tombs are three other tables covered with figures, among which is a man on horfeback preceded by two others, and followed by a third, which is almoft defaced. There are alfo fome figures in the fpace between the two laft works, and three under the third, two of which hold out their hands to each other. One of thefe is a woman, and both of them are half buried in the earth.

Thefe tombs poffefs an extent of 280 paces, and at fixty paces diftance from the firft of them is a little fquare building. The figure of a man on horfeback, between the two tombs, and in the middle of the fourth niche, has his hair fhaped according to our mode, with a crown upon his head, and a pointed bonnet rifing above it. He is dreffed after the Roman manner, and has a large fword by his fide, with the hilt in his left hand ; his right is prefented to a perfon before him. The third figure, which is alfo dreffed in the Roman manner, opens his hands like a fuppliant.

The figures half buried appear on the fide of the third tomb, and two of them have their hands placed in a kind of circle. That in the middle, which is on horfeback, reprefents Ruftan in a Roman drefs ; he has likewife a bonnet and an ornament like a crown, with flowing hair, a large beard, and his left hand upon the hilt of his fword : but notwithftanding the pretence of his prodigious ftature, both he and his horfe are of the common fize. Before him is the figure of a woman with flowing hair ; fhe likewife wears a crown. fhe is dreffed like Pallas, and fupports part of her drapery with her left hand. The third figure reprefents a military man, with a tiara on his head, and his left hand likewife grafps the hilt of his fword. The fifth compartment is an imperfeçt appearance of figures fighting on horfeback. All thefe are carved on the rock.

On the weftern fide of this mountain, at 200 paces diftance, are two tables with figures, likewife cut in the rock. That to the left reprefents two men on horfeback, one of whom grafps a circle, of which the other has quited the hold. Some pretend that the firft is Alexander, and the other Darius, who by this action refigns to him the empire. Others fay, thefe figures reprefent two potent princes or generals, who, after being engaged in a long war, without obtaining any advantage over each other, at laft agreed, that he who fhould wreft this circle out of

his competitor's hand fhould be acknowledged the
victor. But no ftrefs is to be laid on thefe ftories.

The tomb faid to have been that of Naxi Ruftan,
evidently appears to be that made by Darius, Hyfta-
pefs, from its exactly correfponding with the defcription given of it by Ctefias in his hiftory of Perfia,
after Herodotus ; and with that of Diodorus Siculus.

On the 19th of February I left Perfepolis, after
having ftaid there five days, and then proceeding
nine leagues, the next morning reached Schiras, the
capital of the province of Fars, and one of the
greateft and moft confiderable cities in Perfia. It is
fituated between the mountains in a plain between
feven and eight leagues in length, and about four
in breadth ; as fine and as fertile a fpot as imagination can conceive.

The city, which is about two leagues round, is
not furrounded with walls, for they have been fuffered to fall to ruin ; but the gates, which remain
entire, are large, ftrong, and covered with iron
plates. Of thefe there are four, opening to the four
cardinal points. [The city begins to be feen a little
beyond the mountains, which are then to be left 500
paces to the right ; after this you difcover a great
number of cyprefs-trees, with a wall cut out of the
rock, from whence a ftream of water falls like a
torrent after great rains. The road between the
rocks is deep and narrow. This is fituated to the
right, and has a wall of earth on the right and left,
but much impaired on one fide. It is about 300 paces
in length, and joins to the gate, which is five paces
wide at the entrance, and enlarges into ten as you
advance. When you have pafled through this gate,
which is very large and lofty, you come to a narrow
paffage bordered with buildings, moft of which are
in ruins, and the gardens that are filled with cyprefs-trees are run to decay. At the diftance of 1500
paces from the gate, in the middle of the way is a
bafon feventy-two feet in length, and forty-fix in

breadth, lined with ftone. On each fide is a wall in the form of a half-moon, with feats under alcoves, and on the left a mofque, that extends a hundred paces in front. Ninety paces from thence is a ftone bridge of four arches over the river Roetgore. On the other fide of which the way extends to one of the oldeft gates of the city ; a building much impaired, that ferves at prefent for a bazar. It is vaulted, and extends to the length of eighty paces. It affords a paffage into a great ftreet, on the left fide of which is a burying place and a garden, with feveral edifices on the right. This ftreet reaches to the heart of the city,]* which is almoft covered with gardens. The great ftreets are bordered with trees ; thefe are their principal ornaments ; for there are not many grand bazars, nor fine baths. At the end of the ftreets juft mentioned, are feveral others full of fhops, which crofs each other to the right and left. The coffee-houfes are fpacious enough, confifting of fcaffolds built over the running water, to give them a greater coolnefs. As to the mofques, there are nine more fumptuous than the reft, and befides them about three hundred more, that ferve for chapels. [In the heart of the city is a large edifice, the front of which refembles that of a mofque in its portals and two fine towers ; but the upper part is impaired. This ftructure is a public college, where the fciences are taught.

However moft of the buildings of the city are in ruins, and the ftreets fo narrow and dirty, that they are hardly paffable in rainy feafons ; and in feveral places paffengers are obliged to bend their bodies in order to walk under the arches before the houfes, efpecially in the quarter inhabited by the Jews. The ftreets are alfo made extremely offenfive by the many neceffary houfes, in them, which

---

* The paffages enclofed between crotchets thus [ ], are abftracted from Mr. Le Bruyn's Travels.

render the air very difagreeable. The jackals not only infeft the burying grounds, but often commit great diforders in the city, and in the night-time make difmal howlings that refemble an human voice.]

The public gardens at Schiras, which are about twenty, are extremely delightful ; the trees are the largeft of the kind perhaps in the whole world ; thefe are planted without order, and the foil enamelled with flowers, which are in the greateft plenty, and of the brighteft colours. In the king's garden to the fouth of Schiras, I obferved a tree, the trunk of which was eight yards round. The inhabitants, from the great age of this tree, conceive the higheft venerarion for it ; they go to pray under its fhade, and tie chaplets, amulets, and pieces of their clothes to the boughs. The fick, or others for them, come there to burn incenfe, to fix lighted candles to it, and to perform other fuperftitious ceremonies, with the hopes of recovering their health. There are throughout Perfia, many trees thus fuperftitioufly revered by the people.

About a quarter of a league to the eaft of Schiras is the tomb of Sheik Sadi, one of the moft celebrated Perfian authors in profe and verfe, who lived about 400 years ago, and whofe works contain the fineft morals. On one fide of his tomb is a large octagon bafon, the water of which is moderately warm, and contains plenty of fifh confecrated to the Sheik ; but the common people imagine, that if any perfon takes them, he will be punifhed with fudden death : but though I was feveral times at Schiras, I never went thither without having a good plate of thefe fifh with the Carmelite friars, with whom I always lodged.

On the fame fide of the city, by the corner of a mountain, are the ruins of an ancient caftle, and at fome diftance from it a convent of dervifes, near which are two deep holes in the ground. The mouth of one of them is four feet and a half round, and it is of an unfathomabl e, depth. I was told, that on throwing a large ftone into it, one might diftinctly repeat the Lord's prayer, before the noife made by, its falling ceafed ; and this I found to be true by trying the experiment three times fucceffively.

A league beyond thefe ruins, you fee the remains of an ancient building of ftone and marble, whi ch, notwithftanding the folidity of the ftructure, and the durablenefs of the materials, is greatly decayed. It is a fmall temple 38 or 40 paces round, fituated on the declivity of a mountain, with three gates, which are ftill pretty entire, opening to the north, fouth and eaft. They are eleven feet high and three broad : on the fides of each is the figure of a woman done in relief as big as life, refembling thofe at Perfepolis. The Perfians call this place Mador Sulemon, that is, the mother of Solomon ; they pretend, that fhe built the temple, and came thither to pay her devotions. Bizarus relates, that a tomb is found there infcribed with Hebrew characters ; but I faw no fuch thing, and am perfuaded that thefe opinions are ill founded.

[To the north-weft of the city is a delightful avenue extending to the king's garden, which is ninety-five paces wide, and 966 in length. On paffing through the lodge at the end of the garden, you come into another beautiful avenue bordered with cyprefs trees : this is 620 paces long, and twenty broad, and is covered over in the middle with flowers. You there fee a delightful houfe furrounded with a fine canal. At each corner of the building is a fquare fountain, that mingles its ftreams with the water of the canal. This houfe is fpacious, and in the middle of it is a grand hall covered with a dome, filled with niches both within and without. This beautiful avenue is bordered on each fide with feventy-two lofty cyprefs-trees, one of which is 22

2

palms in circumference. We have given a view of the avenue and hall, in the print. Behind the houfe is another avenue bordered with cyprefs and fenna-trees, equal in extent to that of the others. This is called Baeg Siae, or the Royal Garden.]

The fertility of the country about Schiras is very furprifing. It produces the fineft horfes, and the beft paftures. The fheep are fo fat, that their tails weigh eighteen or twenty pounds weight. As to the fruits, among the reft the pomegranates are as large as the head of a new born child : but the beft fruit is the grape, of which there are three principal forts ; one very fmall, which is fweet and delicious, and the feed fo minute and tender that it can fcarcely be perceived : the great white grape ; and a large red grape, the bunches of which weigh twelve or thirteen pounds. Of this grape alone they make the excellent wine diftinguifhed by the name of the wine of Schiras, which, for its fine colour and the richnefs of its tafte, is efteemed the beft, not only in Perfia, but throughout the eaft. It indeed does not pleafe at firft, it appearing to be rough ; but when one has drank it a few days, one cannot help perferring it to all others ; and thofe who are ufed to it can relifh no other wine.

As the ufe of wine is prohibited by the religion of the country, none have the liberty of making it without the king's privilege, and the permiffion of the governor and intendant. At Schiras, the people alfo make rofewater and oil, preferves and pickles.

On the 24th I left Schiras, where I had lodged in the monaftery of the Carmelites, who give a very civil reception to all the Europeans who come to them, without diftinction of nation or religion, and thankfully take whatever any one gives them in return for their hofpitality. We proceeded five leagues, the greateft part through the fine plain in which Schiras is fituated, and lodged at a ruinous caravanfarai at the foot of a mountain.

Two days after, I took up my lodging at a cara-vanfarai named Kafar, fituated by a town of the fame name, that has feveral hundred houfes, and a great number of gardens, in which is plenty of the moft excellent fruits, as peaches, nectarines, figs, and dates. The town is fituated on the bank of a river that runs by in a deep hollow.

On the 27th, I proceeded feven leagues, and the next day reached Jarron, a town confifting of 350 houfes, moft of them built of date wood, which are the only large trees that grow in its neighbour-hood. This town is remarkable for the manufactures of felt bonnets, and for a kind of camblet: but is more particularly famous for its dates, which are efteemed the beft in the world. The adjacent coun-try abounds in water, brought thither by fubterra-neous canals.

The next day we proceeded three leagues over the mountain of Jarron, which is the moft rugged and ftony of any I have feen in Perfia ; in paffing it we frequently came to the brink of moft frightful precipices, where the road is only fecured by a ftone wall two feet high. The defcent is the rougheft I have ever feen, it being covered with large ftones and rocks, among which our horfes could fcarcely fix their feet.

On the firft of March we paffed a mountain not fo high as the former, but the road was even more pain-ful and dangerous, efpecially on defcending it, when we were obliged to walk, for fear of breaking our arms and legs, the horfes not being able to keep their feet. Half way down the defcent, is a bafon, co-vered with large trees ; the rock water is here cool and excellent. We lodged at a large and handfome caravanferai, before which runs a brook fhaded with orange, pomegranate, date, and other trees.

There we ftaid to refrefh ourfelves after the fatigue we had undergone, and on the third of March con-tinued our journey. We proceeded over feveral

2

plains and mountains, and on the 5th arrived at Laer, the capital of the province of the fame name, and not above a hundred years ago the capital of a kingdom of the fame name. It is fituated between the mountains, in 29°. 40' north lat. in a fandy country rendered barren by the heat of the climate. [The houfes for the moft part are very high ; but the moft beautiful of all the buildings is the bazar erected with ftone, in the middle of the city : it is arched over, and full of fhops, and is 216 paces in length. At the end of the bazar is a fine fquare, and below the gate is a place in which the city mufic plays. Oppofite the bazar is a large building that has a fine entrance : this ftructure belongs to the khan or governor. The caftle, which is entirely built of ftone, ftands on the fummit of a high rock. The avenues to the city refemble a wood, the land being covered with palm, orange, and citron trees, which almoft fhroud the city from the eye.]

On the 7th of March I fet out from Laer, at three in the afternoon, and paffing by the village of Chercoff, which is full of gardens, arrived at Gormouth, a town, which, with its gardens, confifting chiefly of date trees, was a league in length, and beyond the town groves of thefe trees extended as far as the eye could reach. The inhabitants of Caramania Deferta, retire, during the fummer, into thefe woods to fhelter themfelves from the heat, which in that feafon is infupportable, as I found in the year 1677, when I paffed through this country at the end of Auguft : for then the wind was fo hot, even in the night, that I was frequently obliged to turn afide my horfe and to cover my face with my handkerchief, to avoid the blafts that could no more be endured than flame. I was once reduced to the neceffity of throwing myfelf from my horfe, and lying with my face to the earth to avoid the fcorching vapours ; but found that thofe which arife from thence were even ftill more fuffocating. In the day I was obliged to continue naked in a caravanferai, from nine in the morning till four in the afternoon, feated or lying on a fkin of Ruffia leather, not only on account of the heat ; but becaufe water inceffantly flowed from my body in fweat, in fuch a manner that I could neither read nor write, and every thing I took in my hand was immediately wet. I had taken two camels at Laer with my ufual baggage, the one to carry wa- ter, and the other provifions ; becaufe the country was deferted, and really for twenty-five leagues, that is, from Gormouth to Cowreftoon, I did not fee a fingle perfon, every body being then retired into the woods of date trees, or into the mountains ; and as the dates were then ripe, the people lived on almoft nothing elfe. This fruit is nourifhing, and wherever it grows there is a certainty of finding water. It is to be obferved that the land which bears dates is al- ways fandy, and that at twelve or fifteen feet beneath the furface, water is to be found : the people there- fore dig pits, and thofe that are laft dug have always the beft water.

I remember, that performing this journey five years before, I happened to lofe my way, and ram- bled into the mountains: I thought myfelf loft, and expected never to return. Having wandered part of the night, I laid myfelf down at the foot of a tree, holding my horfe by the bridle, and waiting till it was light. When the day came, I difcovered a wood of date trees at two leagues diftance, where being arrived, I found I had advanced fix leagues on my way, and a collector of the taxes conducted me to the road. I never fuffered fo much in my whole life : the morning appeared to bring fome coolnefs with the dew, but the heat returning with the fun, at firft confumed this fmall humidity, and affected me fo violently, that I could not even fweat, it feeming to burn and dry up my very entrails. My horfe ftopt at every ftep, not having ftrength to advance ; but what preffed me moft, was my not being able to

keep either my mouth or my eyes open, on account
of the exhalations from the earth which arofe to my
face, like gufts of flame pouring from the mouth of
a lighted oven. I alfo obferved two circumftances in
thefe regions during the heat of fummer ; the one is,
that the fields are entirely burnt up, and there arife
through the whole night and morning vapours excited by the heat of the earth, which cover it in fuch a
manner, that it cannot be difcovered at fifty paces
diftance, it perfectly refembling a fea, or fome great
lake in a calm.

On the 9th I proceeded fix leagues through a
mountainous and-ftony country, where are neverthe-
lefs many ftreams of running water, efpecially in
fpring : thefe are very clear ; but great care muft be
taken not to drink this water, it being almoft as falt
as that of the fea, which proceeds from the land over
which it paffes ; for this land is in fummer white with
the falt which covers it.   We ftopped at Tanguedelan, where are two caravanferais with cifterns.   This
place is between two very high mountains, a quarter
of a league diftant from each other.   One of the caravanferais has a bafon of running water ; but it is
brackifh and not fit to drink ; yet it is brought by a
grand aqueduct to this caravanferai, whence it takes
its courfe towards the oppofite mountain, through
which it paffes by a canal cut in the rock, 300 paces
in length.

On the 12th we reached Cowreftoon, a village that
abounds in dates, and a kind of wild plumbs.   The
inhabitants cultivate tobacco, and fow great quantities of a kind of grain called Zoura, which grows in
bunches fomewhat like the years of Indian corn, on
canes eight or nine feet long.   Of this they make
bread, which is of a reddifh colour : they alfo bake
it like rice.

This day I met a great Lord on the road named
Ali Kouli Khan, who was returning from his government of Gambroon, in order to go to a province

in Perfia, given him by the fhah. He had a grand
train: his women, with all that belonged to them,
were carried on 80 camels, 40 mules; and 20 horfes.
His own retinue and effects were conveyed on twice
as many camels, and mules. Many of the peafants
fled from the villages of the road, for fear that his
men fhould take their provifions by force.

On the 12th, as I was preparing to fet out at five
in the evening, I obferved that the air was darkened
as when the fky is covered with clouds, and confidering that this could not be the cafe, I recollected that
thefe clouds confifted of locufts ; and indeed as they
paffed, a prodigious number of thofe deftructive infects fell to the ground: they were the largeft I had
ever feen, and fo heavy, that they could not rife
again. The peafants gathered them as they fell ;
and told me, that in this feafon fuch clouds appear
almoft every night ; having gathered, they dry and
falt them, after which they live upon them, and fell
them to each other very cheap, as they are their common food.

This day we proceeded five leagues in a very level
country ; but through moving fands into which the
horfes funk. After advancing a league, we paffed
by a fmall village abounding in date-trees and running water ; the inhabitants I found there cutting
their corn ; and as I had feen the people about Perfepolis fowing the land about three weeks before, I
could not help thinking it very remarkable, that I
fhould fee people fow corn after the middle of February, and reap it before the middle of March following. This has happened to me feveral times in my
journeys in Perfia in the like fpace of three weeks.
I have feen them plowing in one place ; two days
after the people have been fowing wheat ; in a few
days I have feen the blade begin to fprout up out of
the ground ; then advancing farther, I have feen the
green corn ; then it has appeared in ear, then ripe,
then cut, and then threfhed : indeed the empire of

Perfia is fo fituated and fo extenfive, that it has fummer and winter at the fame time, the one on one fide,
and the other on the other.

The next day I fet out at two in the morning, and
reached Gambroon, or as it is called by the Perfians,
Bander Abaffie, or the Port of Abas. Gambroon is
fituated to the fouth caft-ward of Schiras, as that
town is of Ifpahan. The diftance between this place
and the laft mentioned city is computed at 183 leagues;
but thefe leagues are very long, and the mountains,
with the badnefs of the roads, render the journey
very tedious.

The houfes of Gambroon are built fo near the
water, that in a high fea they are wafhed by the
waves. It is fituated between the iflands of Ormus
and Kifmis, the one to the left and the other to the
right; and the coaft of Arabia being bordered by
high mountains, may alfo be feen in a clear day to
the right, at twenty leagues diftance. Three leagues
behind Gambroon are alfo very high mountains,
which are far from being barren, they being covered
with trees, and abounding with water. The territory belonging to Gambroon, is, however, dry and
fterile, it confifting of a moving fand. The town
is furrounded by a wall on the land fide, and has
two fmall fortreffes. The houfes are computed at
14 or 1500, one third of which are Indian Gentoos
or idolaters, a few Jews; the greateft part are Perfians, and the reft Englifh, French and Dutch, belonging to their refpective companies. The governor
of the province ufually refides there, and not at the
capital, which is called Neris, and is ten days
journey from thence: he has a pretty large and
commodious palace at the end of the town, at the
greateft diftance from the fea, built with ftone brought
from the ifle of Ormus, and all the houfes have flat
roofs.

This town has no port, but the road is as large,
good and fafe, as any in the univerfe; however, it

has one great inconvenience, which is, that the veſſels that ſtay there during the ſummer, are ſub-ject to be greatly damaged by being eaten with the worms.   The ſhips lie at anchor in four or five fathoms water, in as ſecure a ſituation as if they were in a baſon.

The water of Gambroon is very brackiſh, and drank by none but the poor : it is taken out of pits dug three fathoms deep in the ſand.   The common people drink the water of Mines, a village at the diſtance of a league from the port ; and the people in eaſy circumſtances drink the water of Iſſin, a large and fine village ſituated at the foot of the moun-tains.

As to the air of Gambroon, it is extremely dif-agreeable and unhealthy ; the wind almoſt through-out the year changes four times a day.   From mid-night to break of day it blows from the north, and is cold : from break of day till ten or eleven o'clock in the morning, it blows from the eaſt, and is alſo cold : a ſouth wind ariſes about three o'clock, which is hot, it proceeding from the ſea : this changes to the weſt at ſun-ſet, and blows hot till mid-night. Theſe ſudden changes of the air from hot to cold produce many diſeaſes, that are extremely fatal to foreigners : the moſt common of which are the dyſentery, the bloody-flux, and malignant fevers.

Proviſions are here very good, and in great plenty, particularly fiſh, which are brought aſhore freſh, night and morning : they ſometimes catch antelopes and partridges ; but the natives live chiefly on milk and plants, of which there are here all ſorts.   As to fruits they being brought from a great diſtance, cannot be had very cheap ; the moſt common are nectarines, quinces, citrons, oranges, pomegranates, figs, melons, apples, pears, nuts, almonds and grapes of ſeveral kinds.

On the 13th of March the principal perſon be-longing to the French company took me with him to dine with the governor, who entertained us with great magnificence after the Perfian manner ; that is, we had mufic and dancing, and amongft the reft a young Indian pofture-mafter. The entertainment lafted five hours. It began at ten o'clock with a flight breakfaft ; dinner was ferved up an hour after, at which the governor and fome of his guefts drank to excefs. No body was forced to drink ; but fo many healths were propofed, that it was neceffary to drink a great deal. Swordfmen in the eaft accuftom themfelves to drink wine after our manner ; for when the healths of the kings of France and Perfia with thofe of the principal perfons prefent, were drank, they were accompanied with the difcharge of the cannon of the fortreffes, with thofe of the governor's palace, and of the veffels in the road.

I had not been long at Gambroom before the badnefs of the climate affected all my men, who were taken very ill, and I myfelf was much diforder-ed, when being informed of the danger of our being foon carried off if we ftayed there, I refolved to return to Ifpahan, without waiting any longer for a veffel I expected from India. I therefore fet out ; but was taken fo ill at Tanguedelan, that my life was defpaired of : I however recovered ; reached If-phan, and foon after returned to Europe.

A NEW

HISTORY

OF

THE EAST-INDIES.

Containing an account of Indoftan, the empire of the great mogul;---of the moft remarkable places along the coaft of India;
of the peninfula of India on this fide the Ganges; of the peninfula beyond the Ganges; alfo a defcription of the different
kingdoms, provinces, and cities of thofe countries, with a particular account of the manners and cuftoms of the Inhabitants *.

INDOSTAN or India Proper, is a country of
great extent, fituated to the eaft of Perfia, and is
bounded by Tartary, on the north, by the peninfula
of India within the Ganges, and the bay of Bengal,
on the fouth; and by India beyond the Ganges on
the eaft. It is alfo called Mogulftan or the empire of
the Great Mogul. As the tropic of cancer runs
through the middle of it, the air is exceffively hot;
however in the moft fultry feafon, the rains which
ufually begin at the latter end of June, and laft till
about the end of October, refrefh the earth and cool
the air. When thofe rains fet in, a day feldom paffes
without terrible thunder and lightning; even in the
fair feafon, they have lightning, though without

* In thefe defcriptions we chiefly follow Capt. Alexander Hamilton, who from the year 1688 to 1723, traded and travelled by fea
and land to moft countries in the Eaft-Indies; from Mandeflo's travels, and an excellent work entitled, A New Hiftory of the Eaft-
Indies, ancient and modern.

thunder, for feveral weeks together ; but this does no harm. All the reft of the year, except at this feafon, and the Vernal Equinox, the fky is clear and ferene, and the earth is refrefhed with moderate breezes, fo that the mornings aud evenings are inconceivably pleafant. From the above rains the moft delicious plants fpring forth with incredible fpeed. Rice being of the moft general ufe, is the chief grain cultivated here ; it is fown in May and June, and generally reaped and threfhed in the open fields in November and December : but they have alfo as good wheat and barley in feveral parts of the empire, as any where in the world. Their chief fruits befides thofe brought from Europe, are dates, figs, prunellos, melons, pomegranates, tamarinds, guavas, jaccas, pine-apples, mirabilons, mangoes, cocoas, fugar canes, pepper, oranges, limes, &c.

But though the foil is fo rich as to produce a vaft variety of fruits and flowers, yet the ground is fo light, that feldom more than two oxen are ufed in plowing it. There are here numbers of fine woods that afford timber for building fhips, and redwood for dying. Their mulberry-trees fupply their filkworms with food, the toddy-trees furnifh the inhabitants with liquor ; and of the fruit of the cotton-tree and cotton fhrub, they make their calicoes, muflin, ginghams, &c. the great articles of their clothing and commerce. The country alfo yields for exportatation, Malabar pepper, ginger, fandal-wood, aloes, gum lacque, caffia, camphor, indigo, opium, affafœtida, cardamums, borax, faltpetre, alum, and fulphur ; while the mountains produce jafper, agate, cryfolites, granates, amethyfts, rubies, and diamonds.

Here are plenty of wild and tame beafts : of the former clafs are the elephant, and the rhinoceros, with lions, tygers, leopards, wolves, jackals, elks, apes and baboons. Wild boars, deer, antelopes, hares and foxes, fays Mr. Hamilton, are their wild game, which they hunt with dogs, leopards, and a small fierce creature called a shoegoose. It is about the size of a fox, with long pricked ears like a hare and a face like a cat, a grey back and sides, with a belly and breast white. When they are taken out to hunt, a horseman carries it behind him hood-winked, and the deer and antelopes being pretty familiar, will not start before the horses come very near. He who carries the shoegoose, takes off the hood, and shews it the game, which with large swift springs, it soon overtakes, when leaping on their backs, and getting forward to their shoulders, it scratches out their eyes, and makes them fall an easy prey to the hunters. The leopard runs down his game, and often gives the hunters a long chase, as well as the dogs, who will take to the water when the game betakes themselves to swimming which they frequently do.

The flesh of the Indian hog is reckoned the best butcher's meat of this country; especially that of the wild hogs, of which there are great plenty. These not being the property of any single person, all are at liberty to hunt and kill them; so that though the people have no lands they can properly call their own, the privilege they enjoy in those of the prince is almost an equivalent, the lion being the only beast of the forest which the Mogul reserves the hunting of to himself. They have buffaloes, whose skin is smooth without hair; but their flesh is coarse. To-wards Persia and Tartary they have fine large sheep, with flat tails; but those in the south part of Indostan are thin and long shanked, with a reddish hair on their backs instead of wool, and their flesh is lean and dry. The natives have plenty of good milk from their cows, buffaloes and goats; but their best cream will not every where produce butter, the climate being in some parts too hot to bring it to a due consistence, however, it is said they make good cheese in the north part of India.

They have here plenty of geefe, peacocks, hens, ducks, pigeons, plovers, turtle doves, partridges, quails, parrokeets, &c. but the flefh of their poultry is generally lean and dry. Vultures are no where fo common and tame as here, which is afcribed to their feeding much on the banian-tree. There is a kite here with a white head, to which fome are fo fuperftitious as to pay religious honours. They have bats as big as kites, and an exceeding pretty bird lefs than a wren, which has ravifhing notes and a beautiful plumage. As the monkeys which abound in the woods, are its great enemies, it builds its neft to the extremity of the twigs of the trees, whence they hang like a purfe out of their reach. They have alfo excellent fifh in their rivers and feas.

The people are generally well made, and have good features; towards the fouth they are black, and towards the north of an olive colour; but the natives have every where black long hair, and black eyes, and hardly any of them are deformed. They are ftrong, acute, have a lively fancy and a good genius. They are civil to ftrangers, profoundly fubmiffive to their governors; but not remarkable for their courage. The Indians here are diftinguifhed into Moors, or Moguls, and Gentoos, or original Indians and Pagans. The former are a mixture of Tartars, Perfians, Arabs, and moft of the Mahometan nations, who having the power in their hands, behave as the lords of the country. The Pagans, who are much the greateft number, are as polite, as peaceabic, as ingenious and as inoffenfive a people as any on the face of the earth. Their beautiful chints, and painted calicoes are drawn by the meaneft of the people, from their own fancy; for the chints and calicoes on the Coromandel coaft are painted with a pencil; but thofe to the northward are printed; however, the dye of neither wafhes out. For inlaying in ivory no people excel them. The goldfmiths work curioufly in filligree, and imitate any goldfmith's work made in Europe. The builders ufe a cement made of fea-fhells much harder than bricks, and will terrafs the roof of a houfe, or lay a floor with it, that fhall be like one entire ftone, and be full as hard. They have like-wife as good carpenters, who exactly imitate the Eu-glifh models.

The Indians generally wear a white veft of calico, filk, or muflin, which fold over before, and is tied with ftrings on either fide. The fleeves are clofe to the arms, and fo long that they fit about their wrifts in wrinkles. The upper part fits clofe to their bo-dies ; but from their waifts downwards it hangs in plaits reaching below the knee. They have no ftock-ings, but their breeches reach down to their heels, and they put their bare feet into their flippers. Round their waifts they wear a fafh, in which the bet-ter fort have a dagger. In the north part of the country they have fhirts open before, which hang over their breeches, and in the winter feafon they alfo wear a cloak. The Pagans wear their hair made up in a roll behind ; but the Moors have only a fin-gle lock ; many of them wear their beards, but fome have only wifkers. The Pagan women have their hair adorned with jewels, which they alfo wear in their ears and nofes ; they have bracelets on their wrifts and ankles, and gold, filver, or brafs rings on their fingers and toes ; or if they cannot afford thofe of metal, they have thofe of glafs. The Mahome-tan women are almoft always veiled, and let part of their hair hang on their fhoulders.

The Gentoos are divided into eighty-five different tribes, which do not eat with each other, each tribe herds together, and thofe of one tribe cannot marry into another ; they muft purfue the trade and profef-fion of the family, fo that a goldfmith's fon muft be a goldfmith, and marry a goldfmith's daughter, and a carpenter's fon muft be a carpenter, and fo of the reft. The chief of thefe tribes are the Brachmans, or Bramins who are their priefts ; and the Rajaputes, or Rashboots who profess arms, but do not, like the other tribes, abstain from meat, except it be the flesh of a cow, or some other beasts which they hold sacred.

The bramins or priests of the god brama, persuade those who are ill, to leave legacies to the church, for which they give a receipt, which they put into the dead person's hand ; in this case, says Captain Hamilton, they draw a bill for ten times the value in the other world on some eminent faint, who negociates such bills in paradise. They persuade the vulgar, that their idols eat like men, and in order that they may be plentifully provided with good cheer, they make them of a gigantic stature, and give them a monstrous belly ; and if the people fail in their offerings to these idols, by which the bramins maintain their families, they threaten them with the anger of the gods. The people believe there is something so divine in a cow, that happy is the man who can get himself sprinkled with the ashes of one burnt by a bramin ; and they esteem the man blessed, who in the agonies of death can lay hold of a cow's tail : for they believe transmigration, and think the soul sometimes returns into the body of that beast, which they consider as an high honour. The souls of the wicked they imagine enter the bodies of dogs, swine, and other unclean animals. Hence they abstain from the flesh of all living creatures, and kill nothing that has life, for fear they should dispossess the soul of a friend or relation of its habitation. The learning of the bramins consists in their being able to read and get by heart some ancient books said to be written by Brama.

There is a religious order among them called faquirs and jonges, who make vows of poverty and celibacy, and to obtain the favour of Brama, suffer the most dreadful tortures. They contemn worldly riches, and go naked except a piece of cloth about their loins, and some have not even that. A set of

thefe never comb nor cut their hair, but delighting
in naftinefs, befmear their bodies and faces with
afhes   Mr. Hamilton obferves that he has feen one
of thefe fitting quite naked under the fhade of a tree,
and that a married woman came as a cure for barren-
nefs, to kifs the part which modefty ought to have
taught him to conceal, while he ftroaked their heads,
and muttered prayers over them.   To fuch a degree
do thefe pretented religious impofe on the credulous
muititude.

The aufterities of fome of thefe are incredible to
thofe who have not been eye-witneffes of them. Some
ftand for years on one foot, with their arms tied to
the beam of a houfe, or the branch of a tree.   By
this means their arms fettle in that pofture, and
ever after become ufelefs; and fome fit in the fun
with their faces looking upwards till they are incapable of altering the pofition of their heads. The
people in all thefe cafes making a merit of feeding
them.

Frauds are, however, fometimes practifed; for in
the year 1721, one of thefe zealots pretending to
more fanctity than his neighbours, gave out that he
would be buried alive in a grave ten feet deep, and
that he fhould appear at Amadabat, at about 200
miles diftance, within fifteen days.   The grave was
dug, and going in, he had fome reeds placed about
a foot or two over his head, to prevent the earth
falling in. A large jar of water ftood under the fhade
of a great tree, about ten or twelve yards from the
grave, where a good number of faquirs had for fome
time taken up their quarters, and had perfuaded
many people into a belief of the ftory; but the
governor of Surat ordered a party of foldiers to fee
the faquir buried, and to take care that no impofture
was ufed in his pretended refurrection.   They accordingly fearched narrowly, and fufpecting that
fome place about the root might afford a paffage,
ordered the faquirs to remove a little out of the

way, which they willingly did; but finding nothing,
they ordered the faquirs to remove the great water
jar, which was almoft full : at this they exclaimed
aloud; but their clamours ftrengthened the fufpicions
of the Mahometans ; who either breaking or removing the jar, difcovered a fubterranean paffage that
led within two feet of the grave, on which they fell
upon the faquirs with their drawn fwords, and cut
many of them to pieces ; and the fellow who was
to have arifen from the dead loft his head in the
fray.

Befides the many tribes of Indian idolators, there
is a feft called the Perfees or Gebres, who are wor-
fhippers of fire. Thefe are here bred to trade and
hufbandry, and are very induftrious.

The Banians or Gentoos are often married at fix
or feven years of age, but they do not cohabit before the bride is twelve, and the bridegroom fixteen.
The weddings are celebrated with much pomp. In
the afternoon the bridegroom fends a long train of
meffengers with prefents to the bride, in covered
difhes or bafkets, preceded by a fort of hautboys,
drums, and trumpets, and followed by female flaves,
for the ufe of the married couple, and after them
is carried an empty palanquin to carry the bride to
the bridegroom's houfe. Several nights fucceffively
they are both carried in ftate through the ftreets by
torch-light, dreffed in their beft apparel and jewels,
with mufic, fire-works, flags, and ftreamers before
them, and then the parents of the married couple
fend prefents to their friends. Thefe pompous
cavalcades being over, they proceed to the houfe
of the bride's father, where being feated at a table
oppofite each other, they join their hands, and the
prieft covers their heads with a fort of hood, which
remains fpread over them for a quarter of an hour,
till he has finifhed a prayer and the nuptial benedic-
tion ; and then uncovering their heads, the company is fprinkled with rofe-water and other perfumes

mixed with faffron. If the youth does not happen
to like the girl chofen for him by his parents, he may
keep concubines, and if the wife murmurs at this
he may fet her to work with his flaves, for which fhe
can have no remedy, not even a divorce. The
women of this country pay their hufbands an extraordinary refpect, and are entirely at their difpofal : which is the lefs extraordinary, as among
the richer fort, the hufband purchafes his wife of her
parents.

When a perfon dies, they wafh the corpfe, drefs
it in the common apparel ufually worn by the deceafed, and carrying it a little way out of the town,
place it on a funeral pile generally raifed with wood
near fome river: thofe of fortune ufually mix vaft
quantities of fragrant wood with the reft, and the
whole being reduced to afhes, it is thrown into the
river. As to the cuftom of widows burning themfelves with their hufbands, it feems in moft places
laid afide. Where this is the cafe, the women who
mourn for their hufbands, fhave their heads, and
feeming to abandon themfelves to grief, neglect their
drefs, and never marry again ; but the men never
cut their hair on thefe occafions, unlefs it be for
the death of a father, or fome of their rajas or
princes. When they mourn for other relations, they
generally rend their garments, or rather put on an
old torn veft, and appear quite negligent of themfelves.

The buildings of the common people, efpecially
thofe of the Gentoos, who are at leaft twenty to
one Mahometan throughout the empire are generally
low thatched cottages with clay walls, and only one
floor ; but the bazars, and other public buildings,
with the houfes belonging to the Chriftian and Mahometan merchants, in fome of the ancient cities
are very pompous, being built with brick, timber
and ftone, and fometimes with marble. The houfes
of the more wealthy are two ftories high, and have

flat roofs on which they take the morning and evening air.

The palaces of their princes or rajas are moftly built in one form: before the gate is a large piazza or roof fupported by pillars, open to the front, and upon the right and left towards the gate are banks of earth about a yard high, on which are fpread fine carpets, or pieces of European fcarlet cloth, with cufhions of the fame, on which the raja fits to receive the complaints of his fubjects, to entertain foreigners, or tranfact ftate affairs.

The power of the mogul is fo defpotic, that he has the fovereign difpofal of the lives and effects of his fubjects, and none dare difpute his will. At his command the greateft lords are executed. Few days paffed without his appearing at fun-rifing; and the lords of his court are obliged to be in his apartment, in order to pay him homage. He fhews himfelf alfo at noon to fee the wild beafts fight; and in the evening he appears at a window, from whence he fees the fun fet. He retires with that luminary amidft the noife of a great number of drums and and kettle drums, and the acclamations of the people, wifhing him a long and happy life. None are permitted to enter the palace, but the rajas or princes, and the great officers; who accompany all their difcourfe with continual reverences; they proftrate themfelves before him at taking leave; they put their hands on their eyes, then on their breaft, and laftly on the earth, to teftify that they are only duft and afhes when compared to him. They wifh him all manner of profperity as they retire, and go backwards till they are out of fight.

When he marches at the head of his army, or goes a hunting, or to one of his country palaces, he is accompanied by above 10,000 men. About an hundred elephants covered with houfings of fcarlet, velvet and brocade, march at the head of this little army, each carrying two men, one of whom governs

the animal by touching his forehead with an iron
hook, the other holds a large banner of filk embroidered with gold and filver ; the firft eighty carry
each a kettledrum.   In the middle of this troop the
mogul rides on a fine Perfian horfe, with trappings
of gold, adorned with diamonds and pearls, gold-
bells and fringes, or in a chariot drawn by two
white oxen, whofe large fpreading horns are adorned
with gold ; and fometimes he is carried by men in a
palanquin.   The rajas and officers of his court compofe his retinue, and have 5 or 600 elephants, camels,
or chariots loaded with baggage.   When he rides on
an elephant, he is feated on his back on a ftately
throne, adorned with gold and precious ftones.

His fons have the title of fultans, and his daughters of fultanas, the former are married at thirteen
or fourteen years of age, and when they arrive at
years of maturity, are fent to diftant governments,
none but the heir apparent remaining with his
father.   The firft fon he has by any of his wives, is
confidered heir of the empire, though the longeft
fword generally carries it ; but whenever he obtains
the throne, he inhumanly deftroys his brothers,
and their male iffue.

The mogul has feldom more than four wives,
though his concubines generally amount to above
a thoufand.   His court, according to Tavernier, is
richer than can be imagined.   The great men buy
the fineft diamonds that can be got for their wives
and daughters, whofe head dreffes and other apparel
are amazingly fumptuous.   But thofe for the emperor's own ufe, are the fineft in the world.

Mr. Mandeflo, who wifely lays it down as a rule
to defcribe nothing but what he has feen, obferves,
that the palace of Agra, is four leagues in circumference, and that it is fortified on all fides.   After
having paffed feveral courts and ftreets feparated by
different gates, one comes at laft to the mogul's
apartment, which is in the middle of the building.

In the firſt ſaloon is a baluſtrade of ſilver, where are the officers of the guard, who allow none to enter but the great lords of the court. This leads into the chambers of ceremony, where there is another baluſtrade of gold, encloſing the throne of maſſy gold, enriched with diamonds, pearls and other precious ſtones. None but the king's ſons are allowed to enter within this baluſtrade, or to cool the air and drive away the flies with fans. In this palace is a high tower, the roof of which is covered with plates of gold.

If we may belive Tavernier, this prince had four thrones adorned with diamonds, rubies, emaralds, and the richeſt pearls, made up in ſeveral figures, and that one of them, which was crowned with two peacocks, that had their tails ſet with jewels, coſt thirteen millions ſterling ; and that in this palace are two apartments covered all over with gold, as are alſo the pillars that ſupport the pavillions.

There are two ſolemn feſtivals of which he is the principal object. The firſt at the beginning of the new year, laſts about fifteen days. A theatre is erected before the palace, fourteen feet high, fifty-ſix long, and forty broad, covered with rich tapeſtry, and ſurrounded by a baluſtrade. Near it is a building of painted wood, embelliſhed with mother of pearl, in which ſome of the principal lords of the court ſeat themſelves, though they have at the ſame time tents erected in the firſt court of the palace, where they effect to diſplay all their riches and ſplendor. The prince, attended by ſeven of his miniſters, aſcends the theatre, where he ſeats himſelf on velvet cuſhions, embroidered with gold and pearls, waiting for the preſents that are brought him, which he receives equally from the people, and the grandees of the empire, during the eighteen days the ceremony laſts, and towards the end he diſpenſes among them his bounties ; theſe conſiſt in places and dignities, which he confers on thoſe who have been moſt liberal

to him.   Tavernier fays, he faw him receive at one of
thefe feafts above thirty millions of livres in diamonds,
rubies, emeralds, pearls, gold, filver, fine ftuffs,
elephants, camels, and horfes.

The fecond feftival is the anniverfary of his birth.
He begins the day with all manner of diverfions,
which he breaks off to go to the palace of the Queen
his mother, if fhe be yet alive, and having fhewn
his gratitude to her, he caufes his grandees to make
her magnificent prefents.   After he has dined, he
puts on his fineft robes, covers himfelf with gold and
jewels, and being rather loaded than adorned, goes
into a vaft and fuperb pavillion, where he is waited
on by the principal lords of his court.   He here finds
the great fcales, and the chains which fufpend them,
both of which are of maffy gold adorned with jewels.
He places himfelf in one of the fcales, the other being filled with gold, filver, jewels, pieces of ftuff,
fine linen, pepper, cloves, mace, cinnamon, corn,
pulfe, and herbs, and an exact regifter is kept of the
difference of his weight every year.   If it appears
that he has made any confiderable acquifition of flefh
fince he was weighed laft, there are great rejiocings
throughout the whole kingdom.

This ceremony is followed by his diftributing fmall
pieces of money among the poor ; and in throwing
among the grandees nuts, piftachios, almonds, and
other fruits of gold, but they are fo fmall, and the
gold fo thin, that it is faid a thoufand of them do not
weigh above feven or eight piftoles.   The feftival is
concluded with a magnificent fupper given to the
lords of the court, with whom he fpends the night
in drinking.

But though the treafures of this monarch, and his
revenues from forty kingdoms, which are within his
empire, are immenfely great, yet fpecie is hardly
any where fcarcer than among the private perfons in
this empire.

It is however proper to obferve, that this pompous account was wrote before Nadir Shah ravaged the mogul's dominions: for in the beginning of 1739, that conquorer having defeated the mogul, entered Delly, fecured his perfon, and having feized all his jewels and treafures, of which he obliged him to give a lift, replaced him on the throne ; obliging him to promife to pay him an annual tribute of 6,250,000l. fterling. Among the other plunder feized by the Perfian monarch, was the emperor's bed of ftate, adorned with precious ftones, and the grand imperial throne. In fhort, the value of the plunder taken from the mogul and his nobles, is faid to amount to 111 courons, or 231,250,000l. fterling. It muft be acknowledged, that the largencfs of this immenfe fum may render this account improbable; it is therefore necellary to add, that it is taken from a letter from Perfia, publifhed the fame year in the London Gazette.

Having given a general defcription of the mogul's dominions, we fhall now proceed to defcribe the feveral provinces fituated on the coaft, as being the moft remarkable, on account of the commerce carried on with them by the trading nations of Europe.

The firft port in Sindy, the moft weftern province of India, is Larribundar, fituated five or fix leagues from the fea, on a branch of the river Indus, capable of receiving fhips of 200 tons burden. It is a village of about 100 mud houfes, with a large ftone fort, that has four or five great guns, to defend the merchandize, and prevent its being feized by the Ballowches and other robbers. Tatta, the metropolis of the province, is a large and rich city about three miles long, and one and a half broad, at about 40 miles diftance from the above village. All goods carried from one of thefe places to the other, are tranfported on carriage bealts, as camels, oxen, and horfes. The country, which is almoft level, is over-

grown with fhrubs and bufhes, fit to cover an ambufcade, and often made ufe of by the above robbers,
who fuddently rufh out on a caffila or caravan, and
while the guards and carriers are fighting, another
party drives away the beafts with their packs.

Capt. Hamilton once came to Larribundar, with
a cargo from Malabar worth about 10,000l. where
being unable to fell his goods, he was obliged to
travel to Tatta in a caffila of 1500 beafts, and as
many, or more men and women, befides 200 horfe
for their guard. Having proceeded about fixteen
miles, they were informed by their fcouts that a great
body of robbers were juft before them, Capt. Hamilton had thirteen of his beft markfmen belonging
to his fhip with him in the front, where his beafts
were, and being all mounted on Indian horfes, which
are very fmall, they difmounted, and fet their beafts
on their flanks and front, to ferve for a barricado
againft the fword and target men, who were the
principal ftrength of the robbers. They had not
been long in that pofture, when the robbers fent a
herald on horfeback, who branifhed his fword, and
on his coming within call, threatened, that if they
did not immediately furrender at difcretion, they
fhould have no quarter. Our traveller had two fea-
men who fhot extremely well, and therefore ordered
one of them to fire at the herald, which he inftantly
did, and fhot him through the head. Another came
foon after with the fame threatenings, and met with
the fame treatment. The next that came, the captain ordered his horfe to be fhot in the head, to try
if they could take his rider, that they might know
the enemy's ftrength. The horfe was killed as foon
as he appeared ; but fome of the guard who were
mounted, inftead of bringing him, cut him to pieces.
The horfe guard, who had continued in the rear,
feeing what was done in the front, now took courage,
and getting in among the bufhes, met with fome
who had a defign to attack the flank, and foon

defeated them ; which threw the reft into fuch a panic.
that they betook themfelves to flight, and the horfe,
purfuing them, put many to the fword.

They now travelled without moleftation to Tatta,
where they were received with acclamations from
the populace, and the better fort vifited the Englifh
with prefents of fruit and fweetmeats, afcribing the
fafe arrival of the caffila to their courage and conduct.

He and his men were lodged in a large convenient
room that had large warehoufes. The ftairs from the
ftreet were each of one piece of porphyry ten feet
long, of a bright yellow, and as fmooth as glafs.
They were about ten in number, and led up to a
fquare fifteen yards long, and about ten broad. The
next day the nabob fent them his compliments with
an ox, five fheep, as many goats, twenty fowls, and
fifty pigeons, with fweetmeats and fruit in abundance.
He was then encamped about fix miles from the
town, with an army of eight or 10,000 men, to
punifh thefe bands of robbers. He invited Captain
Hamilton to drink a difh of coffee with him, and the
latter fending him word that he defigned to kifs his
hand, the next day he fent him twenty fine Perfian
horfes well equipped, on ten of which he and his
guard rode, and on the other ten were mounted the
moft confiderable merchants in Tatta, who went to
accompany him out of refpect.

When they came to the camp they would have
alighted ; but an officer informed them, that the
nabob defired they fhould be brought to his tent on
horfeback, and riding before them conducted them
to the door of the pavilion, which the captain entered,
and found the nabob fitting alone. He defiring to
lay a fmall prefent at his feet, this was readily permitted. It confifted of a looking-glafs of about 5l.
value, a gun and a pair of piftols, well gilt, a fabre-
blade, and the blade of a dagger gilt, a glafs tobacco-
pipe, and an embroidered cafe to put it in. The na-

bob fent for all who had accompanied Mr. Hamilton
into the room, and fhewing them the prefent, expa-
tiated on the value of every piece of it; and after
fome encomiums on Mr. Hamilton's valour and generofity, told him, that he was a free denifon of
Tatta, and fhould be exempted from all cuftom on
the goods he had brought or fhould export, and that
he fhould have the power of imprifoning any perfon
who bought any part of his cargo, and did not pay
according to agreement, and if that was not fufficient to induce them to give him fatisfaction, he might
fell their wives and children to difcharge the debt.

Within about four miles of Tatta, are forty-two
fine large tombs, the burying place of fome of the
kings of Sindy, when that country was governed by
its own monarchs. Mr. Hamilton went into the
largeft ; this was built in the form of a cupola, and
in the middle of it ftood a coffin about three feet high
and feven feet long, with fome others of a fmaller
fize. The cupola was of yellow, green, and red
porphyry, finely polifhed, and being fet chequer-
wife, had a very pleafing effect. This tomb is about
30 feet high, and 21 in diameter, and is faid to have
been the burying place of the laft king of the country.

The city of Tatta, ftands in a fpacious plain about
two miles from the river Indus, from which canals
are cut to bring water to the city and the gardens.
Thofe which formerly belonged to the king were at
that time well ftored with excellent fruit and flowers.

The river Indus is navigable for their veffels as high
as Cafmire in 32°. north latitude. One branch runs
to Cabul to the weftward, and others through feveral
large provinces fituated to the eaft. Thefe veffels are
called kifties ; they have one maft, carrying a fquare
fail, and are flat-bottomed. Some of them are 200
tons burthen. The cabbins are built from ftem to
ftern, and in each is a kitchen and a neceffary which
opens into the water. Thefe cabbins are let to paf-

fengers, and the hold being divided into feparate apartments are let out to freighters, fo that every one having a lock on his own cabbin, and apartment in the hold, has his goods always ready to difpofe of wherever he finds a market.

This country never knows the mifery of famine, for the Indus overflows all the low grounds in the months of April, May, and June, and when the floods go off they leave a fat flime. Before the earth dries, it is fown and harrowed, and never fails of bringing forth a plentiful crop.

The people here manufacture. filks, calicoes, cotton cloths of feveral kinds, and alfo chintz and very beautiful coverlets for beds. They make very fine cabinets, both lacquered and inlaid with ivory, and the beft bows and arrows in the world, of buffaloes horns.

The religion eftablifned by law is the Mahometan, but there are ten Gentoos to one Muffulman.

The next maritime country to Sindy is Guzerat, an ifland formed by a branch of the Indus, that runs into the fea at the city of Cambaya. The natives are vaffals to the mogul, though they are ftill pagans. The firft town on the fouth fide of the Indus, is Cutchnaggen. It has fome trade, and produces coarfe cloths, cotton and chonks, a fhell fifh in the fhape of a periwinkle, but as large as a man's arm above the elbow. In Bengal thefe fhells are formed into rings for the ornament of womens arms ; and they are worn in many parts of India. This country is famous for pirates. It has feveral other ports, the moft remarkable of which is Diu, a fmall ifland on the fouth of Guzerat, three miles long and two broad, belonging to the crown of Portugal. The city is pretty large, and fortified by a high ftone wall with baftions at convenient diftances, well furnifhed with cannon. The harbour is fecured by two caftles, that can bring above a hundred large cannon to defend its entrance, and by fea it is fortified by nature with dangerous rocks and high cliffs. This is one of the beft built, and ftrongeft cities in India, and its ftately edifices of free-ftone and marble, are fufficient witneffes of its ancient grandeur and opulence ; but at prefent not above a fourth part of the city is inhabited. It contains five on fix fine churches, which ftanding on a rifing ground of an eafy afcent from the great caftle, and the churches rifing gradually higher than each other, fhew all their beautiful fronts to the fea, where they appear to great advantage ; and within they are well decorated with images and paintings. At prefent there are not above 200 Portuguefe in the caftle and city : the reft of the inhabitants being banyans, of whom there may be about 40,000, but few of them are rich, becaufe the infolence of the Portuguefe renders it unfafe for monied ftrangers to dwell among them. The king of Portugal has about 12,000l. per annum in poll money paid from hence into his treafury, and the cuftoms and land-tax may amount to about fix thoufand pounds more ; but if the ifland were in the hands of fome induftrious European nation, it would be the beft mart-town on the coaft of India, for carrying on a trade up the Indus.

Goga is a pretty large town, that has fome mud wall fortifications. There is fome trade, and ftrangers are admitted to a free commere in fuch merchandize as is fit to be imported or exported to or from Guzerat. The town is governed by an officer of the mogul, whofe forces for the defence of the place amount to about 200.

A peninfula which lies at the bottom of the mouths of the Indus, contains the greateft part of the kingdom of Guzerat. There is not a more fertile province in all the Indies, it produces fruits and provifions in fuch abundance, that it fupplies the neighbouring provinces. Cambay, at the bottom of the gulph of the fame name, and only twelve leagues from Goga, is a fine, large, and agreeable city : its

ftreets are fpacious, handfome and ftraight. Though
it is at leaft two leagues in circumference, it is entirely built of hewn ftone. Without its walls are very
large fuburbs, and fifteen or fixteen public gardens.
It is ftill a place of pretty good trade, though it is
now not half inhabited. The natives are ftrict
obfervers of the doctrine of the Metempfychofis,
and Du Bois fays they maintain three hofpitals, one
for birds, another for goats, and a third for black
cattle. The zealots who eat nothing that had life,
lay food for animals on the high-ways and in the
fields. The banyans carry in their girdles an inftrument to brufh the places where they fit down, or
where they walk, left they fhould crufh the ants,
and other reptiles, that may be found there. Some
of them carry their fcruples and weaknefs fo far as to
eat nothing that is red, for fear there fhould be blood
in it. By the force of money they have obtained
from the great mogul the fingular privilege, that no
calf, bull, or cow, fhall be killed in their city ; and
if a Chriftian, or Mahometan, fhould be found
tranfgreffing the prohibition, his life would be in
danger. Thefe pagans have in this city one of the
moft magnificent temples in the kingdom, full of
idols of all fizes, and, for the moft part, of monftrous figures. It contributes to the wealth and
grandeur of Surat, to which it is fubordinate, and
its vicinity to Amanabat, from which it is only about
150 miles diftant, makes it fhare the advantages of
that great city, which in magnitude and wealth is
but little inferior to the beft towns of Europe. In
this laft city the Englifh have a factory for commerce.

The country abounds in grain, cattle, cotton and
filk. Cornelian and agate are found in its rivers ; of
the former they make rings, and feals, and of the
latter cabinets, fome of which are of one entire
ftone, except the lids. Mr. Hamilton fays, he has
feen fome of them fourteen or fifteen inches long,
and eight or nine deep, the value of each being 30

or 40l. fterling. The natives are the beft embroi-
derers in India, or perhaps in the whole world.

Surat, fituated to the fouth on the peninfula of
India, on the banks of the river Tapta or Tapee,
is the next fea-port town of confequence. The inhabitants are computed at 200,000 fouls, among
whom are many Mahometans and Gentoos, who are
immenfely rich. There are here as many different
religions as in Amfterdam ; that by law eftablifhed
is Mahometanifm, of the feƈt of Ali. There are fome
called Mufey, who obferve the law of Mofes, as well
as the Koran, but the Gentoos are the moft numerous, and are either merchants, bankers, brokers,
accomptants, colleƈtors, or furveyors ; but few of
them are of any handicraft trade, except taylors and
barbers.

Surat is one of the beft, the fineft, the richeft and
greateft marts, not only of the mogul's country,
but of all the Indies. It was one of the firft objeƈts
of European ambition. The Portuguefe eftablifhed
themfelves there by force of arms in the year 1530 ;
the Englifh followed them in 1609 ; the Dutch in
1616, and the French in 1665. All of them have
contributed to embelifh a city, which was already
efteemed the moft fplendid in all the country. Part
of the ftreets are paved with porcelain, and fome
houfes are fronted with it. The houfes are flat on
the top. The rich vie with each other in their
decorations. The furniture of their apartments is
fuperb, and their magnificence is feen even in the
penthoufes of their windows. Thefe confift of feveral
rows of fmall planks joined together obliquely over
the windows, and inlaid with mother of pearl, and
the fhells of tortoifes, crocodiles, &c. Thus they
keep off the heat of the fun, which is extreme, and
by weakening the light they render it more agreeable
by that mixture of colours, which is reflected by its
rays.

The fields about Surat are very fertile, except thofe towards the fea, which are fandy and barren. They have excellent beef, mutton, and fowl daily expofed to fale in the city. Beef is about three farthings a pound, when the bones are bought with the flefh, and about a penny with the bones taken out. Mutton is three half-pence a pound, large fowls are fold for feven-pence half-penny a piece, and live hares at four-pence each. They have great plenty of wild-fowl ; but thofe who would have them muft fhoot them. Their flamingoes are large and good : the pady-bird is alfo good in its feafon, and the corn-bird is excellent. They have good partridges ; but the pheafants are bad. The wild-geefe, ducks and teal, are plenty and good, and feveral forts of turtle-doves are both beautiful and well tafted. They have likewife plenty of good wheat as good as any in Europe, with fome peafe and French beans ; but neither oats nor barley.

There are few or no fine buildings in the city. The French have a little church near the old Englifh factory ; but though there are above an hundred different fects here, they have no religious difputes, each being willing his neighbour fhould worfhip God in that way he believes will pleafe him beft.

The Mahometan women go always veiled when they appear abroad. Their garments differ but little from thofe of the men. Their coats, which alfo ferve both fexes for fhirts, are clofe-bodied ; the men's are gathered in plaits below the navel, to make them appear long-waifted, and the women's are gathered a pretty way above, to make their waifts feem fhort. They both wear breeches which reach to the ankles. The men have only filver rings on their fingers, and generally put one for a fignet. The women wear gold rings on their fingers, and fometimes one on the thumb, in which is fet a fmall looking-glafs ; they likewife often wear gold rings in their nofes and ears. On the other hand, the

Gentoos permit their women to appear bare-faced, and their legs are naked to the knee. They wear gold or filver rings, according to their ability, one in the nofe, and feveral fmall ones in holes bored round the rim, with a large and heavy one in the tip of each ear. They likewife wear rings on their toes, and fhackles on their legs, of thofe metals made hollow; thefe contain glafs beads, in order to rattle when they walk. The men wear gold rings in their ears, and often three or four in a clufter hanging at the tip; fome have them alfo fet with pearls.

From Surat to Daman, a town belonging to the crown of Portugal, at twenty-two leagues diftance, are feveral rivers and villages under the fuperinten-dancy of Surat. Daman was once a place of good trade; but is at prefent reduced to poverty. It is fituated on the fea-fhore at the mouth of a river, and is naturally very ftrong from its being furrounded by a deep marfh; it is alfo encompaffed by a good ftone wall. The town is about half a mile long, and near as broad; the buildings of the city are of ftone, and it has a large cathedral, that may be feen at fea a confiderable diftance. There are two or three other churches, a convent, a monaftery, a nunnery, and an hofpital. On the oppofite fide of the river is a caftle diftinguifhed by the name of St. Salvadore.

At Daman begins the peninfula within the Ganges a large country which nearly refembles the figure of a cone reverfed. It is wafhed towards the eaft, fouth, and weft, by the waters of the ocean; and the country of the great mogul bounds it to the north. It lies in the torrid zone between 7°. 30'. and 21°. north latitude, extending from north to fouth 270 leagues, and from eaft to weft at its greateft breadth 270 leagues, and its outmoft point is called Cape Comorin. The exceffive heats which reign in this country render the colour of the inhabitants

2

much darker than thofe who live in Indoftan ; but with refpect to fertility and riches, both countries are nearly the fame. The country is, however, more celebrated for its numerous harbours, and the immenfe commerce of the European nations.

The weftern coaft which extends from Daman to Cape Comorin, is called the coaft of Malabar, and eaftern fide, which begins at that cape, and ends at the kingdom of Orixa, is the coaft of Cormandel and Golconda. We fhall proceed along the weftern coaft to that cape, and then doubling it, proceed up the eaftern fide to the river Ganges.

From Daman to Baffaim is about eighteen leagues along the fhore. The latter is a fortified city belonging to the crown of Portugal, ftanding on a little ifland feparated from the continent by a fmall rivulet. Its walls are pretty high, and about two miles in circumference. In the middle of the city is a citadel : it has alfo three or four churches, with fome convents and monafteries, a college, and an hofpital. This is a place of fmall trade ; for moft of its riches lie dead in the churches of the Portuguefe, or in the hands of indolent, lazy, country gentlemen, who loiter away their days in eafe, pride and luxury, without having the leaft feeling for the poverty of the reft of the people.

At about half a league diftance is the ifland of Salfett, which is about twenty miles long, and in fome places ten broad. The ifland is cut almoft in two, by a narrow river, near the mouth of which is a fmall town called Verfua, that has a little narrow harbour deep enough to receive fhips of the greateft burthen. It has a fmall trade in dry fifh, which are fold to the inland countries and villages.

Bombay an ifland belonging to the crown of England, is the next place of confequence ; near it is the ifland of Elephanta remarkable for a furprifing temple cut out of a rock.

Farther to the fouth is Chaul, a town belonging
to the Portuguefe, fituated on the fide of a river that
affords an harbour for fmall veffels. The town is
fortified, as is alfo an ifland on the fouth fide of the
harbour. This was once a place of great trade,
particularly for fine embroidered quilts ; but is now
miferably poor.

Paffing by feveral inconfiderable towns on the coaft,
you come to Goa the metropolis of the Portuguefe
dominions in India, fituated in an ifland about
twelve miles long, and fix broad. It has a fine falt
water river, capable of receiving fhips of the largeft
fize, which lie within a mile of the town. The
banks of the river are adorned with noble ftructures,
as churches, caftles, and gentlemen's houfes ; but the
air of the city being reckoned unwholfome, it is not
well inhabited. The viceroy's palace is a fine edifice
within a piftol fhot of the river, over one of the city
gates that opens into a noble fpacious ftreet about
half a mile long, terminated by a beautiful church
called Mifericordia. There are indeed fo many
churches, convents and chapels, that one half of
them would be fufficient for a much larger and
better peopled city. Moft of thefe ftructures are
built and adorned on the infide with aftonifhing magnificence ; the king of Portugal having affigned revenues to all the churches, and penfions to all the
communities in proportion to their numbers. The
Jefuits alone had lately five houfes all very rich.

Of all the churches in and about Goa, none have
glafs windows, except one in the city dedicated to
St. Alexander, the reft have panes of tranfparent
oyfter-fhells, as have likewife all their ftately houfes.
There is here likewife a fine hofpital. Every church
has a fet of bells, fome of which are continually
ringing. The market-place, which ftands near the
church Mifericordia, is about an acre fquare, and in
it are fold moft things produced in that country ;

and in the fhops about it may be had the produce of
Europe, China, Bengal, and other countries of lefs
note. The viceroy generally refides at the powder-
houfe, about two miles below the city, on account
of fome fprings of water, efteemed the beft in the
ifland.

The eftablifhed religion is that of the church of
Rome, and here are its moft zealous bigots. They
have here the court of inquifition, which proceeds
with the greateft feverity againft all whom the mercilefs inquifitors fufpect of being guilty of herefy ;
and yet their Indian converts are indulged in their
abftaining from cows flefh, on account of the peculiar
veneration paid to that beaft by the Gentoos ; and
though the feverity of the inquifition awes both the
clergy and the laity, many Gentoos are fuffered to
dwell in the city, where they are tolerated on account
of their being more induftrious than the Portuguefe
Chriftians ; but the mercantile part of them are very
fubject to the infults of the Portuguefe ; for it is
dangerous for them either to refufe their goods, or
to afk for their money when it is due, for fear of a
baftinado, and fometimes worfe confequences : this
renders the circulation of trade very inconfiderable.

The clergy at Goa are very numerous and illiter-
ate, and a great burthen to the ftate. The firft or
grand inquifitor is always a fecular prieft, who pretends to have the fole right of being carried in a
palanquin, and has much more refpect paid him
than the archbifhop or the viceroy. His authority
extends over all perfons, laymen, and ecclefiaftics,
except the archbifhop, his grand vicar, who is always a bifhop, the viceroy, and the governors who
reprefent him ; but even thefe he may caufe to be
arrefted, and begin their proceffes, after he has informed the court of Portugal of the crimes laid to
their charge. His palace, as well as that of the
viceroy, is very magnificent: his houfhold confifts

of gentlemen, equeraries, pages, footmen, and a great
number of other domeftics. The fecond inquifitor
is a Dominican; and the other officers called deputies
of the holy office, are taken from among the Dominicans, Auguftins, and bare-headed Carmelitics. The
houfes of the Portuguefe are large, and their outfides
magnificent ; but within they are poorly furnifhed,
and they keep very mean tables. Capt. Hamilton
fays, that he has ftood on a little hill near the city,
and counted near eighty churches, convents, and
monafteries, and he was informed that in the city
and its diftricts, which ftretched twenty miles along
the coaft of the continent, and fifteen miles within
land, there are no fewer than 30,000 monks and
churchmen, who live idly and luxurioufly on the
labour of the miferable laity: for here the tyranny
and oppreffion of the domineering clergy are infupportable.

There grows in the ifland of Goa a very fingular
vegetable, called the forrowful tree, becaufe it flou-
rifhes only in the night. At funfet, no flowers are
to be feen, and half an hour after it is quite full of
them. They yield a fweet fmell, but laft no longer
than the fun begins to fhine on the tree, then fome
of them fall off, and others clofe up ; and this continues the whole year. It is nearly as large as the
prune tree, and its leaves refemble thofe of the
orange. It is commonly planted in the courts of
houfes to have the advantage of their fhade and
fmell.

The country about Goa has little corn, but produces fome excellent fruits, particularly the mango
is reckoned the largeft and moft delicious of any in
the world ; their jambo malacca is very beautiful and
pleafant. The little trade they have is mofily for
their arrack, which they diftil from toddy of the co-
coa-nut-tree, which grows in great abundance in the
territories of Goa.

To the fouthward of the kingdom of Vifapour, in which Goa is fituated, is the city of Narfing, which others call Chandegri or Bifnagar. This is the capital of the kingdom of Bifnagar, built on the fummit of a high mountain. It is furrounded with a triple row of walls, the laft of which is more than three leagues in circuit. The prince's palace is lofty, fpacious, magnificent, and environed with large and deep ditches. None are fuffered to enter the fortrefs without his exprefs permiffion. He allows Europeans, and other ftrangers, to pafs fome days in the city in the quality of travellers ; but none are permitted to fettle there for the fake of trade. However, many have ftaid there long enough to inform us that there is no place in the Indies, where juftice is fo impartially adminiftered.

The king of Bifnagar takes the title of king of kings, and hufband of a thoufand wives ; and has fometimes made war to maintain thefe ridiculous titles. He has many fortified places ; but his cannon are not made like ours ; they are formed of thick plates of iron, joined together, and fixed with iron hoops like hogfheads. Every year he vifits his kingdom, and reviews his troops, who honour him as a god. He can raife 100,000 infantry, 30,000 cavalry, and 700 elephants. The inhabitants are pagans, and worfhip the fun in particular, in honour of whom they have a grand feftival every year. In the inland part of the kingdom are many cities ; but it will be fufficient to mention Rafconde above Bifnagar, which is a mine of the richeft diamonds in all the Indies ; Gandecot and Bezouer, famous for the number, fingularity, and magnificence of their pagods ; and many other places whofe fields produce pepper, ginger, rhubarb, fugar, cocoa-nuts, palm-trees, and rice in abundance.

The next place of note is Carwar, which has the advantage of a good harbour, and a river capable of receiving fhips of 300 tons burthen. The Englifh

have a factory here fortified by two baftions, and
fome cannon for its defence. The valleys abound in
corn and pepper ; and the woods on the mountains
with many forts of wild beafts, as tygers, wolves,
monkies, wild-hogs, deer, elks, and cows of a prodigious fize. There are feveral fpecies of the tyger,
the largeft of which is lefs greedy of human flefh than
the others. Mr. Hamilton fays, that he was once
here in the woods with his fuzee, when a fmall rain
happening to fall, damped his powder, which was
only wrapt up in paper : his gun being ufelefs he
ftruck into a foot path, which led from the mountain
to the factory ; but he had not gone far, when he
efpyed a very large tyger in the fame path, with his
face towards him. The tyger no fooner faw him,
than he fquatted with his belly to the ground, and
wagging his tail, crawled flowly to meet him. Mr.
Hamilton, thinking it in vain to fly, walked leifurely
forward, till he came within ten yards of him, and
then clubbing his piece, made what noife he could
to frighten him, on which the beaft rufhed into a
thicket, and leaving the road free, Mr. Hamilton
efcaped with no other harm, than being very much
terrified.

The chief of the Englifh factory is much efteemed
in the country, and when he goes a hunting is generally accompanied by moft of the people of diftinction in
that neighbourhood, attended by their fervants and
vaffals well armed, and with trumpets, hautboys,
and drums. The men with fire arms place themfelves at convenient diftances along the fkirts of a
hill or wood, and others are fent with loud mufic to
rouze the game, who fpread themfelves for a mile or
two, and on a fignal given, ftrike up at once, and
march towards the fkirts of the wood or hill where
the mufketeers are placed. The wild inhabitants,
aftonifhed at the unufual noife, fly before the mufic
and fall into the ambufcade, when many of them are
killed. Mr. Hamilton was prefent at one of thefe

huntings, when a dozen of deer were ſhot; beſides two wild cows, with their calves who would not leave their dead parents, though they had done ſuckling, and four or five ſows, that had above a dozen of pigs, were all killed.

Farther to the ſouth is the province of Canara, which has ſeveral cuſtoms peculiar to itſelf. Its moſt northerly port is Onoar, which has a river deep enough for ſhips of two or 300 tons, and it has an ancient caſtle on a low hill built by the Portugueſe, when they were lords of the coaſt of India; but the raja of Canara blocked them up in the caſtle, until hunger forced them to ſurrender. The eſtabliſhed religion is the pagan, and there is here a temple annually viſited by great numbers of pilgrims. The image is ſometimes carried in proceſſion. This idol, which rather reſembles a monkey than a man, is put into a vehicle in the form of a tower, in which are alſo eight or ten prieſts employed in ſinging his praiſes. This vehicle has four wheels, and is drawn with a thick rope through the ſtreets, by a number of people, attended by a great mob.

This is ſaid to be the country in which the cuſtom of burning widows was firſt introduced, and where it is ſtill practiſed. Mr. Hamilton ſays, that he ſaw it performed ſeveral ways. They dig a pit about ten feet long and ſix broad, which they fill with logs of wood. One great piece is ſet at the brim, ready to fall down on pulling a cord. When all is ready, a great quantity of oil or butter is thrown on the wood, and the corpſe of the huſband placed about the middle of the pile, and fire being ſet to it, it is inſtantly in a blaze. The wife then taking leave of all her friends, the drums, trumpets, and hautboys ſtrike up, when walking two or three times round the pile, ſhe leaps in upon the corpſe.

In other parts they uſe no pits; but a pile is built; the corpſe is laid on it; and the victim dancing round it for ſome time, to the ſound of loud muſic,

leaps in ; and, if fhe hefitates, the priefts pufh her
in with long poles, making fuch an hideous noife
that fhe cannot be heard ; and all the while fhe is
burning, the priefts dance round the fire. 1 heard
a ftory, fays Mr. Hamilton, of a lady who had received addreffes from a gentleman, that afterwards
deferted her, and fhe was obliged by her relations to
marry another, who dying foon after the marriage,
fhe was, according to cuftom, to be laid on the pile.
The fire being well kindled, fhe was going to act
the tragedy on herfelf, when fhe obferved her former
admirer, and beckoned him to come to her. When
he came, fhe took him in her arms, as if fhe had a
mind to embrace him, and being ftronger than he,
rufhed with him into the flames, where they were
both confumed with the corpfe of her hufband.

A very ingenious author of great reputation, takes
notice that there are none of the almoft infinite
number of travellers who have paffed through India,
who do not mention the abominable cuftom of the
women publicly burning themfelves at the death of
their hufbands, in fpite of the mogul Mahometans,
who have endeavoured to abolifh this barbarous ceremony. Mandeflo, a traveller of great learning and
veracity, was prefent at one of thefe funeral rites at
Cambaya, and fpeaks of it thus : " A young woman
" twenty years of age having been informed that
" her fpoufe had died at 200 leagues diftance, refolved
" to celebrate his obfequies by burning herfelf alive.
" In vain was it reprefented to her, that the news
" was uncertain ; nothing was capable of making
" her change the refolution fhe had taken. We
" faw her arrive at the place of her fuffering with
" fo extraordinary a gaiety and confidence, that I
" was perfuaded fhe had ftupified her fenfes with
" opium, which is commonly ufed in the Indies.
" At the head of the retinue which accompanied
" her, was a band of the country mufic, compofed
" of hautboys and kettle drums. After that came

" feveral married women and maids, finging and
" dancing before the widow, who was dreſſed in
" her richeſt clothes, and had her neck, fingers,
" arms, and legs, loaded with rich jewels and brace-
" lets. A troop of men, women, and children
" followed, and clofed the proceſſion. She had
" waſhed herſelf before in the river, that ſhe might
" join her hufband without any defilement or ſtain.
" The funeral pile was made of apricot wood, with
" which they had mixed branches of fanſal and
" cinnamon. She beheld it from afar with an eye
" of contempt, and approached it without being
" difturbed ; ſhe took leave of her friends and re-
" lations, and diſtributed her ornaments amongſt
" them. I kept myſelf near her on horſeback, along
" with two Engliſh merchants. Judging, perhaps,
" by my countenance that I was ſorry for her, to
" comfort me, ſhe threw me one of her bracelets,
" which I luckily catched hold of. When ſhe was
" feated on the top of the pile, they ſet fire to it,
" and ſhe poured on her head a veſſel of fweet fmell-
" ing oil, which the flame immediately feized on :
" thus ſhe was ſtifled in a moment, without being
" obſerved to alter her countenance. Some of the
" affiſtants threw in feveral cruiſes of oil to en-
" creaſe the fire, and filled the air with frightful
" cries. When ſhe was entirely confumed, her aſhes
" were thrown into the river."

It is generally ſaid, that this barbarous cuſtom
was introduced by the Indians to put a ſtop to the
cruelty of their wives, who from jealoufy frequently
poifoned their hufbands. Mr. Grofe, however,
maintains that this opinion is an over refinement of
conjecture, as falſe as it is injurious to the women of
the country, no ſuch practice being either atteſted
by credible tradition, or warranted by the behaviour
of the other Indian women not ſubjected to this cuſtom, and who are generally too foft and tender to
incur even the fufpicion of ſuch deteſtable barbarity.

He rather attributes it to the artifices of the bramins, and the dreadful power of a religious phrenzy ; and Mr. Mandeflo obferves, that they have always had the precaution to animate their courage by alluring them, that thofe who have the noble generofity to facrifice themfelves to the manes of their hufbands, fhall live with them in the other world, feven times as long, and with feven times the pleafure they have done in this.

There are, however, fome faint-hearted girls who have not the courage to accompany their fpoufes into an unknown world ; but rather choofe to live in this though under the badge of infamy and fhame.

The country of Canara is generally governed by a queen, who keeps her court at a town called Baydour, two days journey from the fea. She may marry whom fhe pleafes ; but her hufband never gets the title of rajah, though if fhe has fons, the eldeft of them does : but neither the hufband nor the fons have any thing to do with the management of the government while fhe lives : nor are the queens obliged to burn themfelves with their deceafed hufbands.

The people here obferve the laws fo well, that robbery or murder are hardly ever heard of among them, and a ftranger may pafs with the utmoft fafety through the country. No man is permitted to ride on a horfe or mule, or an elephant, except officers of ftate, and foldiers ; but others are allowed to ride on buffaloes and oxen : and none are permitted to have umbrellas carried over them by fervants ; but if the fun or rain offends them, they muft carry them themfelves. But in all other things they enjoy liberty.

The next fea-port to the fouthward of Onoar, is Batacola, which has the remains of a very large city, that ftands on a fmall river, about four miles diftance from the fea : but there is nothing worth notice,

except ten or eleven fmall pagods or temples covered with copper or ftone. The country produces
good quantities of pepper, and the Englifh company had a factory there : but about the year 1670,
an Englifh fhip coming there to trade, had a fine
Englifh bull-dog, which the chief of the factory
begged of the captain. After the fhip was gone,
the factory, which confifted of eighteen perfons,
going a hunting, took the bull-dog with them; and
paffing through the town the dog feized a cow de-
voted to a pagod, and killed her. The priefts enraged at the profanation, raifed a mob to revenge
the facred animal, who murdered the whole factory ;
but fome natives who were friends to the Englifh,
made a large grave and buried them all in it. The
chief of the Englifh factory of Carwar, afterwards
fent a ftone to put over the grave, with an infcription,
that this is the burial place of John Beft, with
feventeen other Englifhmen, who were facrificed to
the fury of a mad priefthood, and enraged mob.
The Englifh never fettled there again : but often
call there to buy pepper.

The next town to the fouthward of Batacola, is
Barceloar, which ftands on the banks of a broad
river about four miles from the fea. The Dutch have
a factory here only to buy up rice for the Malabar
coaft, about five miles from the river's mouth. The
Portuguefe alfo get fupplies of rice here for Goa,
and bring back in return, horfes, dates, pearls, and
other merchandize of the produce of Arabia. To
the fouthward of Mangulore, is a road leading to
that town eight or ten miles long, planted with four
rows of large trees, which all the way afford the
traveller an agreeable fhade, and in feveral places
are huts where fome old people ftay in the day time,
with jars of fine clear water, for the paffengers to
drink gratis at the charge of the ftate.

Mangulore is the greateft mart for trade in all the
Canara dominions. The Portuguefe have a factory

for rice here, and a pretty large church ; but both
the priests and the laity are very debauched. The
town is poorly built, and is only defended by two
small forts. The fields annually bear two crops of
corn in the plains ; and the higher grounds produce
pepper, betel-nut, and fandal-wood.

Malabar is a pretty large country, divided into
many principalities. It produces little corn, but
has a great number of cocoa-nut and areca-trees,
of the fruit of which the inhabitants make great
advantage. The woods produce several forts of timber, and a variety of drugs ; they are also well stored
with game.

Cananor, a town in this country, formerly belonged to the crown of Portugal ; but in 1660, the
Dutch took the fort, and having added a large curtain with two royal bastions, demolished the town,
and still continuing masters of the fort, they carry
on a small trade there.

Tillicherry is a town situated farther to the south,
where the English East-India company have a factory pretty well fortified with stone walls and cannon.
The town stands at the back of the fort, and is surrounded with a stone wall. The established religion
of the country is paganism ; but there are a few
black Christians that live under the protection of the
factory, and some of them serve for soldiers in the
garrison.

Calicut is the capital of a considerable kingdom on
the coast of Malabar, the sovereign of which takes
the title of zamorin, which in his language signifies
emperor, this city is said to be three leagues in
circuit, though it is not surrounded with walls ; it is
supposed to contain 6000 houses, most of which are
placed by themselves, and at a sufficient distance from
one another to have a garden.

A merchant may purchase a house for twenty
crowns, and those for the common people cost but
two. It is true, they are only built of large pieces

of earth cut in fquares, and dried in the fun, and are
no more than feven or eight feet high ; but the
prince has a palace built of ftone. He is reckoned
the moft powerful fovereign on the coaft of Malabar,
and can bring an hundred thoufand men into the
field, though his dominions do not extend above 22
leagues along the coaft, and at moft 30 or 40 leagues
to the mountains.

When the zamorin marries, he muft not cohabit
with his bride, till the namboury or chief prieft has
enjoyed her ; for which that prieft receives five-hun-
dred crowns, and if he pleafes he may have her
company three nights ; becaufe the fruits of her
nuptials muft be an holy oblation to the god fhe wor-
fhips. The naires or nobles who marry a maid are
fo complaifant as to pay the clergy for the fame favour.

But this is not the only fingular cuftom with refpect
to marriage. The daughters of the naires may marry
feven, and fome fay twelve hufbands ; but they muft
be all of the fame caft or tribe, under the pain of
degradation, if fhe marries into a lower tribe. When
a woman is married to the firft of her hufbands, fhe
has an houfe built for her convenience, and that
hufband cohabits with her till fhe takes a fecond, or
fo many as fhe is prefcribed by law. The hufbands
agree very well ; for they cohabit with her by turn,
according to their priority of marriage, each eight
or ten days, or as they can fix the term among themfelves ; and he who lives with her, during that time,
provides for her fupport. When the man who cohabits
with her, goes into her houfe, he leaves his arms at
the door, and none dare remove them, or enter the
houfe on pain of death ; but if there are no arms to
guard the door, any acquaintance may freely vifit
her. All the time of cohabition, fhe ferves her hufband as purveyor and cook ; fhe alfo takes care to
keep his clothes and arms clean. When fhe proves
with child, fhe nominates its father, who takes care

of its education, after fhe has fuckled it, and taught
it to walk and fpeak: but from the impoffibility of
affigning the true heir, the eftates of the hufbands
defcend to their fifters children, and if there are
none, to the neareft in blood to the grandmother.

This account, however improbably it may appear,
is mentioned by feveral good authors: the celebrated
Baron de Montefquieu treating of this cuftom, accounts for its origin thus. The naires are the tribe
" of nobles, who are foldiers of all thofe nations.
" In Europe, foldiers are forbid to marry: in Ma-
" labar, where the climate requires greater indul-
" gence, they are fatisfied with rendering marriage
" as little burthenfome as poffible ; they give a wife
" among many men, which confequently diminifhes
" the attachment to a family, and the cares of houfe-
" keeping, and leaves them in the free poffeffion of
" a military fpirit."

Calicut is a plain level country, well watered,
and abounding in pepper and ginger. The Englifh
company were formerly fo well refpected here, that
if any debtor went into their factory for protection,
none durft prefume to go there to difturd them. This
factory is now removed to Tillicherry.

Still farther to the fouth is the kingdom of Cochin,
where the Dutch have a fmall fort at Cranganore on
the bank of a large river, at about a league diftant
from the fea. The firft Europeans that fettled in
Cochin, were the Portuguefe, who built a fine city
on the fide of a river, which ftands fo pleafantly,
that they had a common faying, " That China was
" a place to get money in, and Cochin to fpend
" it:" for the great number of canals made by the
rivers and iflands afford the diverfion of fifhing and
fowling ; and the mountains are well ftored with
game. This city was taken by the Dutch in 1660,
who ftill continue mafters of the place, and have fuch
authority, that the king of Cochin may be confidered
as their vaffal.

There is here a place on the fide of a river, called Hell's Mouth. This is a cave about four yards broad and three high, hewn out of a fpungy iron-coloured rock. Capt. Hamilton went into it with a lanthorn, and paffed ftrait forward near two hundred yards; but faw no end to it. It is inhabited by fnakes and bats, who were frighted by the light ; and the captain, as well as thofe who attended him, being tired of their company, they returned back. There is no tradition of the defign for which it was made.

Coilcoiloan and Coiloan, are two fmall principali-ties, in each of which the Dutch have a fort.

At Erwa, two leagues to the fouthward of Coiloan, the Danes have a fmall factory on the fea fide ; but it has a very confiderable trade.

Two leagues farther to the fouth is Aujengo, a fort built by the Englifh on a fandy foundation, and na-turally fortified by the fea on one fide, and a little river on the other ; but there is not a drop of water fit for drinking to be had within a league of it. It is in the dominious of the queen of Attingo. who is an hereditary fovereign. By the conftitution of the conntry, it is to be always governed by a queen, who is not to marry ; but that heireffes of her blood may not be wanting, fhe may chufe whom, and as many as fhe pleafes to admit to the honour of her bed. The handfomeft young men about the court generally compofe her feraglio. The fons are in the rank of nobility, and the daughters alone can pretend to the fucceffion.

From fuch ftrange cuftoms, fays an ingenious au-thor, it might naturally be concluded that the inha-bitants of Malabar are as ignorant as the favages of America. Yet this is far from being the cafe. The Malabars have, in general, a politenefs of behaviour, and a fhrewdnefs in difcerning their own intereft, which thofe who deal or treat with them are fure to experience. Like moft of the Orientals, they are grave, know perfectly how to keep up their dignity, and diſtruſt all verboſeneſs in their public affairs. A king of Travancore, on two ambaſſadors being ſent him by the naick of Madura, a neighbouring prince, and one of them having made a prolix ſpeech, and the other beginning to proceed where the other had left off, auſterely admoniſhed him in theſe words, " Do not be long; life is ſhort."

Moſt of the Malabars, of both ſexes, are particularly fond of having their ears hang almoſt as low as their ſhoulders, which is done while they are young, by boring the lobes, and introducing into them a ſlip of a brab tree-leaf rolled up, and renewed in proportion as the hole grows wider. When greatly ſtretched, they adorn them with heavy pendants, and in the upper part ſtick jewels of value, according to their circumſtances.

Twelve leagues farther to the ſouth is Tegnapatam, where the Dutch have another factory. This country extends to Cape Comorin, and is bounded on the eaſt by the mountains of Gate, which run about 30 leagues from the ſea, through the whole extent of Malabar, and in a manner ſeem to divide the peninſula into two ſeparate worlds ; for all our travellers agree in relating a circumſtance of theſe mountains, which experience alone could have informed them of, they ſeparate as two ſeaſons entirely different at the ſame time. Winter begins on the coaſt of Malabar about the end of June, with a ſouth eaſt wind which blows from the ſea, and rages four months along the coaſt, from Diu to Cape Comorin. The ſea is then no longer navigable, and there are few harbours where the ſhips can ride in ſafety from the ſtorms, attended with terrible thunder and lightning, which prevail at that ſeaſon. Yet at the ſame time on the coaſt of Coromandel, which bounds the peninſula to the eaſt, there is an agreeable ſpring, and the fineſt ſeaſon of the year. Thus when they enjoy the ſereneſt weather at Maſulipatam, at Goa and its neighbourhood they feel all the rigours of

the winter except froft. The fame happens at Men-
galor and Meliapour, Cananor and Pondicherry,
and even at Coulan and Tutucurin, which are only
thirty leagues diftant. Thofe who travel by land
from one coaft to the other, difcover from the top of
the hills of Gate, on the one fide a ferene and temperate air, and on the other a country covered with
tempefts and drowned with rains.

About the end of October, the winter ceafes on the
coaft of Malabar, and almoft generally throughout
the Indies, even in the kingdom of Orixa and Bengal,
and begins on the coaft of Coromandel, where it lafts
four whole months; while in the reft of the country
the heavens are ferene, and the earth pours forth its
beauties and riches in the greateft plenty.

To the fouth of Cape Comorin is a ftreight between.
it and the ifland of Ceylon, famous for the fifhery,
where are caught the fineft pearls in the Indies. We
fhall pafs by feveral fmall factories on the Cape belonging to the Dutch ; and fhall only obferve, that
about the middle of the ftreight is a fmall ifland
named Manaar, which the Dutch company have fortified, and made ufe of as a prifon for the Indian
princes who have the misfortune to difpleafe them.

The firft place that prefents itfelf on leaving the
ftreight, is Negapatan. When the Portuguefe firft
fettled in the Indies, it was only a fmall village, of
which they made a very confiderable city, and furrounded it with walls and a ditch. It had many fine
churches, and a college for the Jefuits ; but after
having kept it about fixty years, the Dutch took it
from them in 1658, by the affiftance of the king of
Tangeor. The country about is full of pagods,
fome richly adorned, but without tafte ; others are
filthy and ill built: all of them are full of horrible
figures, which the poor miftaken natives worfhip as
gods.

From hence fteering farther to the north, you
come to Trangobar, a large city belonging to the

Danes, fortified by a caftle and citadel. It has one
Catholic, and three Proteftant churches, a mofque,
and five large pagods. The king of Denmark maintains Proteftant miffionaries here.

The next place of confequence is Fort St. David,
a colony and fortrefs belonging to the Englifh. The
fort is pretty ftrong, and its territories extend eight
miles along the fhore, and four miles within the land.
The country is pleafant, fertile, and watered by
feveral fmall rivers. The company have a good
garden, and fummer-houfe, where the governor generally refides, and the town has gardens to moft of
the houfes. The place is fubordinate to the Fort St.
George.

Pondicherry, the next place of note on this coaft,
is about five leagues to the northward of Fort St.
David. It was taken by the Dutch in 1693, but reftored to the French at the peace of Ryfwic. According to computation, there are reckoned in
Pondicherry 120,000 inhabitants, Chriftians, Mahometans and Gentoos. The city has feveral great
magazines, fix gates, a citadel, eleven forts or baftions, 405 pieces of cannon mounted upon the walls,
befides bombs, mortars, and other pieces of artillery
in the arfenal. The ftreets are ftraight, and the
houfes of the Europeans built of brick in the Roman
fafhion; but only one ftory high. Thofe of the
Indians, are only of earth mixed with lime, made of
calcined oyfter-fhells, and form ftraight ftreets not
void of beauty. They have fine avenues of trees,
in the fhade of which the weavers work their cotton
ftuffs. The governor's is the principal houfe. Towards the weft are the company's gardens, in which
are viftos of a great length, with a large building
richly furnifhed, where ambaffadors from Indian
princes are lodged. The Jefuits have a fine college,
in which youth are taught reading, writing, and the
mathematics, but no Latin. There are alfo fome
convents, and two pagods, for the ufe of the Gentoos,

who are poor and indefatigably laborious, though, in reality, they are the only fource of the riches of the city and country. The governor general of the company, has twelve horfe guards clothed in fcarlet, with black facings and a border of gold; their captain is clothed in the fame manner, but with lace on the border and feams. He has alfo 300 foot guards called pions. This retinue attends the governor when he receives a king, a prince, or an ambaffador extraordinary, on which occafions he is carried by fix men on a palanquin, the couch and canopy of which are adorned with embroidery and taffels of gold. The company maintain alfo a commandant of the infantry, a major, three companies of French infantry, and between two and three hundred topafes, who are people of the country, clothed and difciplined in the French manner; and who have been inftructed in the Catholic religion. The company, as fovereigns of Pondicherry, and its dependancies, have the privilege of coining money. The city lies about forty or fifty fathoms from the fea, which is here only a road, and fhips being unable to approach nearer the fhore than the diftance of a league, goods are brought from them in boats, which is a very great defect in a city that enjoys many advantages. Living cofts almoft nothing; for butcher's meat, wild fowl, and fifh are exceedingly good, and extremely cheap

The next place of confequence is Fort St. Thomas fubject to Portugal. The city had formerly the beft trade of any place on the coaft of Coromandel; but the Englifh fettling at Fort St. George, were the caufe of its ruin.

Of Fort St. George, or Madrafs, we have already given an account. The Eaft India company now enjoys extraordinary advantages here from the favour of the nabob and the conqueft of all the French fettlements except Pondicherry, obtained by the heroic bravery of General Clive, and the valour of the Britilh navy.

' From thence the Dutch are mafters of the upper coaft, as far as Mafulipatan. They have a factory at Paliacate, to which they have given the name of Gueldres, and have a confiderable trade there as well as at Pottapouli.

Mafulipatan is fituated at the mouth of the river Crifna, and has drawn merchants from all parts of Europe to get the painted calicoes manufactured there, which are more efteemed than any others of the Indies. But notwithftanding its great trade, the city is ill built, though very populous. What is related of the heats felt there is almoft incredible. Annually in the month of May, the weft wind blows during feven or eight hours a day, the heat of which exceeds that of the fcorching rays of the fun, and refembles that felt when one approaches near an houfe in flames. Though their chambers are clofely fhut up, the wood of the chairs, tables and wainfcotting are fo heated, that they are obliged to throw water upon them continually: but the rains which fall plentifully at the end of fummer, lay the whole country under water, and the inhabitants receive the fame benefit that the Egyptians do from the inundations of the Nile ; for they fow their lands, thus prepared, with rice and other grain, without expecting any more rain for eight months. In all that time the trees are green, and alternately loaded with ripe fruits. They have two harvefts of rice ; and there are lands which are reaped three times a year. This plenty, together with the fuperftition of the inhabitants, moft of whom eat rothing that has life, renders every thing cheap. Eight fowls are fold at fourteen fols, a fheep at eleven, and every thing elfe in proportion. All thefe things are ftill cheaper without the city.

The kingdom of Golconda, whofe principal harbour is Mafulipatan, extends from the gulph of

Bengal to the kingdom Vifapour, and from north to fouth contained almoft all the peninfula from the northern extremity of Orixa, to Cape Comorin ; but is now fubject to the mogul, and is governed by princes tributary to that emperor.

The city of Golconda, which gives name to the kingdom, is now two leagues in circuit. Its walls are built of hewn ftone three feet fquare, and furrounded with deep ditches, divided into feveral bafons or ponds, where the water is daily renewed. It has feveral fuperb mofques, in which are the tombs of the kings, and their families. The nabob or prince is of the Mahometan religion, as are alfo a great part of his fubjects, whence the Pagan temples in the country are not filled with fuch monftrous figures as in other parts of the peninfula. The mines of gold, diamonds, faphires and other precious ftones in this kingdom, have filled the palace with immenfe riches. But if any diamond is found above a certain bignefs, the nabob is obliged to have it cut fecretly, left it fhould be demanded by the great mogul.

There are feveral towns of fmall confequence between Mafulipatan and the Ganges. This river, which was the utmoft bounds of the conquefts of Alexander the Great, is much revered by the Indians, from the opinion that its waters efface all the fpots of fin ; whence they go in crowds from the remoteft parts of the country to wafh in its ftream. Nothing is more childifh than the fables related by the brachmans of its fource ; which they reprefent as in heaven, and pretend that it falls from thence to the earth ; the mogul himfelf drinks no other water; but foreigners pretend that it is very unwholefome, and that it cannot be drank unlefs it be firft boiled. On its banks are a great number of fuperb pagods, fome of which are immenfely rich : but what renders this river really valuable, is that it wafhes down gold in its fand ; that it is placed in the firft rank of thofe rivers that produce precious ftones, and that the gulph of Bengal, into which it difcharges itfelf, abounds in pearls and jewels of great value.

Up the river Hughly, which is a branch of the Ganges, is Fort William, a place of confiderable trade, belonging to the Englifh. It is fituated on the moft unhealty fpot in the whole river: and is built without order, every one originally taking in what ground beft pleafed him for gardening, fo that in many places you muft pafs through a garden into the houfe; thofe of the Englifh are built near the river's fide, and thofe of the natives within the land. Fort William is an irregular tetragon of a compofition called puckah, which is a mixture of brick-duft, lime, molaffes, and cut hemp well mixed together, which on its drying, becomes as hard as brick or even ftone. About fifty yards from this fort, ftands the church, built by the merchants refiding there, and the contributions of the fea officers. The governor's houfe is, accordidg to Mr. Hamilton, the beft and moft regular piece of architecture he ever faw in India. Within the fort are alfo many convenient lodgings for factors and writers, ftore houfes for the company's goods, and magazines for their ammunition.

The town has likewife an hofpital, and near it is a garden that furnifhes the governor's table with fruit and herbage; and within it are good fifh-ponds.

Moft of the inhabitants that make any tolerable figure, have the fame advantages. All forts of provifions, as well as clothing, are plentiful, good and cheap. On the other fide of the river are docks for repairing the fhips bottoms, and a pretty good garden belonging to the Armenians.

The kingdom of Bengal in which Fort William is fituated, is well known by its giving its name to the greateft gulph of Afia, which feparates the two peninfulas of the Indies. This kingdom is near 250 leagues from eaft to weft, and is confidered as the moft fertile in all the Indies in fugar, filk, fruits, faltpetre, gum-lac, wax, civet, opium, pepper and rice, with all which commodities it furnifhes the moft diftant provinces. The country is cut through with numerous canals, which ferve both to water it, and facilitate the tranfporting of merchandizes. On their banks are many towns and villages extremely well peopled, and great fields of rice, fugar and wheat, which laft is much larger than that of Europe ; three or four kinds of pulfe, alfo citrons, oranges, and a great quantity of fmall mulberry-trees for the nourifhment of filk-worms. It is chiefly in this country that the rhinoceros and mufk are to be found; and the fineft canes brought into Europe, come from this kingdom.

Ougly, upon the weftern bank of the Ganges, and about twenty leagues from the fea, has become very famous, fince the Dutch have eftablifhed themfelves there. This is next to Batavia, their moft confiderable factory, and where they have the greateft trade. The French company have likewife a factory there. They bring from thence feveral forts of muflins; and pieces for handkerchiefs of filk and cotton. From Daca, on the moft weftern mouth of the fame river, come the beft and fineft Indian embroideries in gold, filver or filk ; embroidered neck-cloths and fine muflins. Chandernagor and Chincora, in the neighbourhood of Ougly, are ftill famous for their commerce and moft of the European nations have factories eftablifhed there. Saumelpour to the north of Bengal, is not lefs important on account of its diamonds, which are found, not as in other places, in the bowels of the earth ; but in the fands of the river Gouel, which they fearch carefully after the month of February, when the waters are low. They begin their fearch at the town of Saumelpour, and carry it up to the moutains, whence the Gouel has its fource : a fpace of about 50 leagues. In this work 8 or 10,000 perfons are employed. From thence come thofe fine lmall diamonds called genuine fparks; but ftones above a certain fize are feldom found.

The capital of the province of Bengal, bears the fame name, and is a city built upon a mountain, whence they carry on a trade in diamonds and other jewels. There is a church here dedicated to St. Thomas, and a fine palace. Its principal cities are Mantipour on the Ganges, and Jagarnat, on the fea fide. In the latter is a Gentoo temple, in which there are idols reprefenting the god Refora, with his wife, his brother, and his fifter. The ftatue of Refora is entirely of gold and jewels, that of his wife of gold without ornaments, and the other two of fandal wood. This temple has revenues for the maintenance of 20,000 men.

The country between the river Ganges and China, is called the peninfula beyond the Ganges; becaufe it ftretches fouthward into the fea. Modern geographers give it 530 leagues from north to fouth, and 360 from eaft to weft. The north, in which are the kingdoms of Azem, Ava, Pegu, Laos, and fome others little known: the fouth, which contains that of Siam; and the eaft which comprehends thofe of Tonquin, Cochin, and Camboia.

The kingdom of Azem lies to the eaft of the great moguls's dominions, and to the weft of the lake Chiamay. It produces every thing neceffary for the fubfiftence of man. Mines of gold, filver, iron and lead are found here, which the king has referved to himfelf, inftead of levying fubfidies from his people, and that he may not opprefs them, he employs none but flaves, whom he purchafes of his neighbours. Thus all the peafants of Azem are at their eafe; while the reft of the Indians are involved in flavery and mifery, in the midft of a country where they ought to live in riches and plenty. It is prohibited by the laws to carry gold out of the kingdom, or to coin it into money: the people, however, ufe it in great and fmall ingots in trade, though it is not permitted to be ufed with ftrangers.   Yet the king caufes pieces of filver of the bignefs and weight cf roupies, and of an octagon figure, to be coined, which may be tranfported any where.

The princes refide in the city of Kemmerof, about 25 or 30 days journey from the ancient capital which bore the fame name ; but their own tombs, and thofe of all the royal family, are in the city of Azoo, on the banks of the river Laquia, where every prince builds a kind of chapel in the great pagod to ferve for his place of burial. Being perfuaded, that after their death they go to another world, and that thofe who die fullied by any crime, fuffer a great deal, chiefly by hunger and thirft, they place food by the head of the corpfe, that it may feed upon it if neceffary. The king is interred with thofe idols of gold and filver, which he worfhipped in his life time, a live elephant, twelve camels, fix horfes, and a great number of hounds, from the belief that they all may be of ufe to him in another world.   In thofe funeral folemnities barbarity is joined to fuperftition, the woman whom he has loved beft, and the principal officers of his houfhold poifon themfelves, that they may have the glory of being interred with him, and of ferving him in the other world.   If a private perfon dies, all his friends and relations muft affift at his funerral : and every one muft throw into the grave the bracelets and other ornaments they wear.

The accounts of thofe who have travelled through the eaft, give us little information about the kingdom of Ava, which is faid to be twice as large as that of France. They only tell us, that the immenfe riches of the king are vifible by the fplendour of his palace, which, though of a vaft extent, is faid to be for the moft part gilded.

Every thing related by hiftorians of the kingdom of Pegu is drawn from Gafper Balbi, a rich Venetian merchant, who traded thither in 1576 ; we fhall therefore take our account of that country from Mr. Hamilton, who vifited the ports of that kingdom, and became inftructed in the manners of the people, partly by converfing with them, and partly from the informations he obtained from fome of the Engiifh company at fort St. George, who carried on a confi-derable trade thither.

The kingdom of Pegu, lies to the fouth-eaft of Azem, and the city of the fame name ftands about 40 miles to the eaftward of the port Syrian or Syri-am, on the fide of the gulph of Bengal. It was the feat of many great and puifant monarchs, but now its glory is laid in the duft, for not a twentieth part of it is inhabited ; but the ditches with which it was fur-rounded, though now dry, and bearing good corn, fhew that few cities exceeded Pegu, in magnitude.

The caufe of the ruin of the kingdoms of Pegu, with Martavan and fome others under its dominion, was told to Mr. Hamilton by fome Peguans, in feveral difcourfes he had with them on that fubject.

A great friendfhip for a long time fubfifted be-tween the kings and fubjects of Pegu and Siam, who being next neighbours, carried on a great trade with each other, till the 15th century : but a Pegu veffel being at Odia, the chief city of Siam, when ready to depart, it anchored one evening near a fmall temple a few miles below the city, when the mafter and fome of the crew going there to worfhip, faw a little well carved image of the god Samfay, and finding the priefts negligent, ftole that idol, and carried it to Pe-gu. The priefts mifling the little idol, lamented their lofs to all their neighbouring priefts, and by their advice carried their complaints to the king of Siam ; and there happening to be a fcarcity of corn that year, the calamity was imputed by the priefts to the lofs of the god Samfay. The king of Siam now fent an embaffy to his brother of Pegu, defiring the reftitution of the image, whofe abfence had been at-tended with fuch fatal confequences : but the king of

2

Pegu refusing to comply with his request, a very
bloody war then ensued between the two kingdoms,
in which the king of Siam ravaged the country, and
annexed the inland countries of Pegu, to his dominions. The king of Pegu in this distress invited the
Portuguese to his assistance, who began to be dreaded in India, and by the great encouragement he gave
them, got about 1000 volunteers into his service:
the use of fire-arms being then unknown in those
countries, they spread terror wherever they came,
and drove the Siamese out of the country. The
king of Pegu then made one Thoma Pereyra, a Portuguese, general in chief of all his forces, and settled
his court at Martavan, near the borders of Siam, to
be ready on all occasions to repel the Siamese forces.
Though the Portuguese, by their insolence, now
rendered themselves hated by the people of all ranks,
Thoma Pereyra was the favourite at court, he had
elephants of state, and a guard of his own countrymen to attend him. One day as he was coming
with great state from the palace, riding on a large
elephant, he chanced to hear music in a burgher's
house, whose daughter, a very beautiful virgin, had
been married to a young man of the neighbourhood.
The general went to the house, wished them joy, and
desired to see the bride. The parents took the general's visit for a great honour, and brought their
daughter to the elephant's side, when being struck
with her beauty, he had the villainy to order his
guards to seize her and carry her to his house. His
orders were but too readily obeyed, and the bridegroom not being able to endure his loss, cut his own
throat ; the disconsolate parents of their injured children, rent their clothes and ran towards the king's
palace uttering their lamentations, and imploring
their gods and countrymen to revenge them on the
insolent Portuguese, the oppressors of their country.
The streets were soon unable to contain the crowds
with which they were filled, and the noise they made

reached the king's ears, who fent to know the caufe
of the tumult, and being informed, he let them know
that he would punifh the criminal. He accordingly
fent for his general ; but he being taken up with the
enjoyment of his new miftrefs, excufed himfelf, by
faying, that he was fo much out of order that he
could not wait on his majefty. The king, provoked
at this anfwer, in the firft tranfport of his rage ordered the whole city to take arms, and make a general maffacre of the Portuguefe, wherever they could
be found. And this order was fo fpeedily put in execution, that in a few hours all the Portuguefe were
flaughtered, except the guilty criminal, who being
taken alive, was made faft by the heels to an elephant's foot, who dragged him through the ftreets,
till the flefh was torn from his bones. There were
only three Portuguefe faved, who were accidently in
the fuburbs near the river ; thefe hiding themfelves
till night, made their efcape in a fmall boat, and
coafting along the fhore, fed on what they found in
the woods and among the rocks, and at length arrived at Malacca.

By thefe wars both kingdoms were much weaken-
ed, they therefore fufpended all acts of hoftility, till
about the middle of the feventeenth century, when
the king of Siam again invaded Pegu, and conquered
feveral provinces tributary to that kingdom. The
king of Pegu now finding that his forces were unable
to protect his more immediate dominions, called in
the affiftance of the king of Barma, a potent prince
whofe dominions lay about 500 miles up the river
from Pegu. Thefe auxillaries drove the Siamefe
from their new conquefts, and afterwards perceiving
the ill difcipline obferved by the Peguan forces, killed the king, broke the Peguan army, and feized the
kingdoms of Pegu and Martavan for their mafter, in
whofe power it continued in the year 1709.

The dominions of Barma, are at prefent very
large, extending about 800 miles from north to fouth,

and 250 from eaſt to weſt ; but they have no ſea-
port except Syriam, where the river of the ſame
name is capable of receiving a ſhip of 600 tons. It
carries on a great trade with the Armenians, Moors,
Gentoos, Engliſh, and Portugueſe. The country
produces elephants teeth, bees-wax, ſtick-lacque,
iron, tin, rubies the beſt in the world, ſmall diamonds, and ſalt-petre. It alſo produces great quantities of corn, fruit and roots, excellent pulſe of
ſeveral ſpecies, abundance of wild game, either
quadrupèd or winged. In the months of September
and October, wild deer are ſo plentiful, that Mr.
Hamilton ſays, he has bought one for three-pence
or a groat, they are very fleſhy, but lean. Swines
fleſh and poultry are both plentiful and good.

The king is deſpotic, and all his commands are
laws ; but he holds the reins of government in his
own hands, and ſeverely puniſhes the governors of
towns and provinces who are found guilty of op-
preſſion. That he may know how affairs paſs in
the ſtate, every province or city has a deputy re-
ſiding at court, which is generally in the city of Ava
the preſent metropolis. Every morning theſe deputies
are obliged to attend the court, and when his majeſty
has breakfaſted, he retires into a room where he can
ſee all his attendants without being ſeen ; mean
while a page waits to call the perſon from whom
the king would have an account of whatever has
paſſed in his province. The deputy approaches the
room with the moſt profound reverence ; and if he
omits any matter of conſequence, which the king
happens to hear of by another hand, he is ſure of
being ſeverely puniſhed.

If he receives information of treaſon, murder or
other crimes, he orders the affair to be tried by
judges of his own chuſing, and on conviction he
aſſigns the puniſhment of the offender ; who is either
to be beheaded, made ſport for his elephants, which

is the moft cruel death, or banifhed for a time to the
woods ; where if they efcape being devoured by the
wild beafts, they may return when their banifhment
is expired, and pafs the remainder of their days in
ferving a tame elephant. For fmaller crimes they
are only condemned for life to clean the ftables of
his elephants.

His fubjects treat him with the moft fulfome adula-
tion. When they fpeak or write to him, they call
him their Kiack, or God, and in his letters to foreign
princes, he affumes the title of king of kings, to
whom all other kings ought to be fubject, as being
near kinfman and friend to all the gods in heaven
and on the earth ; by whofe friendfhip to him all
animals are fed and preferved, and the feafons of
the year keep their regular courfe. The fun is his
brother, and the moon and ftars are his near relations. In fhort, he pretends to be lord over the
ebbing and flowing of the fea ; and after all his lofty
epithets and hyperboles, he calls himfelf king of the
white elephant, and of the twenty-four white umbrellas.

After his majefty has dined, a trumpet is blown
to fignify to all his flaves, as he terms other kings,
that they may go to dinner, becaufe their lord has
already dined. And when any foreign fhips arrive
at Syriam, the number of people on board, with
their age and fex, are fent to him to let him know,
that fo many of his flaves are arrived to partake of
the glory and happinefs of his reign and favour.

The king's palace is a very large ftone building,
with four gates. Ambaffadors enter that to the
eaft, which is called the golden gate, becaufe all
ambaffadors appear before him with prefents. The
fouth gate is named the gate of juftice, where all
people enter that bring petitions, accufations or
complaints. The weft is the gate of grace, where
all that have received favours, or have been cleared from crimes pafs out with honour ; and the

north gate fronting the river, is the gate of ſtate, through which his majeſty. paſſes, when he thinks fit to honour his people by ſhewing himſelf.

When an ambaſſador is admitted to an audience, he is attended by a large troop of guards, with trumpets ſounding, and heralds proclaiming the honour the ambaſſador is about to receive, in going to ſee his majeſty's face, the glory of the earth : and between the gate and the head of the ſtairs that lead to the chamber of audience, the ambaſſador is attended by the maſter of the ceremonies, who inſtructs him to kneel three times in the way thither, and to continue ſo with his hands over his head until a proclamation is read. To what a height is human pride capable of being carried ! the empty vanity of this monarch, in attempting to raiſe himſelf above all the reſt of his ſpecies, in reality ſinks him beneath them ; and this real meanneſs can only be equalled by that of his ſlaviſh flatterers.

Though the palace is very large, it is a mean building, and though the city is of great extent and very populous, the houſes are only built of bamboo-canes, thatched with ſtraw or reeds, and the floors are of teak plank, or ſplit bamboos.

In all the cities and towns the governor ſeldom ſits in council, but appoints his deputy, and twelve judges who hear cauſes at leaſt once in ten days. They meet in a large hall, the floor of which is raiſed about three feet from the ground, and ſurrounded with benches for people to ſit or kneel upon. This hall being built on pillars, is open on all ſides, and the judges ſit on mats in the middle, and as they form a circle, there is no place of precedence. Every one has the privilege of pleading his own cauſe, or of giving his defence in writing, to be publickly read; but if another doubts his own abilities, he may get a perſon to plead for him ; and there are no fees, the court being maintained by the town. Every ſuit muſt be determined at three ſittings.

The judges have a peculiar garb; their hair being permitted to grow long, is tied on the top of their heads with a cotton ribband wrapt about it, and ſtands upright in the form of a ſharp pyramid. Their coat is thin cotton, ſo that their ſkin may be eaſily ſeen through it, and about their loins they wear a large faſh tied with a great bunch before, with the ends reaching to their ancles; but ſtockings and ſhoes are not uſed in Pegu.

The original natives of Barma imprint ſeveral devices on their ſkins with the point of a bodkin and charcoal duſt; and as the Peguans do not diſcolour their ſkins, the natives of each nation are eaſily diſtinguiſhed. The men are of an olive colour; they are generally pretty plump, though not fat, and have a good ſhape and features. The women are much fairer than the men, and have uſually pretty plump faces; they are of ſmall ſtature, but are very well ſhaped. Their hands and feet are likewiſe ſmall, and their arms and legs well propertioned. Their headdreſs is their own black hair tied up behind, and when they go abroad, they wear a piece of white cotton cloth on the top of their head. They have a frock of cotton cloth, or ſilk, that ſits cloſe to their bodies and arms, and the lower part reaches half way down the thigh. Under the frock they have a ſcarf doubled four fold, made faſt about the middle, the ends hanging down almoſt to the ancles.

The women are courteous and kind to ſtrangers, and are very fond of marrying Europeans. They prove obedient and obliging wives, and take the management of affairs within doors wholly in their own hands. If a wife is convicted of diſhonouring her huſband's bed, he may cauſe her hair to be cut off, and have her ſold for a ſlave.

The talapoins, or clergy of Pegu, are ſtrict obſervers of the laws of humanity and charity. There are a great number of temples built in the country; but theſe are moſtly of wood, becauſe it is not only

plentiful, but moft eafily takes varniſhing and guild-
ing; for they are gaudily painted both within and
without. Every one has free liberty to build a temple, and when it is finiſhed it is the general practice
to beſtow a few acres to maintain a certain number
of prieſts and novices, who cultivate the ground for
their own ſupport, and in the garden they have a
convent built, for the conveniency of lodging and
ſtudy. Theſe are their ſettled benefices: they are
no charge to the laity; for by their induſtry in managing their garden, they have generally enough
for themſelves, and ſomething to ſpare for the poor
among the laity: but if their garden is too ſmall,
or too barren for their ſupport, they ſend ſome
novices abroad dreſſed in a large orange-colour man-
tle, with a baſket hanging on their left arm, a little
drum in the left hand, and a little ſtick in the right.
When they come to the peoples' doors they beat
three ſtrokes with the ſtick on the drum, and if none
come to anſwer, they beat again, and ſo on to the
third time, and then if no body gives them any
thing, they proceed to the next houſe without ſpeak-
ing a word; but they are ſeldom ſuffered to go without a ſupply of rice, pulſe, fruit, or roots, which
are their only food; and what they receive more than
they have preſent occaſion for, they diſtribute to the
poor, who by age, diſtreſs, or other accidents, cannot maintain themſelves: but none who are able to
work, partake of their charity; nor do they ever
take care for the morrow. If a ſtranger has the mif-
fortune to be ſhipwrecked on the coaſt, he is by the
laws of the country the king's ſlave, but by the
mediation of the prieſts, the governors overlook that
law. When any unfortunate ſtrangers come to their
temples, they are hoſpitably ſupplied with food and
raiment; if they are ſick or maimed, the prieſts,
who are alſo the chief phyficians of Pegu, keep them
till they are cured, and then furniſh them with
letters of recommendation to the prieſts of another

convent, on the road they defign to travel. They
never enquire after the religion of a ftranger ; he has
the human form, and that renders him the objeƈt of
their charity. They hold all religions to be good,
that teach men to be good, and believe that the Gods
are pleafed with a variety of worſhip ; but with none
that is hurtful to man ; becaufe cruelty muſt be difagreeable to their nature. Hence they have not the
leaſt idea of perfecution.

The Pegu clergy are all mediators in cafes of difpute and contention between neighbours. They
never leave mediating till they procure a reconcilia-
tion, and in token of friendſhip, according to an
ancient cuſtom, the parties eat champock from one
another's hand, which feals the friendſhip. This
champock is a kind of tea of very difagreeable taſte,
it grows like other tea, on buſhes, and on fuch occafions is ufed all over Pegu.

They frequently preach to numerous auditories,
and have images of the inferior gods in their temples,
which are placed crofs-legged under domes. Their
faces are longer than the human ; their ears are large,
and the lobes very thick. The congregation bows
to them when they come in and go out, and that is
all the oblation they receive. But they make no
images of the great god. The fubjeƈt of their difcourfes is that charity is the moſt fublime of all virtues, and ought therefore to extend not only to mankind, but to animals, which they therefore neither
kill nor eat.

The country is healthful and fertile, and the air
fo good, that when ftrangers go thither in a bad ftate
of health, they feldom fail of a fpeedy recovery ; but
the fmall-pox is extremely dreaded, and in the province of Kirian is efteemed fo infeƈtious, that if any
one is feized with it, all the neighbourhood remove
to the diftance of two or three miles, and build new
houfes with bamboos and reeds, which they have in
great plenty. They leave with the fick perfon a jar

of water, a basket of rice, and some earthen pots to
boil it in, and then bid him farewel for twenty days. If
the patient has strength enough to rise and boil his
rice, he may then recover, if not he must die without
attendants ; but if he survives the twenty days they
take him away ; conduct him to their new built town,
and make him a free burgess. It is observed here
that while a person is afflicted with that distemper,
the tyger, notwithstanding his ravenous nature, will
not touch him.

The ordeal trial is much practised here for disco-
vering secret murder, theft, or perjury, One way is
to make the accuser and accused take some raw rice
in their mouths, when he who is guilty of the crime
alleged, or of false accusation, he is supposed not to
be able to swallow it, while the innocent swallows it
easily. Another way is driving a stake into a river,
and making the accuser and the accused take hold of
it, and keep their heads under water, when he who
continues longest without breathing, is the person to
be credited ; and whoever is convicted by this trial,
either for the crime alleged, or for malicious slander,
must lie on his back three days and nights, with his
neck in the stocks, without meat or drink, and is besides fined. They have likewise the custom of dipping the naked hand in boiling oil, or melted lead, to
clear them, when accused of attrocious crimes ; and
if the accuser scalds himself he must undergo the pu-
nishment due to the crime, which makes people very
cautious how they calumniate one another.

The people here make sky-rockets of an incredible
size ; and they have various sorts of musical instruments, the most esteemed of which are the tabor and
pipe ; they have also stringed instruments ; and an
instrument formed in the shape of a galley, with
about twenty bells of several sizes, placed on the upper part. The instrument is about three feet long,
eight or ten inches broad, and six deep; they play
upon these bells with a stick of heavy wood, and make
no bad music.

Martavan, once a principal fea-port, was one of the moft flourifhing towns for trade in the eaft, it having the benefit of a noble river that afforded a good harbour for fhips of the greateft burden; but after the king of Barma had conquered it, he caufed a number of veffels filled with ftones to be funk in its mouth, fo that it is now unnavigable, except for fmall veffels. They make earthern-ware there ftill, and glaze them with lead ore ; Mr. Hamilton fays he has feen jars made there big enough to contain two hogfheads. They have alfo a fmall trade in fifh.

According to father Marini, the talapoins or priefts of the kingdom of Lao or Laos, are very different from thofe of Pegu. They are confidered as the fcum of the people, and as enemies to labour. Their convents are fo many colleges of vicious men blinded by pride, and nothing can be more fenfelefs than the opinions they inftil into the minds of the people, who would probably be as vicious as the priefts, did not the feverity of the laws put a reftraint on their licentioufnefs. The propenfity of the Langians to paffion and bloodfhed, has forced their kings to punifh not only thofe who give a blow, but even thofe who put themfelves in a rage. Nay, to infpire the greater terror, the innocent are often punifhed with the guilty : thus, if the chief of a family is convicted of a great crime, all his kindred of whatever degree, are degraded, deprived of their offices, and reduced to gather grafs for the king's elephants, to carry it to his ftables, and to watch them all night.

There are eight principal pofts in the kingdom : that of general viceroy is the firft. His employment confifts in taking charge of the public affairs, and affifting the prince in the government. At the king's death, he affembles the ftates, and acts as fovereign till the fucceffor is chofen. The kingdom being divided into feven provinces, there are feven other viceroys, each of whom has equal power in the government entrufted to him. Thefe provinces have their

particular militia, who fubfift on the revenues affign.
ed them, both in peace and war.

Laos produces great quantities of benjoin, of a
better kind than what is found any where elfe in the
eaft, but the felling it to ftrangers is prohibited.
Lacque is likewife found here. There is no country
where more ivory is to be had, elephants being fo
numerous, that the inhabitants have thence taken
their name; for it is faid that the word Langians
fignifies a thoufand elephants. Many kinds of animals, and particularly cows and buffaloes are very
common; the rivers abound with fifh of an enormous
bulk; vaft quantities of rice, garden fruits, and
falt formed of a kind of foam which the great rains
leave upon the earth, and is hardened by the fun,
are the other advantages of this kingdom.

To the fouth of thefe countries lies Siam, the moft
famous kingdom of all the Indies : but the accounts
of the miffionaries and ambaffadors fent thither by
the French about the end of the laft century, frequently contradict each other, and fometimes themfelves. Some feem at a lofs for words to defcribe the
opulence of the country, while others talk of nothing
but the mifery and indigence of the inhabitants.

Europeans have given the name of Siam to the
capital of the kingdom, called by the natives Crung
fi ayn thaya, that is, the excellent city. It is built
on the river Menan, which fignifies the fea of waters,
and is contained in an ifland two leagues in circuit.
It is furrounded by a ftrong wall, and is capable of
fupporting a fiege of feveral months againft an army
of 50,000 men : one great addition to its ftrength is
the everflowing of the river every fix months, which
muft oblige an army to retire. The city has the
advantage of canals running through all the ftreets,
by which means they tranfport their effects quite
from the fea, and conveying them in boats, land
them at their warehoufes ; and this has drawn traders
thither from moft parts of the world. The Portu-

guefe were firft mafters of the commerce; but were
driven from thence by the Siamefe and Dutch: they
are not however, entirely expelled; for they, as well
as the Englifh, French, Chinefe, and Moors, have
boufes there. The other nations are faid to refide in
two large rich fuburbs that lie to the eaft and weft
of the city.

The riches of the country are chiefly difplayed in
the pagods, and the prince's palace, by the quantity
of the workmanfhip in gold, with which they are
adorned; by their prodigious bulk, their admirable
ftruɛture, and incredible colleɛtions of jewels.

The magnificence of the pagods furpaffes every
thing of the kind to be feen in the Indies. The moft
celebrated of thefe is that in the king's palace. While
the fpeɛtator is ftartled at feeing on one fide of the
portal an horrible monfter, and on the other a cow,
his eyes and imagination all at once lofe fight of thofe
objeɛts, and are dazzled with the fplendor of the
walls, the ceiling and pillars, and of an infinite
number of figures fo properly gilt, that they feem
covered with plates of gold. Having advanced fome
fteps, a fmall elevation appears in the form of an altar, on which are four figures faid to be of maffy gold,
nearly as big as the life, fitting crofs-legged; beyond
it is a kind of choir, where there is the richeft pagod
or idol in the kingdom; for they give that name
indifcriminately to the idol, or the temple in which
it is contained. This ftatue is about 45 feet in height,
and being in a ftanding pofture, touches with its
head the vault of the choir. But what is moft aftonifhing, it is faid to be of folid gold, and according to a
curfory eftimate ought to be above 12,500 pounds
weight. It is alfo pretended that this rich coloffus
was caft in the place where it ftands, and that afterwards they built the temple about it. On its fides
are others of lefs value, which are alfo of gold, and
enriched with jewels.

At an hundred paces from the palace is another temple, which though not fo rich, is a regular and beautiful ftruĉture, adorned with five cupolas, of which that in the middle is larger than all the reft : the roof is covered with gilt pewter. Forty-four pyramids furround and adorn the temple : thefe are placed in three rows, and in different ftories. In the circuit which enclofes thefe buildings, all along the galleries, are above four hundred clay ftatues gilt.

The principal pagod in the city contains near four thoufand idols all gilt, befides the three principal ones faid to be of maffy gold. That which paffes for the fecond is fix leagues from the city, and is only open for the king and the priefts ; the people remain proftrate before the gate, with their faces to the earth. The third is in the Dutch ifland, where the principal idol is furrounded by above three hundred others of different dimenfions, in all manner of poftures.

According to the fame authors, the king's palace both within and without, is even more fplendid than the temples. It is fituated on a fmall eminence, and extends to the banks of the river. Though in extent it may be compared to a city, all its towers, pyramids and elevated buildings are gilt. The apartments of the king and queen contain inconceivable riches, gold and precious ftones fhine on all fides ; and there is nothing in all the eaft fo magnificent, except at Indoftan and China.

Such were the notions propogated by Father Tachard, and the Abbe de Choify, who, in 1685 accompanied M. de Chaumont in his embaffy to Siam ; but the Count de Forbin, one of the commanders of the fquadron fent on this occafion obferves, that the Siamefe minifter omitted nothing that could impofe upon thofe gentlemen. He fhewed them all the riches of the royal treafury, which are indeed worthy of a great king ; but he forbore to tell them that the quantity of gold, filver and jewels, was

collected by a long fucceffion of kings; it being
cuftomary at Siam, and in other of the eaftern
nations, to value their kings only in proportion as
they have enriched the treafury, while at the fame
time, (however great be their neceffity) they are not
permitted to touch it. He took them to fee the fineft
pagods of the city and country : when they beheld
the enormous ftatues, which they were told were of
maffy gold : this they believed ; for they are finely
gilt, and they could not touch them, moft of them
being placed very high, and the reft fhut up within
iron grates that are never opened, and are not to
be approached within a certain diftance.

In the long ftay the Count de Forbin made at
Siam and Louvo, he had time to be acquainted with
the truth, and did not overlook the real mifery that
prevails in the country. Of this we may form a
judgment by the poverty of the madarines, who
are the chief of the Siamefe nation. He was extremely furprized at the fituation in which he found thofe
of the court of Louvo : they were feated in a circle
on mats of flender ofier, with only one lamp before
them; and when one of them wanted to read or
write, he took the end of a yellow candle out of his
pocket, lighted it, and put it on a piece of wood,
which turning from fide to fide on a pivot, ferved
them for a candleftick.

De Forbin had the honour to be made lord high
admiral and general of the forces of his Siamefe
majefty ; but his fortune ill fuited the pompous titles
beftowed on him. They gave him a houfe as plain
as it was little, whither they fent thirty-fix flaves
to ferve him, and fix elephants. The maintaining
of his houfhold coft him only five fols a day, fo
temperate are the men, and fo cheap the provifions.
He himfelf had his table at the minifter's ; his
houfe was furnifhed with a few very inconfiderable
moveables ; to which were added twelve filver plates

2

and two filver cups, all very thin ; four dozen of
cotton napkins, and two yellow wax candles a day.

In fhort, there is none rich but the king, and
nothing elfe in Siam appears with the leaft fplendor
but the royal palaces and temples. M. Ceberet
obferves that the whole kingdom, which is very·
large, is nothing but a vaft defert, and that in proportion as one advances into the country, nothing is
to be feen but forefts and wild beafts. The people
dwell on the banks of the rivers, and prefer that
fituation to any other, becaufe the lands which are
overflowed fix months in the year, produce great
quantities of rice almoft without culture. In this
rice confifts all the riches of the country. As to
the king, haughtinefs, defpotifm, and an abfolute
government, are the only marks by which he choofes
to be diftinguifhed from all other fovereigns. The
refpeĉt he requires from his people extends almoft to
adoration. Even in the council, which fometimes
lafts four hours, the minifters of ftate and the mandarines are continually proftrate before him. They
never fpeak to him but on their knees, with their
hands raifed to their heads, making every moment
profound reverences, and accompanying their difcourfe with pompous titles, celebrating his power
or his goodnefs. They receive his words as oracles,
and his orders are inftantly executed without the leaft
oppofition. When he goes abroad all are obliged
to keep within doors ; and that law was thought fo
important, that even the French ambaffadors were
obliged to fubmit to it. His fubjeĉts are flaves who
poffefs nothing but what belongs to him. Even
nobility is not hereditary, it confifting only in
honours and employments which the prince beftows,
and may withdraw whenever he pleafes.

The natives of both fexes go bare-headed ; their
hair is cut within two inches of the fkin, gummed,
and combed upwards, which make their heads feem
very large, and all in briftles, like a boar's back.

The men are of an olive complexion, and have but little hair on the chin ; but the complexion of the women is a ftraw colour. They are well fhaped, and have a large forehead, a fmall nofe, and a hand-fome mouth, with plump lips. Their talapoins or priefts are diftinguifhed from the laity by wearing a cinnamon or orange coloured cloak, and by having their heads, beards, and eye brows kept clofe fhaved. They are forbidden to marry, or to meddle with money, and if any of the priefthood is convicted of incontinence he is burned alive. The children are carefully educated by priefts fet apart for that purpofe, fo that there are few Siamefe who cannot write ; afterwards the children are put to fuch bufineffes as fuit beft with their genius and quality; and there is generally a reciprocal harmony between the parents and children. In marriages, they pay no regard to confanguinity; except between father and daughter, mother and fon, brother and fifter ; for all other degrees are lawful.

The punifhments inflicted on criminals are very fevere : for robbery and theft, they are commonly beheaded. For rebellion and mutiny, they are ripped up alive, their entrails taken out, and their bodies faftened in a kind of wicker bafket, and ex-pofed to the birds and beafts of prey ; and for murder, the condemned perfon is made faft to a ftake driven into the ground ; an elephant is then brought, which twines his trunk round the perfon and ftake, and pulling them with great violence, toffes them both into the air, and in coming down receives the man on his teeth ; then fhaking him off, he puts one of his fore-feet on the carcafe and fqueezes it flat.

In the mountains of Siam are mines of iron, tin, lead, filver and gold : but they all belong to the crown. The plains produce rice and other grain ; and as good, if not the beft oranges, lemons, and limes, to be found in the world. In the woods are abundance of wild animals, as elephants, rhinocerofes, leopards, and tygers; and the natives have tame cattle, as cows, buffaloes, and fwine in plenty about their farms.

The king's dominions extend fouthward to the neighbourhood of Ligor, where the kingdom of Malacca begins. It is thus that the peninfula or tongue of land is called that lies between the ftreight of that name, and the kingdom of Siam.

The inhabitants of Malacca are extremely favage. The heat of the climate in which they dwell, which is almoft under the line, renders their colour very fwarthy; and they are fo fond of the Europeans on account of their whitenefs, that as foon as they arrive on their coafts, they offer them their wives and daughters, that they may have children like them. But notwithftanding the barbarity of their manners, their language is reckoned the fineft in all the Indies, where it is at leaft as common as the French in Europe. But of this country we have already given an account.

To the eaftward of the peninfula beyond the Ganges, is the kingdom of Camboia, or Cambodia, which is bounded on the north by that of Laos, on the eaft by thofe of Cochin China, and Ciampa ; on the fouth and weft by the fea, and the dominions of the king of Siam. This country which is entirely watered by the river Mecon, produces in great abundance all that is necelfary to the life of man, as flefh, rice, cocoas, and fruit of all other kinds ; yet it is ill peopled, and its trade very inconfiderable.

Camboia, the capital, is the only city in the kingdom worthy of notice. The prince refides in a mean palace, furrounded with a palifade that refembles a partition-wall ; but it is defended by a great number of Chinefe cannon, and other pieces of artillery faved from the wreck of two Dutch veflels thrown upon the coaft. There is a temple here of a

very particular ſtructure, whoſe beauty is much com-
mended. It is ſupported by wooden pillars varniſhed
with black, and adorned with gilded foliages and
reliefs, and the pavement is covered with mats. The
prieſts who ſerve in it hold the firſt rank in the ſtate.

The Cambodians are of a light brown complexion;
they are well ſhaped, and have long hair and thin
beards. Their women are handſome, but not very
modeſt. Their dreſs is a petticoat reaching below
the ancles, and a jacket which ſits cloſe to their
bodies and arms. The men wear a veſtment like
our night-gowns, but nothing on their heads and
feet.

To the eaſtward is Cochin China, which extends
along the coaſt of the ſea 700 miles from the river of
Cambodia to that of Quambin. There is no country
in the torrid zone wherein the four ſeaſons are better
diſtinguiſhed. Though 'the rivers are not conſiderable, they are the ſource of its plenty. During the
months of September, October, and November,
they riſe every fifteen days, overflow all the fields for
three days, and render them ſo fertile, that the
natives ſow and reap twice a year : the ſoil produces
rice, ſeveral ſorts of fruit and herbs, pepper, cinnamon, benjoin, eagle and calembawood. Gold, ſilver,
ſilk, cotton, and porcelain, are likewiſe to be found
here. Among the animals are rhinocoroſes, and
elephants of an extraordinary ſize and ſurpriſing
docility. The ſea abounds with excellent fiſh. There
are ſixty good harbours, which induce the inhabitants to apply themſelves to trade and navigation.
That of Faiſo, ſituated a little above the mouth of a
navigable river, is one of the moſt conſiderable, and
is defended by a fortreſs. It is inhabited by Chineſe
and Japaneſe, who carry on a free trade under the
protection of the prince.

The abbe Choiſi, in his travels has given a very
pompous deſcription of this country ; which appears
to be entirely fabulous. He repreſents their gallies

as covered on the outfide with a black varnifh, and
within with a red, that fhines like a mirror. According to him, the failors commonly wear nothing
but drawers of white filk, and a hair cap ; but when
they prepare for battle, they put on their heads a
fmall gilt head-piece, and on their body a fine clofe
coat : but what is moft extraordinary, this clofe coat
leaves the right arm, fhoulder, and fide entirely
naked. The guards of the king and prince, fays he,
are clothed in velvet, and have arms of gold and
filver: but we are not writing a romance, and fhall
therefore not attempt to dazzle the reader with fuch
abfurd defcriptions.

To the northward of Cochin China lies the kingdom of Tonquin, which was once fubject to the vaft
empire of China ; but a famous robber named Din,
put himfelf at the head of a body of men of his own
profeffion, whom he infpired with the refolution of
throwing off the Chinefe yoke : when being joined
by others, he fucceeded in his attempt, and thofe
who had engaged in the revolt, out of gratitude,
placed the crown on his head. But the happinefs of
independency was foon loft, by the people becoming
involved in a long train of civil wars, the laft of which
was concluded by a treaty, wherein the competitor of
the king Lé being lefs defirous of the title of fovereign than of real power, left him all the external
fplendour of a monarch, on condition he fhould have
the abfolute command in the armies, with the greateft part of the revenues of the kingdom, and that their
defcendants fhould fucceed to the fame privileges. By
virtue of this agreement there are two forts of kings ;
he who receives the title and honours of royalty is
called Bau, and the other, who has all its advantages,
is termed the Choud. The Bau, fenfible of the fmallnefs of his power, is feldom feen out of his palace.
He is almoft conftantly taken up in giving audience
to his fubjects, in hearing their complaints, and de-
termining their private differences. This is the ut-

moſt extent of his authority; for he can publiſh no edict relating to the government, without the Choua's conſent. The princes his ſons are attended by offi-cers appointed by the Choua, and never leave the palace above ſix times a year, and that only ſix days each time. In the firſt of theſe days of liberty, they viſit the temples; in the two following, they take the diverſion of hunting; and during the three laſt, they ſail on the river, in gallies magnificently adorned. The ſovereign nominates which of his ſucceſſors ſhall ſucceed him: this is no ſooner made known than the Choua, followed by his principal officers, and the council of ſtate, do him homage, and take an oath to place him on the throne after the Bau's death.

The Tonquineſe are affable, and naturally formed to the laws of reaſon. Both ſexes are clothed after the ſame manner; their dreſs is a long robe, pretty ſtrait, with a cloſe neck, and reaching down to the heels; it is faſtened round the waiſt by a ſilk girdle, or one of gold or ſilver tiſſue; but the military dreſs reaches no lower than the knees. It is the common cuſtom of the country to walk barefooted all the year. The Tonquineſe ladies are as modeſt and reſerved, as thoſe of the common rank are libertine in their con-duct. They wear a ſort of hat, the borders of which are extremely large and ſolid; it is made of the leaves of a tree that grows in the country. Both ſexes wear their hair as long as it will grow, and the women dreſs theirs with great care. The people are of a ſtrong and hardy conſtitution; their ſtature is not extraordinary; but they are well proportioned, and have agreeable features. Thoſe who live in the cities are rather white than brown; but the country peo-ple are almoſt all olive coloured.

Nobility, with ſuitable revenues, is the reward of thoſe who excel in the knowlege of the laws, or mathematics, aſtronomy, and natural philoſophy. Several days in the year are ſet apart for the exami-nation of thoſe who preſent themſelves. The king honours this ceremony with his prefence; he confers nobility on thofe who have given fatisfaction to the queftions of the mandarines; he caufes a robe of violet-fatin to be given them, and appoints the cities and villages that are to produce the rents which he affigns them. During one part of the year, all the tradefmen whatever, except the citizens of Keco, the capital, are obliged to work three months in the year for the royal family, and two more for the mandarines or great lords: fome of their moft laborious employments are, lopping the trees, and feeding the elephants belonging to the king and the army.

Their principal riches confift in filk, mufk, and aloes wood, which they fell to foreigners. They value themfelves much on their fairnefs in trade: which is the more furprizing, as they are neighbours to the Chinefe, and are not only nearly of the fame religion, but have frequent dealings with thofe cunning people, who are verfed in all manner of deceit. The Tonquinefe having no mines of gold or filver, coin no money; but make ufe of plates of gold and filver as they come from China, which they cut in pieces, and weigh according to the prices of what they purchafe.

A

DESCRIPTION

OF

CHINA.

BY

LOUIS Le COMPTE, and P. Du HALDE.

Containing their appointment by the French king;—their adventures till their arrival in China;—their reception at court;—
alfo the buildings, religion, manners and cuftoms of the Chinefe,
with an account of the climate, vegetables, mines, &c. of that
country.

THE French king having refolved to fend fix
Jefuits to China, under the charaćter of his majefty's
mathematicians, I was appointed one of them, and
in the beginning of the year 1685, we all fet fail in
a fhip which carried Monf. Chaumont, who was fent
as ambaffador extraordinary to the court of Siam.
We had a very agreeable voyage. The king of Siam
who pretended to be fkilled in aftronomy, was defirous of affifting at our aftronomical obfervations, and
admiring the exaćtnefs with which we foretold an
eclipfe of the moon, endeavoured to perfuade us to
ftay at his court; but at length confented that four

* The paffages from Du Halde are enclofed in crotchets, thus [ ]

of us fhould depart for China, provided one of us would return with his ambaffador, to defire Louis XIV. to fend him more mathematicians, and that in the mean while I would remain with him.

The prieft with the Siamefe ambaffadors arrived in fafety at Paris ; but the four fathers who fet fail for China, fuffered fhipwreck, and after undergoing feveral hardfhips returned to Siam, in an Englifh veffel.

At that time a rebellion had broke out at Siam, which facilitated my departure ; we fet fail in a fmall Chinefe veffel ; but though the king gave orders for our being treated with kindnefs, it is not eafy to conceive a more difagreeable voyage than we were obliged to endure. We had no fhelter againft the weather, and were fo ftreightened for want of room, that we could not lie at our length. We were placed near an idol, black with the fmoak of a lamp continually burning to its honour, and daily worfhipped by the deluded crew. The fun fhone directly over our heads, and we had fcarce any water to quench the extreme thirft caufed by the exceffive heat of the climate. Indeed we had a daily allowance of three meals of rice, and the captain often afked us to eat meat with him ; but that being always firft offered to the idol, we looked upon it with more horror than appetite.

In this manner we fpent above a month. It is true, we fometimes, by the help of an interpreter, attempted to convince them of the abfurdity of that worfhip in which they had the unhappinefs to be educated. One day in particular, they flocked about us, and the difpute grew fo warm, that we were obliged to give it up. Seamen are generally untractable ; thefe took great offence at what we had faid of their idol, and foon came towards us armed with lances and half pikes, with looks that feemed to threaten our deftruction. We were inftantly filled with apprehenfions ; but at laft were delivered from this painful fufpenfe, by finding that they were only

preparing for a proceffion in honour of their idol;
perhaps to appeafe the anger they fuppofed fhe might
have conceived at what we had faid to her difadvan-
tage.

There is fcarce a nation under the fun more fuperftitious than the Chinefe, who worfhip the very compafs by which they fteer, continually offering it meat
and incenfe. Twice a day they regularly threw into
the fea little pieces of guilt paper in the form of money, as it were to bribe it to be favourable. Sometimes they would prefent it with little paper boats,
that being bufy in toffing and ruling them, fhe might
neglect our fhip. But when that unruly element, in
fpite of their courtfey, grew troublefome, from its
being agitated as they imagined by the Dæmon who
governs it, they burnt fome feathers, with which
they made fuch a ftink, as was fufficient to drive
away any fiend that had the fenfe of fmelling.

Once paffing near an hill on which one of their
temples is erected, their fuperftition was carried to
the utmoft length; for befides the ufual ceremonies
confifting of meat offerings, burning of candles and
perfumes, throwing little baubles of guilt paper into
the fea, and an infinite number of other fopperies, all
hands were employed for five or fix hours in making
a little veffel refembling the fhip, of about four feet
in length, with the mafts, tackling, fails, and flags:
it had likewife its compafs, rudder and fhallop; its
arms, utenfils for dreffing provifions, the provifions
themfelves, with the cargo and book of accounts:
befides they daubed as many fmall pieces of paper as
we were men in the fhip, which were difpofed of in
the fame place we were in. This veffel with all its
appurtenances, being placed on two ftaves, was, at the
noife of a tabor and brazen bafon, raifed up in view
of the whole crew. A feaman in the habit of a
bronze, or prieft, was the chief man among them, he
playing feveral apifh tricks with a quarterftaff, and at

intervals fhouting aloud. At length the myfterious toy was committed to the waves, and gazed at as far as the fight could reach, accompanied with the ac· clamations of the bronze, who roared with all his might.

Soon after an accident happened, which at firft gave them lefs pleafure, though in the end it proved an equal diverfion to us all. The mariners imagined they faw through their perfpectives a fhip in a part of the fea much infefted by pirates : they diftinguifh- ed the mafts, the fails, nay fome faw the very tackling, and even perceived by the manner of her failing, that fhe intended to pay us a vifit. The Chinefe, who, of all men, love beft to fleep in a whole fkin, were in great confternation ; and the fear we faw painted in their faces while they prepared their fcymeters, pikes and mufkets, filled us with terror, for we imagined ourfelves in danger of being im- mediately ftrangled, by villains who gave no quarter to fuch as fall into their hands, and which we could no otherwife efcape but by leaping into the fea. A remedy which was fomewhat violent and not much better than being ftrangled. Our perfpec- tive glaffes were often ufed, and to our no fmall furprize, the mighty veffel as it came nearer leffened, as did our ill grounded fears ; for we now doubted whether it was a fhip or no. At length it grew a floating ifland, then a fea horfe, and then I know not what, till at laft being full in fight, it proved to be a tree, which a violent wind had torn from the coaft. The earth and pebbles about its root made it fwim upright, fo that its trunk, which was very high, refembled a maft, fome branches fpread on each fide, had been taken for a yard, and the leffer boughs, for ropes, while the wind and fea beating about it formed a track not unlike that made by a fhip. The dreadful enemy being now no more, the Chinefe exprefied very heroically their

vexation and difappointment at lofing fuch an opportunity of fhewing their courage.

At length after a navigation of thirty-fix days,
which the continual dangers and hardfhips to which
we were expofed, had rendered very tedious, we
came within fight of the city of Nimpo in China.
The fight infpired us with joy ; but though we were
fo near, it was not eafy for us to enter it. The
captain of our veffel, on our arrival, confined us in
the hold, where the heat, which increafed as we
came nearer the land, and feveral other inconveniences, rendered our condition almoft infupportable.
We were, however, difcovered by an officer of the
cuftoms, and foon after brought before a mandarine,
whom we found in a large hall attended by his
officers with a multitude of people, who are more
curious of feeing an European, than we fhould be
here of viewing a Chinefe.

We were no fooner entered, than we were informed that we muft kneel to the mandarine, and
bow our heads nine times to the ground. His countenance was very fevere, and our dread was increafed
at the fight of his executioners, who, like the Roman
lictors, attended with chains and great fticks, ready
to bind and cudgel whom he thought fit. Having
paid our devoirs, he afked us, who we were, and
our bufinefs there. On which we informed him,
that hearing in Europe that feveral of our brethren
had laboured with fuccefs in fpreading the knowledge
of our holy religion in thofe remote parts, the fame
zeal had infpired us with the defire to procure them
the knowledge of the true God, the only thing
wanting to complete the grandeur of fo flourifhing
and renowned a nation. We did not know that we
were in a city where there was not one Chriftian.
The mandarine, however, exprefled his defire to ferve
us ; but added, that he muft confult with the governor ; and in the mean while we muft return to
our fhip.

Some days after the general of the milita in and about the city, defiring to fee us, entertained us very kindly, and on our leaving him to wait upon the governor, fent an officer to defire him to ufe us kindly. The governor exprefled fome refpect for us, but letting us know that he could determine nothing till he had firft conferred with the chief officers of the city, we were forced to return again on board our hated fhip. Eight days being fpent in confultations at the cuftom houfe, we were fent for, together with our goods, which confifted of feveral bales and trunks of books, images, and mathematical inftruments ; and having opened three of them, we were told that we might lodge in the fuburbs, till they had heard from the viceroy, to whom the governor had wrote about us. Of this civility we gladly accepted, and in our new habitation enjoyed that reft and liberty which is always grateful after long fatigue and confinement.

The port of Nimpo is fituated in the moft eaftern part of China, and has a very difficult entrance ; but from thence a very confiderable trade is carried on to Japan. This city is one of the firft clafs ; it is walled round, and very populous. It is remarkable for the great number of triumphal arches to be feen there, which indeed are very common in the other parts of China ; but they are here fo numerous as to be inconvenient, though they afford an agreeable profpect at a diftance. They confift of three great arches together, built of marble, that in the middle being much the higheft. The four pillars by which they are fupported are fometimes round ; but oftner fquare, formed of a fingle ftone, generally placed on an irregular bafe. They have no capitals, the trunk being faftened into the architrave, if that name may be given to fome figures cut over the pillars. The frieze, which is too high, in proportion to the reft, is adorned with infcriptions and relievos, finely executed, with knots wrought loofe one within another, adorned with flowers and birds flying as it were from the ftone. But while fome of thefe edifices cannot be fufficiently praifed, others are not worth notice.

Some time after, we had intelligence that the viceroy of the province was much offended at our being fuffered to land, and was refolved to fend us back. He wrote a fhort reprimand to the governor of Nimpo, and at the fame time fent to inform the grand tribunal of Pekin, intrufted with the care of foreign affairs, that we were five Europeans, who for fome private ends defigned to fettle there, in oppofition to the fundamental laws of the kingdom ; fo that the court decreed that we fhould be banifhed ; and according to cuftom he fent an order to that effect to the emperor, for his fignature. Had this order been confirmed, we fhould have been ruined, and probably the mandarines of Nimpo, for treating us fo favourably. The viceroy who had as great love to our money, as he had hatred to our belief, would have feized our bales, aud have punifhed the captain who brought us, by feizing his merchandize, and ordering him to be gone, and to take us with him ; while he would have thrown us overboard as the authors of his ruin. But we had wrote to father Intorcetta, an Italian miffionary, the general of nor order in thofe parts, who on receiving our letters wrote to a friend at court, to inform his majefty, who was then in Tartary, of our arrival, and by a wilful miftake caufed his letters to be put into a pacquet, which he knew would be delivered into the emperor's own hand. Thus the emperor opened and read it ,and therefore when the tribunal's decree was delivered to him, he anfwered, that he would confider of it at Pekin. On his arrival at that city he was informed by one of our order, that by our fkill in the mathematics we might be of ufe to his majefty, on which, by the advice and confent of his privy council, he fent for us up to court ; and it happened that the very perfon who had endeavoured to turn us fhamefully out of China, was himfelf obliged to introduce us.

The viceroy left our journey as far as Hamtcheou to the governor's care, who provided boats for us, and that we might want for nothing, he commanded an inferior mandarine to attend us. We reached that city, and afterwards, on our leaving it, the viceroy, who was afraid left he fhould be informed againft, prefented us ten piftoles ; fent fome chairs to carry us to an imperial barge he had provided for us, and ordered fome trumpets and hautboys to attend us, at the fame time he gave us an order from court, in purfuance of which all the places through which we paffed, were, while we went by water, to find us boats well maned, and fixty or more porters, in cafe the froft obliged us to go by land ; befides each city was to give us the value of about half a piftole ; this being allowed to the chief mandarines, who are faid to have their charges borne by the emperor, though this will not amount to the tenth part of the expence.

The barge provided for us was a fecond rate, containing fixteen feet in breadth, and feventy in length. Befides the cook-room, that of the mafter and his family, that for the crew, and another for our men, there was a pretty large cabin wherein we dined, and three rooms, in which fix perfons might lie at their eafe, all which were painted, gilt and varnifhed.

As to our manner of proceeding up the river: as foon as the anchor was weighed, the trumpets and hautboys founded a march, and then took their leave by firing a kind of cheft, in which were three iron barrels, that were difcharged one after another, the mufic founding between each. This was repeated whenever we met a mandarine's barge, or came to a town, or when either night or a contrary wind obliged us to come to an anchor. Every night ten or twelve inhabitants of the town neareft to the place

where he caft anchor, appeared in one row on the
fhore, when the mafter coming on the deck, made a
fpeech on their obligations to preferve all who belonged to the emperor, and to watch for the fafety
of the mandarines, who took care of the ftate. He
then enumerated all the accidents to which we were liable, as fire, thieves, and ftorms, exhorting them to be
vigilant, and telling them they fhould be anfwerable
for all the mifchief that happened. They anfwered
each fentence with a fhout, and then retired as to
form a guard, leaving only one centry, who continually ftruck two fticks againft each other, and was
hourly relieved by others who made the fame noife,
to let us know that they did not fall afleep, which we
would gladly have allowed them to do, on condition
we might have done fo ourfelves.

On the third of January we arrived at Yamtchcoy,
when the froft forcing us to leave the great canal, we
had horfes provided for our men, and porters for our
goods. As for ourfelves, the cold and fnow to which
we were unaccuftomed, made us chufe to go in litters.
We changed our porters at every city or large town,
and found to our furprize, that we could get above
a hundred with as much eafe and fpeed as in France
we could have got five or fix   The cold now hourly
encreafed, and at length became fo fharp, that we found
the river Hoambo, one of the largeft in China, almoft
frozen over : a whole day was fpent in breaking the
ice, and we paffed it with much trouble and difficulty.

On our arrival at Pekin, we found the court in
mourning for the emprefs dowager ; the courts of juftice were fhut up and the emprefs gave no audience :
but the 27 days of mourning being over, in which the
fovereign himfelf is obliged by the law to remain in
folitude, he fent one of his officers to fee how we did,
and to afk us fome queftions ; fome time after we were
fent for by the tribunal who had paffed the fentence
of banifhment upon us : where the prefident, gave us

a finall piece of varnifhed board, wrapped up in taffety, and on this board was written, among other things, that we might ufe our inftruments, and fettle in what part of the empire we pleafed. We had not yet had the honour to attend on his majefty ; for thefe formalities were to precede our audience: but we had fcarcely thus got our difcharge, when two eunuchs entered, to inform the prefident, that he muft attend with his brethren in a particular court of the palace ; and we were informed of the ceremonies ufed on fuch occafions.

We were then carried in chairs to the firft gate, whence we went on foot through eight courts of a prodigious length, built round with houfes of different kinds of architecture ; but the buildings of none of thefe courts were very extraordinary, except the large fquare ftructures over the arches through which we paffed from one court into another. Thefe indeed made a ftately appearance, they being built of white marble, though worn rough with age. Through one of thefe courts ran a rivulet, over which were feveral finall bridges of the fame kind of marble, but of a whiter colour and better workmanfhip.

The grandeur of this palace does not confift in the noblenefs and elegance of the architecture ; but in the prodigious number of its buildings, courts and gardens, all regularly difpofed. What chiefly ftruck me, as being moft fingular, was the emperor's throne, of which the beft defcription my memory will afford me is the following ; in the midft of one of thefe courts is a fquare bafe or folid building of an extraordinary extent, adorned on the top with a baluftrade much in the European fafhion, this fupports another fmaller bafe, alfo encompaffed with a baluftrade, over which are placed three more of the fame kind, each leffening in bulk, as it arifes above the other. On the uppermoft is a large hall, the roof of which is covered with gilt tiles, and fupported by the four walls, and as many rows of varnifhed pillars, between which is feated the throne. Thefe vaft bafes, with their baluftrades of white marble, thus rifing above each other, with a palace on the top glittering with gold and varnifh, have a very fine appearance, efpecially as they are thus placed in the midft of a fpacious court, furrounded by four ftately rows of buildings: and were its beauty enhanced by the ornaments of the Greek and Roman architecture, and by that noble fimplicity, fo much valued in our buildings, it would be doubtlefs as magnificent a throne as ever was raifed by art.

After a quarter of an hour's walk, we at length came to the emperor's apartment, the entrance of which was not very fplendid ; but the anti-chamber was adorned with marble, fculpture, and gildings, the neatnefs of the workmanfhip being more value-able than the richnefs of the materials. But the fecond mourning not being over, the prefence cham-ber was ftill difrobed of all its ornaments, and could boaft of none but the prefence of the fovereign, who fat on a fopha raifed three feet from the ground, covered with a plain white carpet, that took up the whole breadth of the room. By him lay fome books, paper and ink. He was clothed with a veft of black fatin furred with fable, and on each hand ftood a row of young eunuchs plainly habited, and unarmed, with their legs clofe to each other, and their arms extended downwards along their fides, which is efteemed the moft refpectful pofture.

Being come to the outer door, we hafted, for fuch is the cuftom, till we came to the end of the chamber oppofite to the emperor. Then ftood for a moment all abreaft in the pofture the eunuchs were in. Next falling on our knees, and joining our hands, we lifted them up to our heads, in fuch a manner that our arms and elbows were of the fame height. We bowed thrice to the ground, then rifing ftood as be-fore. The fame proftration was repeated a fecond and a third time, when we were ordered to come for-

ward, and kneel before his majefty, who treated us
with the greateft good nature, and having afked us
fome queftions relating to the grandeur of France,
the length of the voyage, and the manner in which
we had been treated by his mandarines, let us know
that he was difpofed to grant us frefh favours, and
then difmiffed us. He was fomewhat above the middle ftature, and though pretty corpulent, was lefs fo
than a Chinefe would wifh to be, he was full vifaged,
disfigured with the fmall pox : had a broad forehead,
little eyes and a fmall nofe. In fhort, though he had
not an air of majefty, he had a look of great good
nature.

From his apartment we went into another, where
a mandarine treated us with tea, and prefented us
from the emperor, a fum worth about an hundred
piftoles ; this prefent might feem but inconfiderable
from fo great a prince ; but in China it is a very
extraordinary one where it is a maxim with the great,
to take as much, and give as little as they can. On
the other hand, he loaded us with honour, and ordered one of his officers to wait on us to his houfe.

Pekin, which fignifies the north court, is the chief
city of China, and ufual feat of the emperors it
being thus named to diftinguifh it from Nankin,
or the fouth court, where the emperor formerly re-
fided, it being in the fineft and moft commodious
fituation of any city in the empire ; but the continual incurfions of Tartars obliged the emperors to
fettle in one of the northern provinces; where he
might be always ready to oppofe them. Pekin was
the place fixed upon for this purpofe, it being fituated
in the 40th degree of north latitude, at a fmall diftance from the famous Chinefe wall. Its neighbourhood to the fea on the eaft, and the great canal on
the fouth, afforded it a communication with feveral
fine provinces, from which it draws part of its fubfiftence.

The city of Pekin, which is exactly fquare, was formerly four leagues round ; but the Tartars fettle-ing there, forced the Chinefe to live without the walls, where they foon built a new town, which, with the old one, compofes an irregular figure.   Thus Pekin confifts of two cities, one called the Tartar's, becaufe they permit none elfe to inhabit it; and the other the Chinefe, which is as large, and more populous than the firft ; both together being fix leagues in circumference.   So that the city of Paris, which is 10,000 paces round, is but half as big as the Tartar's town, and but a quarter as large as all Pekin.   Indeed their houfes are generally no more than one ftory high, and thofe of Paris are, one with another, four. The ftreets of the former city are wider, the em-peror's palace, which is of a vaft extent, is not half inhabited ; befides, there are in that city magazines of rice for the fupport of 200,000 men, and large courts filled with houfes, in which thofe who are candidates for their doctors degree are examined; which alone would form a very confiderable city. But on the other hand the Chinefe live fo clofe to-gether, that twenty or more of them dwell in as little room as ten perfons at Paris.

The multitude of people in the ftreets is quite amazing ; even thofe that are wideft are not free from confufion; and at the fight of fuch numbers of camels, horfes, mules, waggons, chairs, paffengers, and rings of one or two hundred perfons gathered here and there round the fortune-tellers, one would ima-gine, that fome unufual fhew had drawn all China to Pekin.   For the moft populous cities in Europe appear a wildernefs to this : hence fome have imagined that as only the men are here to be feen, the num-ber of the inhabitants of both fexes muft amount to fix or feven millions of fouls.

This is however, a very erroneous computation ; and the following obfervations will fhew the number of the inhabitants muſt not be gueſſed at from the crouds ſeen in the ſtreets. As no river comes up to Pekin, the neceſſary proviſions and commodities brought there by land, daily cauſe a great reſort to that city of peaſants, camels, horſes, mules, waggons, &c. Almoſt all the artiſicers work at the houſes of their cuſtomers, and even the ſiniths carry with them their furnace, anvil and tools, and return home at night. All perſons above the vulgar never go abroad but on horſeback, or in chairs, with a numerous retinue ; the mandarines are conſtantly attended by the inferior officers, following them with all their formalities in a kind of proceſſion. In ſhort, the princes of the blood, and the lords of the court, who are obliged to go almoſt daily to the palace, are always attended with a great guard of horſe. The cuſtoms, which are peculiar to China, greatly encreaſe the throng, and make the city appear more populous than it really is : however, I think I ſhall not be very wide of the truth if I allow the inhabitants to amount to two millions.

Almoſt all the ſtreets are built in a direct line, the largeſt being about 120 feet broad, and a league in length, and the ſhops where they ſell ſilks and China ware, which generally take up the whole ſtreet, form a very agreeable viſta. The Chineſe have a cuſtom which adds to their beauty : each ſhopkeeper puts out before his houſe, on a kind of pedeſtal, a board about twenty feet high, painted, varniſhed, and often gilt, on which are written in large characters the commodities in which he deals. Theſe kind of pilaſters, thus erected on each ſide the ſtreet, and almoſt at an equal diſtance from each other, have a very pretty effect. This is cuſtomary in almoſt all the cities of China, and in ſome places I have ſeen them ſo neat, that the whole ſtreet has appeared like the decorations of the ſtage. How-ever, the houſes are neither well built, nor of a ſufficient height ; and beſides, are always peſtered with mud or duſt.   There is ſo much of the latter, that the city is generally covered with a cloud of it, which makes its way into the cloſeſt cloſets, and notwithſtanding their ſtriving to allay it, by continually ſprinkling the ſtreets, it is not only offenſive, but prejudical to·the health.

It is ſurprizing to ſee the perfect tranquility maintained among ſuch an almoſt infinite number of Chineſe and Tartars ; for it ſeldom happens in many years that a houſe is broke open by thieves, or any murder committed.   Indeed ſuch ſtrict order is obſerved, that it is next to impoſſible ſuch crimes ſhould be committed with impunity.   All the great ſtreets, which are drawn by a line from one gate to another, have ſeveral corps de garde. Day and night, ſoldiers with their ſwords by their ſides and whips in their hands, are ready to chaſtiſe thoſe who make the leaſt diſturbance, and have power to take into cuſtody whoever raiſes any quarrel.   The little ſtreets that come into the greater have gates made in the form of a latice, which affords a view of all who paſs along: they are guarded by the corps de garde placed over againſt them in the great ſtreets.   The latice gates are ſhut at night by the corps de garde, and are ſeldom opened but to perſons known, who carry a lanthorn in their hand, and give a good reaſon for their going out.   As ſoon as the firſt ſtroke is given by the watch on a great bell, a ſoldier or two muſt go from one corps de garde to another ; and as they walk along they play continually on a ſort of rattle. Whoever is found walking in the ſtreets in the night, is examined, and if his buſineſs is not of a very extraordinary nature, he is taken into cuſtody.   To this it muſt be added, that the governor is obliged to take his rounds when leaſt expected ; and that the officers who keep guard on the walls, and on the pavilions of the gates, where the watches are, beat on great drums of braſs, ſend ſubalterns to examine the quarters belonging to their

refpective gates, and that the leaft neglect is punifhed the next day, and the officers broke. By this
beautiful order, peace, filence, and fafety reign
throughout the city.

Of all the buildings of which this city confifts,
the moft remarkable is the imperial palace, of which
1 have already taken fome notice : but it is proper
here to add, that it includes not only the emperor's
houfe and gardens, but a little town inhabited by
the officers of the court, and a multitude of artificers employed and kept by the emperor ; for none
but the eunuchs lie in the inner palace. The outward town is defended by a very good wall without,
and divided from the emperor's houfe by one of lefs
ftrength. However, all the houfes of the courtiers
and artificers are low and ill contrived, and even
worfe than thofe in the Tartars city.

The inner palace is formed of nine vaft courts
built in one line. The arches through which you
go from one to another are, as already mentioned,
of marble, and over each is a large fquare building,
of a kind of Gothic architecture, wheie the timbers
of the roof projecting beyond the wall, are formed
by other pieces of wood into a kind of cornice, that
at a diftance looks very fine. The fides of each
court are clofed by leffer apartments ; but when you
come to the emperor's lodgings, the porticos fupported by ftately pillars, the white marble fteps by
which you afcend to the inward halls, the gilt roofs,
the carved work, varnifh, gilding and painting, appear extremely fplendid. [The whole is covered
with fhining tiles of fuch a beautiful yellow, that at
a diftance they appear as bright as if they were gilt.
Another roof as bright as the former, fprings from
the walls, and ranges all round the buildings, and
this is fupported by a foreft of beams, joifts, and
fpars, all japaned with gold flowers on a green
ground : this fecond roof, with the projection of the
firft, make a fort of crown to thefe ftructures, which

has a fine effect.   The terraces on which the apart.
ments are built contribute to give them an air of
grandeur.   They are fifteen feet high, cafed with
white marble, and adorned with baluftres of pretty
good workmanfhip, open only at the fteps placed
on each fide, and in the middle and corners of the
front ; but the afcent in the middle is only a flope of
marble, with neither fteps nor landing-place.

  The hall appointed for ceremonies has large maffy
veffels of brafs placed on the platform before it, in
which perfumes are burnt during any ceremony, and
alfo candlefticks in the fhape of birds, large enough
to hold flambeaus.   This hall is about 130 feet long,
and almoft fquare: the ceiling is carved, japaned
green, and charged with gilt dragons: the pillars.
that fupport the roof are about fix or feven feet in circumference at the bottom, incrufted with a kind of
pafte, and japaned with red ; the pavement is partly
covered with an ordinary fort of carpets, in imitation
of thofe of Turkey ; but the walls are deftitute of all ornament ; they are very well whited, but have neither
tapeftry, looking-glaffes, fconces or paintings.   In
the middle of this room is a throne under a lofty al-
cove ; very neat, but neither rich nor magnificent.
There are two other leffer halls hid by the former,
one of them a pretty circular room with windows all
round, and fhining with japaned work of various colour : the other is of an oblong form.]   In the view
of thefe buildings the different pieces of architecture
dazzled the eyes of the beholder.   But the imperfect
notion the Chinefe have entertained of all arts, is be-
traye by the moft unpardonable faults.   The ornaments are not only irregular and puerile, but the
apartments are ill contrived, and want that connec-
tion which forms the beauty and conveniences of the
palaces in Europe ; and cannot fail of difgufting all
who have the leaft notion of architecture.

  The guards placed at the gates and avenues have
no other arms but their fcymitars.   Formerly the

The Porcelain Tower at Nankin.

whole palace was inhabited by eunuchs, whofe power and infolence grew to fuch a height, that they became infupportable to the princes of the empire ; but the laft Chinefe emperors, efpecially thofe defcended from Tartary, have fo humbled them, that the youngeft are made to ferve as pages, while the tafk of the others is to fweep the rooms and keep them clean ; and for the leaft fault they are feverely punifhed by their overfeers.

The emperor's houfe is the only one at Pekin that deferves the name of a palace ; the others are extremely mean, and thofe of the grandees, like all the reft, but one ftory high ; however, the great number of rooms for themfelves and their fervants, make fome amends for their want of beauty and magnificence. The nobility, are, indeed, like thofe of other nations, fond of making a great appearance ; but they are curbed by the cuftoms of the country, and the danger of being taken notice of. While I was at Pekin, one of the chief mandarines built himfelf a houfe fomewhat more lofty and magnificent than the reft. For this crime he was accufed before the emperor, when being afraid of the confequence, he pulled it down while the affair was under examination.

The halls in which they plead, have few advantages above the other houfes. Indeed they have fpacious courts and lofty gates, fometimes embellifhed with tolerable ornaments ; but the inward halls and offices are neither magnificent nor even cleanly.

Amongft the moft remarkable buildings, is the famous imperial obfervatory, fo celebrated by travellers, one of whom fpeaks of it in this manner : "Nothing in Europe is to be compared to it, whether for the magnificence of the place, or the fize of thofe vaft brazen machines, which having been during 700 years expofed on the platforms of thofe large towers are ftill as fair and entire as if they were but juft caft. The divifions of thofe inftruments are moft exact ; the difpofition moft proper for their

" defign, and the whole work performed with an
" inimitable neatnefs." Filled with thefe high ideas
we vifited this famous place, and firft entered a court
of a moderate extent, where we were fhewn the
dwelling houfe of thofe who look after the obfervatory. Then turning to the right, we afcended a very
narrow ſtair-cafe to the top of a fquare tower, fuch as
were formerly ufed to fortify our city walls: indeed
it is joined on the infide to that of Pekin, and raifed
only ten or twelve feet above the bulwarks. Upon
this platform the Chinefe aftronomers had placed their
inftruments, which though but few took up the
whole fpace : but father Verbieft having judged them
ufelefs, had prevailed on the emperor to have them
pulled down, and to have new ones put up of his
contriving: they were therefore in a hall near the
tower, buried in duft and oblivion. We faw them
only through a window fecured with iron bars ; when
they appeared to be very large and well caft ; however, we had an opportunity of examining more narrowly a celeftial globe of about three feet diameter
left in a by-court, when we found that it was of a
form inclining to an oval, divided with little exactnefs, and the whole work very coarfe. In fhort, this
obfervatory, which was of little worth, with refpect
both to its ancient machines, and its fituation, is now
enriched with feveral brazen inftruments fet up by
father Verbieft. Thefe are an armillary fphere fix
feet in diameter, fupported by four dragons heads,
whofe bodies after feveral windings are faftened to
the ends of two brazen beams laid acrofs, that bear
the whole weight of the fphere. Four lions of the
fame metal ftand under the ends of thefe beams. The
circles are both in their interior and exterior furface
divided by lines into 360 degrees each, and each degree into fixty minutes, and the latter into portions
of ten feconds each.

     An equinoxial fphere fix feet in diameter, fupported
by a dragon who bears it on his back, and ftands on

four brazen beams fupported by four fmall lions. The defign is well executed.

An azimuthal horizon of the fame diameter, alfo fupported by dragons.

A quadrant whofe radius is fix feet. A dragon folded in feveral rings, and wrapped up in clouds, feizes on all parts the plates of the inftrument to faften them together.

A fextant, whofe radius is about eight feet, and a fine celeftial globe of fix feet diameter ; both likewife decorated with dragons.

But the Chinefe would never have been perfuaded to leave their old inftruments, and make ufe of thefe, which are infinitely fuperior to them, without the exprefs orders of their emperor ; for they are more fond of the moft defective pieces of antiquity, than of the moft noble improvements. It is faid that they have watched the motions of the ftars above 4000 years ; but it is a fhame that in fo long a time they have made no greater improvements. However, they ftill continue their obfervations, and five mathe-maticians fpend every night on the tower, one gazing towards the zenith, another to the eaft, a third to the weft, the fourth to the fouth, and the fifth to the north, that nothing may efcape their obfervation. They take notice of the winds, the rain, the air, and all unufual phænomena, eclipfes, the conjunction and oppofition of planets, and of fires and meteors. Of thefe they keep ftrict account, which they bring in every morning to the furveyor of the mathematics, to be regiftered in his office. Thefe aftronomers, are, however, very unfkilful, they take little care to improve the fcience, and provided their falary be paid, give themfelves no great trouble about the changes that happen in the fky.

In treating of Pekin it would be doing that great city injuftice to pafs over in filence its noble gates, and ftately walls. The former are not like the other public buildings in China, embellifhed with ftatues or other carving, all their beauty confifting in their prodigious height, which at a diftance·has a fine appearance. They confift of two large fquare edifices, built feparately, but bound together by two thick and lofty walls forming a fquare fufficient to contain above 500 men in battle, the firft building which refembles a fortrefs, faces the road. There is no way through it; but you enter in at the fide wall, where there is a gate proportionable to the reft; you then turn to the right, and meet with the fecond tower which commands the city, and has a gate like the former; but the gate-way is fo long that it grows dark in the middle. There they conftantly keep a guard, and a fmall magazine of ftores. Though thefe gates are deftitute of the embellifhments of architecture, yet on approaching Pekin, thefe immenfe buildings have an air of magnificence preferable to our ornaments. The arches are built with marble, and the reft with very large bricks, cemented with excellent mortar.

The walls are anfwerable to the gates, fo lofty that they hide the whole city, and fo thick that centeries are placed upon them on horfeback. Square towers are raifed at the diftance of a bow-fhot from each other. The ditch is dry, but very broad and deep, and the city is as regularly defended by a ftrong garrifon, as if the people were under the continual apprehenfions of a fiege.

[Among the moft fumptious buildings of China, we ought not to omit their temples or pagods, erected to fabulous deities by the fuperftition of the princes as well as of the people. Of thefe there are a prodigious number, the moft celebrated of which are built in barren mountains, to which, however, the induftry of the people has given the beauties and advantages denied them by nature: the canals cut at a great expence to conduct the water from the heights into refervoirs made for that purpofe; with gardens, groves, and grottos made in the rocks for fhelter, againft the exceffive heat of the climate, render their folitudes delightful. We have given a view of one of thefe ftructures in the province of To-kien.

Thefe temples confift partly of porticos, paved with large fquare polilhed ftones, and partly of halls or pavili ons that ftand in corners of courts, and communicate by long galleries, adorned with ftatues of ftone, and fometimes of brafs. The roofs of thefe buildings fhine with beautiful tiles japaned with green and yellow, and at the corners are adorned with dragons of the fame colour, projecting forward. Moft of thefe pagods have a great tower ftanding by itfelf, and terminating in a dome, to which they afcend by a handfome ftaircafe that winds around it. A fquare temple commonly occupies the middle of the dome, which is often adorned with mofaic work, and the walls covered with ftone figures of animals and monfters in relievo. This is the form of moft of the pagods, and thefe are the habitations of the bonzes or the priefts of the idol.]

The frontier towers, efpeciaally thofe near Tartary, are fortihed with good bulwarks, towers, brick walls, and large and deep ditches filled with running water: in thefe all the fkill of the Chinefe engineers confifts, which is no wonder, fince none elfe were known in Europe before cannon were in ufe. Their moft fingular fortification is the great wall, which extends from the eaftern ocean, to the province of Chanfi, and if all its windings be reckoned, is no lefs than 500 leagues long. It is fortified with towers, much like thofe of the cities; and where the paffes might be more eafily forced, they have raifed two or three bulwarks one be hind another, of an enormous thicknefs; thefe with the forts that command all the avenues, being guarded by a great number of forces, protect the Chinefe from all attempts on that fide. As China is divided from Tartary by a chain of mountains, this wall has been carried not only

through the valleys, but over the higheft hills : it is
every where of a great height, but rather lower than
the walls of their cities, and only four or five feet in
thicknefs : it is moftly buiit with brick, and bound
with fuch ftrong mortar, that though it is 1800 years
fince it was built, it is fcarce the worfe. This work
was at once one of the greateft and the moft ridiculous,
ever made by man : for notwithftanding its being
extremely prudent thus to guard all the paffes and
the eafieft avenues, how abfurd was it to carry this
wall to the top of fome precipices, which the birds
can fcarely reach with their flight, and to which it is
impoffible that the Tartarian horfe fhould ever afcend ? Befides, if they could fancy it poffible for
any army to clamber up thither, how could they
imagine that fo thin and low a wall could be any defence. Yet it is amazing how the materials were
conveyed thither, which was not done without a
vaft expence, and the lofs of more men than would
have perifhed by the greateft fury of their enemies.
It is faid, that during the reigns of the Chinefe emperors, this wall was guarded by a million of foilders;
but as that part of Tartary now belongs to China,
they are contented with manning well the worft
fituated, but beft fortified parts.

There are in China above a thoufand fortreffes of
the firft rate ; but though the reft fcarcely deferve the
name, they are all well garrifoned whence fome judgment may be formed of the vaft armies conftantly
kept on foot.

But what is far more aftonifhing, is the number,
the largenefs, and the government of their trading
towns. Thefe are generally divided into three claffes,
the firft confifting of above an hundred and fixty,
the fecond of two hundred and feventy, and the third
of near twelve hundred. Befides, there are near
three hundred walled cities, which they confider as
not worth notice, though moft of them are populous,

and places of trade. The largeneſs of theſe cities is no leſs amazing than their number.

Pekin is not to be compared to Nankin, or as it is now called, Kiam-nin, which was formerly encloſed within three walls, the outermoſt of which was ſixteen leagues round ; and though this city has loſt much of its former ſplendor, yet including thoſe who live in its ſuburbs, and on the canals, it is ſtill more populous than Pekin. The ſtreets are of a moderate breadth, and very well paved ; the houſes are low, but cleanly, and the ſhops very richly furniſhed with ſilks, and other coſtly goods. Thither all the curioſities of the empire are brought. There the maſt famous doctors, and the mandarines out of employment, uſually ſettle, on account of the convenience of ſeveral libraries filled with choice of good books. Their printing is fairer, their artificers more ſkillful, the language more polite, and the accent ſmoother than elſewhere. Beſides the river Kiam, on which it is ſituated, is the largeſt, deepeſt, and moſt navigable in the whole empire.

Nankin is famous for what is called the China tower. Of which it may be proper to obſerve, that there is without the city a houſe named by the Chineſe, The Temple of Gratitude, built 300 years ago by the emperor Yonlo. It is erected on a maſſive baſis built with brick, aud ſurrounded with a rail of unpoliſhed marble. Round it are ten or twelve ſteps, by which you aſcend to the lowermoſt hall, the floor of which ſtands one foot higher than the baſis, leaving a walk two feet wide all round it. The front is adorned with a gallery and ſome pillars. The roofs, which in China are generally two, one next the top of the wall, and a narrower over that, are covered with green ſhining tiles ; and on the inſide the ceiling is painted, and formed of little pieces differently wrought one within the other, and this the Chineſe eſteem very ornamental. Indeed ſuch a medley of beams, joiſts, rafters, and pinions, ap-

pear furprifingly fingular, from our judging that fuch
a work muft be very expenfive : but it only proceeds
from the ignorance of the workmen, who are un-
acquainted with that noble fimplicity, which renders
our buildings at once folid and beautiful.

The hall has no other light than that admitted
at the doors, of which there are three very large
ones, that open into the China tower. This laft
firucture joins to the temple, and is of an octagonal
figure, each fide fifteen feet wide. A wall in the
fame form is built round it, at the diftance of two
fathoms and a half, and being of a moderate height,
fupports one fide of a penthoufe which iffues from
the tower, forming a pretty kind of gallery. The
tower is nine ftories high, each ftory being adorned
with a cornice three feet wide at the bottom of the
windows, and diftinguifhed by little penthoufes like
the former, but narrower, and like the tower, de-
creafing in breadth as they increafe in height. The
wall which, at the bottom, is at leaft twelve feet
thick, and above eight feet and a half at the top,
is all over incrufted with coarfe China ware, which
has in a great meafure retained its beauty, though
the tower has been erected three hundred years.
The flair cafe within is narrow, and the fteps
high. Each ftory has a room with a painted
ceiling, and in the walls of the upper rooms are
feveral fmall niches, in which are carved idols gilt.
The firft floor is the moft lofty, and all the reft of
an equal height. This tower, from the bottom of
the bafe to the top of the cupola rifes at leaft two
hundred feet from the ground. Towers of the fame
kind are erected in almoft every city, and are fome
of their greateft ornaments.

Nankin was once famous for the largenefs of its
bells ; but their weight brought the whole fteeple
to the ground. One of thefe which is ftill entire, is
eleven feet in height, and that of its ear is two feet,
and its outward circumference is twenty-two feet,

But this is nothing, when compared with feven bells at Pekin, caft 300 years ago, each of them weighing 120,000 pounds ; thefe are eleven feet wide, forty round, and twelve high, befides the ear, which is at leaft three feet : but as much as their bells exceed ours in fize, ours exceed theirs in found ; which is perhaps chiefly owing to their clappers being of wood. Thefe bells are ufed to diftinguifh the watches of the right, of which they ufually reckon five. They begin the firft with ftriking once, which they repeat a few moments after, and thus continue till the fecond watch, when they ftrike two ftrokes ; at the third watch they ftrike three, and fo on ; fo that thefe bells ferve as fo many repeating clocks, which every minute inform you of the time of night. For the fame purpofe they in the fame manner beat very large drums.

Of all the public works in China, none do the people fo much honour as their canals and bridges ; nor is any thing more worthy of the attention of the curious. [By means of thefe canals the whole trade of the empire is carried on, with the advantage of water carriage, and in this manner one may travel from Canton, the moft fouthern city, to Pekin the moft northern, without travelling above one day by land. This, which is called the great canal, is 160 leagues in length. The number of thefe canals is very furprifing ; they are often lined on each fide to the height of ten or twelve feet, with fine fquare ftone, and in fome places with a kind of marble of the colour of flate. The banks of fome of them are twenty or twenty-five feet high on each fide, and fome extend above ten leagues together in a ftraight line. But what moft charms the eye is the great number of beautiful imperial barks, loaded with the beft productions of different provinces ; many of them eighty tons burthen.]

As in an extent of 400 leagues in length, the earth cannot be every where level, there are feveral cata-

racts, where the water is precipitated with greater or
lefs violence, according to the difference of the level;
but the induftry of the Chinefe has found out a means
of remedying the inconveniences that might arife
from them with refpect to navigation. At each of
thefe waterfalls live a number of men, who are employed in raifing the barks. Thefe having drawn
cables to the right and left, to lay hold of the veffel,
in fuch a manner that it cannot efcape from them;
they have feveral capfterns, by the help of which they
raife it by little and little, till it be in the upper canal, and in a condition to continue its voyage.

In fome places where the waters of two canals have
no communication, they have a method of making
the boats pafs from one to the other, though the
level may be above 15 feet different. At the end of
the canal they have built a double floping bank of free-
ftone, which uniting at the top, extends on both fides
to the water of each canal. The bark is hoifted up
the flope by means of feveral capfterns, till being
raifed to the top, it flides down the other bank, like an
arrow fhot from a bow, and entering the other canal
fkurs away with prodigious fwiftnefs. There are no
fuch obftructions in the grand canal, and, indeed, the
emperor's barks, which are as large as our frigates,
could not be thus raifed.

[Thefe canals are at proper diftances covered with
bridges of three, five, or feven arches; that in the
middle is fometimes 36, and even 40 feet wide, and
fo high that barks may pafs through without taking
down their mafts; thofe on each fide are feldom lefs
than 30, and diminifh in proportion to the flopings
of the bridge. Some of thefe bridges have but one
arch, which is fometimes femi-circular, and built of
arched ftones, five or fix feet long, and only five or
fix inches thick. Thefe arches not being thick at the
top, cannot be ftrong; but then carts never pafs over
them; for the Chinefe make ufe of porters to carry their
bales. Several bridges have three or four great ftones

from 12 to 18 feet long placed on piers, like planks. There are a confiderable number of this fort neatly built over the great canal, whófe piers are fo narrow, that thefe bridges feem to hang in the air.

Many of thefe bridges are very handfome: one two leagues and a half from Pekin, was one of the fineft that ever was feen, before part of it was broken down by a land flood. The whole was of white marble. On each fide were feventy pillars, feparated by cartridges of fine marble, curioufly carved in flowers, foliages, birds, and feveral forts of animals. On each fide of the entrance at the eaft end were two lions of an extraordinary fize, on marble pedeftals, with feveral lions of ftone, fome climbing on the backs of the great ones, fome getting off them, and others creeping between their legs. At the weft end flood on marble pedeftals, the figures of two children, carved with the fame fkill.

One of the moft extraordinary bridges is built over the point of an arm of the fea. It is 2500 Chinefe feet in length, and 20 in breadth. It is fupported by 252 ftrong piers, 126 on each fide. All the ftones are of the fame bignefs, as well thofe laid from pier to pier, as thofe that are laid crofswife. It is difficult to conceive how ftones of fuch an enormous fize fhould be placed with fuch regularity, or even raifed to the top of fuch high piers.

In the way leading from Han-tchong-fou to the capital, the Chinefe have levelled mountains, and made bridges from one mountain to another, and when the vallies were too wide, they erected pillars to fupport them ; thefe bridges which form part of the road, are fo high, that one cannot look down without horror : four horfemen can ride abreaft upon them, and for the greater fecurity, they have rails on each fide.]

[Kircher obferves, that in the fame province is a bridge of one arch, extending from mountain to mountain, whofe length is 400 cubits, and its perpendicular height 500 above the Saffron river, which runs under it. Of this laſt aſtoniſhing ſtructure a better idea may perhaps be formed from the annexed plate, than from the moſt accurate verbal deſcription.]

To theſe extraordinary inſtances of induſtry, it will be proper to add, that the road from Signanfu to Hamtchoum, is ſaid to be one of the ſtrangeſt pieces of work in the world. I have been told, that upon the ſide of ſome mountains that are perpendicular, and have no ſhelving, the inhabitants have fixed large beams into them, upon which they have formed a kind of balcony without rails, extending along the ſides of ſeveral mountains. Thoſe unuſed to theſe kind of galleries, cannot travel over them without great apprehenſions ; but the people of the place who have mules uſed to theſe roads, travel with as little fear and concern over theſe ſteep and hideous precipices, as they could do in the plaineſt heath.

One cannot imagine the care that is taken of the common roads, theſe are as fine as poſſible, and are generally 80 feet broad. At about a mile and a half diſtance from each other, are erected wooden ſtructures about 30 feet high, reſembling triumphal arches, with three gates, over which is wrote upon a large frieze, in characters of an extraordinary ſize, the diſtance from the place you left, and how far it is to the town to which you are going.

The origin of the empire of China is as obſcure as the ſource of thoſe rivers that can ſcarce be diſcovered. The vulgar hiſtory of its monarchy. is indeed manifeſtly falſe, ſince forty thouſand years are ſuppoſed to have paſſed ſince its foundation : but according to their regular hiſtory, which none of their learned men ever queſtioned, China has had its kings for above four thouſand years. It ſeems probable that the children or grand children of Noah diſperſed themſelves into Aſia, and at length penetrated into the moſt weſterly part of China, where they

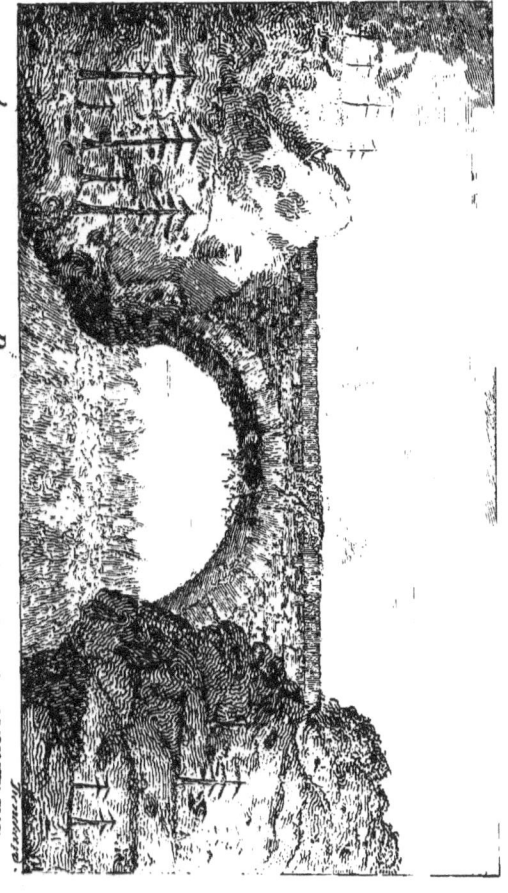

A REMARKABLE BRIDGE THAT JOINS TWO MOUNTAINS.

lived at the beginning in families, and the kings were fathers, to whom a long fucceffion of years, abundance of flocks, and other paftoral riches, added authority. The foundation of the monarchy was laid by Fohi, whofe wifdom, power, reputation and virtue, together with his great age, made the people liften to him as to an oracle. He regulated all private as well as political, and religious affairs ; thus the ftate foon became in a flourifhing condition. His fubjects at firft poffeffed the province of Honan, and fome years after all the lands and territories that extend as far to the fouth as the fea.

The people now principally applied themfelves to the education of their children, and to agriculture, for which they had the higheft efteem ; they were laborious to excefs. The judges and governors of provinces were grave and fober, and by the equity of their decifions gained the love and refpect of all the people ; while the emperor placed his higheft felicity in rendering his fubjects happy, and did not fo much confider himfelf the fovereign of a grand empire, as the father of a numerous family. By this means the Chinefe acquired fuch reputation, that they were confidered by all the neighbouring nations as the oracles of wifdom ; and it is probable that from their firft origin they confidered themfelves as fuperior to all other men ; an opin on which they ftill entertained after they had fuffered as great revolutions in morals as in politics ; and became fo vain, that they fancied heaven had placed them in the centre of the univerfe to give laws to mankind, the wretched outcafts who had been placed on the extremities of the creation, and who had fcarcely the human form. But perceiving the Europeans inftructed in all the fciences, they were ftruck with aftonifhment. How can it be poffible, faid they, that a people fo far remote from us, fhould have any wit or capacity ? they have never perufed our books; they were never inftructed by us, and yet like us,

they ſpeak and reaſon right. On ſeeing our ſtuffs,
clocks, watches, and mathematical inſtruments, their
ſurprize encreaſed ; for they had imagined that expert artificers were no where to be found but in China.
They ſaw that we were not ſo barbarous as they had
imagined, and in a joking way cried, " We ſuppoſed
" all other people to be blind, and that nature had
" beſtowed eyes upon none but the Chineſe ; that is
" not univerſally true ; for though the Europeans
" do not ſee ſo clearly as we, they have at leaſt each
" of them one eye."

The countenance, air, language, diſpoſition and
manners of the Chineſe, differ not only from ours,
but alſo from thoſe of all other nations. Of the perſons of the Chineſe in general we may form a pretty
diſtinct idea, by conſidering that they entertain of
beauty. They would have a man to be tall and fat,
with a broad forehead, ſmall eyes, a ſhort noſe,
great ears, a mouth of a middling ſize, a long beard,
and black hair. They are naturally as fair as we,
eſpecially towards the north ; but their faces being
continually expoſed to the ſun, commonly renders
them as tawny as the Portugueſe in the Indies.
Thoſe in the ſouthern provinces are of an olive complexion. The learned, eſpecially if of baſe extraction,
never pare the nails of their little fingers, letting
them grow an inch long or more, to ſhew that they
are not driven by neceſſity to work for their living.

The men ſhave their heads all over, except the
crown, where they ſuffer a long lock to grow ; but
they continually wear a bonnet or cap, which civility
forbids their pulling off. That worn in ſummer is
in the form of a cone, round below and above terminating in a point. It is lined with ſatin, and the
top covered with a fine mat, much worn in the
country : to which they add a piece of red ſilk, that
falls round about it and reaches to the edges ; but
when they walk, this ſilk flows irregularly on all
ſides, and the continual motion of the head gives it

a particular pleafing grace. Sometimes inftead of filk they wear long hair of a vivid fhining red, and this is more efpecially ufed when they ride. This hair grows upon the legs of certain cows, and is naturally white ; but they give it a tincture that makes it dearer than the fineft filk. In winter they wear a plufh cap, bordered with fable or fox-fkin ; the reft is of fine black or purple fatin, covered with a flake of red filk like fatin. Nothing can be hand-fomer than their caps; but they are fo fhallow, that they always difcover the ears. When the mandarines are dreffed in their formalities, the upper part of the bonnet has a diamond, or fome other precious ftone ill cut, but inchafed in a gold button very curioufly wrought.

Their habit confifts of a veft that reaches to the ground, the fkirts or fides of which are folded before, in fuch a manner that the uppermoft is extended to the left fide, where it is faftened by four or five gold or filver buttons. Their fleeves are wide towards the fhoulder, but grow narrow to the wrift. They in a manner cover the whole hand, leaving nothing to be feen but the fingers ends. They keep the veft clofe about the body with a broad filk fafh, the two ends of which hang down to their knees. The Tartars ftick a handkerchief to it on each fide, with a fheath for a knife and fork ; a purfe, a tooth-pick, and other things. In fummer they have the neck quite bare ; but in winter they cover it with a fatin collar faftened to the veft, or with a tippet of fable or fox fkin, about three or four fingers broad, faften-ed before with a button.

Over this they wear an upper garment with fhort wide fleeves like thofe of the barrifters gowns ; the ftudents wear them very long ; but the gentlemen, and efpecially the Tartars, have them fhort. As for their under garment, they ufe in fummer, only a fingle pair of drawers of white taffety, under a very broad fhort fhirt of the fame ftuff; but in winter they

have a linen fhirt, and under it breeches of coarfe
fatin, quilted with cotton or raw filk. But what appears more extraordinary, the Chinefe are always
booted, and when any one pays them a vifit, they
make them wait till they have drawn them on. The
form of thefe boots is fomewhat different from ours:
thofe made for riding long journeys are of leather,
or thick, black, pinked cotton ; but in the city they
ufually wear them of fatin, with a coarfe border of
plufh or velvet upon the knee ; befides they have no
heels. Thefe boots are fo extremely hot and cumberfome in fummer, that no people befides the Chinefe
would be able to endure them, and indeed the working people fcarce ever wear them. Thefe people in
public, and perfons of quality within doors, inftead of
fhoes, wear a kind of flippers of black linen, or fome
pretty filk, made to fit clofe to the foot by a border
that covers the heel. Befides their ufual garments
they fometimes travel in an upper coat of a kind of
green oil-cloth made of coarfe taffety. The mourning
habit is fomewhat fingular, the bonnet, veft, furtout,
ftockings and boots being made of white linen, and
from the prince to the handicraftsman, none dare wear
any other colour.

Ridiculous as this drefs may appear to us, ours
appears much more extravagant to them ; in particular the large curling peruke is a conftant fubject of
ridicule ; on this account they look upon us as no
wifer than a foolifh fet of people, who for want of a
beard, fhould get an artificial one clapped to their
chin, that fhould reach down to their knees. This
phantaftical head-drefs, fay they, with that prodigious
heap of curled hair may be proper upon the ftage,
for a man that would reprefent the devil : but no
perfon can have the form of a man who is thus dif-
guifed. On the other hand, nothing can perfuade
them that the difcovery of long fhanks, with a ftock-
ing drawn ftraight, and clofe breeches, can look either
grave or handfome.

As to the women, they have little eyes, fhort nofes, and pretty fair complexions, which they take great care to preferve. A little collar of white fatin faftened to a veit covers the neck all over. Their hands are always hid in long fleeves Their head-drefs ufually confifts of feveral locks buckled up, and interlaced with flowers of gold and filver. They, as well as the men, wear a long veft of red, blue or green fatin or cloth of gold ; but the elderly ladies drefs in purple or black. Over this they have an upper garment, the fleeves of which are extremely wide, and trail upon the ground, when they have no occafion to hold them up. But what diftinguifhes them from all the women in the world, is the fmallnefs of their feet, in which lies the moft effential part of their beauty.

The girls are no fooner born, than the nurfes take care to tye their feet extremely hard, for fear of their growing ; but what appears moft furprizing is, that this violence offered to nature, does not feem to impair their health. Their fhoes of fatin, embroidered with gold, filver, and filk, are extremely neat; and though they are exceedingly fmall, yet they ftudy to fhew them as they walk ; for walk they do, though one would fcarce believe it poffible, and indeed would willingly walk all day long, had they the liberty to go abroad.

When perfons of quality pay vifits, when they are upon journeys, or when they wait upon the emperor, they always appear with a grandeur that fills a ftranger with aftonifhment. The mandarines richly dreffed, are carried in an open gilt fedan, upon the fhoulders of eight or fixteen perfons, accompanied by all the officers of the tribunal, who furround them with umbrellas, and other marks of their dignity. Some walk two and two before them, bearing chains, rods and efcutcheons of varnifhed wood, upon which are in large gold characters all the titles of honour annexed to their places of truft, with a bafon on

which they beat a certain number of ſtrokes, according to the rank they bear in the province. Other
officers follow in the fame order, and fometimes
four or five gentlemen on horſeback bring up the
rear.

Thoſe that belong to the army commonly go on
horſeback, and if they are of confiderable rank, appear at the head of 25 or 30 men well mounted.
The princes of the blood at Pekin, are preceded by
four of their officers, and followed by a ſquadron of
troops that march without order. The domeſtics
wear no liveries, but according to the quality of their
maſter are dreſſed in black ſatin or painted linen.
Though their horſes are neither fine nor well managed
their trappings and harneſſes are very magnificent;
the bit, bridle, and ſtirrups are gilt, or elſe of ſilver.
Inſtead of leather they make bridles of two or three
twiſts of courſe pinked ſatin two fingers broad. Under the horſe's neck hang two great taſſels of that
curious red hair they wear on their bonnets, which
are faſtened to two very large braſs buttons, gilt or
waſhed with ſilver, hung at rings of the fame metal.

The mandarines appear with the greateſt magnificence when they travel by water: their barges are of
a prodigious ſize adorned with carving, painting,
gilding, and decorated with their arms, flags, and
ſtreamers.

The emperors of China never appear in public
without that ſplendor that may be neceſſary to attract
the reſpect and veneration of the people. They formerly ſeldom ſhewed themſelves; but the Tartars,
who at preſent poſſeſs the throne, take more popular
meaſures. The preſent emperor never marches, but
at the head, or in the midſt of an army, accompanied
by all the lords of the court. Nothing is to be ſeen
but ſilks, gildings, and precious ſtones: the arms
the harneſs of the horſes, the umbrellas, the ſtreamers, and a thouſand other badges of the royal dignity,
or of the particular quality of the princes, ſparkle

Every one, on thefe occafions, knows
rank, and that man would lofe his
t his fortune, who fhould prefume to
order of the march,
kes a progrefs through the provinces
he commonly rides poft, attended
:s who are his confidents, and a few
all the cities, and at all the difficult
iny troops are drawn up in order of
feems to ride poft hafte through an

:s goes into Tartary to take the di-
ing, when he is attended by an army
who endure great hardfhips, and in
)ilfome huntings there fometimes die
an he would lofe in a pitched battle;
the lofs of 10,000 horfes as nothing.
:s attended by thirty or forty petty
ces who come to pay him tribute,
cafions the train, habits, and tents of
are furprifingly magnificent.
oes the emperor difplay greater fplen-
pomp with which he goes to the tem-
rifices to heaven. The particulars of
ave been given by Father Magalhens,
re worthy to be repeated here, as the
in all public ceremonies in China, is
t the very emperor dares not add or
ft article. It begins with twenty-four
ned with gold coronets, and twenty-
ch ranked in two files; twenty-four
; fix or eight feet long, varnifhed and
the fame order. Then come 100
halberts, on each of which is a femi-
n the form of a crefcent, followed by
mace, and two officers bearing pikes
d varnifh, with flowers, and figures in
)ear 400 lantherns curioufiy wrought,
of a gilt wood that flames like our

torches, 200 lances charged with huge tufts of filk, twenty-four banners on which are painted the figns of the Zodiac, and fifty fix others that reprefent the celeftial conftellations: there are alfo to be feen 200 large fans, with the figures of dragons and other animals; 24 umbrellas ftill more magnificent, and a kind of beaufet filled with utenfils of gold, and borne by the officers of his palace. The emperor then appears on horfeback, richly dreffed, furrounded by the white horfes, whofe harnefs is covered with gold and precious ftones, and by 100 of his life-guards and pages, who bear an umbrella that fhades him and the horfe, and dazzles the fight with all the ornaments that man could poffibly invent. The emperor is followed by all the princes of the blood, by the mandarines of the firft order, by the viceroys and principal lords of the court, all in their formalities. After them appear 500 young gentlemen of quality, attended by 1000 footmen, dreffed in carnation filk bordered with flowers, and fpotted with ftars of gold and filver. Immediately after appear thirty-fix bearing an open triumphal chariot, and 120 bearers fupport another clofe one, fo large, that it might be taken for an entire apartment. Then come four chariots, the two firft drawn by elephants, and the other two by horfes, each of thefe carriages is guarded by a company of fifty men: the charioteers of the four laft are richly dreffed, and the elephants as well as the horfes are covered with embroidered houfings. At length this pompous cavalcade is clofed by 2000 mandarine officers, and 2000 officers of the army all in rich habits, and marching with a folemn gravity. The court is not at much expence for this pomp; for whenever the emperor is pleafed to make known his intention to offer facrifice, they are always ready to attend him.

But notwithftanding this parade, the houfes of the great have neither looking-glaffes, tapeftry, hangings, nor wrought chairs; and even gildings are only

uſed in the apartments of the emperor and princes
of the blood : all their magnificence conſiſts in their
cabinets, tables, and varniſhed ſkreens, in their pictures, which are not very extraordinary, and in having ſeveral pieces of white ſatin inſcribed with a moral ſentence on each in large characters, hung here
and there in the chamber. Beſides theſe, porcelain
or China ware is the ornament of every houſe ; it is
found on the tables, ſide-boards, and even in the
kitchen ; for theſe are the ordinary veſſels, out of
which they eat and drink. There are likewiſe many
huge flower-pots of it. The very architects cover
roofs with it, and ſometimes make uſe of it to incruſt
buildings.

The Chineſe painters are very deficient in the art
of drawing, particularly of human figures, and they
have a very imperfect knowledge of perſpective.
Though ſtrangers are not admitted into the bed-chambers, yet their beds are very fine ; in ſummer they
have taffety curtains powdered with flowers, trees,
and birds, in gold, ſilk, and embroidery. Others
have curtains of the fineſt gauze. In winter they make
uſe of coarſe ſatin worked with dragons, and other
figures ; and their counterpanes are in the ſame taſte.
They ſleep on thick cotton quilts inſtead of feather
beds ; and their bed-ſteads are joiner's work, ſometimes finely wrought in figures.

The emperor's authority is unbounded : he is almoſt adored by his people, who ſtile him the ſon of
heaven, and the only maſter of the world. His
words are conſidered as oracles ; he is ſeldom ſeen,
and never ſpoke to but on the knee. In which poſ-
ture the grandees of the court, the princes of the
blood, nay, his own brothers bow to the ground, not
only when he is preſent, but even before his throne.
All places in the empire are at his diſpoſal, he confers them on whom he thinks fit, and none of them
are ever ſold ; honeſty, learning, long experience,

and a grave and fober behaviour are the only qualifica-
tions in the candidates; but if he diflikes their management, he difmiffes them without ceremony. He has
even the liberty of chufing his fucceffor, whom he
may nominate not only from the royal family, but
from amongft the pooreft of his fubjects. The old
law-givers have from the firft foundation of the go-
vérnment, made it a ftanding maxim, that a king is
the father of his people, and not the mafter of flaves.
This title they therefore efteem the greateft honour.

    Yet every mandarine may tell the emperor of his
faults, provided it be in a fubmiffive manner : and
if he has any regard for his reputation, the manner
in which their hiftories are written, is alone fufficient to keep him in due bounds. A certain number
of men, who from their learning and impartiality are
chofen to this office, obferve all his words and actions,
having feparately wrote their remarks without confulting each other, on a loofe flip of paper, each puts
it through a chink into an office appointed for that
purpofe. '' Such a day, fay they, his behaviour
'' was unfeafonable and intemperate ; he fpoke after
'' a manner that did not become his dignity. The
'' punifhment he inflicted on fuch an offender, was
'' rather the refult of paffion, than of juftice.'' Or
'' elfe, '' He gave fuch and fuch marks of his love
'' to his people. Notwithftanding the commenda-
'' tions of his flatterers, he was not puffed up, but
'' behaved with his ufual modefty ; his words were
'' tempered with fweetnefs.''

    That thefe men may be neither biaffed by fear
nor hope, this office is never opened during the
prince's life, or while any of his family fit on the
throne : but when the crown goes to another line,
which often happens, thefe loofe memoirs are gathered together, and by comparing them they compofe
the hiftory of that emperor, to propofe him as an
example to pofterity, if he has acted wifely, or to

expofe him to the public cenfure, if he has been
negligent of his own duty, or the good of his
people.

The emperor has two fovereign councils ; one
compofed of the princes of the blood alone, and the
other into which the minifters of ftate are alfo admitted. Befides thefe there are at Pekin fix fovereign
courts, whofe authority extends over all the provinces of China, and who have different apartments
affigned them. One prefides over all the mandarines ;
another has the management of the treafury, and
the care of raifing the taxes : another has the care of
religion, arts, fciences, and foreign affairs ; another
prefides over the army ; another over the public
buildings and palaces, and another takes cognizance
of all criminals. In each of thefe courts is a cenfor,
who, though he is not of the council, is prefent at
all the affemblies, and accufes the mandarines for the
faults they commit both in their private capacities
and in the execution of their office. 'Tis faid, that
he who undertakes this office can never accept of
another, that the hope of preferment may never
tempt him to be partial to any one, nor the fear of
lofing his place deter him from accufing the guilty.
Of thefe officers even the princes of the blood ftand
in awe.

The provinces are under the immediate infpection
of two forts of viceroys ; one fort has the government of only one province ; and the other have
under their jurifdiction, two or three, and fometimes four provinces, all of whom have courts of
the fame nature as thofe of Pekin, but are fubordinate to them. The viceroy, in whom refides the
imperial authority, convenes the principal mandarines of his province to take cognizance of the good
or bad qualities of the governors, lieutenants, and
inferior officers, and privately informs the emperor
of thofe who mifbehave themfelves, who are either
deprived of their offices or cited to appear and juftify

their conduct.　On the other hand the power of the viceroy is counterpoifed by that of the great mandarines, who may accufe him when he acts inconfiftently with the good of the public, and even the people when oppreffed by him, may petition the emperor for his removal.　The leaft infurrection is laid at his door, which if it continues three days he muft anfwer for at his peril.　It is his fault, fay the laws, if difturbances fpring up in his family, that is, in the province over which he has the charge.

[Caufes are generally decided and fentence given by a fingle mandarine, who, after a fhort procefs, and the examination of both parties, orders the lofer to be baftinadoed, either for carrying on an unjuft profecution, or maintaining a caufe contrary to equity.　This is the common punifhment for the meaner fort ; but cannot be inflicted on a mandarine, till he is deprived of his office.

The next punifhment is a collar, made of two pieces of wood hollowed in the middle, and fmaller or greater, according to the nature of the crime; this is put on the delinquent's neck, and fealed with the feal of the tribunal with a piece of paper denoting the nature of the crime, and the duration of the punifhment.]

Thefe, except imprifonment, are all the punifhments, which the Chinefe laws permit the mandarines to inflict on criminals: they may indeed condemn to exile ; but their fentence muft be examined by the fupreme courts.　The capital punifhments are ftrangling.　Mean and ignoble perfons are beheaded ; for in China the feparation of the head from the body is difgraceful.　On the contrary perfons of quality are ftrangled, which is a more honourable death : but if their crimes are very great, they are punifhed like mean perfons, and fometimes their heads are cut off, and hung on a tree in the highway.　Rebels, traitors, the children who murder a parent, and the fervants who murder their mafter are cut in pieces. After the executioner has tied them to a poft, he cuts the fkin of their foreheads, and tears it by force till it hangs over their eyes, that they may not fee the torments they are to endure. Afterwards he cuts off the flefh from their bodies wherever he thinks fit, and when tired of this barbarous employment, he leaves them to the tyranny of their enemies, and the infults of the mob.

As the emperor is confidered as the father of his people, the greateft refpect is paid to the parental authority, and one cannot imagine how far this firft principle of nature is carried. There is no fubmif-fion, no point of obedience which a father cannot com-mand, he is an abfolute fovereign in his own family while he lives, and at his death, is honoured as a God. He is not only abfolute mafter of his eftate, which he may diftribute to whom he pleafes; but alfo of his concubines and children, whom he may even fell to ftrangers, if their behaviour difpleafes him; and if a father accufes his fon of any crime before a mandarine, there needs no proof of it; for if a father complains, they make no doubt but that the fon is in the fault. If a fon is fo wicked as to mock his parents, or if he arrives at fuch a height of madnefs as to lay vi-olent hands on them; the province where it is done is alarmed: the emperor himfelf judges the criminal: all the mandarines near the place are turned out, efpecially thofe of that town, who have been fo negli-gent in their inftructions. The neighbours are all reprimanded for neglecting, by former punifhments, to ftop the iniquity of the criminal before it arofe to fuch a height; for they fuppofe fuch a diabolical dif-pofition muft have fhewn itfelf on other occafions, and that it is impoffible to arrive at fuch a pitch of wicked-nefs at once. As to the criminal, they caufe him to be cut in a thoufand pieces; they burn his mangled corpfe, deftroy his houfe to the ground, and even thofe that ftand near it, and fet up monuments and memorials of fo horrid an action.

To preferve peace and order, the utmoft modefty and civility are inculcated ; they have prefcribed forms of falutation and addrefs, and in paying vifits a great number of troublefome ceremonies, kneeling, cringing and geftures are to be obferved. Their feafts are ceremonious even to the moft extravagant and ridiculous excefs.

Every gueft has a feparate table without table-cloth, napkin, knife or fpoon ; for every thing is ready to cut their hands ; and they never touch any thing but with two little inftruments tipped with filver, which the Chinefe handle very dexteroufly. They begin their feafts with drinking wine, which is given to every gueft at one and the fame time, in a fmall filver or China cup, which all the guefts lift with both hands as high as their heads, thus pre-fenting their fervice to each other without fpeaking, and inviting each other to drink firft. After the firft cup a large veffel of hafhed meat is fet on the table. Then every one obferves the motions of the mafter of the feaft, according as he gives the fign, they take their two little inftruments, brandifh them in the air, and after twenty different motions, ftrike them into the difh, from which they bring up a piece of meat, which muft neither be eaten too haftily nor too flowly : in all this you muft obferve time, that all may begin and eat at once. Soon wine is again brought, which is drank with the fame ceremonies as before. Then comes a fecond mefs, which they dip into as into the firft, and thus the feaft is continued, drinking between every mouthful, till there have been twenty or twenty-four different difhes at table, and they have drank as many cups of wine ; but they drink as little as they will at a time, and their wine is fmall. When all the difhes are ferved, no more wine is brought, and the guefts may take out of any of the difhes before them ; but it muft be done when the reft of the guefts take out of fome of the difhes ; for order and uniformity are held facred.

At this time they bring in rice and bread ; for as yet nothing but meat has been brought ; they alfo bring fine broths made of flefh or fifh, in which the guefts may mingle their rice. They fit at table grave and filent, till the mafter feeing them all done gives the fign to rife, on which they retire into the hall or garden ; but in about a quarter of an hour return, when they find the tables covered with fweetmeats and dried fruit, which they keep to eat with their tea. This entertainment is followed by the entrance of a company of ftrollers, who act a long tedious play.

The Chinefe have alfo their folemn feafts, which they celebrate with great pomp. One of the principal of thefe is on the 15th day of the firft month, called the feaft of lanthorns, from the multitude and grandeur of the lanthorns exhibited in the evening ; many grandees retrenching every year fomethings from their tables, apparel, and equipage, to fhew the greater magnificence in the lanthorns ufed on this occafion, fome of which coft 2000 crowns. The largeft are above twenty feet in diameter, and are lighted by an immenfe number of wax candles and lamps: but thofe that are more common are of a middling fize. Thefe are generally compofed of fix faces, or panes, each of which has a frame of varnifhed wood adorned with gildings, four feet high, a foot and a half broad, covered on the infide with fine tranfparent filk, on which is painted flowers, trees, rocks, and fometimes human figures. The painting is very curious, the colours lively, and the wax-candles give the painting a beautiful fplendor. Thefe fix pannels joined together, compofe an hexagon, furmounted at the extremities by fix carved figures that form its crown. Around it are hung broad ftrings of fatin of all colours, with other filken ornaments, that fall upon the angles without hiding the light or the pictures. The feaft of lanthorns is alfo celebrated by bonfires and fireworks, which though very agreeable, are far from being fo fine as fome authors have reprefented them.

Notwithftanding the excellent conftitution of the Chinefe government which teaches all the rules of civility, the people are far from being remarkable for humanity add integrity. Though gaming be forbidden to perfons in all ranks, it does not hinder the Chinefe from playing fo long till they have loft all their eftate, their houfes, their children, and their wives, which they fometimes hazard on a card ; for there is no degree of extravagance to which avarice will not carry them ; but they take great care to conceal their gaming.

The men do not follow their own tafte in the choice of a wife ; for they never fee her before-hand, but take her parents word, or that of fome old women, who are a kind of infpectors, and are employed for that purpofe ; but are in general in fee with the girl's parents, who reap an advantage from their daughter's being thought beautiful, witty, or genteel : for as the Chinefe buy their wives, they give more or lefs, according to their fuppofed good qualities, The parties having agreed on the price, the contract being made, and the money paid down, both fides prepare for the marriage. When the day arrives, the bride is carried in a fumptuous chair, preceded by hautboys, drums and fifes, and followed by her parents, relations and friends. All the portion given by her father is her clothes, and fome houfhold goods. The bridegroom ftands at his door richly drefled to receive her : he opens the fedan, and having conducted her into a chamber, delivers her to feveral women invited thither for that purpofe, who fpend the day together in feafting and fports, while the hufband entertains his friends in another room. This being the firft time in which the bride and bridegroom fee each other, both, or one of them frequently difliking their bargain, it is a day of rejoicing to their guefts, but of forrow to themfelves. The woman muft fubmit, though fhe don't like the man ; but the hufband is not always fo complaifant; for fome on opening the chair to receive the bride, repulfed by her fhape and afpect, have fhut it again, and fent her back to her friends, chofing rather to lofe their money than take pofleffion of fo bad a purchafe.

When the Tartars in the late war took Nankin, they formed a defign which made the Chinefe merry, notwithftanding all their misfortunes. Among the diforders committed by the victors they endeavoured to feize upon all the women of the province, in order to make money of them ; they carried them to that city; and fhut them up together in the magazines with other goods. As they were of all ages and degrees of beauty, they refolved to put them into facks ; to carry them to market, and to fell the difagreeable and the handfome at the fame price, without the facks being opened. Two crowns were the value fet on each fack, for which the purchafer in this lottery was to have the chance of obtaining a woman either in the bloom of youth, a matron, or a wife wrinkled with age. Thus did thefe foldiers, ever infolent in profperity, abufe their victory, and fhew themfelves more barbarous in one of the moft polite cities in the world than they had been in the deferts of Tartary.

On the day of fale there was no want of purchafers. Some came with the hopes of recovering their own wives and children, who were among the captives, and others were led thither with the flattering expectation that fortune would favour them, and that for fo trifling a fum they might obtain a woman blooming with youth and beauty. In fhort, the novelty of this affair brought a great concourfe from all the adjacent parts. An ordinary fellow who had but two crowns in the world, purchafed a fack like the reft, and carried it off; but was no fooner out of the crowd, than curiofity, or a defire to relieve the perfon in his fack, made him liften to her entreaties, and he could not forbear to open it. When, to his amazement and confufion he found it contained an old woman, whom age, grief, and ill treatment had rendered extremely difagreeable. In the firft tranf-port of his rage he refolved to throw both the woman and the fack into the river, and thus to comfort him-felf for the lofs of his money, by the barbarous gra-tification of his revenge on the innocent caufe of his vexation. But fhe inftantly ftopped his hand. Son, faid fhe, be of good cheer, your lot is not fo bad as you imagine ; take care of my life, and I will render your's happy. Somewhat pacified at thefe words, he took her into a houfe hard by, where fhe let him know that fhe belonged to a mandarine of note in the neighbourhood, to whom fhe wrote im-mediately. He fent her an equipage agreeable to her quality ; fhe carried her deliverer along with her, and was afterwards fo good a friend to him, that he had never reafon to complain of his having laid out two crowns in the purchafe.

But to proceed, a hufband cannot divorce his wife, except for adultery, and in a few other cafes that feldom happen ; the hufband may then fell his wife ; but if he difpofes of her without juft reafon, both the buyer and feller are feverely punifhed : yet the hufband is not obliged to take her again. The Chi-nefe are generally fo extremely jealous, that they will not fuffer their wives to be a moment in private even with their own brothers. The men may have as many concubines as they pleafe, and their children have an equal claim to the eftate ; they are indeed efteemed the children of the wife, and they accord-ingly call her mother. She indeed is the fole miftrefs of the houfe ; and the concubines ferve and honour her.

Yet the people who are diftreffed by want are per-mitted to expofe their children. Thus when the family feels the diftrefs of penury, when the mother falls fick, or when fhe has no milk, it is common to condemn the poor helplefs innocent to perifh in the

ftreets ; and frequently they are fo void of humanity
as to engage their midwives to ftifle the females in a
bafon of water, as foon as they are born, In all this
the Chinefe, notwithftanding their boafted politenefs,
are as favage as the untutored Hottentots.

[As the whole frame of the Chinefe government
is founded on filial piety, they pay the greateft honour to their deceafed parents. The ufual time of
mourning is three years ; but it is commonly reduced
to 27 months, during which they cannot exercife any
public office: fo that a mandarine is obliged to quit
his government ; to live retired, and give himfelf up
to grief. The mourning colour is white. The funeral
is pompous and expenfive, and a fon will fometimes
fell himfelf to buy a magnificent coffin for his father.
They are prohibited from burying their dead within
the walls of a city, but are permitted to keep them in
their houfes, which they often do for feveral months,
and even years, enclofed in their rich coffins daubed
on the infide with pitch, and without japaned : however, if a fon does not, at laft, caufe the corpfe of
his father to be laid in the tomb of his anceftors,
however diftant it may be, he will lofe his reputation.]

The Chinefe are Pagans of feveral fects ; one of
the principal of which is compofed of the worfhip-
pers of Foe or Fo; a religion brought from India.
Thefe believe tranfmigration, and their bonzes, or
priefts, who are frequently great hypocrites, grofly
impofe on the credulity of the people. Two of thefe
bonzes one day feeing two large ducks in a rich
farmer's yard, fell on their faces before the door,
and burfting into bitter lamentations, the good
woman, who faw them from the chamber window,
came down to afk the caufe of their affliction. They
informed her, that the fouls of their fathers inhabited the bodies of thofe creatures, and that the dread
of her killing them, was what they could not fupport.
The woman anfwered that fhe intended to fell them,

but as they were their fathers, fhe would keep them
fafe. But, perhaps, faid the bonzes, your hufband
will not be fo charitable, and then if any accident
fhould happen to them it would kill us. At laft,
after a long difcourfe, the good woman was fo far
moved by their tears and importunity, that to comfort them, fhe committed the ducks to their care,
and allowed them to keep them for fome time. They
took them with the appearance of the greateft refpect ; and proftrated themfelves before the uncon-
fcious ducks ; but that very evening made an entertainment for fome others of their order, and the
ducks were eaten for fupper.

They likewife get money from the people by
public acts of penance, which are fure to procure
them the efteem and compaffion of the ignorant
multitude. I have feen them dragging a long iron
chain, as thick as one's arm, and about thirty feet
long, faftened to their neck or legs. Thus it is,
fay they, at every door as they pafs, that we expiate
your faults, and fure this deferves fome alms. Others
in public places ftrike their heads with large bricks,
till they are almoft covered with blood. One day I
met in the middle of a town, a young bonze, of a
good mien, and with fuch an ingenuous and modeft
look as might eafily move compaffion. He ftood
upright in a fort of fedan, the infide of which was
like a barrow, full of nails with the points ftick-
ing inwards, fo that he could bend no way without
being wounded. Two fellows were hired to carry
him from houfe to houfe, while he endeavoured to
excite compaffion, by telling the people that he was
fhut up in that chair for the good of their fouls, and
was refolved never to leave it till they had bought
all the nails, of which there were above 2000, at the
value of fix-pence each ; the fmalleft of which, he
faid, would derive incomparable bleffings on themfelves and families ; fince their charity would be
beftowed on the god Fo, to whofe honour, they

were going to build a temple. The bonze directing this difcourfe to me, I advifed him to leave his prifon, and go to the temple of the true God, to be inftructed in heavenly truths, where he might fubmit to penances lefs fevere, but more wholefome. He calmly replied, that he was obliged to me for my advice ; but would be much more fo, if I would buy a dozen of his nails, which would certainly procure me a good journey. Here, hold your hand, faid he, take thefe, on the faith of a bonze, they are the beft in all my fedan for they prick me the moft, yet you fhall have them at the fame rate, at which I fell the others. The tone in which he uttered thefe words would, on another occafion, have made me laugh ; but I left him with a mixture of pity and contempt.

The Chinefe are, however, fometimes weary of paying ufelefs addreffes to their idols, which are very numerous: for it often happens, that if after wor- fhipping them a great while, the people do not obtain the blefling they defire, they ufe them in the moft reproachful manner ; fome load them with hard names, and others with hard blows: We lodge you, fay they, in a magnificent temple, we cover you with gold, and offer to you food and incenfe, and after all you are fo ungrateful as to refufe our requefts. They then tie the idol with cords, pluck it down, drag it along the ftreets, through all the mud and dunghills. Yet if they foon after obtain their defire, they then take the idol, and with great ceremony carry it back, and place it again on its niche, after they have wafhed it clean, fallen down before it, and made excufes for what they have done ; promifing that if it will forget what is paft, they will gild it again.

Thefe fects are, however, only tolerated ; the re- ligion of the court, and that of the mandarines, confifts in following the precepts and doctrines of Confufius, an excellent moral philofopher, and thofe of the other fages of antiquity ; which they have intermixed with many idolatrous and fuperſtitious cuſtoms. They are far from abſtaining from fleſh, and almoſt all the people, not only feed on the animals that are uſually eaten in other countries ; but on cats, dogs, and horſes; and even on ſuch creatures as die of themſelves ; though their principal food is hogs.

The Chineſe in writing do not uſe pens made of quills, like the Europeans, nor canes or reeds like the Arabians, nor crayons like the Siameſe ; but only hair pencils. When they ſit down to write, they have upon the table a piece of poliſhed marble, with a hollow at one end that contains a little water, into which dipping a ſtick of Indian ink, they rub it upon the ſmooth part of the marble, and into the liquid ink thus made, dip their pencil. Every word has a different character ; for they have no idea of expreſſing ſounds on paper, by the letters of an alphabet. They write from the right to the left, and end their books where we begin ours ; ſo that our laſt page ſtands in the place of their firſt.

The Chineſe paper is made of the inner bark of the bamboo, which is ſoft and white : this they beat in clear water ; after which it is formed into ſheets by being taken up in long and broad frames. Some of theſe ſheets are ten or twelve feet long ; they are exceeding white and ſmooth, and each ſheet is dipped into alum water, inſtead of ſize. They have alſo paper made of cotton, which is, indeed, the whiteſt, fineſt and moſt uſed.

Printing, which is in a manner in its infancy in Europe, has been uſed from all antiquity in China: but their manner of printing is very different from ours. As they have no letters, they are obliged to cut the marks which ſtand for words on even blocks of wood. He who intends to print a book has it fairly wrote, and then the wood cutter glues each leaf upon an even ſmooth pear-tree board, and cuts out whatever is not to appear when printed, leaving the characters as perfect as thofe of the original. Having thus prepared the block, they rub it over with a brufh dipped in ink, and placing the paper upon it, they rub a dry brufh gently over the back of the paper, preffing it down a little, that it may imbibe the ink, and take the impreffion. All this is done with great expedition. They print only on the one fide of the leaf, and finifh a whole book in the manner here defcribed ; after which it is bound, and covered either with a neat fort of grey pafteboard, or with fine fatin or flowered filk, which coft little, and fome are covered by the binders with red brocade, interfpered with gold and filver flowers.

The Chinefe have a variety of books on morality, medicine, of agriculture, of plants, of the military art, of hiftory, aftronomy, philofophy, and the mechanic arts; romances, comedies, tragedies, and abundance of treatifes compofed by the bonzes, on the worfhip of the deities of the country : fo that fome of their public libraries are faid to contain 30,000 volumns.

The Chinefe are well fkilled in the management of the filk-worm, and in raifing and manufacturing the richeft filks ; in making cabinets refembling thofe of Japan; and are particularly famous for their porcelain, fo well known in Europe by the name of China.

Among the other inftances of their ingenuity, that practifed in fifhing appears not the leaft extraordinary. Befides, the line, nets, and the ordinary inftruments ufed in Europe, which they employ as well as we, they have two methods that appear extremely odd. The one is practifed in the night by moonfhine; they take two long ftraight boats, and nail the fides from one end to the other, a board about two feet broad, painted white, and finely varnifhed. This plank flopes outward, and almoft touches the furface of the water ; in order to anfwer their purpofe, they turn towards the moon, that the reflection of that luminary my increafe its brightnefs :

when the fifh playing and miftaking its colour, for that of the water, fpring up towards it and either fall upon it, or into the boat. So that the filher-men with very little trouble foon fill their boat.

The fecond manner of fifhing feems at firft equally furprifing : as the Europeans and others breed up hawks to fly at the game, and catch birds, they train cormorants to catch fifh : one fifherman can eafily look after a hundred of them : he keeps them perched on the fides of his boat, waiting patiently for their orders, till they are come to the place defigned for fifhing in, and then at the firft fignal each takes its flight, and flies the way affigned it. It is pleafant to fee them divide amongft themfelves the whole breadth of the river, or of the lake : they feek up and down, they dive, come up again, and hover over the water till they perceive their prey ; when they inftantly dart upon it, feize it with their beak, and bring it to their mafter. When the fifh is too big, they help one another interchangeably, one taking it by the tail and another by the head, in which manner they carry it to the boat, where the men hold out long oars or ftrong canes for them, on which they pereh with their fifh, which they do not part with till they go in fearch of others. When they are weary they let them reft a while ; but give them nothing to eat till the fifhing is over ; during which time the throat of each cormorant is tied with a fmall cord, for fear they fhould fwallow the fmall fifh, which might prevent their having any inclina-tion to return.

As the land of China is incapable of maintaining its inhabitants, the dread of want puts every body in motion, and they have a thoufand methods of getting money which other nations would never think of. If indeed, they would accompany labour and natural induftry with a little more honefty, efpecially with refpect to ftrangers, they would make complete merchants ; but they feldom fail to cheat whenever

It is in their power. They falfify almoft every thing they fell ; and in particular they are faid to counterfeit gammons of bacon fo artfully, that people are often miftaken in them, and when they have boiled them a long time, they find nothing, when they fit down to eat them, but a piece of wood under a hog's fkin. It is certain that a ftranger will be always cheated if he buy alone, let him take what care he will : he fhould employ a trufty Chinefe, who knows all the tricks of his countrymen ; and indeed even then you will be very happy if he that buys for you and he that fells, do not colleague together to your coft, and go fhares in the profits *.

The following inftance will perhaps give a more perfect idea of their character. An Englifh captain having bought fome bales of filk of a merchant of Canton ; on opening them he found that they were almoft all filled with rotten filk ; upon which he reproached the Chinefe in the fevereft terms, for his difingenuity and knavery ; while the other heard him very unconcernedly, and only made this reply : Blame, Sir, your rogue of an interpreter ; for he protefted to me, that you would not examine the bales.

Their fubtlety in deceiving is ftill more extraordinary in their thieves and robbers, who break through the thickeft walls, burn gates, and make great holes in them, by the help of a certain engine that fires the wood without any flame. Thus they penetrate into the moft private receffes, and having, it is faid, a cer-

* Du Halde obferves, that generally fpeaking, they are not fo knavifh as Le Compte here reprefents them; bnt acknowledges, that when they have to do with ftrangers, they feldom fail to cheat them if they can ; and that they have the art to open the breaft of a capon, and taking out all the flefh to fill up the hole, and clofe it fo nicely, that the cheat is not perceived till the fowl comes to be eaten. Thefe tricks he, however, obferves, are feldom practifed on any but ftrangers; and that at a diftance from the coaft, the Chinefe themfelves will fcarce believe them. The brave commodore Anfon found to his coft, that they were guilty of many other artifices equally mean and difingenuous.

tain drug, the fume of which ftupifies the fenfes, and
cafts perfons into a deep fleep, they enter into the
very bed-chambers without being perceived ; and
when the people awake in the morning, they are
amazed to find their bed without curtains ; thei
chamber unfurnifhed ; and the tables, cabinets, cof
fers, and every thing removed without any footftep
being feen of the thieves but the hole in the wall, a
which they went out with all the moveables of the
houfe.

There are, however, fome few exceptions to thi
general charaƈter of the Chinefe : honefty and difin
tereftednefs are fometimes to be found among them
but the examples are very rare : we, however, me
with a fingular inftance of it in one who had not em
braced the doƈtrines of Chriftianity ; for on our firf
arrival, offering a prefent to a commiffioner of the
cuftoms, he protefted, notwithftanding all our earnef
entreaties, that he would never receive a prefent from
any man while he was in his office ; but if one day he
fhould chance to be in another ftation, he would
with all his heart, receive from us fome Europeai
curiofity.

China is, from north to fouth, of greater lengtl
than Tartary ; but is not equal to it in breadth
from eaft to weft. Yet in the narroweft part it ex
tends 360 leagues, or 1080 miles.

It is remarkable, that though the northern pro
vinces of China do not extend to above 42 degree
north latitude, yet the rivers and canals are frozei
four months in the year ; that is, from the middle o
November to the middle of March : but when the
wind does not blow from the north, the froft is no
attended with that piercing cold, which at fuch a time
is felt in Europe. This may be attributed to the ni
trous exhalations arifing from the earth, efpeciall
when the weather is clear, which is fo conftant, tha
during the winter, the fun is very feldom obfcured
The rainy feafon is only towards the end of July, and

the beginning of Auguſt ; but though it ſeldom
rains at any other time, the dew that falls in the night
moiſtens the earth ; but this moiſture dries at the
riſing of the ſun, and is ſucceeded by the air being
filled with a dry duſt that penetrates the cloſeſt re-
ceſſes ; and has ſuch an effect on thoſe that travel on
horſeback, that they who have tender eyes are obliged to cover their faces with a looſe veil. In the
ſouthern parts of China the heats, during the ſummer,
are very exceſſive.

China being of great extent, the nature of the ſoil
is different, according to its ſituation. The land,
like all others, is divided into hills and plains ; but
the latter are ſo even, that one would imagine that
the Chineſe have ever ſince the foundation of their
monarchy, been employed in nothing but leveling
them ; and their manner of meliorating their ground
being to let water through it, they could not think
of a better way of rendering the whole country
fertile, than that they have taken ; for was it not for
their numerous canals, thoſe parts that lie higheſt
would have been ſubject to continual drought, and
the reſt have lain always under water. Their mountains are cut out like a pair of ſtairs, from the top
to the bottom, that the rain-water may ſpread equally,
and not waſh down the ground with its ſeeds. A
long ſeries of ſuch hills, ſurrounded with ſuch ter-
raſſes, loſing in breadth as they gain in height, afford
a very entertaining landſcape.

Their mountains are, for the moſt part, leſs ſtony
than ours, and covered with a mould that is light,
porous, and eaſily cut ; and what is moſt ſurpriſing,
ſo deep, that in moſt provinces you may dig three
or four hundred feet in depth before you come to the
hard rock. Nature, however, has not every where
equally diſtributed her favours ; [for ſome places are
naturally ſo fertile, as to yield two crops a year ;
while others owe their fruitfulneſs to the indefati-
gable labour of the huſbandmen.] She has been leſs

lavifh of her favours in the provinces of Chenfi, Honan, Canton, and Fo-kien : yet even there the mountains are covered with a variety of ftraight and lofty trees, among which are tall cedars. They have other mountains, that produce gold and filver, iron, tin, and mercury. Their filver mines are not now worked ; but as for their gold, the torrents wafh great quantities of it into the plains, and a number of people are folely employed in looking for it among the fand and mud, where it is found fo pure as to need no refining.

The mines of common copper fupply the empire with fmall money. But the moft extraordinary fort of this metal is white copper, which is of that colour when dug out of the mine, and more fo on the infide than without. It appears by many experiments made at Pekin, that its colour is owing to no mixture : on the contrary, all mixtures diminifh its beauty ; for when it is rightly managed, it looks exactly like filver ; but there is a neceffity of mixing a fmall quantity of fome other metal with it, to foften it and prevent its brittlenefs ; and therefore thofe who would have it keep its fine colour, mix it with a fifth part of filver.

There are in China alfo many mines of pit-coal, of which there is a very great confumption. In the mountains are found lapis armenus, cinabar, vitriol, allum, jafper, rubies, rock cryftal, load ftones, porphyry, and quarries of different kinds of marble.

The canals of China have been mentioned among the works which fhew the art and induftry of the inhabitants , and the rivers from whence they derive their fcources are very confiderable. The river Kiam rifes in the province of Yunnan, and after having watered three other provinces, and run a courfe of four hundred leagues difcharges itfelf into the eaftern fea. The Chinefe have a proverb, that " The fea " has no bounds, and the Kiam no bottom :" and indeed in fome places they have found none ; but

as their pilots never carry a cord of above fifty or
fixty fathoms in length, the impoffibility of finding
a bottom with their ordinary plummet, probably
gave rife to this hyperbole. This river is in many
places extremely rapid, and the paffage along it is
very dangerous.

The moft confiderable river, next to the former,
is the Hoamho, or the Yellow River, fo called,
becaufe the earth it fweeps away with it, efpecially
in heavy rains, gives it that colour. The Hoamho
has its fource at the extremity of the mountains
that bound the province of Soutchouen in the weft :
from thence it runs into Tartary, where it flows for
fome time along the great wall, and then re-enters
China between the provinces of Chanfi and Chenfi ;
it then waters feveral other provinces, and after
flowing 600 leagues, difcharges itfelf into the eaft
fea, not far from the mouth of the Kiam. This
river is very broad and rapid, but neither very deep
nor navigable : befides thefe, there are abundance
of other rivers in China, that are more commodious
for trade and commerce ; but as they afford nothing
uncommon, we fhall not enter into a particular
defcription of them.

China alfo abounds with lakes, one of which
named the Jau, is thirty leagues in circumference,
and is like the fea, fubject to ftorms : indeed almoft
every province has lakes of a prodigous extent ;
thefe have a communication with the rivers and canals
and are well ftocked with fifh.

The plains are extremely beautiful, they are all
cultivated, and fo afraid are the inhabitants of lofing
an inch of ground, that they have neither hedge nor
ditch. All the northern and weftern provinces bear
wheat, barley, feveral kinds of millet and tobacco,
with black and yellow peafe, with which they feed
their horfes, as we do with oats ; the plains to the
fouth, being a watery country, produce rice. The
hufbandmen firft fow it like other corn, and when

it is grown about two feet from the ground, pull it up by the roots, and fet it in ftraight lines checquer-wife, in fmall parcels like fheaves, that the ftalks may fupport each other, and the eafier refift the wind.

The foil is proper for all manner of fruits ; it produces apricots, peaches, pears, apples, figs, grapes of all kinds, and efpecially excellent mufcadines. There are alfo pomegranates, walnuts, chefnuts ; and in general all that we have in Europe ; but as the Chinefe are ftrangers to the art of grafting, they are for the moft part inferior in goodnefs to ours, and there is no great variety among each diftinct fort.

In the fouthern provinces grow other fruits that are in greater efteem among the natives ; for befides oranges of feveral kinds, lemons, and citrons, which were many years ago brought into Europe, there are other fruits that have a fine tafte and flavour, that feem peculiarly natives of the country ; particu-larly what they call the lichi, which is of the fize of a date, and has a foft pulp of a very agreeable tafte, which it partly lofes on its becoming dry and wrink-led like a prune. Ananas, guavas, bananas and cocoas have been tranfplanted from the neighbouring iflands. Befides thefe there is a tree which bears a fmall fruit that in fhape, colour, fhell, and tafte, is extremely like a pea. This tree is common in feveral provinces, and in refpect to its height, its fpreading branches, and the thicknefs of its trunk, is excelled by few.

But among the trees that are moft likely to raife the envy of the Europeans are the four following. The firft is the varnifh tree, which is of a fmall fize, and has a leaf refembling the wild cherry : a gum diftils from it drop by drop like the tears of the tur-pentine-tree ; and if an incifion be made in it, it yields a greater quantity of liquor ; but then it foon deftroys the tree. The varnifh is much ufed, and is greatly efteemed by the artificers ; it takes all colours alike, and if it be well managed, neither lofes its luftre by the changes of the air, nor the age of the wood to which it is applied.

There is alfo another tree from which a liquor is obtained that differs but little from varnifh.

Another is termed the tallow tree. This is as large as a high cherry-tree; the leaves are of a lively red, and the fhape of a heart ; fruit is contained in a rind, which, when ripe, opens in the middle like a chefnut: it confifts of white kernels of the fize of a hazel-nut, whofe pulp has the properties of tallow, and of which candles are accordingly made.

The white wax-tree is no lefs extraordinary. It is not fo tall as the tallow-tree ; and has longer leaves and a whiter bark. A fmall kind of worm fixes it-felf to the leaves, and forms a fort of combs much fmaller than an honey-comb, the wax of which is very hard and fhining, and of far greater value than the common bees-wax.

They have moft kinds of wood that are to be found in Europe, and feveral others, among which is the tfe-tam, or rofe-wood, which is of a reddifh black, and full of fine veins that feem painted. This wood is fit for the fineft fort of joiner's work.

[Among the fhrubs, the moft extraordinary is that of tea, which is diftinguifhed into feveral different forts. One of the principal of them is the fong-lo, which we call green tea. It is planted in the manner of vines, and if not cut will grow feven or eight feet high. The flower is white, and in the fhape of a rofe, in the autumn, when it drops off, there appears a berry in the fhape of a nut, a little moift and of no bad tafte.

There is another fort of the tea fhrub which grows in the province of Fo-kien, and is called vui, or bohea. The only difference between this tea and the former is, that the leaves of that are longer and fharper pointed, and thofe of the latter of a darker colour. This laft being efteemed more falutary is moft generally ufed throughout the empire.

From this fhrub are prepared three forts of tea ; the firft, of the tender leaf when newly planted, which is feldom expofed to fale ; but ferves to make prefents of, and to fend to the emperor ; this is called man-cha, or imperial tea. The fecond confifts of leaves of a fenfible growth, and is efteemed a very good fort. The remaining leaves are fuffered to arrive at their full growth, and this makes a third fort; and a fourth is made of the flower itfelf.

There are alfo feveral other kinds of teas ; but they are very little different from the two principal forts, except in what is owing to the nature of the foil in which they are planted.

The flowering trees and fhrubs are very numerous throughout the empire. In thefe the Chinefe have the advantage of the Europeans, as the Europeans have of them with regard to flowers that fpring from feeds, and fmall roots. Large trees are to be feen there that perfectly refemble tulips ; the flowers of others are like rofes, which intermixed with the green leaves make a very beautiful appearance,

Among the animals is an odoriferous deer, which is without horns ; the hair is of a blackifh colour ; and its mufk-bag is compofed of a very thin fkin, covered with exceeding fine hair : the flefh is good to eat, and ferved-up at the beft tables.

Among the other animals are horfes, which are very indifferent, fmall affes and mules, fome cows and buffaloes, white goats and black hogs, which laft are excellent food, greatly fuperior to the pork of Europe. There are alfo a prodigious number of bucks, does, wild boars, elks, hares, rabbits, and fquirrels.

In the fouthern provinces are parrots of all forts, exactly refembling thofe brought from America. They have the fame plumage, and the fame aptnefs for talking : but they are not comparable to the bird called the golden hen. There is no bird in Europe any thing like it. The livelinefs of the red and yellow, the plume on the head, the delicate fhadowing of the tail, the variety of colours in the wings, together with a well fhaped body, render it the moft beautiful of the feathered kind: befides, the flefh is more delicate than that of the pheafant.

But it is certain that the Fongwhang, whofe figure is often painted, and fet off with a vaft number of ornaments, is only a fictitious bird like the phœnix.

There are prodigious numbers of tame ducks in China, and the natives hatch the eggs in an oven, or in dung, and putting the young ones in boats, carry them to the fea fhore at low water, where they feed on oyfters, and other fhell-fifh: feveral boats go together, whence many flocks of thefe ducks are intermixed upon the fhore; but as foon as the men ftrike on a bafon, it is faid, that each flock returns to its own boat as pigeons do to their houfes.

There are alfo in fome parts of China, abundance of wild and tame peacocks; and likewife, geefe, woodcocks, partridges, pheafants, quails; all thefe laft are very common, and are fold exceedingly cheap.

There are butterflies in the province of Quangtong fo much efteemed, that the largeft and moft uncommon are fent to court, where they become a part of certain ornaments in the palace. Their colours are furprizing lively and diverfified. In the day time they appear without motion on the trees, and are eafily taken; in the evening they begin to flutter about, much like our bats, and fome of them, when their wings are extended, feem to be as large.

There is fcarce any fort of fifh in Europe, but what is to be met with in China, as lampreys, carps, foals, falmons, trouts, fturgeons; befides many of an excellent tafte, that are quite unknown to us.

One of thofe moft efteemed is the armour fifh, fo called from its back, belly, and fides being covered with fharp fcales, regularly placed in rows one over another, much like the tiles on the roof of a houfe. It is an admirable fifh of about forty pounds weight ; it is exceeding white, and in tafte refembles veal.

In calm weather they catch another fort of delicate fifh, called by the people of the country the meal fifh, from its exceeding whitenefs. There are fuch prodigious fhoals of them in the fea near the province of Cyang-nan, that they commonly take 400 weight of them, at one draught of the net.

One of the beft fort of fifh China affords, refembles a fea-bream, and weighs five or fix pounds, and is fo cheap, that it is commonly fold for the value of about a farthing a pound, and for only about twice as much on its being carried twenty leagues up the country.

In the province of Kyang-nan, are very large fifh, which coming out of the fea, or yellow river, throw themfelves into vaft plains covered with water ; but matters are fo ingenioufly contrived, that when the plains are fufficiently ftocked with thefe aquatic animals, the people drain off the water, and the fifh being left on dry land, are taken without difficulty, falted, and fold to the merchants, at a very cheap rate.

In the river Yang-tfe-kyange, the natives catch a variety of excellent fifh, and among others, one called whan-yu, or the yellow fifh, which is of an extraordinary fize, fome of them weighing upwards of 800 pounds ; they are alfo of an exquifite tafte ; but they are only to be caught at certain feafons, when they come out of the lake Tonting-hu, into this river.

To thefe I fhall only add the gold or filver fifh, as being remarkable on account of its beauty, whence it is kept by the grandees in bafons in their courts or gardens. They are commonly of a finger's length, and proportionably thick, the body being finely fhaped. The male is of a beautiful red, from the head to above half way down the body, and the remaining part, together with the tail, is gilded ; but accompanied with fuch a bright and dazzling luftre, that our beft gildings fall vaftly fhort of it. The female is white, the tail and fome part of the body perfectly refembling filver. The tail of either kind is fmooth and flat, like that of other fifh ; but form a fort of thick and long tuft, that adds a particular beauty, to this little creature.

[We cannot conclude our account of this fpecies of animals, and of China in general, without mentioning a fingular method by which all kinds of fifh are difperfed into different provinces even before they have life. About the month of May the Chinefe draw mats acrofs the great river Yang-tfe-kyange in order to ftop the fpawn, which they know how to diftinguifh at firft fight, though the water is fcarce altered by it, with this water mixed with fpawn, they fill many veffels, which they fell to the merchants, who go thither at that feafon in great numbers to buy it, and tranfport it into different provinces. This they fell by meafure to thofe who have fifh-ponds belonging to their houfes. In a few days the young fry begin to appear in little fhoals ; but the different kinds of fifh cannot be foon diftinguifhed.

A

DESCRIPTION

OF

GUINEA.

Containing a particular account of the Slave Coaſt and Gold Coaſt
of Guinea;--of the kingdom of Great Benin, with the religion,
cuſtoms, dreſs and manners of the inhabitants of thoſe countries.

GUINEA is a large country that extends
ſeveral hundred miles along the weſtern coaſt of
Africa, and is divided into many kingdoms and
commonwealths. The Gold Coaſt reaches about 330
miles : it beginning, according to Mr. Smith, at the
river Mancha, and extending to the Volta ; comprehending the countries of Axim, Ante, Adom, Jabi,
Commani, Fetu, Saboe, Fantyn, Acrin, Agona,
and Aquambo ; each containing a village or two on
the ſea-ſhore ; but their moſt populous towns are generally within the land.

To begin with Axim, the inhabitants of this country are generally rich, from their driving a great
trade with the Europeans for gold, which they chiefly
diſpoſe of to the Engliſh or Dutch. They employ
themſelves either in trade, fiſhing, or the cultivation
of rice, which is tranſported from thence all over
the Gold Coaſt ; and they receive in return, millet,

jammes, potatoes, and palm oil, The river Anco-
ber, on the borders of this province, has a winding
courfe ; and its banks are adorned with fine lofty
trees, that afford a moft agreeable fhade, and defend
the traveller from the fcorching beams of the fun,
It is very pleafant to obferve the birds beautifully
variegated with the brighteft colours, and the fpor-
tive apes, diverting themfelves on the boughs of the
trees.

The Dutch fort of St. Anthony is at the mouth
of this river ; and about feven or eight leagues to the
fouth-eaft, they have alfo a large beautiful fort which
belonged to the king of Pruffia; but was taken by the
Dutch in the year 1724.

In the next province, which is that of Ante, the
Englifh have a fort called Dickfcove, which is a
handfome regular fortification with four good batteries, on which are mounted twenty pieces of ordnance This, and all the other Englifh forts, are
fubordinate to Cape Coaft Caftle. There are alfo
feveral Dutch forts. This country, as well as the
Gold Coaft, abounds in hills covered with lofty and
beautiful trees. Between thefe hills, the valleys are
wide and extenfive. The earth produces in great
abundance, very good rice, the richeft fort of millet,
which has a red grain ; fugar canes of an extraordinary fize ; and the palm-trees, which afford the
inhabitants the moft excellent wine and oil. There
are here all forts of tame and-wild beafts. This
country is watered by a river that is navigable three
miles from its mouth ; but the cataracts above that
diftance render it impaffable beyond it. It affords
great plenty of fifh notwithftanding its being peftered
by incredible numbers of crocodiles. On each fide
of this river grow a fort of trees great and fmall
intermixed, whofe branches fhoot directly into the
water, where they are immediately covered with
oyfters, which are at firft of the bignefs of fhell-

fnails; out in a fhort time grow to their natural fize.

The countries of Adom and Jabi are extremely fertile in maize, and have feveral mines of gold.

In the country of Commani or Commenda, is a town thus named, where is the largeft and ftrongeft of any fort belonging to the Englifh on the Gold Coaft, except Cape Coaft Caftle, and within a mufket-fhot is alfo a good Dutch fort. The gardens are very good, and there are large villages of negroes belonging to both forts.

In the next province named Fetu is Cape Coaft Caftle, which being a place of great confequence belonging to England, deferves a particular defcription. This caftle was founded by the Portuguefe about the year 1610, upon a large rock, which projects into the fea, forming a head-land, to which they gave the name of Cabo Corfo. In a few years they were difpoffeffed by the Dutch, who enlarged and beautified it. The parade which is twenty feet perpendicular above the furface of the rock, forms a kind of quadrangle, open on the eaft fide towards the fea, which renders it very cool, airy and pleafant, and affords a fine view of Queen Anne's Point, and of the fhips in Anamaboe road, which has a platform of thirteen pieces of heavy cannon. The other three fides contain many neat and fpacious apartments and offices, particularly on the fouth fides is a large well-built chapel, the back part of which joins to the caftle wall. The negroe town is very large and populous. The inhabitants, though Pagans, are a very civilized fort of people: their chief employment is fifhing, at which they are very dexterous, and it is a pleafing fight to behold eighty or 100 canoes going out to fifh in the morning, and returning in from the fea well freighted in the evening, which may be feen every day during the dry feafon, except Tuefday, which is their Fetifh day, or Sabbath. The garden of Cape Coaft Caftle is very large

A View of Cape coast CASTLE: a part of the NEGRO·TOWN.

and pleafant, it being eight miles in circumference: it is no where circumfcribed by either walls or hedges, except on the fouth-fide next the town ; but all in general is called the Garden as far as any regular walks are planted. It produces every thing that grows within the torrid zone, as pine-apples, oranges, lemons, limes, citrons, guavas, plantanes, papas, bonanas, cocoa-nuts, cinamon, and tamarinds; alfo many forts of European fruits and falads.

By the fide of the garden, on the top of a fteep hill, is a little round tower, that mounts feven guns ; which from its being built by General Phipps, is called Phipps's Tower ; it is three quarters of a mile to the north-weft of the caftle. At the fame diftance to the eaft by north is another Englifh fort called Fort Royal, which formerly belonged to the king of Denmark, and is every way inacceffible through the fteepnefs of the hill, except by one narrow path, which a fingle gun may defend.

The Dutch have likewife feveral forts in the country of Fetu, the principal of which is the caftle of St. George del Mina, fituated near the town of Mina ; this according to Mr. Bofman, has not its equal in all the Gold Coaft. It is built fquare with very high walls, and has four good batteries within, and another on the out-work of the caftle : on the land fide it has the advantage of two canals cut in the rock on which it ftands, which are always furnifhed with rain or frefh water fufficient for the ufe of the garrifon and fhips. Befides, within the caftle are three very fine cifterns, containing feveral hundred tuns of rain-water. Below the caftle is the town of Mina, called by the natives Oddena ; but though it is but indifferently built, the houfes are of ftone, wherein they differ from thofe of the other towns on the coaft, which are ufually only raifed with wood and clay.

The next country is Saboe, in which is a Dutch fort named Naffau, that is almoft fquare, but is broad-eft at the front; it has four batteries, and eighteen pieces of cannon: the curtain takes in two fea batteries, and is equally fpacious and convenient. The village of Moxiree, which lies under it, is not fo large as Mina, but is more populous: the greateft part of the inhabitants are fifhermen; four or five hundred of whom go out every morning in canoes to fifh; who, upon their return, are obliged to pay every fifth fifh as a toll to the Dutch factor.

In Fantyn, the next divifion, the English and Dutch had feveral fmall forts. The inland inhabitants, befides trading, are employed in tillage, and the making of palm-wine. The country is very populous, and befides its being rich in gold, pro^ duces the neceffaries of life; and more efpecially corn, which the inhabitants fell in large quantities to the fhips that arrive there. Here is no king, the government being in the hands of a chief comman^ der, whom they term their braffo or lea er. He is a kind of chief governor, and has greater power than any other fingle perfon in the country; but his authority is reftrained by the old men, who compofe a kind of parliament.

The remainder of the Gold Coaft contains the kingdoms of Acron, Agonna, and Aquamboe; the firft of which borders on Fantyn, and has a Dutch fort in the middle of the coaft, that has two batteries, on which are mounted eight pieces of cannon; under it is a fmall village inhabited only by fifhermen. The people of Acron feldom or never enter into war; for having chofen the Fantynians for their protectors, none dare injure or attack them; which afford them an opportunity of tilling their land in quiet, and they accordingly have annually a plentiful harveft; a great part of which they difpofe of to other countries. Harts, hares, partridges, pheafants, and other wild-fowl and quadrupedes, are here very good and in great abundance.

A little below the above fort, is a falt river that abounds both in fifh and fowl. About a mile further eaftward, is a very high hill, called the Devil's Mount, faid to contain vaft quantities of gold. About this hill begins the country of Agona, which furpaffes Acron in largenefs, power, and riches, though in fertility and pleafantnefs they are nearly equal.

We come next to the laft country on the Gold Coaft, that of Aquamboe, the greateft part of which is fituated within the land ; but the king extends his power over the Negroes of the coaft for above twenty miles, though they are governed by feveral diftinct fovereigns. The Aquamboe Negroes are haughty, arrogant and warlike, and their power fills moft of the neighbouring countries with terror.

The Englifh, Danes, and Dutch have each a fort at Acra in this province. Mr. Bofman fays, that the king and his favourites are fo rich in gold and flaves, that he is of opinion, this country poffeffes greater treafures than all the countries on the coaft we have hitherto defcribed : but though the foil is fufficiently fertile, the inhabitants commonly fall fhort of provifions before the end of the year.

The countries where moft of the gold is obtained, are fituated fome diftance within land, the beft gold is found in or between particular hills ; where the Negroes dig pits, and feparate it from the earth dug up with it. It is alfo found about fome rivers and water-falls, where after heavy rains it is wafhed down from the mountains by the violence of the torrents which fometimes fall, and bring down great quantities of earth that carry the gold with it. It is likewife gathered on the fea-fhore, particulariy at Mina and Axim, where are little branches of rivers, into which the gold is driven from mountainous places. In the morning after a rainy night, thefe places are fure to be vifited by hundreds of Negro women, who have no other covering but a cloth tied round the waift, each is furnifhed with two callabaſhes, one of which they fill with earth and ſand. This they waſh with many waters, by often turning the callabaſh round, till it waſhes over the brims ; while the gold, if there be any, ſinks to the bottom by its own weight : and thus they continue till they have waſhed all away, except two or three ſpoonfuls at the bottom ; this they carefully take out and lay by in the other callabaſh ; then they fill the other again, and waſh on till about noon, when the callabaſh that receives the ſettlings, being pretty well filled, is carried home, and what remains is deligently ſearched, when they ſometimes find a ſhilling's worth of gold, or ſometimes as much as is worth half a guinea, and ſometimes none at all.

The gold obtained by digging, or thus found, is of two ſorts, one called gold duſt, which is the beſt ; the other conſiſts of pieces of different ſizes ; ſome being hardly of the weight of a farthing, and others weighing as heavy as twenty, or thirty guineas: few indeed are found ſo large as theſe ; but the Negroes ſay, that they have in the country pieces that will weigh one or two hundred guineas ; but the multitude of ſmall ſtones which always adhere to them, occaſion great loſs in the melting.

The Negroes of theſe countries are, however, ſaid to be artiſts in adulterating gold, and ſometimes impoſe upon the unexperienced tradeſman.

The Gold Coaſt being ſituated within the fifth de-gree of north latitude, the heat is exceſſive during the months of October, November, December, January, February, and March ; but it is more tem-perate during the ſix remaining months. The coaſt is extremely unhealthful, owing to the heat of the day and the coolneſs of the night ; with the thick and ſulphureous miſts which ariſe in the mountains. Indeed few come who are not ſeized by a ſickneſs which frequently proves fatal : but ſince Dr. James's diſcovery of his admirable powder, and its being tried on this coaſt, the danger of going thither is in a manner removed.

Mr. Bofman, whofe only fault as an hiftorian, feems to be his writing with too much acrimony, fays, that all the Negroes on this coaft are without exception, crafty, fraudulent, and feldom to be trufted ; being fure to flip no opportunity of cheating an European, or even one another.

The richeft of the natives adorn their hair with a fort of coral called conte de terra, which they efteem much more valuable than gold ; and with a fort of blue coral called by the natives accori. They are very fond of our hats, for which they will pay a great price. Their arms, legs and waifts are adorned with gold and coral, and their arms in particular are adorned with rings of gold, filver and ivory. Round their waift they wrap three or four ells of filk, cloth, perpetuana, or other ftuff, which hanging from the navel, covers half the leg. Their other ornaments are ftrings of gold, or chains of gold, filver, fhells, &c. which they wear round their necks. But their Caboceros or chief men, who have a fhare in the government, wear only a handfome cloth round their waifts, a cap made of deer-fkin, with a ftring of coral about their heads, and always appear with a ftaff in their hands.

The common people have fome an ell or two of cloth round their waifts, others have only a kind of girdle to which is faftened a piece of ftuff which paffes between their legs, and ferves to cover their nakednefs ; to this the fifhermen add a cap made of deer-fkin or rufhes, or an old hat purchafed of fome European failor.

The women of rank fhew themfelves more fkilled in the ornaments of drefs than the men. The cloth they wear round the waift is much longer, and faftened with greater neatnefs about their bodies. Their hair is more beautifully adorned with gold, coral, and ivory. Gold chains and ftrings of coral not only hang about their necks, but their arms, legs, and waifts are in a manner covered by thefe fplendid ornaments ; befides on the upper part of their bodies they frequently caft a veil of filk, or fome other fine ftuff.

The kings, while in their own houfes, are not diftinguifhed by the leaft grandeur. Their clothes are fometimes not worth a fhilling ; and they eat the fame food as the meaneft of their fubjects ; for bread, oil, and a little ftinking fifh make up their bill of fare ; and water is their moft common drink ; but they have brandy, which they purchafe of the Europeans, and palm-wine, which they receive from the inland country. They have no guard at the palace gates, nor any but their own wives and their flaves to wait on them ; and when they go abroad in their town, they are ufually attended by only two boys, one of whom carries the king's fabre, and the ether his feat. But in cafe they go to pay a vifit to a confiderable perfon in another town, or are to receive a vifit from another great man, they take care to fhew their grandeur ; on fuch occafions they and their wives are richly adorned ; they are accompanied by armed men, and have umbrellas held over their heads.

The arms ufed by the troops are mufkets, of which vaft numbers have been bought of the Europeans, and in the ufe of which they are extremely expert ; their other weapons are a kind of affagays, and a fort of fabres ; they alfo wear large fhields four or five feet long, and three broad, made of ofiers, fome of which are covered with tyger fkins, or other materials ; and fome again have broad thin copper plates at each corner and in the middle, to ward off the affagays and arrows of an enemy. They fight without the leaft order, and are chiefly intent on obtaining prifoners, in order to make them flaves, and to obtain from them ornaments of gold and coral.

Almoft all the Negroes believe in one God, to whom they attribute the creation of the world, and all things in it. It alfo appears that they have fome

dea of the immortality of the foul. Every one has
what he calls a fetifh, which is fome ornament worn
)n the head, or any other fubftance dedicated to God,
md to which they pay the greateft reverence ; for
:hinking themfelves too mean to offer their petitions
immediately to the Supreme, they ignorantly efteem
it more modeft to addrefs them to their fetifhes. Each
fetifher or prieft, has his peculiar idol prepared in a
particular and different manner; which is moftly a
large wooden pipe filled with earth, oil, blood, the
bones of dead men and beafts, feathers, hair, and
all fuch kinds of excrementitious fubftances thruft
into the pipe : by thefe mixtures the prieft may probably convey the idea of fome fecret myftery, or
fome powerful charm, that has all the powers of ne-
cromancy. If a Negro is to take an oath before this
fetifh, he firft afks the prieft its name, each having a
peculiar one ; then calling the fetifh by it, he repeats
what he is to confirm by an oath, and defires the
fetifh to punifh him with death if he fwears falfely ;
then going round the pipe, he afterwards ftands in
the fame place, and repeats the oath a fecond time,
in the fame manner as before, and fo a third time ;
after this the fetifher takes fome of the ingredients
out of the pipe, with which he touches the perfon's
head, arms, belly, and legs, and holding it above
his head, turns it three times round. He then cuts
a bit of the nail of one finger in each hand, and one
toe on each foot, and fome of the hair of the head,
all which he puts into the pipe ; and thus the ceremonies of the oath are concluded.

Befides when their fifhery is at a low ebb, they make
offerings to the fea ; and almoft every village has a
fmall facred grove to which the governors, and principal inhabitants frequently repair to make their
offerings. They are faid to have fome notion of the
devil, but are fo far from paying him any kind of
worfhip, that they have a cuftom of banifhing him,
which they perform annually with abundance of

ceremony at a time appointed for that purpofe. This is done after a feaft of eight days, in which they take the greateft liberties with each others characters, and particularly with their fuperiors. This time of licence being ended, they hunt out the devil with an horrid cry; all running after one another, and throwing ftones, dirt, and every thing that comes in their way at the fuppofed fiend. When they have driven him far enough out of town, they return to their houfes, on which the women immediately wafh and fcour all their wooden and earthen veffels very neat, to cleanfe them from all pollution.

Marriage is not here obftructed by previous ceremonies. If a man likes a young women, he has nothing more to do, than to afk her of her parents, who feldom refufe fo reafonable a requeft, efpecially if he be in the leaft agreeable to their daughter. The bride brings no fortune ; but the man keeps an exact account of the expences of the wedding day, and of the prefents he makes to the bride or her friends, that if ever fhe become fo far difgufted with him as to leave him, he may demand the whole again. But if he puts her away, he can demand nothing of her or her relations, unlefs he produces very good reafons why he difmiffes her. They allow of a plurality of wives, and fome are faid to have even twenty ; but thefe are obliged to cultivate the earth, and to drefs provifions for their hufbands, who generally fpend their time in loitering about, and drinking palm-wine : however, thofe who are rich have two wives that are perpetually exempted from labour. Thefe are the firft wife, who has the chief command, and the care of houfe-keeping ; the fecond is confecrated to their God, and is called the fetifh wife. Of this laft they are generally very jealous ; with her they lie on the night following their birth-day ; and on that day of the week, which they call their fetifh day. Each wife ufually endeavours to pleafe her hufband in order to obtain the greateft fhare in his affections, and fhe who is fo happy as to be pregnant, is fure to be waited on and refpected by her hufband.

The women are delivered with very little pain, even without the affiftance of a midwife, and it is ufual for them to go as foon as they are delivered to wafh in the fea. The child is no fooner born than the fetifher or prieft is fent for, who binds a number of cords, pieces of coral and other things about the infant's head, body, arms and legs, which are to fecure it from ficknefs and ill accidents, and thefe are all the clothes it is to wear till it is feven or eight years old, at which age it puts on a fort of apron of half an ell of cloth. The number of females born is faid greatly to exceed that of the males, which may render their having fuch a multiude of wives fomewhat more excufeable.

As the people are naturally inactive from the heat of the country, they are mafters of but few manual arts; however, befides building their houfes, or rather huts, making their canoes; and being fkilled in managing them and in fifhing; they employ themfelves in the making of wooden bowls, and earthen veffels; and in forming rings and chains for their arms and legs, of gold and filver and ivory: but they are moft expert at fmiths work; for by means of a fmall pair of bellows with two or three pipes, which is entirely their own invention, they with a great ftone for an anvil, make not only fwords and other offenfive weapons: but feveral inftruments of agriculture, with hooks, and harping irons for fifhing, and knives and tools for making their canoes, the largeft of which are about thirty feet long. They alfo make feveral forts of mufical inftruments, the principal of which are a kind of horns made of elephants teeth; drums made of the hollow trunks of fmall trees, covered at one end with fheep-fkin, and a fmall ftringed inftrument refembling a harp. But they have not the leaft idea of letters.

What is moſt commendable among the Negroes, is their having no beggars ; for when one of them finds himſelf ſo poor that he perceives it difficult to procure ſubſiſtence, he binds himſelf for a certain ſum of money ; or his friends do it for him, and the maſter to whom he engages himſelf, ſets him a taſk that is far from being ſlaviſh ; it being chiefly to defend him in caſe he ſhould be attacked, and at his leiſure time to aſſiſt him in tilling the earth. But yet all the people in general, from the king to the meaneſt of his ſubjects, freely beg whatever they like of the Europeans.

In ſickneſs they have firſt recourſe to remedies; but not thinking them alone ſufficient to preſerve life and reſtore health, they apply to their ſuperſtitious worſhip, as more effectual. The phyſician being alſo the fetiſher or prieſt, he eaſily perſuades the patient's relations that he cannot be recovered without ſome offerings, and therefore propoſes a ſheep, a hog, a cock, or whatever he likes beſt ; but this ſacrifice he always proportions to the ability of the perſon to be ſerved. If the diſeaſe increaſes, more expenſive offerings are made. It frequently happens that one phyſician is diſcharged with a good reward, and another called in his ſtead ; and this charge of phyſicians ſometimes happens twenty times or more ſucceſſively, each of whom has the benefit of making freſh offerings, and of appropriating them, as they always do, to their own uſe.

Such boys as are ſlaves or ſervants to the Europeans, if they think they have a good maſter, will, on his being ſeized with the leaſt indiſpoſition, go without his knowledge to make offerings for him, that he may recover his health ; and accordingly there are ſometimes found on the beds, or in the chambers of the Europeans, things conſecreated by the fetiſher, laid there to defend their maſter from death : but as they know that the Europeans are diſpleaſed with ſuch marks of their gratitude and affection,

they always do it privately, and conceal them fo
well, that they are feldom difcovered before the perfon is dead, when they have not time to remove
them.

The chief medicines ufed here are lemon or lime
juice, the grains of paradife, the roots, branches,
and gums of trees, and about thirty forts of herbs,
impregnated with fanative virtues; and with thefe
they fometimes perform very extraordinary cures.

When a perfon has breathed his laft, his relations
and friends fet up a difmal cry, and the youth of his
acquaintance now generally fhew their refpect by
firing mufkets. If the deceafed be a man, his wives
immediately fhave their heads very clofe, fmear their
bodies with white earth, put on an old worn-out
garment, and run about the ftreets making difmal
lamentations, continually repeating the name of the
deceafed, and the great actions of his life ; and this
lafts feveral days fucceffively till the corpfe is interred.
While the women are lamenting abroad, the neareft relations fit by the corpfe making a difmal noife,
and wafhing and cleaning themfelves : the diftant
relations alfo affemble from all parts to be prefent at
thefe mourning rites. The town's people and acquaintance of the deceafed, come likewife to join
their lamentations, each bringing his prefent of gold,
brandy, fine cloth, fheets, or other things, to be
carried to the grave with the corpfe ; and the larger
the prefent is the more does it redound to the honour
of the perfon who makes it. During this ingrefs
and egrefs of all forts of people, brandy in the
morning, and palm-wine in the afternoon are very
brifkly filled out ; fo that the funeral of a rich Negro
becomes very expenfive : for after this the body is
richly dreffed and put into the coffin with fetifhes of
gold, the fineft corals, and feveral other things of
the greateft value, which it is fuppofed the deceafed
will have occafion for in the other world. After two
or three days, the relations and friends being all met,

the corpfe is carried to the grave, followed by a number of men and women without the leaft order, fome filent, others crying and fhrieking. At the fame time many young foldiers running about, load and difcharge their mufkets, till the deceafed is laid in the ground. The corpfe being interred, the multitude go where the pleafe; but moft of them return to the houfe to drink and be merry; this lafts feveral days fucceffively, fo that every thing now rather refembles a wedding than a time of mourn· ing.

They fometimes keep a king, or very great perfon a whole year above ground, when, to prevent putre· faction, they lay the corpfe upon a wooden frame like a gridiron, that ftands over a very gentle clear fire, which by flow degrees dries it. When a king is to be publicly buried, notice is firft given, not only to the people of his own nation, but to other countries, which bring a furprifing concourfe of people, and all are as richly dreffed as poffible. In thefe funerals feveral of the flaves of the deceafed are inhumanly killed, that they may ferve him in the other world, as are alfo thofe whom he has dedicated to his falfe gods, which are one of his wives, and one of his principal fervants; and even fome poor wretches, who, through the infirmities of age, or other incidents, are rendered incapable of labour, are fold, in order to be victims in thefe horrid offer· ings, and who are put to death with every circum· ftance of inhumanity. With the utmoft horror, fays Mr. Bofman, I faw eleven perfons killed in this manner, among whom was one, who after hav· ing endured the moft exquifite tortures, was deliver· ed to a child of fix years of age, who was to cut off his head, which the boy was about an hour in performing, he not being ftrong enough to wield the fabre. But human facrifices are only in ufe among thofe Negroes who are not fully fubject to any European government, and are at a diftance from our forts.

The Negroes generally build a fmall cottage, or plant a little garden of rice on the grave, into which they put fome of the goods of the deceafed ; but no houfhold furniture, as fome authors have pretended.

Of the trees and plants of this country we have already given fome account in treating of the Gold Coaft in general. There are here cocoas, and palm-trees of various kinds ; the cabbage tree, orange-trees, lemon-trees, bananas, pepper, ananas, water-melons, and many others. Among thofe for timber are many of an extraordinary height and fize, and others of different coloured wood, fit for the fineft cabinet-makers work : of the corn, there is maize, or Indian wheat ; but there is little rice or other corn on this coaft : Among the leguminous plants are feveral kinds of beans, one fpecies of which is of a bright red, and grows in pods three quarters of a yard in length, and another fpecies grows on trees of the fize of a goofberry-bufh ; and among the roots, are potatoes, yams, and feveral others fit for food, as well as fome ufed in medicine.

In the inland countries are great numbers of cows and goats ; but only a few of them are brought to the coaft ; however, at Axim, El Mina and Acra, great herds of them are bred ; but they are fo light and fmall, that a full grown cow does not ufually weigh above 250 pounds, and both the beef and veal are very indifferent meat. There alfo many fheep along the coaft ; but they are dear, and not above half as big as ours: they have no wool, but that want is fupplied with hair: however, thefe fheep are very dry and difagreeable meat. As to the goats, they are innumerable, and both fatter and more flefhy than the fheep of Europe, though they are exceeding fmall. There are likewife many hogs ; but thofe bred by the Negroes are extremely bad.

There are no horfes on the coaft ; but there are great numbers of fmall ordinary ones in the inland country : but the affes, which are pretty numerous on the coaft, are larger, and handfomer than thofe horfes. Among the wild beafts the elephant, on account of its fize, deferves the firft place. Thefe beafts, which are heie twelve or fourteen feet high, are very prejudical to the fruit-trees, efpecially to the orange, banana, and fig-trees, and with refpect to the two laft, eat both the fruit and the ftem ; but though thefe animals are of fuch ufe in the Eaft Indies both in war, and as beafts of burthen, none of them are here tamed. However, when unprovoked they feldom hurt any body; and it is frequently not very 'eafy to put the elephants of this coaft in a rage. Mr. Bofman, from whom this defcription of Guinea is chiefly taken, gives the following account : " In December 1700, at fix in the morn-
" ing an elephant came here to El Mina, walking
" eafily along the fhore under the hill of St. Jago.
" Some Negroes were fo bold as to go to him with-
" out any thing in their hands ; he fuffered them
" to encompafs him, and went quietly along with
" them under Mount St. Jago, where one of our
" officers fhot him above the eye : but this, and
" the following fhots, which fome Negroes now
" poured on him, did not even make him mend
" his pace, and he only feemed between whiles
" to threaten the Negroes by pricking up his ears,
" which were of a prodigious fize. He, however,
" went on, and foon entered our garden. This drew
" the director general and myfelf thither, and we
" were foon followed by fome of our people. He
" had broke down four or five cocoa-trees, and in
" our prefence he brought down five or fix more;
" when the ftrength he feemed to ufe in breaking
" down a tree, might be fitly compared to the force
" exerted by a man in knocking down a child of
" three or four years of age. While he ftood here

" above an hundred fhot were fired at him; which
" made him bleed as if an ox had been killed. But
" this did not make him ftir, he only fet up his ears,
" and made the men apprehend that he would fol-
" low them. At length a Negroe going fottly
" behind him, wantonly got hold of his tail, and
" was going to cut off a piece of it ; but the ele-
" phant giving the Negro a blow with his trunk,
" and drawing him to him, trod upon him two or
" three times, and as if that was not fufficient, gored
" two holes in his body with his teeth, large enough
" for a man's double fift to enter. He then let him
" lie, and even ftood fill while two Negroes ventured
" to fetch away the body, without offering to hurt
" them. At length the elephant, after he had
" been about an hour in the garden, wheeled about
" as if he intended to fall on us, on which we all
" flew to the fore door, in order to make our efcape;
" but he followed none of us ; but going to the
" back door, threw it to a great diftance; then turn-
" ing from it, walked through the garden hedge,
" and proceeding flowly to the river by Mount St.
" Jago, bathed himfelf. Having thus refrefhed
" himfelf a little, he came out of the river, and ftood
" under fome trees, by fome of our water tubs ;
" where he alfo cooled himfelf, and then broke the
" tubs in pieces, as he did alfo a canoe that lay by
" them. The firing was here renewed till the ele-
" phant at laft fell ; after which they cut of his
" trunk, which was fo hard and tough, that it coft
" the Negroes thirty ftrokes before they could fepa-
" rate it, which muft have been very painful to the
" elephant, fince it made him roar ; which was the
" only noife I heard him make. He was no fooner
" dead, than the Negroes fell on him in crowds,
" each cutting off as much as he could, fo that he
" furnifhed great numbers with food. Thofe who
" pretended to underftand elephant fhooting, after-
" wards told us, that we ought to have fhot iron

" bullets ; indeed our's were not only of lead but too
" fmall, and therefore moft of them had rebounded
" from his hide, and very few penetrated his fkull."

Tygers are here numerous, and of feveral fpecies,
fome of wich are very large, and they are all extremely
fierce and voracious ; but happily for the natives,
while they can fatisfy their appetites on the flefh
of brutes, they will not attack any of the human
race.

The jackal is next in fiercenefs to the tyger, and
is fo bold, that it devours whatever comes in its way,
whether man or beaft.

There are alfo wild boars ; but they are very few,
and not fo rapacious as thofe of Europe. Thefe are
excellent meat.

There are prodigious numbers of apes, of which
there are a great variety of fpecies. The moft common fort are of a pale moufe-colour, and grow to
the height of five feet. Some of the Negroes are
firmly perfuaded that they can fpeak ; but that they
will not for fear of being fet to work. Another
fpecies is fo fmall, that four of them put together
would not weigh one of the former. There is a
third fort very beautiful. Thofe of this fpecies
grow to the height of about two feet : their hair is
as black as jet, and above a finger's length, and they
have a long white beard. Befides thefe there are
many other kinds.

There are feveral forts of wild cats, among which
is the civet cat. The Negroes are great lover's of
dog's flefh ; which they prefer to that of cattle:
their dogs are very ugly, and it is remarkable, that
thofe brought from Europe foon degenerate, and
their ears grow long and ftiff like thofe of foxes, and
in three or four broods, their barking turns into a
howl.

Among the wild beafts, there are incredible numbers of deer all along the Gold Coaft, efpecially at
Arte and Acra, where herds of an hundred together

are fometimes feen. Of thefe there are many different fpecies, fome as large as cows, and others no
bigger than cats ; but all of them are good to eat,
particularly a fort about two feet long, the flefh of
which is efteemed very delicate. One is about four
feet in length, and of a flender fhape with a long
head and ears, and is a beautiful creature of an
orange-colour, ftreaked with white.

There are likewife hares and porcupines. Thefe
laft, which, as well as the former, are efteemed good
food, are great enemies to the fnakes, and will
attack the largeft and moft dangerous of thofe
reptiles.

Befides thefe, there are feveral other quadrupeds,
and among the reft the floth, one of the moft loth-
fome animals in the world, it being almoft impoffible
to look on it without horror.

Among the feathered tribe there are cocks and
hens, thofe at Axim are fat and good, though fmall ;
but about El Mina, and other places on the coaft,
they are extremely dry and lean. There are alfo tame
and wild ducks, pigeons, vaft numbers of partridges,
plenty of pheafants; fnipes, herons, parrots ; great
numbers of large and fmall birds, fome which are
extremely beautiful, their plumage being finely
variegated with the brighteft colours, and their
heads crowned with tufts of feathers. There are
likewife eagles, falcons, kites, and many others of
the birds of Europe, as well as thofe that feem
peculiarly the natives of the Torrid Zone.

Let us now take a view of the amphibious animals
and reptiles: we have already obferved, that the
rivers fwarm with crocodiles ; befides thefe, there is
an animal of nearly the fame form, though it feldom
exceeds four feet in length, its body is black, fpeck-
led with a round fort of eyes, and the fkin is very
tender. It injures neither man nor beaft ; it however fometimes makes great flaughter among the
poultry. Its flefh is fometimes eat by the Europeans,

and all who have tasted it agree, that it is much finer than that of a young cock or a hen.

In this class of animals we may reckon the lizards, of which there are every where many thousands, especially by the walls of the forts; and of these there are various species, differing in size, shape, and colour: there are likewise great numbers of cameleons, which are far from living on air alone.

Frogs and toads are as numerous as in Europe; but the latter are in some places as large as a pewter plate. These are mortal enemies to the snakes, with which they have frequent engagements. Of these last reptiles there are not only great numbers, but a prodigious variety, and some of them are of a hideous size. Mr Bosman says, that the largest of those taken while he was on this coast was twenty feet long, and he even believes that they are still larger within land; and we have frequently found, says he, in their entrails, not only harts and other beasts, but also men.*

Some of my servants, says the above-mentioned author, once going to the country beyond Mouree, found a snake seventeen feet long, and very bulky, lying about a pit of water; near which were two porcupines, between which and the snake began a very sharp engagement, each shooting very violently in their way, the snake his venom, and the porcupines their quills of two spans in length. My men having seen this fight a considerable time, without being perceived by the furious combatants, in the heat of the battle loaded their muskets, and let fly at the three champions to so good a purpose, that they killed them all, and brought them to Mouree, where they were devoured by them and their comrades, as very great delicacies.

* It must be confessed that this account at first sight shocks probability, and yet the concurrent testimony of many authors of reputation render the fact indisputable.

Moſt of the ſnakes are venomous ; but one is ſo to an extraordinary degree: this is ſcarce a yard long ; it is two ſpans thick, and variegated with white, black, and yellow. The ſnakes not oniy infeſt the woods, but the dwellings of the Negroes, and even the very bedchambers within the forts.

The country alſo produces ſcorpions, millepedes of a poiſonous nature ; but whoſe ſting is noto dangerous as that of the ſcorpions on this coaſt. But none of the reptiles and inſects of this country appear more extraordinary than the ants. " Theſe vermin, ſays the above travellers, make neſts about twice the height of a man, of the earth which they turn up in the fields and hills, and ſometimes build large neſts on the trees, from which places they ſometimes come to the forts in ſuch prodigious ſwarms, that they frequently oblige us to quit our beds in the night. They are ſtrangely rapacious, and no animal can ſtand before them : they have often in the night attacked one of my live ſheep, and before morning have made it ſo perfect a ſkeleton that no human hands could have performed the work with ſuch art. They ſerve chickens and other fowl in this manner : and the rat, notwithſtanding its ſwiftneſs, cannot eſcape them ; for as ſoon as one of them attacks a rat, he is inevitably gone ; for attempting to run away, he is aſſaulted by ſeveral others, till ſo many fall upon him that he is over-powered. Theſe ants are of various ſizes and colours. The ſting or bite of the red ant raiſes an inflammation that is more painful than that of the milliepedes. The white are as tranſparent as glaſs, and bite with ſuch force, that in one night they will eat through a thick wooden cheſt of goods.

The want of fleſh and neceſſary proviſions in this country, renders it neceſſary for the natives to ſubſiſt principally on fiſh, and it ſeems a particular favour of providence that the ſea and rivers ſeem to contend which ſhall produce the beſt. There are here many ſorts found in Europe, as pike, plaice, flounders,

bream, thornback, lobfters, crabs, prawns and
fhrimps ; befides a great variety of excellent fifh that
feem peculiar to thefe feas.

The Slave Coaft begins about Rio Volta, probably
fo called from the rapidity with which that river runs
into the fea; for being very broad a few miles within land, and narrow at its mouth, where the fhore
rifes high, it difcharges its waters with an amazing
impetuofity.   The country affords nothing very
extraordinary till we come to the kingdom of Whydah*, which is one of the moft delightful places in
the world.   The great number and variety of tall,
beautiful and fhady trees on the coaft, feem as if they
were planted in fine groves, for the fake of ornament,
and are without under-wood or weeds.   The verdant
fields are every where cultivated, and no otherwife
divided than by thefe groves, and by villages, each
encompaffed by a low mud wall, and regularly placed
over the face of the country.   In fhort, every thing
contributes to render the profpect the moft delightful that imagination can form.   Not a mountain, or
even an hilloc interrupts the view; the whole country
being a fine, eafy, and almoft imperceptible afcent,
for the fpace of forty or fifty miles from the fea ;
fo that from any part of this kingdom you may have
a profpect of the ocean, and the farther you go from
it, the more beautiful and populous is the country.
Yet the air is extremely unhealthful with refpect to
foreigners.

All the fruits produced on the Gold Coaft grow
here, befides which there are abundance of tamarinds,
citrons, and fome others ; European feeds grow up
to great perfection ; and here might be planted the
fineft falad gardens in the world.

The cattle are cows, fheep, goats, and hogs, all
which are but little different in fhape and fize from

* This country is called Fida by the Dutch, Juda by the French,
and Whydah by the Englifh, Portuguefe and natives.

thofe of the Gold Coaft, but are more flefhly and of
a more agreeable tafte. There are alfo horfes, but they
are very indifferent ones ; and farther within land,
there are elephants, buffaloes, feveral forts of deer,
hares, and tygers. There are here alfo vaft numbers
of apes, of different kinds.

There are no other forts of tame-fowl but a few
turkeys and geefe, cocks and hens, of which laft
there are great plenty, which though fmall are fat
and good. The whole country feems covered with
wild fowl, as geefe, ducks, fnipes, turtle-doves,
and twenty other forts of birds that are both good
and cheap.

Among all the birds in this country, there is one
that has this remarkable circumftance attending it,
that whenever it moults it changes its colour, fo that
thofe that are black this year, become blue or red
the next ; they will be yellow the following year,
and afterwards green : but they never vary from
thefe five colours, which are always very bright, and
are never mixed *.

The natives are better dreffed than thofe of the
Gold Coaft. The drefs of the king and that of the
great officers, is nearly the fame. It confifts in a piece
of white linen about three ells long, which encom-
paffes the waift, and hangs down to their feet like a
petticoat. Upon this they wear a garment of filk of
the fame fize and form : and over this laft they have
a richer piece of filk fix of feven ells in length, which
they tie by the two corners, and making a great
bunch on the right hip, the reft hangs down to the
ground fo as to form a train : but none are allowed
to wear red, except the royal family. They wear
necklaces and bracelets of pearl, gold and coral, with
chains of gold. Moft of them never wear any thing
on the head, to fhelter them from the rain or the

* This and moft of the following particulars relating to Whydah,
are abridged from Le Voyage du Chevalier des Marchais en Guinee.
Tom. II.

. heat of the fun ; but a few of the great put on a hat
and feather.

The common people have generally only a few
herbs or a piece of cotton of the fize of a napkin
faftened round their wafts, to cover what modefty
teaches them to conceal : but the women of the fame
rank, have five or fix cloths round the waift, the
longeft of which covers half the leg, and the others
which are over it, are each fhorter than the other.

The king's wives, and thofe of the grandees, are
like all the others, naked from the girdle upwards,
and from the girdle downwards have two or three
coverings of cotton and filk, the longeft of which
reaches to the ankles, and the others are a little fhorter
They are very large and form a roll about the hips,
that makes them feem as if they wore a hoop-petticoat.
They are adorned with necklaces, and with ftrings
of pearls, gold and coral from the wrift to the elbow,
and wear on their heads a cap of plaited and coloured
ftraw which is very light, and refembles the pope's
tiara.

Thefe people are remarkable for their civility to
ftrangers, and the extraordinary refpect they fhew
each other. If any of them goes to vifit a fuperior,
or meets him by chance, he immediately falls on his
knees, and three times kiffes the earth, and clapping .
his hands, wifhes him a good day or night, which
the fuperior anfwers only with clapping his hands,
and returning the wifh. The fame marks of refpect
are paid by the younger to the elder brother ; by the
children to the father, and by the wives to their hufbands, none of whom receive any thing from the
other but on the knee, with their hands joined ; or if
they fpeak to them one hand is always put before the
mouth, that their breath may not be offenfive.
When two perfons of equal condition meet, they
both fall on their knees, clap their hands, and mu-
tually wifh each other a good day; which ceremonies

are alfo nicely obferved by their followers and de-
pendants on each fide.

But notwithftanding this fervile complaifance, they
are next to the Chinefe, the moft artful thieves in
the world ; like them, they are extremely addicted
to gaming, after having loft their whole fubftance,
they play for their wives and children, and when
they have loft them, ftake their own liberty, and
thus become flaves to their countrymen, who fometimes fell them to the Europeans; and like the Chinefe
they are indefatigably induftrious. Befides agriculture, from which the king and a few great men only
are exempted, they fpin cotton, weave cloths, make
calabafhes, wooden veffels, affagays, hardware, and
feveral other things, which are done to greater perfection here than on the Gold Coaft. While the men
are thus employed, the women make a kind of beer,
which they carry to market to fell, together with
their hufband's merchandize.

The meaner fort carry the goods from the fhore to
the king's village, and with a burthen of a hundred
pounds on their heads, they run a fort of continual
trot fo faft that it is difficult to keep up with them,
without any load at all.

Thofe who are very rich, befides hufbandry, in
which their wives and flaves are employed under
them, drive a very confiderable trade, not only in
flaves, but in many other commodities.

Thefe flaves are generally prifoners of war, which
are fold by the victors as their booty. When thefe
flaves come to Whydah, they are put in prifon all
together, and are afterwards brought out into a large
plain to be fold to the Europeans, who before they
purchafe them, examine every limb with the greateft
care. The invalids and maimed being thrown out
the remainder are numbered. In the mean while a
burning-iron with the arms or name of the companies
lies in the fire, and with this iron the Englifh, French,
and Dutch brand thefe unhappy wretches both men

and women, to prevent their being exchanged.
After this they are returned to their prifon, where
they are kept at the charge of thofe who have bought
them, on bread and water, till they are ready to be
taken on board, before which their former mafters
ftrip them entirely naked ; in which condition they
are ftowed in the holds of the fhips, and carried to
America, where they are again fold to the planters
in the European colonies.   I gladly drop this dreadful commerce, fo inconfiftent with Chriftianity, and
fo difhonourable to human nature.

It is remarkable that the natives of Whydah are
fo expert in accounts, that they reckon very confie
derable fums as quick, and as juftly by the head alon-
as we do with the affiftance of pen and ink, which
makes it very eafy to trade with them, and not half
fo troublefome as it is to deal with other Negroes.

A plurality of wives is here carried to a greater
length, than on the Gold Coaft, or perhaps in any
country in the world, fo that if the females do not
vaftly exceed the males in number, it is evident that
multitudes of the latter muft for ever be excluded
from marriage.   It is faid that private men have often
forty or fifty ; that their chief captains have three
or 400, and the king as many thoufands.   Thefe
wives may be confidered as only fo many flaves, and
indeed the greateft part of them are probably captives,
who happen to pleafe their mafters, who therefore
rather chufe to keep them, than to fell them to the
Europeans.   The chief part of them till the ground
for their hufbands, while the moft beautiful ftay at
home, where they are not excufed from working ;
but the men are fo extremely jealous of them, that
on the leaft fufpicion they fell them to the Europeans.
On the Gold Coaft, it is common for the hufband to
fhare with his wife the profits of her proftitution; but
here adultery is punifhed with death, if the perfon
injured be a rich man, the crime is fufficient to plunge
the whole family into flavery.

There are feveral claffes among the king's wives. She who has brought forth the firft male infant is at the head of the firft. This is the queen, or as they term her, the king's great wife. All the others treat her with refpect, all in the feraglio are under her command, and fhe has no fuperior but the king's mother, whofe credit is greater or lefs according to the degree of his majefty's affection for her, or her power of managing him. She is properly of no clafs; fhe has a feparate apartment in the palace, flaves of her own fex to wait upon her, and revenues for her fupport. When fhe has great credit with her fon, fhe receives many prefents from thofe who ftand in need of her protection; but fhe is obliged to live in a ftate of celibacy, and is not allowed to marry again.

If a man accidently touches any part of the body of one of the king's wives, his head, or at leaft his liberty is forfeited, fhe is defiled, and being unfit to return to the palace, both are doomed to perpetual flavery. Hence the king is entirely ferved by his wives, and no man is permitted to enter the apart-ment inhabited by them ; and when any of them go to work in the field, which they do by hundreds, whenever they fee a man they call out ftand clear, on which he immediately falls on his knees, or flat on the ground, and thus waits for their palling by with-out prefuming fo much as to look at them. The king on the leaft difguft fells eighteen or twenty of them ; but this does not leffen their number: for the officers to whom the government of the feraglio is intrufted, fupply their places with frefh ladies ; and whenever they fee a beautiful virgin, they prefent her to the king, none daring to oppofe them ; and if a lady happens to pleafe his majefty, he does her the honour to lie with her two or three times, after which fhe is obliged to pafs the remainder of her life like a nun : which in this country is confidered by the women as a moft dreadful punifhment.

Upon the father's death the eldeſt ſon inherits not only all his goods and cattle ; but his wives, which he keeps and enjoys as his own ; excepting only his own mother, for whom he provides a ſeparate apartment, and ſufficient ſubſiſtence. This cuſtom prevails both among the great and the commonalty.

The kingdom of Whydah is hereditary ; the eldeſt ſon ſuccecding his father, unleſs the great have ſome extraordinary reaſons for excluding him, and placing the crown on the head of one of his brothers, as was the caſe in the year 1725. The king's eldeſt ſon is therefore preſumptive heir of the crown; but then he muſt have been born after the king's acceſſion ; for thoſe he had before he aſcended the throne, are only conſidered as private perſons.

But they have here a cuſtom that is much more extraordinary ; though it is a law never to be vio- lated. The ſucceſſor is no ſooner born, than he is carried by the great men into the province of Zingua on the frontiers of the kingdom, where he is educat- ed as a private perſon, without knowing his birth, or having the leaſt knowledge of ſtate affairs. None of the great are allowed to viſit or receive viſits from him. He is to continue at Zingua under the care of a private man, who though he is intruſted with the ſecret of his birth he is not to reveal it to him on pain of death, and is to treat him in the ſame man- ner as if he was his own ſon. Thus on his aſcending the throne, knowing neither the intereſts nor the maxims of the ſtate, he is obliged to abandon the government to the management of the great, and their ſucceſſors ; for their poſts are hereditary, and the eldeſt ſon always ſucceeds them.

The ſtate of abaſement and ignorance, from which the preſumptive heir of the crown is thus raiſed, makes him long ſenſible of the pleaſure of royalty, when he ſees himſelf thus unexpectedly placed on the throne. Indeed that moment is no ſooner arrived than he is no longer conſidered as a man ; he becomes in an inftant a kind of deity, who is never approached, but with the moft profound reverence. As foon as a perfon is arrived at the gate of the hall of audience, he proftrates himfelf on the earth, and advances, creeping on his hands and knees, till he comes within a certain diftance of the throne, and the king allows him to fpeak by gently clapping his hands. He then utters what he has to fay in a low voice, and in few words, with his face towards the earth. Nobody is exempt from this inconvenient and humbling ceremonial; the greateft lords in the kingdom are fubject to it, as well as the others, and none but the chief captain of the feraglio, and the high prieft can enter the palace without leave ; but if they fpeak to the king, they, as well as the others, are obliged to do it in the above pofture.

When one of the great men would fpeak to the king, and has obtained his permiffion, he goes to the palace, attended by all his men in arms, and with drums, trumpets and flutes. When he arrives at the gate of the hall of audience, his men make a general difcharge of their mufkets, the drums, flutes and trumpets ftrike up, and all the men fhout aloud. In this manner he enters into the firft court, and there ftrips off all his clothes, and hides his nakednefs with herbs put round his waift ; he alfo takes off his bracelets, necklaces, and rings, and in general all his jewels. In this condition he proceeds to the hall of audience, where he proftrates himfelf, advances creeping to the foot of the throne, fpeaks with his face towards the earth, and when his audience is ended, retires, creeping backward, without changing the pofture he took in entering. On his rejoining his men who wait for him in the court, he dreffes and puts on his ornaments, and the king is informed of his departure by the firing of guns, the found of the inftruments of mufic, and the loud cries of joy uttered by his people.

The king never comes to the hall of audience but when the directors of the companies, or his

great men have affairs to communicate to him, and
are to receive his orders, or when he would admini-
ster juftice to his fubjects.   He paffes the reft of his
time in the feraglio, accompanied by his women,
fix of whom ftay with him ; thefe are magnificently
adorned, and kneel before him with their heads
almoft touching the floor. In this pofture they entertain and endeavour to divert him ; they drefs him,
and wait upon him at the table ; and ufe every art
to render themfelves beloved.   When he would be
alone with one of his wives, he touches her flightly,
and gently claps his hands : immediately the five
others retire, and having fhut the door of the room
where the king remains with their companion, they
keep it, till the happy woman leaves it.   Then fix
others take the places of the former, and thus they
relieve each other.

The king's palace is now plentifully provided
with European furniture, while the great men and
rich merchants in this refpect endeavour to furnifh
their houfes in the fame manner. They have magnificent beds, eafy chairs, canopies, looking-glaffes,
and in a word, every thing fit to adorn a houfe in
that climate.   There are here cooks inftructed by
thofe of France, fo that when an entertainment is
given to an European, he finds the tables of the
Negro lords ferved with as many delicacies as thofe
of Europe.   Wine is brought them from Spain, the
Canaries, Madeira, and France ; they are alfo fupplied with brandy, fweetmeats, tea, coffee and cho-
colate ; and their tables fhew no remains of their
ancient fimplicity. They are covered with fine linen,
and they have veffels of filver, and fervices of china.
But this politenefs is confined to the great and the
wealthy, the common people preferving their ancient
manners.

Notwithftanding the fervility with which the king
is treated by his fubjects, when the directors of companies or the captains wait upon him, he receives

them in the hall of audience, caufes eafy chairs to
be brought them, and even drinks and fmokes with
them.

We have already obferved that the people are
extremely jealous, and that adultery is punifhed
with death : but if a man is furprized with one of
the king's wives nothing can fave them ; the king
aimfelf pronounces fentence againft them on the
fpot. The officers of the palace inftantly caufe two
pits to be dug, fix or feven feet long, four broad,
and five deep, fo near together that the criminals
may fee and fpeak to each other. In one of thefe
pits a poft is fixed, to which the woman is faftened
with her hands tied behind her. Two wooden forks
are fixed at the end of the other pit, and the man
being ftripped naked, is faftened to a great iron bar
like a fpit, with iron chains, in fuch a manner that
he cannot move. The king's wives then bring fag-
gots, which they put into the pit, and before they
are lighted, the fpit to which the man is faftened,
is put upon the two forks, and fire is put to the wood
in fuch a manner, that only the extremity of the
flames can reach his body. He is thus left to burn
by a flow fire ; a cruel punifhment that would laft
for a long time, had they not the charity to turn
him with his face downwards: in which fituation he
is foon ftifled by the fmoke. When he no longer
gives any fign of life, they undo the chains, and
letting him fall into the pit cover him with earth.

The man being dead, about fifty or fixty of the
king's wives efcorted by a party of mufketeers, and
accompanied with drums and flutes, come from the
palace with each a large earthen pot of fcalding
water on her head, which they pour one after another
on the head of the poor wretch who is tied to the
poft, and afterwards throw the pots on her head
with all their force. Dead or not, all the water, and
all the pots that come from the palace are thrown on
the body of this unhappy woman ; after which,

whether she be still alive or dead, they cut the cords that fasten her to the post, pull that up, and bury her in the pit, under a heap of earth and stones.

When the wife of a great man is taken in adultery, he may either sell her to the Europeans, or put her to death: if he chuses the latter, he causes her head to be cut off, or has her strangled by the public exe. cutioner, and is acquitted by informing the king of what he has done, and paying the executioner's fee. But as he has no power over the man who has dif- honoured him, unless he catches him in the very act, in which case he kills them both, he is obliged to demand justice of the king, who never fails to con. demn the guilty to suffer death.

This severity is only inflicted with respect to marri- ed women. The unmarried are not subject to it, and a man runs no danger in being caught with one of them; for no body has any fault to find with him, because she is supposed to be her own mistress. It is so far from being infamous for her to have children before marriage, that she is sure this will cause her to be sooner married, because it is a proof of her fruitfulness, which is a very important con- sideration in a country where the fathers consider children, especially the males, as the greatest riches, and the support of their families: and it must be observed, that they never sell their own children for slaves.

When the king of Whydah is dead, the queen, or great wife of the deceased, lets the grandees know it, who are obliged to keep his death secret for three months, during which they assemble in order to consult whether the king's eldest son be worthy to ascend the throne. This term being expired, the king's death is made public, on which every thing falls into confusion: law, policy, justice, seem to have expired with the king, and the most dreadful disorders are committed: but this state of confusion lafts only five days; during which, the prince is fought for who is to fill the throne, and is put in poffeflion of the palace A number of great guns are now fired to inform the people that they have a king, and immediately tranquillity and good order are reftored ; the markets are open, and every body applies to bufinefs.

It being cuftomary to pull down the palace in which the king dies, within three months after his death another is built, to which the new king is brought with all the wives belonging to his father, which now become his. None but the mother of the deceafed, and that of the reigning king are exempt from this law.

The new king immediately orders the funeral of the late monarch, by caufing five cannon to be fired at break of day, five at noon, and five at fun-fet. The noife of the laft is followed by dreadful cries and howlings, which refound through the whole palace. The high prieft, who fuperintends the funeral, caufes a pit to be dug fifteen feet fquare and five deep, in the middle of which they hollow out a vault eight feet fquare, in the centre of which the king's body is placed with great ceremony. The high prieft then chufes eight of the favourite wives of the deceafed to go and ferve him in the other world. Being dreffed in their richeft apparel, and loaded with provifions, which they are to carry to the late king, they are conducted to the vault in which they are fhut up alive, and left there to perifh : but their death is fpeedy, they being foon covered with earth.

After the death of thefe women they bring the men, who are alfo to go and ferve the late king, the number of whom is not fixed, it depending on the will of the prefent monarch and the high prieft. As it is not known on whom the lot will fall, his late majefty's domeftics endeavour to fly or hide themfelves, and do not appear till four or five days after the ceremony is over. They are then reproached with having eaten the king's bread while he was living, and with receiving an infinite number of favours from him, and yet wanting the gratitude to accompany him into the other world. To this they ufually reply that the thoughts of death are dreadful, and that being of an age capable of enjoying the pleafures of life, they could not think of quitting it fo foon. With fuch excufes they obtain pardon, and are entered into the fervice of the new king, promifing that if he happens to die, they will be more faithful to him.

Among all the officers or domeftics of the king who muft infallibly follow him to the other world, his favourite is the principal. The perfon who is honoured with this title has no particular office in the palace; he is not even permitted to enter it: when he has any favour to afk, he muft addrefs himfelf to the high prieft, who makes known his requefts to the prince, who always grants them immediately. He has a right to take out of the market whatever pleafes him. He is dreffed in a long robe with large fleeves, and wears a hood, it may be of white linen, filk or Indian ftuff, adorned with flowers; and when he appears in public, holds a cane in his hand. He is treated with great refpeɛt, and exempted from the payment of all taxes. He lives a happy life; but it ends with that of the king; for nothing can difpenfe with his accompanying his mafter into the other world, and he is the firft who lofes his head, after the king's favourites are fmotherd in the cave. All the other men who were deftined to ferve the late king, have alfo their heads cut off, and according to the high prieft's order, their bodies are laid down, or placed fitting, with their heads befide them, and buried about the cave of the king.

When all the bodies are covered up, they raife above them a great heap of earth, which terminates in a pyramid, at the top of which they place the arms which the king was accuftomed to ufe, and furround them with a number of fetifhes, or little earthern figures, that are the tutelar deities to guard them.

Thofe would be very much to blame who fhould accufe the Negroes of Whydah of having no religion they practife circumcifion, but this does not here feem to be a religious rite, for they know no better reafon for it, than its being practifed by their fathers and grand-fathers, who learned it from their anceftors; and that they ought therefore to follow their example.

The moft fenfible men of Whydah have a confufed idea of the exiftence, and unity of God ; whom they fuppofe to be in heaven, and fay, that he rewards the good, and punifhes the wicked ; and that it is he who makes the thunder roll in the fky : but imagining that it would be prefumption in them to addrefs their petitions to him, they have feveral inferior deities, and befides the fetifhes, which they have in common with the Negroes on the Gold Coaft, they have four principal objects of religious worfhip ; the ferpent, which holds the firft rank ; the trees, which are of the fecond clafs; the fea, which is only in third rank ; and Agoya, who is the god of counfels.

The worfhip of the ferpent is accounted for in the following manner: the people of Whydah being ready to give battle to the king of Ardrah, a neighbouring nation, a great ferpent came from the enemy's army, to furrender itfelf to that of Whydah, and appeared fo gentle, that far from biting, it fawned upon every body ; which the high prieft obferving, ventured to take it in his hands, and to hold it up on high, to fhew it the whole army ; who being aftonifhed at the prodigy, proftrated themfelves before the harmlefs animal, and then fell upon the enemy with fuch courage, that they gained a complete victory. This the foldiers attributed to the ferpent. They carried it away with them, built a

houfe for it, brought it provifions, and in a little time
the new god eclipfed all the others, even the fetilhes,
which were the firft and the moft ancient gods of the
country, and its worlhip increafed in proportion to
the imaginary favours they fuppofed they had received
from it ; thus it did not long remain in the firft houfe
they had built for it ; they erected a more fumptuous
one, with many courts, and fpacious lodgings. They
appointed it a high prieft, and an entire order of marabouts to ferve it. But this was not all, they dedicated
to it the moft beautiful women, and that it might
never want fervants, chofe new ones every year.

It is remarkable that the moft fenfible Negroes,
very gravely affert, that the ferpent they now worfhip is really that which came to their anceftors, and
gave them the celebrated victory that delivered them
from the oppreffions of the king of Ardrah. The
pofterity of this ferpent have multiplied extremely,
and have not degenerated from the good qualities of
their father. They do no injury to any one ; but
fuffer the people to place them in their bofoms, to
put them about their necks, and into their beds.
The only refentment they lhew is againft the vene-
mous ferpents, which they always endeavour to deftroy, and there is no danger of the people's miftaking
one for the other. Thefe laft are all black, and refemble vipers ; they are four yards long, and an inch
and an half in diameter ; but the beneficent ferpent
is not commonly above feven feet and a half in length,
but it is of the thicknefs of a man's leg. It has a
large round head, and a pointed tail. Its fkin is very
beautiful, it being of a whitifh colour, marked in
waves very agreeably with yellow, blue and brown.

The people efteem themfelves happy when one of
thefe honours their houfe with its prefence, they give
it a bed, and if it be a female with young, they
make her a little houfe, to which fhe retires to bring
them forth, and when fhe or her young want food,

they fetch it them till they are big enough to take care of themfelves. The perfon that fhould kill one of them would fuffer a cruel death.

Every body knows that ferpents or fnakes multiply extremely, and that they live for a long time: one would therefore imagine, that the earth would be covered with them, but the black ferpents give them no quarter, and without refpect to their divinity, kill and eat them: the fwine do the fame, and this diminifhes their number; but it always cofts the life of thofe animals when they are caught in the fact; nothing can hinder a hog from being immediately put to death; the people have no refpect to thofe to whom they belong, for though they are the king's they are killed on the fpot, and their flefh belongs to thofe who flaughter them.

The ferpent of Whydah, from which all the others of the fame fpecies are faid to be defcended is wor-fhipped in his houfe or temple, upon every occafion: therefore the offerings and facrifices made to him are not confined to bulls and rams, to loaves of bread, fruit, or a few gold rings. The high prieft often prefcribes a confiderable quantity of valuable merchandize, barrels of bougies*, powder, brandy, hecatombs of bulls, fheep, fowl, and fometimes even human facrifices are offered to his honour. All this depends on the fancy and avarice of the prieft.

. The marabouts or the priefts of the grand ferpent are of one family, of which the high prieft, who is one of the grandees, is the chief. All the other marabouts receive his orders, and pay obedience to him. But befides the men and women of this family, a number of girls are confecrated to the ferpent, which procures them univerfal refpect, and confers upon them many extraordinary privileges, one of

* Thefe are the fame with the fhells called cowries, vulgarly termed blackmoor's teeth, which are brought from the Maldiva iflands, and on the coaft of Guinea pafs for fmall money.

which is a right to tyrannize over their hufbands, when they can find a man fuch a fool as to marry one of them.

But to proceed to the other deities : Agaya, or the god of counfels, is confulted by the people before they undertake any thing. This god is a paltry little idol of black earth, which rather refembles a mifhapen monfter than any thing elfe. It is reprefented feated or crouching on a kind of pedeftal of red earth, on which there is a piece of red cloth, adorned with cowries, and he has about his neck a fcarlet band, to which hang four cowries. His head is crowned with lizards, ferpents and red feathers. This idol is placed on a table in the high prieft's houfe, with three calabafhes before him, in which are fifteen or twenty balls of earth. Thofe who would confult him, addrefs themfelves to a marabout, tell him the fubject that brought them thither, give him the offering defigned for the god, and the price of confulting him, after which the queftion is determined by throwing the balls from one calabafh into another a certain number of times, when if there be an odd number in each, the marabout boldly pronounces that the oracle has declared in his favour, and the man may undertake the affair on which he has confulted the god.

When the fea is agitated in an extraordinary manner, fo that merchandize can neither be embarked, nor brought afhore, they confult the high prieft, and by his advice facrifice a bull or a fheep on the bank of the fea, fuffering the blood to run into the water, and throw a gold ring into the waves, as far as they are able. The ring and blood are loft; but the body of the facrificed beaft belongs to the prieft, who caufes it to be carried to his houfe.

It cofts lefs to render the trees favourable. It is commonly the fick that have recourfe to them, who make them an offering of millet, maize or rice, which the marabout places at the foot of the tree to which the fick man pays his devotions.

The kingdom of Ardrah, is but of fmall extent on the coaft, where the kingdoms of Whydah and Popo are taken out of it. It reaches only twenty-five leagues along the fhore ; but within land it extends from eaft to weft from the river Volta to that of Benin, which is above 100 leagues, and it reaches ftill farther from north to fouth.

The manners, cuftoms and religion of thefe people are in fome refpects the fame as thofe of Whydah, except their not worfhipping the ferpent. On the contrary, they fearch for the tame and gentle ferpents, in order to kill and eat them.

However, the people here offer up neither prayers nor facrifices. They feem to have no idea of another life, and only dread the accidents that may render this life unhappy. The great marabout appoints for every family the fetifhes they are to honour, in order to fecure themfelves from thefe misfortunes. The fetifhes of the king and the court are certain black birds almoft like the crows of Europe. With thefe the gardens of the palace are filled, and they are fed as well, though they are not treated with the fame refpect, as the ferpents of Whydah.

Private perfons have for their fetifhes fome a mountain, others a tree, a ftone, a piece of wood, or any other inanimate fubftance, which they regard with a kind of refpect ; but as we have already obferved, offer no prayers to them.

The great marabout has in every town a houfe to which he invites by turns the wives of all the free-men, to learn fome religious excercifes. They ftay there five or fix months, and are inftructed by old women in a fort of finging and dancing. They make them enter by bands, which fucceed each other day and night, in a hall appointed for that purpofe, and after having tied fmall irons and brafs plates to their legs and feet, in order that they may make the greater noife, they dance and fing with all their force. This dance confifts of ftamping and performing all the agitations and motions of the body that are moft fatiguing, and moft difficult to fupport. They accompany it with a fong, mixed with cries and howling, performed in cadence, and continue this violent exercife till they faint away, when in an inftant their old miftrelles fubftitute another fet of fcholars in the room of thofe who are out of breath, who begin the fame dance, the fame fong, and the fame cries, to the great difturbance of the neighbourhood.

The Sieur d'Elbée, who was there in 1670, obferves, that in the great marabout's houfe he faw a figure made to reprefent the devil, which was of the fize of a child of four years of age, and painted white, and he afferting that the devil was black, the marabout gravely replied, that he was miftaken, for he was fure he was very white, for he had feen and fpoke to him feveral times.

The above gentleman found at Affem fome Negroes who were Chriftians, and came to afk him for chaplets of beads, and to afk if he would not order mafs to be faid in his apartmemt. It is probable that thefe Negroes had been baptized by the Portuguefe while they were eftablifhed in the kingdom.

Ali the men of rank wear two fhort petticoats of taffety or other filk, and have filk fcarfs in the form of fhoulder-belts. Moft of them go with their heads and feet naked; they may, however, wear bonnets or hats, and fandals, except in the king's palace. The men of the common rank are covered from the girdle to the knees with a piece of ferge, that goes twice round them, the ends wrapping over at the navel. The poor and thofe who gain their living by their labour, have only a fmall piece of cotton cloth, or fome grafs to cover their nudities, and have the head and feet naked.

The women of rank have petticoats and fcarfs like the men, and as they feldom leave their houfes, they commonly wear nothing on their heads and feet. The poor women have fhort cloths tied about their waifts, and have their heads and feet always naked.

The city of Affem, the capital of the kingdom, is furrounded by four walls of earth which are very high and thick. This earth is red, and forms a fub-ftance as firm and even as plafter, though it does not appear to be mixed with lime. Each wall has a large and deep ditch, not on the outfide but within it, and over thefe ditches are wooden bridges.

The palace when Mr. d'Elbée was there*, was very large and compofed of many great courts, entirely furrounded with porticos, above which were apartments, that had fmall windows. In fome of thefe chambers the floor was covered with large Turky carpets, and in others with mats. A fingle eafy chair was in each room, and they were likewife furnifhed with fkreens, chefts, cabinets and porcelain brought from China. There was no glafs in the windows, but only frames of white linen, and taffety curtains. The gardens were very fpacious, and confifted of long viftas of thick trees, to afford a cool and fhady retreat.

The king always eats alone, and when he drinks an officer makes a fignal with two fmall rods of iron, in order that all who are within fight may turn away and not look at his majefty ; for feeing him drink is thought a crime worthy of death. The very officer who prefents the glafs is faid to turn his body and head, and to prefent it backward. This they fay is done to prevent the effects of forcery at that moment.

The king is always ferved on the knee, and this refpect is fhewn even to the provifions fet on his table.

---

* This country has been fince ravaged by the king of Dahomey, who in 1724, made a conqueft both of Whydah and Ardrah, which has probably produced fome confiderable changes.

Thofe who happen to be in the way of the officers who carry them, proftrate themfelves with their faces to the earth, and dare not raife them up, till the diſhes are out of fight.

The commerce of the ſtate confiſts only in ſlaves and proviſions : the ſlaves are of feveral kinds ; fome are prifoners of war, others are paid to the ſtate by the neighbouring kingdoms, dependant on that of Ardrah. Some are condemned to be fold for ſlaves, for having violated the laws of their country. Some are ſlaves by birth, as are the children of all ſlaves ; and there are others who not being able to pay their debts, are fold for the benefit of their creditors. Thofe who have difobeyed the king's orders are inévitibly condemned to fuffer death, and their wives and kindred, to a certain degree, become ſlaves to the king, who fells them to whom he pleafes.

The common people can neither read nor write, they therefore in buying and felling make ufe of cords tied in knots, each of which has a particular fignification. Thefe knots are in ufe among many of the favages of America. But the great underſtand the Portuguefe tongue, which they read and write very well.

About fifty miles eaſt of Ardrah are fituated the cape and river of Formofa, otherwife called Benin, from the kingdom of Great Benin on its banks. The country by the fides of this river, is very unhealthful, and peſtered with muſketoes, which are very troubleſome to the Europeans, who have had factories in three vilages up the river.

The natives feem very civil to each other ; and at the fame time are prudent and referved, efpecially in the management of their trade, always pretending to be poorer than they really are, in order to efcape the rapacious hands of their governors.

The habit of the Negroes is neater and more ornamental than that of the Negroes on the Gold Coaſt. The rich wear a white calico or cotton cloth, about

a yard long, and half a yard broad, which ferves
them for drawers. Over this they wear a finer white
cotton drefs, which is commonly 16 or 20 yards long,
this is wrapped about them ; over this is a fcarf,
about a yard long, and two fpans broad, the end of
which is adorned with fringe or lace. In thefe clothes
they appear abroad ; but at home they wear a coarfe
cloth about their waifts inftead of drawers, and
above all a great painted cloth, of the manufacture
of the country, which they wear like a cloak. The
meaner fort are drefled in the fame manner, only the
ftuff they wear is coarfer.

The wives of the great lords wear fine calico cloths
round their waifts, handfomely chequered with feveral colours. The upper part of the body is covered
with a beautiful cloth about a yard long. Their
necks are adorned with necklaces of coral, very
agreeably difpofed ; their arms are dreffed up with
bright copper, or iron bracelets ; as are alfo the legs
of fome of them, and their fingers are as thick
crowded with copper rings as they can poffibly wear
them. The meaner fort differ from the rich only in
the goodnefs of their clothes.

Almoft all the children go naked; the boys till
they are ten or twelve years old, and the girls till nature difcovers their maturity : till then they wear
only ftrings of coral twifted about their middles,
which are not fufficient to hide their nudities.

The men let their hair grow in its natural form,
except buckling it in two or three places, in order
to hang a great coral to it ; but the women's hair is
artfully turned up into great and fmall buckles, and
divided at the crown of the head like a cock's comb
inverted, by which means the fmall curls are placed
in exact order. Some divide their hair into twenty
plaits and curls.

The king is an abfolute monarch, his will being
a law. Next to him are three great lords, to whom

all muſt addreſs themſelves who want to apply to
his majeſty ; but as they are ſure to inform him only
of what they themſelves pleaſe, the whole adminiſtra-
tion of the government depends on them. Next to
theſe are the Are de Roes, or ſtreet kings, ſome of
whom preſide over the commonalty, and others
over the ſlaves; ſome over military affairs; and others
over the affairs relating to the cattle, and the fruits
of the earth, &c.

From theſe Are de Roes are choſen the viceroys
and governors of the countries ſubject to the king ;
who are recommended by the three great lords, and
are reſponſible to them. The king preſents to each of
them a ſtring of coral, as a mark of their honour:
but this ſtring they are obliged to wear about their
necks, without ever daring to put it off on any
account whatſover, and if they are ſo unhappy as
to loſe it, or careleſsly ſuffer it to be ſtolen, they are
certainly condemned to die. The king keeps theſe
corals, which are factitious, in his own poſſeſſion ;
and the counterfeiting, or having any of them,
without his grant, is puniſhed with death. They
are made of a ſort of pale red earth or ſtone, and
are ſo well glazed, that they look like ſpeckled marble.

The king has a great revenue ; for his territories
are very large. He keeps his court in the city of
Benin, whence the river and the whole kingdom
derives its name. This city is of great extent, and
the ſtreets are very long and broad ; and beſides are
kept very clean and neat, every woman cleaning
her own door. Formerly it was cloſely built, and
in a manner overſtocked with inhabitants, but half
the houſes are now in ruins. Thoſe that are ſtill
ſtanding are large and tolerably handſome, but are
built with clay walls, there not being a ſtone in the
whole country as big as a man's fiſt They are
covered at the top with reeds, ſtraw or leaves. Markets are kept every day in the ſtreets, either of

corn, cotton, elephants teeth, or European wares, but the inhabitants are all natives, foreigners being not permitted to live there.

The palace, which forms a principal part of the city, is built upon a large plain, and has no houses joining to it. The firſt place you come to is a very long gallery, (if it may be called by that name,) fuſtained by fifty-eight ſtrong planks, about twelve feet high, inſtead of pillars ; theſe are neither ſawed nor plained ; but only hacked out. On paſſing this gallery, you come to a mud wall that has three gates, at each corner one, and one in the middle ; this laſt is adorned on the top with a wooden turret, about ſixty or ſeventy feet high, ornamented on the top with a large copper ſnake, well caſt. Entering one of theſe gates, you come into a large ſquare, almoſt a quarter of a mile over, and encloſed by a low wall, at the oppoſite ſide of which you come to another kind of gallery, which has a gate at each end ; and paſſing through one of them, a third gallery appears, differing from the foimer only in the planks which ſupport it, that have ſome little reſemblance to human figures, but wretchedly executed. Going through a gate of this gallery you enter another greater ſquare, and a fourth gallery, beyond which is the king's dwelling houſe, where is another brazen ſnake. The firſt apartment is the king's audience chamber, where he fits on an ivory couch, under a canopy of Indian ſilk ; this room is adorned with ſeven elephants teeth, made perfectly clean, and placed on ivory pedeſtals.

As to the religion of the inhabitants of Benin, they aſcribe to God the attributes of omnipreſence, omniſcience, and inviſibility, and ſay that he governs all things by his providence ; but like the other Negroes on this coaſt, they offer up their petitions to things conſecreated for that purpoſe, as elephant's teeth, and the like ; and yet they think it abſurd to make any corporeal repreſentation of the Deity.

They make daily offerings of a few boiled yams, mixed with oil, which they lay before their subordinate deities; and sometimes they offer a cock; but then the idol has only the blood; because they like the flesh themselves. They are laid to observe a kind of sabbath every fifth day, on which the great sacrifice cows, sheep, and goats; while the commonalty kill dogs, cats, and chickens; and of whatever is killed large portions are distributed to the necessitous, in order to enable them to celebrate this festival. They have a great feast in May, called the coral feast, which is the only time when the king appears publicly. On this occasion, he comes magnificently dressed to the second square of the palace, where he is seated under a fine canopy, his wives and great officers placing themselves around him. Soon after they begin a procession, and the king rises in order to offer sacrifices, during which he is saluted with the loud acclamations of the people. In about a quarter of an hour the king returns to his place, where he stays about two hours, in order to give the people time to perform their devotions; which being done, he returns home. The remainder of the day is spent in feasting, and the king causes all sorts of provisions to be distributed to all in common, and the great follow his example: so that on that day nothing is seen throughout the whole city, but all possible marks of rejoicing. The reason of this festival is unknown.

One day in the year they have likewise an expensive festival in honour of their deceased ancestors.

The men marry as many women as their circumstances will allow them to keep; they have scarce any marriage ceremonies among either rich or poor, except only, that the first treat the bride's friends more splendidly than the others. They are very jealous of their wives with their own countrymen, but place greater confidence in the Europeans;

for they fuffer the latter freely to converfe with them; but no Negro is allowed to come near the women's apartment. All the difference between the wives of the great and thofe of the meaner fort, is, that the former are always fhut up very clofe ; while the latter go every where.

Adultery is here punifhed different ways: If one of the commonalty furprizes his wife in the fact, he may lawfully feize all the effects of the paramour, which he may immediately apply to his own ufe ; while he punifhes his wife with a cudgel ; and then turns her out of doors to feek her fortune. The rich revenge themfelves the fame way ; but the women's relations, to avoid the fcandal that might fall upon the family, reconcile the injured hufband by giving him a good fum of money, to induce him to reftore her again to favour. But if the governors furprize a perfon debauching their wives, they kill both on the fpot, and then throw out their dead bodies, that they may become a prey to the wild beafts.

If a woman bears two children at a birth, it is believed to be a good omen, and the king is immediately informed of it, who caufes the public joy to be expreffed by all forts of mufic. This is the cafe in all the territories of Benin, except at Arebo, where both the woman and the twins are cruelly facrificed to a certain dæmon which they fuppofe inhabits a wood near the town. But if the man happens to have an extraordinary affection for his wife, he generally buys a female flave, and facrifices her in her ftead. At prefent the men, when the time of their wives delivery approaches, fend them to another place where this inhuman cuftom is not obferved.

When the child is feven days old, the parents make a fmall feaft, imagining that the infant is paft its greateft danger ; and in order to prevent the evil fpirits doing it any mifchief, they ftrew all the

ways with provisions ready dreffed, in order to appeafe them.

Eight or fourteen days after the birth of their
children, both males and females are circumcifed;
the former are berelt of their prepuce, and the latter
of a fmall part of their clitoris; befides they make
fmall incifions all over the bodies of the infants, in
a fort of regular manner, expreffing fome figures;
and notwithftanding the cruelty of thus torturing
the poor innocents, this cuftom is univerfally obferved among the inhabitants of Benin.

If they fall fick they have immediately recourfe to
the prieft, who here, as well as on the Gold Coaft,
acts the phyfician. If his remedies prove ineffectual,
he has recourfe to facrifices, and if the patient recovers is much efteemed. But the priefts are here
generally poor, becaufe on common occafions each
perfon offers his own facrifice, and performs the
fervice of his idols, without troubling them.

The cattle and productions of the country are
much the fame as in the other parts of Guinea, only
the country contains great numbers of elephants,
and lions, as well as tygers.

When any perfon dies, the corpfe is wafhed and
cleaned, and if a native of Benin happens to die at
a very diftant place, the body is perfectly dried up
over a gentle fire, and put into a coffin, whofe planks
are clofe joined with glue, and brought the firft opportunity to that city, in order to be buried. The
neareft relations, wives and flaves, go into mourning
for the deceafed; fome fhave their beards, others
half their heads. The public mourning commonly
lafts fourteen days. Their lamentations and cries are
accomodated to the tunes of feveral mufical inftruments; with large intermediate ftops, during which
they drink very plentifully. When the funeral is over,
each perfon retires to his own houfe, and the neareft
relations, who continue in mourning, in this manner bewail the dead, during feveral months.

Their mufical inftruments chiefly confift of large and fmall drums not very different from thofe of the Gold Coaft : they have befides a fort of iron bells on which they play ; and calabafhes hung round with cowries, that ferve them inftead of caftagnets ; all which together afford a very difagreeable and jarring found. Befides thefe they have a kind of harp, ftrung with fix or feven extended reeds, upon which they play with much art ; at the fame time they fing to it very agreeably, and dance in fuch a juft manner as is very diverting.

The natives here are not at all addicted to gaming, for they only play for diverfion ; but never for money.

They divide the time into years, months, weeks, and days ; and reckon fourteen months in the year.

They are entirely ignorant of the art of war ; and it is with the greateft reluctance they are brought to face an enemy. Their weapons are a fort of hang-ers, fmall poniards, affagays, bows, and poifoned arrows. They have light fhields made of fmall bamboos, but as they cannot ward off a forcible blow they are of little fervice.

They are well fkilled in making feveral forts of dyes, as green, blue, red, yellow, and black. The blue they prepare from indigo, but the other colours they extract from trees. They fpin cotton, and weave cotton cloths in fuch quantities, that many thoufand pieces are exported every year. Befides weaving, they have few mechanical arts ; their other workmen are moftly fmiths, carpenters, and leather dreffers : but their workmanfhip is fo clumfy, that an ingenious boy who had been but a month or two learning in Europe would excel them; though perhaps the mafters themfelves might be unable to outdo them had they only their tools.

If poffeffed of wealth, the people live well ; their common diet being beef, mutton and chickens, with yams for bread ; which after they have boiled they beat very fine, in order to make cakes of it. They frequently treat one another, and generoufly impart a portion of their fuperfluity to the necellitous. The meaner fort content themfelves with fmoaked or dried fifh : their bread is alfo yams, bananas, and beans, and their drink, water and pardon wine, which is none of the beft.

The king, and the great lords, and every governor, who is but indifferently rich, fubfift feveral poor at their refidence ; employing thofe who are fit for any work, and charitably fupporting thofe incapable of labour without working ; fo that there are here no beggars, nor do we find any among them remarkably poor. They fhew their liberality by mutual prefents of all forts of goods which they fend to each other, and likewife fhew their hofpitality by giving the Europeans prodigious quantities of refrefhing provifions.

TRAVELS

INTO

THE INLAND PARTS OF AFRICA.

BY

FRANCIS MOORE.

Containing the author's arrival at James's Fort in the river Gambia, an account of the company's factories there; a defcription of the different nations inhabiting the banks of that river, with their manners, cuftoms, religion, and the climate of the country.

I LEFT England in July 1730, on my being appointed a writer in the fervice of the royal African company, and on the 9th of November came to an anchor in the mouth of the Gambia. As we faiied up that river near the fhore, the country appeared very beautiful, being for the moft part woody ; and between the woods were pleafant green rice grounds, which after the rice is cut, are ftocked with cattle. On the eleventh we landed at James's ifland, which is fituated in the middle of the river, that is here at leaft feven miles broad. This ifland lies about ten leagues from the river's mouth, and is about three quarters of a mile in circumference. Upon it is a fquare ftone fort regularly built, with four baftions ; and upon each are feven guns well mounted, that command the river all round ; befides, under the

walls of the fort facing the fea, are two round batteries, on each of which are four large cannon well
mounted, that carry ball of twenty-four pounds
weight, and between thefe are nine fmall guns
mounted for falutes.

Befides the fort, there are feveral factories upon
the river, fettled for convenience of trade ; but they
are all under the direction of the governor and chief
merchants of the fort. For this purpofe the company have here three or four floops of about thirty
tons each, and about the fame number of long-boats;
fome of which are conftantly employed in fetching
provifions and water from the main for the ufe of
the garrifon, and the reft are employed in carrying
goods up to the factories, and bringing from them
flaves, elephants teeth, and wax.

On my arrival, I had a good apartment given me
near the compting-houfe. I dieted with the reft of the
writers, at what was called the fecond table ; and we
had frefh provifions in plenty, there being a beaft
killed every other day ; fowls were brought daily by
the natives to fell to the governor, and he allowed
every perfon who did not care for beef, to have them
at a very eafy rate. Our table, as well as that of the
governor's, was almoft every day fupplied with greens
from the company's garden at Gillyfree, for which we
paid nothing. Flour we were well fupplied with by
the company, and having a baker on the ifland we
had very good bread made us every day. Oyfters we
had when we pleafed, for at low-water we could get
them at the N. N. W. point of the ifland. We had
wine and brandy at a moderate price, and when the
governor had any quantity of beer, we had a pretty
good fhare of it. In fhore, we wanted for nothing
that was neceffary in regard to diet; but every one
who come there ought to bring bedding, clothes and
chefts. As foon as a perfon arrives, it is ufual to
agree with fome women at Gillyfree, on the oppofite

continent, to wafh their linen, which they do by the month, with good foap of their own making

On the 16th, Mr. John Hamilton, my fhipmate, was ordered up to manage the factory at Tancrowall, fettling their chiefly for bees-wax. This town is divided into two parts, one for the Portuguefe, and the other for the Mundingoes. The former live in large fquare houfes, the latter in round huts, made of a good fat binding clay, which foon hardens: they are about twenty feet diameter, and about eight feet high, with a roof like that of a beehive made either of ftraw or palmetto leaves, fo well fitted together, that the rain cannot penetrate, nor the heat of the fun ftrike through them. Tancrowall is the refidence of the prieft annually fent over from St. Jago, one of the Cape de Verd iflands, who has a church here, in which, during the prieft's ftay, mafs is faid almoft every day. Here are many of the defcendants of the Portuguefe, who fend canoes up the river to trade once or twice a year: by which means they have made this town a place of great refort, and the richeft in the whole river. It is about half a mile in length, and pleafantly fituated by the water-fide, with a woody hill behind it.

A night or two after, I fupped upon oyfters that grew upon trees: this being fomewhat remarkable, it may be though worthy of an explanation. Down the river where the water is falt, and near the fea, the river is bounded with trees called mangroves, whofe leaves being long and heavy, weigh the boughs into the water: to thefe leaves the young oyfters faften in great quantities, where they grow till they are very large, and then you cannot feparate them from the tree; but are obliged to cut off the boughs, with the oyfters hanging on them, refembling ropes of onions.

On the 20th, I went to St. Domingo on the main land, which was the firft time of my landing upon the continent of Africa. I walked from St. Domingo

to Gillyfree, which is about a mile and a half, all
the way through grafs eight or nine feet high. By
the way we faw a great number of lizards, fome of
which have heads as yellow as gold. St. Domingo
lies on the north fide of the river, directly oppofite
to James's ifland, and confifts only of a few round
huts belonging to the company, in which fome of
their caftle-flaves live who cut wood for the ufe of the
fort, take care of a well, and fill the cafks daily
brought over from the fort for that purpofe.

On the 22d of February, one of the kings of Fonia came to the fort, and on his landing, was faluted
with five guns. He came to fee the governor, or
rather to afk for fome powder and ball, in order to
enable him to defend himfelf againft fome people
with whom he was at war; he was a young man,
very black, tall, and well fet, was drefled in a pair
of fhort, yellow cotton-cloth breeches, and wore on
his back a garment of the fame cloth, made like a
furplice: he had on his head a very large cap, to
which was faftened part of a goat's tail, which is a
cuftomary ornament with the great men of this river,
but he had no fhoes nor ftockings. He and his retinue came in a large canoe holding about 16 people,
all armed with guns and cutlafles. With him came
two or three women, and the fame number of Mundingo drums, which are about a yard long, and a
foot, or twenty inches diameter at the top, but lefs
at the bottom; made out of a folid piece of wood,
and covered only at the wideft end with the fkin of a
kid. They beat upon them with their left hand,
ufing only one drum-ftick; and the women will dance
very brifkly to the found. They ftaid at the fort all
night, and then returned home; having nine guns
fired at their going off.

It may be here proper to obferve, that there are
many different kingdoms on the banks of the Gambia,
inhabited by feveral races of people, as Mundingoes,
Julloiffs, Pholeys, Floops, and Portuguefe. The

moſt numerous are called Mundingoes, as is likewiſe the country they inhabit: they are generally of a black colour, and well ſet. When this country was con-quered by the Portugueſe about the year 1420, ſome of that nation ſettled in it, who have cohabited with theſe Mundingoes, till they are now very near as black as they : but as they ſtill retain a ſort of baſtard Portugueſe language called Creole and as they chriſten and marry by the help of a prieſt annually ſent thi-ther from St. Jago, one of the Cape de Verd iſlands, they ſtill eſteem themſelves Portugueſe Chriſtians, as much as if they were actually natives of Portugal, and nothing angers them more than to call them Negroes, that being a term they uſe only for ſlaves.

On the north ſide of the river Gambia, and from thence in-land, are a people called Jolloiffs, whoſe country extends even to the river Senegal. Theſe people are much blacker, and handſomer than the Mundingoes ; for they have not the broad noſes and thick lips peculiar to the Mundingoes and Floops.

In every kingdom and country on each ſide of the river are people of a tawny colour, called Pholeys, who reſemble the Arabs, whoſe language moſt of them ſpeak ; for it is taught in their ſchools, and the koran, which is alſo their law, is in that language. They are more generally learned in the Arabic, than the people of Europe are in Latin; for they can moſt of them ſpeak it, though they have a vulgar tongue called Pholey. They live in hoards or clans, build towns, and are not ſubject to any of the kings of the country, though they live in their territories ; for if they are uſed ill in one nation, they break up their towns, and remove to another. They have chiefs of their own, who rule with ſuch moderation, that every act of government ſeems rather an act of the people than of one man. This form of government is eaſily adminiſtered, becauſe the people are of a good and quiet diſpoſition, and ſo well inſtructed in what is juſt and right, that a man who does ill, is the abomination of all.

In thefe countries the natives are not avaricious of lands: they defire no more than what they ufe ; and as they do not plough with horfes or cattle, they can ufe but very little. Hence the kings are willing to allow the Pholeys to cultivate the land, and live in their dominions. They plant tobacco near their houfes, and all round their towns they plant cotton ; beyond that are their corn fields, of which they raife the four kinds ufually produced all over this country ; that is, maize, or Indian corn, rice, and the larger, and lefler Guinea corn. In Gambia is no wheat, barley, rye, oats, nor any other European grain; but they have a kind of pulfe between the kidney-bean and pea, and alfo potatoes and yams. The Indian corn they fet in holes, about four feet diftance from each other, fo that it grows up like hops and fhoots about eight or ten feet high in large canes, with the ears growing out of the fides. The rice which is efteemed their choiceft food, they fet in rills, as we do peafe ; it grows in wet grounds, and the ears refemble thofe of oats. The largeft Guinea corn is round, fand about the fize of the fmalleft peafe : they fow it as we do wheat and barley : it grows to nine or ten feet high, upon a fmall reed, and the grain is in a large tuft at the top. The lefler Guinea corn, called by the Portuguefe manfaroke, is fowed by hand, and fhoots to the fame hight, on a large reed, on the top of which the corn grows on a head like a bulrufh : the grain is very fmall, and like canary feed, only larger.

The natives make no bread, but thicken liquids with the flour of the different grains. The maize they moftly ufe when green, parching it in the ear, when it eats like green peas. Their rice they boil in the fame manner as is practifed by the Turks ; and make flour of the Guinea corn and manfaroke, as they alfo fometimes do of the two former fpecies, by beating it in wooden mortars. The natives never bake cakes or bread for themfelves, but thofe of their women who live among the Europeans learn to do both.

The Pholeys are the greateft planters in the country, though they are ftrangers in it. They are very induftrious and frugal, and raife much more corn and cotton than they confume, which they fell at reafonable rates, and are fo remarkable for their hofpitality, that the natives efteem it a blefling to have a Pholey town in their neighbourhood : befides their behaviour has gained them fuch reputation, that it is efteemed infamous for any one to treat them in an inhofpitable manner. Though their humanity extends to all, they are doubly kind to people of their own race; and if they know of any one of their body being made a flave, all the Pholeys will unite to redeem him. As they have plenty of food, they never fuffer any of their own people to want, but fupport the old, the blind and the lame, equally with the others. They are feldom angry, and I never heard them abufe each other ; yet this mildnefs does not proceed from want of courage ; for they are as brave as any people of Africa, and are very expert in the ufe of their arms, which are the affagay, fhort cutlaffes, bows and arrows, and even guns upon occafion. They commonly fettle near fome Mundingo town ; there being fcarce any one of note, efpecially up the river, that has not a Pholey town near it. They are ftrict Mahometans ; and fcarcely any of them will drink brandy, or any thing ftronger than fugar and water.

They breed cattle, and are very dexterous at managing them, fo that the Mundingoes leave theirs to their care. The whole herd belonging to a town feed all the day in the favannahs, and after the crop is off, in the rice grounds. They have a place without each town for the cattle, in the middle of which they raife a ftage about eight feet high from the ground, and eight or ten feet wide ; to this is a ladder, and over it a roof thatch, with the fides all open. Round

this stage they fix a number of stakes, and every
night the cattle are brought up, and each beast tied
to a separate stake, with a strong rope made of the
barks of trees. The cows are then milked, and
four or five men stay upon the stage all night with
their arms, to guard them from the lions and other
wild beasts. Their houses are built in a very regular
manner, and placed at a distance from each other,
to avoid fire.

They are likewise great huntsmen, and not only
kill lions, tygers, and other wild beasts ; but often
go 20 or 30 in a company to hunt elephants, whose
teeth they sell, and whose flesh they smoke-dry and
eat, keeping it several months together. The elephants, they say, generally go one or two hundred
in a drove, and do great mischief by pulling up the
trees by the roots, and trampling down the corn ; to
prevent which, the natives when they have any suspicion of their coming, make fires all round their
corn to keep them out.

The Pholeys are almost the only people who make
butter, and of whom cattle can be purchased at some
distance up the river. They are very particular in
their dress, and never wear any clothes but such as
are of white cotton, which they make themselves.
They are always very clean, especially the women,
who keep their houses exceeding sweet. However,
in some things they are superstitious, in particular if
they know any body boils the new milk bought of
them, they will not on any consideration, sell that
person any more, because they say, that boiling the
milk makes the cows dry.

On the south side of the river, opposite James'
fort, in the empire of Fonia, and but a little way
inland, are a sort of people called Floops, who are
in a manner wild : they border on the Mundingoes, who are bitter enemies to them. Their
country is of vast extent, but they have no king :
each of their towns is fortified with a double row of

ftakes drove all round them and filled up with clay :
but though they are independent of each other, and
under the government of no one chief ; they unite
fo firmly, that all the force of the Mundingoes cannot get the better of them.

The moft general language ufed in thefe countries
is the Mundingo ; and if you can fpeak it, you may
travel from the river's mouth up to the country of
the Joncoes, or the merchants, a people fo called,
from their annually buying a great number of flaves
there, and bringing them down to the lower parts
of the river, to fell them to the Europeans ; though
I believe their country cannot be lefs than fix weeks
journey from James' fort.

The next language moftly ufed here is called the
Creole Portuguefe, though I believe it would be
fcarce underftood at Lifbon ; it is, however, fooner
learnt by Englifhmen, than any other language
ufed on the banks of this river, and is always fpoken
by the linguifts or interpreters ; and thefe two I
learnt whilft in the river. .

The Arabic is not only fpoken by the Pholeys,
but by moft of the Mahometans in the river, though
they are Mundingoes ; and it is obferved, that thofe
who can write that language are not only very ftrict
at their devotions three or four times a day ; but are
fo remarkably fober and abftemious in their manner
of living, that they would rather die than drink
ftrong liquors, and rather faft, than eat any thing
that is not killed by one of their own way of thinking.
All the Mundingoes pay them great veneration, and
if any of them are ill, they apply to one of thefe
Mahometans for a cure ; not by inward potions ;
but only by a note wrote on a fmall piece of paper
to wear about them, imagining, that while they
carry a paper wrote by a holy man, no ill can happen
to them, or continue long with them ; but the worft
of it is, they pay a great price for thefe papers ; by
which means the Mahometans, commonly called

Bufherines, are generally richer, and plenty than moft of the other Mundin

Befides the above languages, there culiar to every kingdom; fuch is that the Banyoons, the Jolloiffs, and Bu latter is ufed very high up the river in country.

On the 4th of April I went to Gi is a large town, a little below Ja habited by Purtuguefe, Mundingoes hometans, who have here a pretty The Englifh company have a factory fituated, facing the fort, and alfo, as obferved, fome gardens that fupply greens and fruit. The country round tl fine fhooting, and were it not too f be pleafant walking Here are grea plantain and banana trees; guavas lime-trees; and among the birds are i which are as large as a goofe, and fame colour: they have a very long b it is a very large bag. They live u therefore are commonly near the rive

A native here took me to his houf me a great number of arrows, daube black mixture, faid to be fo venemou arrow did but draw blood it would be the perfon who made the mixture had it; for the man obferved, that there w ous herbs, whofe effects might not be the application of other herbs.

On the 11th, came down the river manded by Captain Pyke, a feparate Joar, loaded with flaves, among whon of an elegant figure, named Job Ben S was of the Pholey race, and fon to t of Bundo, in Foota, a place about ter from Gillyfree. This perfon was tra fouth fide of the Gambia, with a ferva twenty or thirty head of cattle, which induced the king of a country a little way within the land to feize not only the cattle, but Job and his man, both of whom he fold for flaves to Captain Pyke. The Pholeys, his humane countrymen, would have redeemed him; but they had the mortification to find that he was carried out of the river before they had notice of his being a flave, and Captain Pyke failed with him to Maryland. Job, who was a perfon of extraordinary abilities, and diftinguifhed merit, was not fo' unhappy as he had reafon to expect ; but his adventures will be hereafter related, when I fhall have occafion to mention his return to this country.

On the 4th of June two Jolloiffs came to James' ifland to fell cotton clothes : thefe they make very fine, and in large quantities: their pieces are generally twenty-feven yards long ; but are never above nine inches broad ; but they few them neatly together to make them ferve for broader cloths. They clean the cotton from the feed by hand, and then fpin it with a fpindle and diftaff, after which they weave it with a fhuttle and loom of very coarfe workmanfhip. In order to drefs themfelves with thefe cloths, they make them into pairs, one about three yards long, and a yard and a half wide, to cover their fhoulders and body; the other almoft of the fame .width, and but two yards long, to cover them from the waift downwards. This pair of cloths is the clothing of either a man or woman, the only difference being in the manner of wearing them. I have feen a pair of thefe cloths fo fine, and of fo bright a dye, as to be worth 1l. 10s. fterling. Their colours are either blue or yellow, fome very lively : the firft is dyed with indigo, and the other with the bark of trees.

On the 29th, the governor and I fet out for Vintain, where we arrived in three hours, though it lies about fix leagues from James' Fort. Some part of the way is up the river of the fame name.

The town belongs to one of the kings of Fonia, and is pleafantly fituated on the fide of a hill clofe to the river. It is inhabited both by Portuguefe and Mahometans, the latter of whom have a hand-fome mofque. Is is noted for plenty of provifions, great quantities of which are brought by the Floops, who border on it ; and the company have a fmall factory there to buy bees-wax : above the town is fine grafs, and fome trees, that render its fituation very pleafant.

On our coming to the town, the alcade, and all the principal inhabitants came to welcome us, and foon after came the prince, in whofe dominions the town is fituated. The common people were dreffed with a cloth round their waifts that reached to their knees, and another cloth over their right fhoulder ; for the men have commonly one fhoulder bare, which the women have not; the clothes of the latter generally reach as low as the fmall of their legs. They are very proud of their hair ; fome wear it in tufts and bunches, others cut it in croffes, and others again firing coral or beads upon it. The men have commonly caps of cotton cloth, fome plain, and fome adorned with feathers and goats tails. The women general'y wear handkerchiefs tied round their heads, leaving the crown bare, and for want of a handkerchief, they ufe a flip of blue or white cotton cloth : a great many of them, efpecially up the river, wear on the crown of the head a good number of fmall horfe bells.

Their towns confift of a number of huts built promifcuoufly together; each hut is generally four-teen or fifteen yards in circumference, built with clay, and covered with long grafs, or palmetto leaves. They generally keep their houfes very clean ; but the ftinking fifh, and other things they keep in them, prevent their being very fweet.

The inhabitants are not very curious in their furniture ; for the moft that any of them have is a ſmall cheſt for clothes, a mat raiſed upon poſts from the ground, to lie on ; a jar to hold water, a cala-baſh to drink it with ; two or three wooden mortars, in which they pound their corn and rice; a baſket which they uſe as a ſieve, and two or three large clabaſhes, out of which they eat with their hands inſtead of ſpoons. They are not very careful of laying up ſtore againſt a time of ſcarcity ; but chuſe rather to ſell what they can, as upon occaſion they can faſt two or three days without eating ; but then they are always ſmoaking tobacco, which is of their own growth. The boll of their pipes is neatly made of a reddiſh coloured clay ; but the ſtems are only a piece of reed or a ſmall ſtick bored through with a hot iron wire, and ſome of them are ſix feet long. After they have bored, they poliſh them with rough leaves till they are very ſmooth, white and handſome. They faſten the boll and ſtem together with a piece of red leather, and ſometimes have a fine leather taſſel hanging to the middle of the pipe. The mer-chants who travel much, carry with them pipes of ſo large a ſize, that the bolls of ſome of them hold no leſs than half a pint.

But to proceed : the governor expecting to receive orders for appointing me a factor, ſent me on the 28th of Auguſt to Joar, to learn the nature of the trade. Joar is ſituated in the kingdom of Barſally about three miles from a large town called Cowar, in a fine ſavannah, ſurrounded with woods that har-bour wild beaſts, which you may hear howling and roaring every night. It is about two miles from the Gambia, and inhabited by a few Portugueſe ; it conſiſts only of ten houſes, beſides one belonging to the king of Barſally, and the Engliſh factory ; but the two laſt take up as much ground as all the others. About a mile from it is a ledge of high and rocky hills covered with trees, which the natives ſay, run a hundred leagues up the country. In the ſummer it is pleaſant walking on theſe hills : but

the wild beaſts being driven thithei
ſeaſon, by the low ground being covei
one cannot walk there without dar
ſeaſon, the frogs, of which there are
much larger than thoſe of England
night, as much noiſe as a pack of l
a good diſtance, the ſound is not v
About the above ſavannah are plenty
loes, wild hogs, partridges, geeſe, duck
which are very good eating, and a
natives themſelves. It is remarkable
tridges here have ſometimes two larg
leg. There is here a remarkable bird
ſize of a pigeon, which comes abroac
has four wings.

Here are alſo cameleons, and gre
crocodiles, which the natives kill and
mire both them and their eggs, wh
quently ſecn them eat, when they ha
in them as long as my finger. This
niceſt diſhes.

Whilſt I was here, I ſaw an oſtric
riding upon its back, who was goin
fort; it being a preſent to the governe
our factors, who bought it at Fatatei

Soon after my arrival at Joar, the k
came thither, attended by three of
above 100 horſemen, and as many ſoc
he had a houſe of his own in the to
lying at the factory. Mr. Roberts,
who were factors, and I were all the
The king immediately took poſſeſſion o
bed, and then having drank branc
drunk, ordered Mr. Roberts to be
himſelf took out of his pocket the key
houſe, into which he and ſeveral of hi
and took what they pleaſed: he ſearc
brandy; of which there happened 1
anker; he took that, and having dra

dead drunk, was put to bed. This anker lafted him three days; and it was no fooner empty, than he went all over the houfe to feek for more. At laft he entered a room, in which Mr. Harrifon lay fick, and feeing there a cafe that contained fix gallons and a half, that belonged to him and me, he ordered Mr. Harrifon to get out of bed and open it ; he, however, told him with great gravity, that there was nothing in it but fome of the company's papers ; and that it muft not be opened, but the king was too well acquainted with liquor cafes to be fo eafily deceived ; and therefore ordered fome of his men to hold Mr. Harrifon in bed, while he himfelf took the key out of his breeches pocket. He then opened the cheft, took out all the liquor, and was not fober while it lafted : but he often fent for Mr. Harrifon and me to drink with him. At length it being all drank, he talked of going home, on which his people, and even his chief minifters, who were his general, and the keeper of the ftores, amufed themfelves with taking whatever they liked, and had the affurance to open even chefts and boxes, this we could not help, for what refiftance could three men make againft 200 ? What they took amounted to 20l. fterling.

Sometimes the king would ride abroad, and take moft of his attendants with him : but when he was gone we were plagued with the company of two of his brothers, who were, if poffible, worfe than his majefty. Once during his abfence Boomey Haman Benda, one of thefe princes, laid hold of a mug of water and pretending to drink, took a mouthful, and then fetting the mug on the table, fpurted the water in my face. Upon which confidering that if I fuffered fuch infolence to pafs unrefented, it would render me liable to be continually infulted, I took the remander of the water, and threw it into his breeches. Upon this he pulled out his knife, and endeavoured to ftab me, but was prevented by his favourite attendant, who held his arm, and foon after reprefented to him the unhandfome manner in which he had treated me, and the provocation I had received to wet him. This made him fo afhamed, that coming up to me, he laid himfelf down on the floor without his garment, took my foot, and placed it on his neck, and there lay till I defired him to rife: after which no man appeared more my friend, nor fhewed greater willingnefs to oblige me.

This king, as well as his attendants, are of the Mahometan religion, notwithftanding their being fuch drunkards, and this monfter, when he is fober, even prays. He dreffes like moft of the other kings of this country, in a garment like a furplice, that comes no lower than his knees. He has a pair of breeches of the fame fort of cloth, about feven yards wide gathered round his waift ; he wears a pair of flippers, but not ftockings. His head is covered with a fmall white cotton cap, and he commonly wears a pair of gold ear-rings. His people, as well himfelf, always wear white clothes and white caps, and as they are exceeding black, this drefs makes them look very well.

This tyrant is tall, and fo paffionate that when any of his men affront him, he makes no fcruple of fhooting them ; and fometimes when he goes aboard a company's floop at Cohone, where he ufually refides, he inhumanly fhews his dexterity by fhooting at the canoes as they pafs by, frequently killing one or two men in a day. He has many wives, but never brings above two or three abroad at a time with him. Among his brothers, there are fome to whom he feldom fpeaks, or permits to come into his company ; and when they obtain this favour, they pull off their caps and garments and throw duft upon their heads, as all except white men do, who come into the king's prefence.

The dominions of this prince are very extenfive, and divided into feveral provinces, over which he appoints governors, called Boomeys, who annually come to pay him homage: but though they have almoſt an unlimited power, they are beloved, as well as feared by the people.

At length the king and his guards to our great joy, left the factory, in order to return to Cohone ; but they firſt ſtript Mr. Roberts's chamber, and took away his clothes and books, which late they offered to ſell to a Mahometan prieſt ; but he being a friend to Mr. Roberts, told them he believed they were books in which he kept the account of his goods, and that to take them would inevitably ruin him : upon which they gave him leave to return them.

However five months after the king of Barſally paid us another viſit, and ſtaying about a week, during which he behaved much in the ſame manner as before, he and his attendants again left us: but ſome of them firſt broke open my bureau, and took out things to a conſiderable value, and the ſame fate attended Mr. Roberts : beſides which they took a great quantity of the company's goods.

In the interval which paſſed between theſe two viſits, I had been made factor, and had received orders to take charge of the factory ot Joar ; but I was unwilling to accept of this office, as that factory was liable to ſo many inſults from a drunken monarch, void of every principle of juſtice, and deſtitute of the feeling of humanity ; I therefore took an inventory of the goods the company had there, in January 1723, and taking a letter to the governor from Mr. Roberts, my colleague, returned to James' fort.

In March I returned to my factory: but Mr. Hugh Hamilton being ſent up the river to ſettle a factory at Fatatenda, I was permitted to accompany him, and accordingly on the 9th of April we left Joar, and proceeded in a ſloop up the Gambia. The next day we arrived at Yanimarew, which is the pleaſanteſt port in the whole river, the country being delightfully ſhaded with palm and palmetto trees. The

company have here a fmall houfe, with a black factor
to purchafe corn for the ufe of the fort.

From thence we proceeded to Caffan, a fmall town
on the north fide of the river, in an agreeable fituation, about a mufket fhot from the water fide, and
fortified with a wall of clay fupported by flakes, with
holes left for mufkets, and watch towers at proper
diftances.

From Caffan we fteered up to Dubocunda, which
lies on the fouth fide of the river, and is divided into
two parts, or diftinct towns ; one of which is fortified
with a wall made by a vaft number of palmetto trees
fixed in the ground, and clay laid in between, fo that
it is little inferior to a brick wall. The other town
is only encompaffed by a fence of canes, formed like
hurdles, and faftened by a number of ftakes, in which
manner moft of the towns on the Gambia, and even
the factories are furrounded. The people live in the
open town, in time of peace ; but when they are at
war, and find it in danger of being attacked by an
enemy, they fhut themfelves up in that which is
moft ftrongly fortified.

On our leaving this town we proceeded up the river
feveral days, and at length reached Yamyamacunda,
where I ftaid while Mr. Hamilton proceeded up to
Fatatenda. When I had been there fome time I took
horfe and rode to the port of Baffy, in my way to
Nackway, where we had a Portuguefe fervant who was
fettled there, in order to trade for the company : the
reafon of my going thither was to infpect into his
behaviour, and examine his accounts.

The port of Baffy is in the kingdom of Tomany,
on the fouth fide of the river Gambia. All the way
to it is very woody. I lay at night in one of the
huts of the natives, and the next morning leaving
my horfe there, croffed the river in a fmall canoe,
and walked to Nackway, which is almoft feven miles.
Half the way led through woods, and the other
through a fine large favannah, without any trees,

except a few fcattered at a diftance from each other ; and in the rainy feafon it is generally under water.

On my arrival at Nackway, the natives welcomed me with the mufic of the balafeu, which, at about a hundred yards diftance founds fomething like a fmall organ. It is compofed of about twenty pipes of very hard wood finely polifhed ; which diminfhes by little and little, both in length and breadth, and are tied together by thongs of very fine leather. Thefe thongs are twifted about fmall round wands, put between the pipes to keep them at a diftance, and underneath the pipes are faftened twelve or fourteen calabafhes of different fizes. This inftrument they play upon with two fticks, covered with a thin fkin taken from the trunk of the palmetto tree, or with fine leather, to make the found lefs harfh. Both men and women dance to this mufic, which they much admire, and are highly delighted to have a white man dance with them.

Having finifhed my bufinefs here, I returned to Yamyamacunda, and having continued there about three months, proceeded ftill farther up the river to Fatatenda. The Gambia is there as wide as the Thames at London-Bridge, and feemed very deep; but what is moft extraordinary, the tide in the dry feafon rifes three or four feet, though that place is 600 miles from the river's mouth. The land on both fides of the river is covered with wood ; the fouth fide is low ; but the factory is fituated on a high and fteep rock on the north fide, and has a fine profpect of the courfe of the river feveral miles up and down, and on the oppofite fide you may fee great part of the kingdom of Cantore : but I was every night difturbed by the howling and roaring of the wild beafts.

Having ftaid there a few days, I thought of going to Nackway along the north fide of the river, but could not, the creeks being fo much out that it was impoffible to pafs them. I therefore croffed the river Gambia ; and went on the fouth fide. That day I rode over the fteepeft hill I ever faw in my life, it being almoft a continued rock of iron ftone, and yet it is full of trees About fun fet I got to Baffy port, and having croffed the river, walked to Nackway by moonlight, and the next morning returned to Yamyamacunda, which I believe to be near 40 miles by land from Fatatenda. The river being now fallen, the women flocked to it, and were exceeding bufy in catching fmall fifh like fprats. This is done in a bafket like a hamper, by putting a little bail of pafte at the bottom of it; holding it a fhort time under water, and then raifing it gently, they bring up the fifh and lay them on a clean fpot of ground to dry; after which they pound them in a wooden mortar to a pafte, then make them into bails of about three pounds each, and thus keep them all the year round. A fmall quantity of them goes a great way; they do not drefs them by themfelves, but mix them with rice or corn, and this is food I have feveral times eat with a good appetite.

At the latter end of October, the weather, which had been exceffive hot, began to grow cool and pleafant. The mornings and evenings were very foggy, and the women were bufy in cutting their rice, which is here their own property; for after they have fet by a fufficient quantity for their family ufe, they fell the remainder and take the money themfelves, the hufbands not interfering. They obferve the fame cuftom with refpect to fowls which they breed in great numbers when they find they can difpofe of them.

About this time I fhot a green fnake two yards long, though it was not above three inches in circumference. Thefe fnakes are not at all venomous; but there are fuch numbers of others that are fo, that the natives feldom go out without a medicine to apply in cafe they are bitten. They are very much afraid of the black fnakes, which I have feen three yards long, and as thick as the fmall of my leg. They fay among the venomous fnakes there are fome with a comb on their heads, like a cock, and tncîe they pofitively affirm crow like one. There are alfo plenty of guanas, a very ugly creature, that has fome refemblance to an alligator. They are about a yard long, and are eat both by the natives and fome Europeans as a great dainty.

On the 20th of November in the evening was a total eclipfe of the moon, and the Mundingoes told me, the darknefs was occafioned by a cat's putting her paw between the moon and the earth. The Mahometans in this country were finging and danc ing the whole time, becaufe they expect their prophet to come in an eclipfe.

On the 4th of September, 1733, the Gambia rofe fo high, that it entered the inclofure that furrounded the factory houfe, and was of fplit cane ten feet high, ftrengthened by long flakes. This was towards the end of the rainy feafon : the next day finding the houfe was furrounded, I employed all the fervants to build me a hut in the middle of the town of Yamyamacunda, which was the higheft fpot of ground in that neighbourhood: the walls of the factory being built only of a binding clay, which began to crack, I made all the difpatch I could, and the following day removed the company's effects to my new hut in the town; I now thought it advifeable to leave the factory, there being frogs, toads, fnakes, and fifh continally coming into it, and about midnight fome of the walls fell, but the roof ftill ftood. For the ten following days we daily faw vaft numbers of floating iflands come down the river, fome of them twenty or thirty yards long, with ftumps of trees, and fometimes many fmall trees growing on them ; with the birds hopping on the boughs. The roots being thick and interwoven one within another and faftened with earth, made the iflands float : they being only parts of woods torn away by the force of the floods. All the neighbouring valleys

were under water: the rich grounds were almoſt
ſpoiled by being long covered with it: canoes went
from place to place over the very roads which in the
dry ſeaſon the natives travel on foot, and proviſions
were ſo ſcarce that I was ſometimes two days without
a poſſibility of getting any, for want of canoes,
without which I was unable to go twenty yards
from my hut ; and the natives told me, that they
had not had ſuch an inundation for eight years paſt.
However, none of the company's effects were either
loſt or damaged ; nor was the company put to any
charge, except for repairing the factory-houſe, which
was inconſiderable. On the 20th the water began
to fall apace, and a week after I removed with all
the company's goods to the factory ; but it was ſo
much damaged, that we were ſoon after obliged to
rebuild it.

Having pitched upon a riſing ground about fifty
yards diſtance from the river, I marked out a place
for the houſe forty feet ſquare. The beſt trees for
upright poſts and ridge poles being mangroves, they
were brought from below Joar, of thoſe the frame
of the houſe was built, the roof projecting about
four feet, in order to ſecure the walls from wet.
We next began to build the walls of clay, which
the Negroes trod with their feet, and tempered extremely well that it might not crack. The walls
were then laid a foot and a half thick, and one foot
high, all round the houſe, and then left to dry, till
they were hard enough to bear a ſecond layer ; thus
they were raiſed foot by foot, till they were ten feet
high, leaving one foot diſtance between them and
the roof for air. At the ſame time we made the
partition walls of clay of the ſame thickneſs, working the clay cloſe up to the doors and window frames;
and afterwards we formed a porch at the door ; for
the natives ſay, that they have a right to a porch at
every factory, to afford them acceſs and ſhelter.
Having covered the roof with a kind of thick mats

made of ftraw, wc floored the ftore-houfe with clay hard rammed. Thus we finifhed our houfe, in which we had a large hall, three ftrong ftore-houfes, and two lodging-rooms, without any iron work, trowels, fquares, or carpenter's rules, with fcarcely any ex-pence to the company, ; for it was done by their fervants, without any other help than one man who was hired to lay and fmooth the clay. Yet the infide was not only convenient and free from ver-min, but very clean, and had a cool look ; for clay is hard, clofe, fmooth, and takes white-wafh very well.

On the outfide of the houfe were two fhady bifhelo trees, and a piece of ground containing about an acre, which we inclofed with a fence ten feet high made of fplit cane, wove like hurdles. Within this fence, at proper diftances from the factory, we built four houfes after the Mundingo fafhion, one for a kitchen, one for a falt-houfe, another for a ftore-houfe for corn, and the other for the lodging of the company's black fervants. The ground between we ufed for a garden, and fome part of it, for fowls and other ftock.

Speaking of the poultry reminds me of the Gui-nea fowl, which are of a dark colour, with white fpots, and fome blue and red about the head. Thefe are generally thought to be the tame fowl of Africa ; but that is a miftake ; for they are as wild as the pheafants in England, only much more plentiful. The only tame fowl of this country are of the fame dunghill breed as thofe in Europe, and the natives have great plenty of them ; but here are no turkeys, tame geefe, or ducks.

I ftaid at the new factory houfe I had caufed to be built at Yamyamacunda, till the 5th of May, 1734; and was employed in the company's fervice in dif-ferent parts of the river till the 13th of July follow-ing, when I was defired to come down to James' Fort, where I was on the 8th of Auguft, when the Dolphin

fnow arrived, with four writers, and Job Ben Solomon, on board. We have already mentioned his
being robbed and caried to Joar, where he was fold
to Captain Pyke, by whom he was carried to Maryland. Job was there fold to a planter, with whom
he had lived about a twelve month, in all which
time he had the happinefs not to be ftruck by his
maiter, and had then the good fortune to have a letter
of his own writing in the Arabic tongue, conveyed
to England. This letter coming to the hand of Mr.
Oglethorp, he fent it to Oxford to be tranflated;
which being done, it gave him fuch fatisfaction, and
infpird him with fo good an opinion of the author,
that he immediately fent orders to have him bought
of his mafter. This happened a little before that
gentleman's fetting out for Georgia, and before his
return from thence, Job arrived in England, where
being brought to the acquaintance of Sir Hans
Sloane, he was found to be a perfect mafter of the
Arabic tongue, by his tranflating feveral manufcripts
and infcriptions on medals. That learned antiquary
recommended him to the duke of Montague, who
being pleafed with his genius and capacity, the
agreeablenefs of his behaviour, and the fweetnefs of
his temper, introduced him to court, where he was
gracioufly received by the royal family and moft of
the nobility, who honoured him with many marks of
favour. The African company and the chief merchants of the city ftrove who fhould ofteneft invite
him to their tables. His good fenfe engaged their
efteem, he freely difcourfed on every fubject, and attended the churches of the moft celebrated divines.
When he had been in England about fourteen
months, his ardent defired to fee his native country
made him prefs for his departure. He had wrote
from England to the high prieft his father, and
earneftly longed to fee him. Upon his fetting out
from England, he received many noble prefents
from queen Caroline, prince William, the duke of

Montague, and the earl of Pembroke, feveral ladies of quality, Mr. Holden, and the royal African
company, and the latter ordered all their agents to
fhew him the greateft refpect.

On the arrival at James' Fort, Job defired that I
fhould fend a meffenger to his country to let his
friends know where he was. I fpoke to one of the
blacks whom we ufually employed, to procure me a
meffenger, and he brought me a Pholey, who not
only knew the high prieft his father, but Job himfelf,
and expreffed great joy at feeing him fafely returned
from flavery, he being the only man, except one,
ever known to come back to his country, after being
once carried a flave out of it by white men Job
gave him the meffage himfelf and defired that his
father fhould not come down to him, and obferving
that it was too far for him to travel ; and that it was
fit the young fhould go to the old, and not for the
old to come to the young. He alfo fent fome prefents
to his wives, and defired the man to bring his
little one, who was his beft beloved, down with
him.

Job having a mind to go up to Joar, to talk with
fome of his countrymen, went along with me. We
arrived at the creek at Damafenfa, and having fome
old acquaintances at the town of that name, Job
and I went in the yawl : in the way going up a narrow
place for about half a mile, we faw feveral monkeys
of a beautiful blue and red, which the natives told
me never fet their feet on the ground, but live entirely among the trees, leaping from one to another,
at fuch great diftances, as would appear improbable
to any but an eye witnefs.

In the evening as my friend Job and I were fitting
under a great tree at Damafenfa, there came fix or
feven of the very people who three years before, had
robbed and made a flave of him, at about thirty
miles diftance from that place. Job though naturally
poffeffed of a very even temper, could not contain

himfelf on feeing them ; he was filled with rage and
indignation, and was for attacking them with his
broad fword and piftols, which he always took care
to have about him. I had much ado to diffuade him
from rufhing upon them ; but at length reprefenting
the ill confequences that would infallibly attend fo
rafh an action, and the impoffibility that either of us
fhould efcape alive. I made him lay afide the attempt, and perfuaded him to fit down, and pretending not to know them, to afk them queftions about
himfelf ; which he accordingly did, and they told him
the truth. At laft he enquired how the king their
mafter did ; they replied that he was dead, and by
farther enquir we found that amongft the goods
for which he fold Job to Captain Pyke there was a
piftol which the king ufed commonly to wear flung
by a ftring about his neck ; and as they never carry
arms without their being loaded, the piftol one day
accidently went off, and the balls lodging in his
throat, he prefently died. Job was fo tranfported at
the clofe of this ftory, that he immediately fell on
his knees, and returned thanks to Mahomet for
making him die by the very goods for which he fold
him into flavery. Then turning to me, he cried.
" You fee now, Mr. Moore, that God Almighty
" was difpleafed at this man's making me a flave, and
" therefore made him die by the very piftol for which
" he fold me : yet I ought to forgive him, becaufe
" had not I been fold, I fhould neither have known
" any thing of the Englifh tongue, nor have had any
" of the fine, ufeful and valuable things, I have
" brought with me ; nor have known that there is
" fuch a place in the world as England ; nor fuch
" noble, good, and generous people as queen Caro-
" line, prince William, the duke of Montague, the
" earl of Pembroke, Mr. Holden, Mr. Ogelthrope,
" and the Royal African company."

    After this Job went frequently with me to Cower,
and feveral other places about the country. He

always fpoke very handfomely of the Englifh, and what he faid removed much of that horror the Pholeys felt for the ftate of flavery amongft them ; for they before generally imagined, that all who were fold for flaves, were at leaft murdered, if not eaten, fince none ever returned. His defcriptions alfo gave them an high opinion of the power of England, and a veneration for the Englifh, who traded amongft them. He fold fome of the prefents he brought with him for trading goods, with which he bought a woman flave, and two horfes, which he defigned to take with him to Bundo. He gave his countrymen a good deal of writing paper, a very valuable commodity amongft them, and the company had made him a prefent of feveral reams. He ufed frequently to pray, and behaved with great affability and mildnefs to all, which rendered him extremely popular.

The meffengers not returning fo foon as was expected, Job defired to go down to James' Fort, to take care of his goods, and I promifed not only to fend him word when the meffenger came back, but to fend other meffengers, for fear the firft fhould have mifcarried.

At length the meffenger returned with feveral letters, and advice that Job's father was dead ; but had lived to receive the letters his fon had fent him from England, which gave him the welcome news of his being redeemed from flavery, and an account of the figure he made in England. That one of Job's wives was married to another man ; but that as foon as the new hufband had heard of his return, he thought it advifeable to abfcond ; and that fince Job's abfence from his native country, there had been fuch a dreadful war, that the Pholeys there had not one cow left, though before Job's departure his countrymen were famed for their numerous herds. With this meffenger came many of Job's old friends, who he was exceeding glad to fee; but notwithftand-

ing the joy their prefence gave him, he fhed abundance of tears for the lofs of his father, and the
misfortunes of his country. He forgave his wife,
and the man who had taken her; "For Mr. Moore,
"faid he, fhe could not help thinking I was dead;
" for I was gone to a land from whence no Pholey,
" ever yet returned ; therefore neither fhe, nor the
" man is to be blamed." During three or four
days he converfed with his friends without any in-
teruption except to fleep or eat.

As I have brought this account almoft to the time
of my leaving this country, it will be neceffary to
give a more particular defcription of it with refpeét
to the climate, the general cuftoms of the natives,
and the trade carried on there.

As the mouth of the Gambia lies in the latitude
of 13°. 20'. north, and in 15°. 20'. weft longitude,
there is no wonder that the climate is exceffive hot,
but the greateft heats are generally about the latter
end of May, a fortnight or three weeks before the
rainy feafon begins. The fun is perpendicular twice
a year, and the days are never longer from fun
rifing. to fun-fet than thirteen hours, nor ever.
fhorter than eleven. What at firft feemed to me
ftrange, was that as foon as it grew light, the fun
arofe, and it no fooner fet than it grew dark.

The rainy feafon commonly begins with the month
of June, and continues to the latter end of September, or the beginning of Oétober. The wind comes
firft, and blows exceffive hard, for the fpace of half
an hour or more, before any rain falls, fo that a
veffel may be fuddenly furprized and overfet by it :
a perfon may however perceive the figns of its coming; for the clouds grow very black, and the lighten-
ings darting from them, have an awful appearance:
both the thunder and the lightening are exceeding
dreadful, the flafhes fucceeding each other fo fwiftly,
as to render it continually light, while the thunder
at the fame time fhakes the very ground. During.

the rain the air is generally pretty cool ; but the
fhower is no fooner over than the fun breaks out
exceffive hot, which induces fome people to caft off
their clothes, and lie down to fleep ; but before they
are awake another tornado perhaps comes, when the
cold ftrikes into their very bones, and gives them
fits of illnefs, which to the Europeans are very fatal.
During the rainy feafon, the fea breezes feldom blow,
but inftead of them, eafterly winds, which in the
months of November, December, January, and February generally blow very frefh, and fometimes
the evenings and mornings are exceeding cold, and
the middle of the day very hot.

Four months in the year are unhealthful, and
very tedious to thofe who come from a colder climate;
but a perpetual fpring, in which you commonly fee
ripe fruit and bloffoms on the fame tree, makes
fome amends for that inconvenience. Befides, the
heat of the air is frequently moderated by pleafant
and refrefhing breezes.

The Gambia is of fuch a length as to be navigable
for floops above 600 miles, the tides reaching fo far
from its mouth. The land on each fide of this great
and fine river is for the moft part flat and woody
about a quarter of a mile beyond its banks, and
within that fpace are pleafant open grounds, on
which the natives plant rice, and in the dry feafon
it ferves the cattle for pafture. Thus within land it
is generally very woody ; but near the towns there
is always a large fpot of ground cleared for corn.
Near the fea, no hills are to be feen ; but high up
the river are lofty mountains. Thefe are chiefly
compofed of iron ftone, and though they are fometimes little elfe but a continued hard rock, they are
full of trees, and ferve greatly to beautify the face of
the country.

In every kingdom there are feveral perfons called
lords of the foil, who have the property of the palm
and palmetto trees, fo that none are allowed to draw

any wine from them, without their knowledge and confent. Thofe who obtain leave to draw wine, give two days produce in a week, to the lord of the foil ; and white men are obliged to make a fmall prefent to them, before they cut palmetto leaves, or grafs, to cover their houfes.

The palm is a fine ftraight tree that grows to a pro-digious height, and out of it the natives extraƈt a fort of white liquor like whey, called palm wine: by making an incifion on the top of the trunk, to which they apply gourd bottles, and into thefe the liquor runs by means of a pipe made of leaves. This wine is very pleafant as foon as it is drawn, it being extraordinary fweet ; but is apt to purge very much: however, in a day or two it ferments, and grows rough and ftrong like Rhenifh wine; when not being at all prejudical to the health, it is plentifully drank by the Negroes. It is very furprifing to fee how nimbly the natives will go up thefe trees, which are fometimes fixty, feventy, or a hundred feet high, and the bark fmooth. They have nothing to help them to climb, but a piece of the bark of a tree made round like a hoop, with which they enclofe themfelves and the tree, then fixing it under their arms they fet their feet againft the tree, and their backs againft the hoop, and go up very faft ; but fometimes they mifs their footing ; or the bark on which they reft breaks or come untied, when falling down, they lofe their lives.

The ciboa or palmetto tree refembles the palm and grows to a great height : the leaves which grow on the top, are ufed in covering houfes, and the natives extraƈt wine out of the palmetto, in the fame man-ner as out of the palm. It is not quite fo fweet as the palm wine ; but taftes not unlike it.

The people here, as in all other hot countries, marry their daughters very young ; even fome are contraƈted as foon as they are born, and the parents can never after break the match ; but it is in the power of the man never to come and claim his wife, and yet without his confent fhe cannot marry another. Before a man takes his wife, he is obliged to pay her parents two cows, two iron bars, and 200 cola, a fruit that grows a great way within land ; it is an exceeding good bitter, and much refembles a horfe-chefnut with the fkin off.

When a man takes home his wife he makes a feaft at his own houfe, to which all who pleafe come without the form of an invitation. The bride is brought thither upon men's fhoulders, with a veil over her face, which fhe keeps on till fhe has been in bed with her hufband, during which the people dance and fing, beat drums, and fire mufkets.

After the wife is brought to bed, fhe is not to lie with her hufband for three years, if the child lives fo long ; for during that term the child fucks, and they are firmly perfuaded that lying with their hufbands would fpoil their milk, and render the child liable to many difeafes. The women alone are fubject to all the mortifications attending fo long an abftinence ; for every man is allowed to take as many wives as he pleafes ; but if the wife is found falfe to her hufband, fhe is liable to be fold for a flave. Upon any diflike, a man may turn off his wife, and make her take all her children with her ; but if he has a mind to take any of them himfelf, he generally chufes fuch as are big enough to aflift him in providing for his family. He has even the liberty of coming feveral years after they have parted, and taking from her any of the children he had by her. But if a man is difpofed to part with a wife who is pregnant, he cannot oblige her to go till fhe is delivered.

The women are kept in the greateft fubjection ; and the men, to render their power as complete as poffible, influence their wives to give them an unlimited obedience, by all the force of fear and terror. For this purpofe the Mundingoes have a kind of image eight or nine feet high, made of the bark of trees, dreſſed in a long coat, and crowned with a wiſp of ſtraw. This is called a mumbo jumbo; and whenever the men have any diſpute with the women, this is ſent for to determine the conteſt, which is almoſt always done in favour of the men. One who is in the ſecret, conceals himſelf under the coat, and bringing in the image, is the oracle on theſe occaſions. No one is allowed to come armed into his preſence. When the women hear him coming they run away and hide themſelves; but if you are acquainted with the perſon concealed in the mumbo jumbo, he will ſend for them all to come, make them ſit down, and afterwards either ſing or dance, as he pleaſes; and if any refuſe to come, he will ſend for, and whip them. Whenever any one enters into this ſociety, they ſwear in the moſt ſolemn manner never to divulge the ſecret to any woman, or to any perſon that is not entered into it; and to preſerve the ſecret inviolable, no boys are admitted under ſixteen years of age. The people alſo ſwear by the mumbo jumbo, and the oath is eſteemed irrevocable. There are very few towns of any note that have not one of theſe objects of terror, to frighten the poor women into obedience.

About the year 1727, the king of Jagra having a very inquiſitive woman to his wife, was ſo weak as to diſcloſe to her this ſecret, and ſhe being a goſſip, revealed it to ſome other women of her acquaintance. This at laſt coming to the ears of ſome who were no friends to the king, they dreading leſt if the affair took vent, it ſhould put a period to the ſubjection of their wives, they took the coat, put a man into it, and going to the king's town ſent for him out, and taxed him with it; when he not denying it, they ſent for his wife, and killed them both on the ſpot. Thus the poor king died for his complaiſance to his wife, and ſhe for her curioſity.

The women pay fuch refpeĉt to their hufbands, that when a man has been a day or two from home, his wives falute him on their knees, and in the fame pofture they always give him water to drink.

When a child is new born they dip him over head and ears in cold water three or four times in a day, and as foon as he is dry, rub him over with palm oil. particularly the back-bone, the fmall of the back, the elbows, neck, knees, and hips. When they are. born they are of an olive colour, and fometimes do not turn black till they are a month or two old.

I do not find that they are born with flat nofes ; but the mothers when they wafh the children, prefs down the upper part of the nofe: for large breafts, thick lips, and broad noftrils, are efteemed extremely beautiful. One breaft is generally larger than the other.

About a month afterwards they name the child, which is done by fhaving its head, and rubbing it over with oil, and a fhort time before the rainy feafon begins, they circumcife a great number of boys, of about twelve or fourteen years of age, after which the boys put on a peculiar habit ; the drefs of each kingdom being different: from the time of circumcifion to that of the rains, they are allowed to commit what outrages they pleafe, without being called to an account for them ; and when the firft rain falls, the term of this licentioufnefs being expired, they put on their proper habit.

I have already obferved, that the Mundingoes are fond of the flefh of crocodiles, and their eggs, but their moft common food is called coofcoofh, which is pounded corn fifted through a fine bafket, till it is of the finenefs of coarfe flour ; and this is put into an earthen veffel full of holes like a cullender, luted to an earthen pot, in which is boiling water, and fometimes broth, the fteam of which cures the flour, and when it is done, they mix it with the water or broth, and eat it with their hands. Fifh dried in the fun or fmoked, is a great favourite of theirs ; but the ftronger it fmells the more they like it. They are fo little delicate with refpect to their provifions, that there is fcarce any thing which they do not eat ; large fnakes, guanas, monkeys, pelicans, bald eagles, and fea horfes, are efteemed excellent food.

The people are naturally very jocofe and merry, and will dance to a drum or ballafeu, fometimes four and twenty hours together, now and then dancing very regularly, and at other times ufing very odd geftures, ftriving always to outdo each other in nimblenefs and activity.

The behaviour of the natives to ftrangers is really not fo difagreeable as people are apt to imagine ; for when I went through any of their towns, they almoft all come to fhake hands with me, except fome of the women, who having never before feen a white man, ran away from me as faft as they could, and would not by any means be perfuaded to come near me. Some of the men invited me to their houfes, and brought their wives and daughters to fee me, who then fat down by me, and always found fomethig to wonder at and admire, as my boots, fpurs, clothes, or wig.

Some of the Mundingoes have many flaves in their houfes, and in thefe they pride themfelves. They live fo well and eafily, that it is fometimes difficult to know the flaves from their mafters and miftreffes ; they being frequently better clothed, efpecially the females, who have fometimes coral, amber, and filver about their waifts to the value of 20l. or 30l. fterling.

In almoft every town they have a kind of drum of a very large fize, called a Tangtong, which they only beat at the approach of an enemy, or on fome very extraordinary occafion, to callthe inhabitants of the neighbouring towns to their affiftance ; and this in the night-time may be heard fix or feven miles.

There was a cuftom in this country which is not thoroughly repealed, that, whatever commodity a man fells in the morning, he may, if he repents his bargain, go and have it returned to him again, on his paying back the money any time before the feting of the fun the fame day: this cuftom is ftill in force very high up the river ; but below it is pretty well worn out.

Whenever any factories are fettled, it is cuftomary to put them, and the perfons belonging to them, under the charge of the people of the neareft large town, who are obliged to take care of it, and to let none impofe upon the white men, or ufe them ill, and if any body is abufed, he muft apply to the alcalde, the head man of the town, who will fee that juftice is done him. This man, is up the river, called the white man's king ; and has befides very great power. Almoft every town has two common fields, one for their corn, and the other for their rice, and he appoints the labour of the people : he fees that the men work in the corn fields, and the women and girls in the rice grounds, and afterwards divides the crop among them. He likewife decides all quarrels, and has the firft voice in all conferences relating to any thing belonging to the town.

The trade of the natives confifts in gold, flaves, elephants teeth, and bees-wax. The gold is finer than fterling, and is brought in fmall bars, big in the middle, and turned round into rings, from ten to forty fhillings each. The merchants who bring this, and other inland commodities, are blacks of the Mundingo race, called Joncoes, who fay, that the gold is not wafhed out of the fand, but dug out of mines in the mountains, the neareft of which is twenty days journey up the river. In the country where the mines are, they fay there are houfes built with ftone, and covered with terrafs ; and that the fhort cutlafles and knives of good fteel, which they bring with them, are made there.

The fame merchants bring down elephants teeth, and in fome years flaves to the amount of 2000, moft

of whom they fay are prifoners of war ; and bought
of the different princes by whom they are taken.
The way of bringing them is by tying them by
the neck with leather thongs, at about a yard diftance from each other, thirty or forty in a ftring,
having generally a bundle of corn, or an elephant's
tooth upon each of their heads.   In their way from
the mountains they travel through extenfive woods,
where they cannot for fome days get water ; they
therefore carry in fkin bags enough to fupport them
for that time.   I cannot be certain of the number of
merchants who carry on this trade ; but there may
perhaps be about a hundred, who go up into the inland country with the goods, which they buy from the
white men,   and with them   purchafe, in various
countries, gold, flaves, and elephants teeth.   They
ufe affes, as well as flaves in carrying their goods,
but no camels or horfes.

Befides the flaves brought down by the Negro
merchants, there are many bought along the river,
who are either taken in war like the former, or condemned for crimes, or ftolen by the people : but
the company's fervants never buy any which they
fufpect to be of the laft fort, till they have fent for
the alcalde, and confulted with him.   Since this
flave trade has been ufed, all punifhments are changed into flavery ; and the natives reaping advantage
from fuch condemnations, they ftrain hard for crimes,
in order to obtain the benefit of felling the criminal;
hence not only murder, adultery and theft are here
punifhed by felling the malefactor ; but every trifling
crime is alfo punifhed in the fame manner.   Thus at
Cantore, a man feeing a tyger eating a deer, which
he himfelf had killed and hung up near his houfe,
fired at the tyger, but unhappily fhot a man : when
the king had not only the cruelty to condemn him
for this accident ; but had the injuftice and inhumanity to order alfo his mother, his three brothers,
and his three fifters to be fold.   They were brought

down to me at Yamyamacunda, when it made my heart ache to fee them ; but on my refufing to make this cruel purchafe, they were fent farther down the river, and fold to fome feparate traders at Joar, and the vile avaricious king had the benefit of the goods for which they were fold.

Indeed the cruelty and villainy of fome of thefe princes can fcarcely be conceived. Thus, whenever the king of Barfally, fome of whofe villainies I have already mentioned, wants goods or brandy, he fends to the governor of James' fort, to defire him to fend a floop there with a proper cargo, which is readily complied with. Mean while the king goes and ranfacks fome of his enemies towns, and feizing the innocent people, fells them to the factors in the floop, for fuch commodities as he wants, as brandy, rum, guns, gunpowder, ball, piftols and cutlaffes; for his attendants and foldiers, with coral and filver for his wives and concubines, but in cafe he is not at war with any neighbouring king, he then falls upon one of his own towns, which are very numerous, and ufes them in the fame manner, felling them for flaves, whom he is bound by every obligation to protect.

Several of the natives of thefe countries have many flaves born in their families : thus there is a whole village near Brucoe of 200 people, who are the wives, flaves, and children of one man. And though in fome parts of Africa, they fell the flaves born in the family ; yet this is here thought extremely wicked ; and I never heard of but one perfon who ever fold a family flave, except for fuch crimes as would have authorifed its being done had he been free. Indeed, if there are many flaves in the family, and one of them commits a crime, the mafter cannot fell him without the joint confent of the reft : for if he does, they will all run away to the next kingdom, where they will find protection.

Ivory, or elephants teeth, is the next principal article of commerce. Thefe are obtained either by hunting and killing the beafts, or are picked up in the woods. This is a trade ufed by all the nations hereabouts ; for whoever kills an elephant, has the liberty of felling him and his teeth : but thofe traded for in this river are generally brought from a good way within land. The largeft tooth I ever faw weighed 130 pounds.

The fourth branch of trade confifts in bees-wax. The Mundingoes make beehives of ftraw fhaped like ours, and fixing to each a bottom board, in which is a hole, for the bees to go in and out, hang them on the boughs of trees. They fmother the bees in order to take the combs, and preffing out the honey of which they make a kind of metheglin, boil up the wax with water, ftrain it, and prefs it through hair cloths into holes made in the ground.

At length, on the eighth of April 1735, having delivered up the company's effects to Mr. James Conner, I embarked on board the company's floop: among other perfons, Job came down with me to the floop, and parted with me with tears in his eyes, at the fame time giving me letters to the Duke of Montague, the royal African company, Mr. Oglethorpe, and feveral other gentlemen in England, telling me to give his love and duty to them, and to acquaint them, that as he defigned to learn to write the Englifh tongue, he would, when he was mafter of it, fend them longer epiftles ; defiring me, that as I had lived with him almoft ever fince he came there, I would let his grace and the other gentlemen know what he had done ; and that he was going to the gum-foreft, and would endeavour to produce fo good an underftanding between the company and the Pholeys, that he did not doubt but that the Englifh would procure the gum-trade : adding, that he would fpend his days in endeavouring to do good to the

Engliſ by whom he had been redeemed from
ſlav⸗, and from whom he had received innumer-
aſ⸗ favours.

Soon after he returned on ſhore, while I ſailed to
England, and at length, on the 13th of July. landed
ıt Deal.

U u

RELIGION

OF THE

MAHOMETANS,

WITH A

DESCRIPTION OF MECCA AND MEDINA.

BY

JOSEPH PITTS.

INTRODUCTION.

THOUGH many learned and ingenious authors have wrote on the religon of the Mahometans, none feem fo qualified for the tafk as Mr. Pitts of Exeter, who when a youth was taken a captive by the Algerines, and by the force of torment, in a ftrange country, where he had no Chriftian friend to comfort and ftrengthen him, was unhappily compelled to feem to embrace the religion of the country. Perfecution may, indeed, fhake the refolution of the mind ; but can never convince the judgment. Thus it happened with our author ; he was ftill a Chriftian : yet as he affumed the garb and manners of a Mahometan, he was admitted into their mofques, and allowed to vifit the fuppofed facred places of Mecca and Medina.

HAVING a ftrong inclination to the fea, I entered in the year 1678, when I was about fourteen or fifteen years of age, on board the Speedwell, at Lymfom, near Exeter, Mr. George Taylor, mafter, on a trading voyage to Newfoundland, from thence to Bilboa, from thence to the Canaries, and fo home; but on our coming near the coaft of Spain, we had the misfortune to be taken by an Algerine rover, and carried to Algiers.

On our landing we were carried to the captain's houfe, where we were allowed only bread and water. The next morning we were driven to the dey's, who having chofen an eighth part of the flaves for the fervice of the public, the reft of us were driven to the market place for the fale of Chriftians, who are difpofed of by way of auction; but after the bidders have done bidding, the flaves are driven again to the dey's houfe, where any that are difpofed to advance above what was bidden at the market, may: but then whatever exceeds the bidding in that place belongs not to the pirates, but to the Dey.

I was bought by a man who treated me with the utmoft cruelty, and though it is very uncommon for the Algerines to trouble themfelves about the religion of their flaves, my patroon, or mafter was continually beating me in order to force me to become a Mahometan. With this cruel man I lived about two or three months, and he then fent me to fea. I gladly went on board, flattering myfelf with the hopes of our being taken by fome veffels belonging to the Chriftians. We were out two months, in which we took only one Portuguefe fhip; and my heart funk within me on its being refolved to return to Algiers, where I expected to be treated with the fame cruelty by my inhuman mafter, who had ftaid on fhore. But to my great fatisfaction, in a few days after my return to that city, he fold me to a perfon who lived in the country and had many flaves, both Chriftians and Negroes.

My fecond patroon had two brothers in Algiers, and one at Tunis; I was bought in order to be given to the latter, and was very handfomely dreffed to en-hance the value of the prefent. Soon after my pa-troon and I failed for Tunis, where we arrived with-in fourteen or fifteen days. We immediately went to the houfe of my mafter's brother. The next day a young man, my patroon's nephew, being proud of having a Chriftian to wait upon him, made me walk after him, to which I readily confented, from my defire to fee the city. As I was attending my new mafter through the ftreets, I met with a gentleman dreffed like a Chriftian, who afked me, if I was an Englifhman? I anfwered, yes. He then enquired, how I came thither? to which I replied, I came with my patroon. He then defired to know if I was a flave, and I let him know that I was, and that I came from Algiers. Not being willing to enter into farther difcourfe in the public ftreet, he invited the young man on whom I waited to come to fee him at fuch an hour of the day, and to bring me to his houfe, which the youth readily promifed.

The gentleman was no fooner gone, than my young mafter, to my no fmall pleafure, told me, that he was the Englifh conful. We went at the time ap-pointed, and I was directed to his chamber while the young fpark was eating and drinking in another room. The conful afked me many queftions, and among the reft, whether I could write and un-derftood arithmetic; and telling him I could do both tolerably well, he called for pen, ink, and paper, and bid me write a line, on which I wrote, The Lord be my guide, in him will I truft. He feemed pleafed, and after fome farther converfation, kindly told me that if I were left in Tunis, he would order matters to my fatisfaction ; but if my patroon defigned to carry me back again to Algiers, I fhould let him know it. Telling me, if I had fo much liberty, I fhould be welcome to come every day to his houfe,

When I had been at Tunis about thirty days I, to my great grief, heard that my patroon's brother would not accept of me, and that I muft return to Algiers. This news I communicated to the conful, who endeavoured to remove my concern, by telling me, that he and two other Englifh merchants would the next day endeavour to procure my redemption ; this, indeed, they attempted, and agreed to give 300 dollars for me; but my patroon infifting on 500, the conful, when I faw him again, told me that I muft have patience, for a hundred pounds was a confiderable fum to be contributed by three only. Upon this, burfting into tears, I returned him a thoufand thanks for his generous good-will: when the conful laying his hand upon my head, bid me ferve God, and be cheerful, and when he returned to England he would prefer a petition to the king for me.

Thus were all my hopes vanifhed. My patroon returned with me to Algiers ; and fome time after being made captain of a troop of horfe, took me with him to the camp, when his brothers being alfo in the army, the youngeft was continually perfuading me to turn Mahometan ; and finding all his arguments ineffectual, he applied to my mafter, telling him, he had been a debauched man, and a murderer; but that making me a profelyte would atone for his paft crimes. Upon this my mafter, the elder brother, began alfo to perfuade and threaten me, and one day when his barber came to fhave him, he bid me kneel before him, which I did. He then ordered the barber to cut off my hair: I miftrufting them, began to ftruggle ; but by mere force they cut off my hair, and then the barber ftrove to fhave my head, my patroon all the while holding my hands, I kept fhaking my head, and he kept ftriking me in the face. My head was at length with difficulty fhaved, and my patroon would then have me take of my clothes, and put on the Turkifh habit ; but I plainly told him I would not : whereupon I was dragged away to another tent, where we kept our provifions, and there the cook and the fteward, ftripped me, and one of them held me, while the other put on me the Turkifh garb. All this while I kept crying, and told my patroon, that though he had changed my habit, he could not change my heart.

The following night, he ufed entreaties that I would gratify him by renouncing my religion. I told him it was againft my confcience, and defired him to fell me and buy another boy, who might perhaps be more eafily won ; but for my part, i was afraid of being everlaftingly damned, if I complied with his requeft. He told me, he would pawn his foul for mine, and made ufe of many other importunate ex-preffions. At length, I defired him to let me go to bed, and I would pray to God, and if I found better reafons fuggefted to my mind for changing my opinion by the next morning, I did not know what I might do ; but if I continued in the fame mind, I defired him to fay no more on that fubject.

To this he agreed, and I went to bed. But he had not patience to ftay till the morning for my anfwer. He awoke me in the night, and afked me what were my fentiments now. I told him they were the fame as before : on which he feized my right hand, and endeavoured to make me hold up the fore-finger, as they do in uttering the Mahometan creed ; but I bent it down with all my force. When feeing nothing was to be done without violence, he called two of his fervants, and commanded them to tie up my feet with a rope to the poft of the tent, which being done, he with a great cudgel beat me on my bare feet, and being a ftrong man, his blows fell very heavy. I roared out with pain ; but the more I cried the more furioufly he laid on, threatning that he would baftinado me to death, if I did not turn, and ftamping with his foot on my mouth to ftop the noife of my crying. At which I begged him to difpatch me out of the way; but he continued beating me. Having endured this mercilefs ufage till I was ready to faint and die under it, and yet faw him as mad and implacable as ever, I begged him to forbear, and I would turn. Breathing awhile, he urged me to fpeak the words La Allah ellallah, Mohammed Rezul Allah: that is, There is but one God, and Mahomet the prophet of God. But I held him in fufpence, and at length told him, that I could not fpeak them: at which he was more enraged than before, and fell upon me again in the moft barbarous manner. I again befought him to hold his hand, and gave him frefh hopes of my turning Mahometan; but after a fhort refpite I told him, as before, I could not do what he defired. Thus I held him in fufpenfe three or four times, infatiable unlefs I turned, but at laft finding his cruelty and overcome by pain and terror, I fpoke the words, holding up the fore finger of my right hand. Prefently I was had to a fire; care was taken of my feet, and I was put to bed; but was unable to ftand for feveral days.

. All the ceremony ufed by one who turns Mahometan by compulfion is only holding up the forefinger of his right hand, and pronouncing the above words: but when any perfon voluntarily turns from his religion to the Mahometan, a great deal of formality is ufed. In this cafe he goes to the court, where the dey and divan fits, and declaring his willingnefs to be a Mahometan, he is mounted on a fine horfe, adorned with rich trappings; and is very handfomely dreffed with a turbant on his head; but nothing of this is to be called his own; only there is given him two or three yards of broad-cloth, which is laid before him on the faddle. Thus he rides all round the city, carrying an arrow in his

right hand, which he holds straight up, thus sup-
porting the fore-finger of his right hand, which he
holds up against it. He is attended with drums, and
other music, with twenty or thirty persons, who
march in order on each side of the horse, with
naked swords in their hands. There is also a
person on each side of the street, as he marches
through, to receive what people are pleased to
give him; and one here and there drops perhaps
the value of a farthing or a halfpenny. Mean-
while the cryer goes before, giving thanks to God
for the proselyte that is made. A few days after the
circumciser comes and performs his office, and then
he is a Mahometan to all intents and purposes. It is
pretended by some writers, that who any thus
voluntarily turns Mahometan, he throws a dart at
the picture of Jesus Christ, in token of his disown-
ing him; but there is no such custom.

About two or three months after I was taken a
slave, I had found means to send a letter to my father,
giving him an account of what had happened; to
which I received a kind and affectionate answer, a
few days after I had been thus induced by my patroon's barbarity to turn from my religion: but in
this answer he tenderly exhorted me to let no
methods of cruelty prevail on me to deny my blessed
Saviour; and observed that he would rather hear of
my death, than of my being a Mahometan.

This letter threw me into the greatest dejection
of mind, and a few days after, I wrote a second
letter to my father, in which I let him know that I
was forced by the cruelty of my master to turn Mahometan; but that I was a Christian in my heart,
and that as soon as ever I could find an opportunity
I would endeavour to make my escape. After this
several other letters past between us.

Notwithstanding what I had done, I still lived a
miserable life with my patroon, and I was often so
beaten by him, that my blood ran upon the ground;

for a Chriftian flave does not by turning Mahometan become free. Befides he now hated me, from his fuf-pecting my fincerity, and on that account I fared in manyrefpects worfe than my fellow flaves. I lay with them in the ftable, and alfo ftill eat with them. Our provifions were very coarfe, and moftly barley bread with four milk : but if a fheep happened to die, the flefh came to our fhare.

Though a Mahometan of this country have all the outward appearance of religion, yet almoft all kinds of wickednefs, except murder and theft, are left unpunifhed. They are generally very ftrict in pray-ing five times a day; and in their numerous ablutions, in which they are extremely exact. I fhall more particularly defcribe the worfhip of the mofques, which Chriftians are not allowed to enter. Even the female fex of their own religion are excluded from having any fhare in the public worfhip.

The clerk having called from the fteeple of the mofque, the people immediately hafte thither. The infides of thefe buildings have neither pews nor feats, but a plain floor fpread over with mats, except near the Imam where carpets are fpread. The gal-leries are likewife fpread with mats. In the mofques are weither pictures nor ftatues, for they utterly abhor images, and the walls are all white. On coming to the door the men put off their flippers, walk in barefoot, and putting the foles of their flippers to-gether, place them before them, and kneeling reft upon their heels. The iman is raifed above the people ; his back is towards them ; but the mezzins or clerks are placed in a gallery by themfelves, where they obferve his motions, and begin with much the fame words as they had before ufed in calling from the fteeple: that is, " God is great. " God is great. I teftify that there is no God befides " God. I teftify that Mahomet is the meffenger of " God. I teftify that Mahomet is the meffenger of " God. Hafte to prayers. Hafte to prayers. Hafte

" to a good work. Hafte to a good work. Now
" prayers are beginning. Now prayers are begin-
" ning. Now prayers are beginning. God is great.
" There is no God befides God." On his faying the
" laft words, all the congregation bring their two
thumbs together, and kifs them three times, and at
every kifs they touch their forehead with their
thumbs, and then rifing up all on their legs, they ftand
exactly clofe to each other in even ranks.

They all imitate the iman in the front, who is no
fooner on his feet than he brings his two thumbs to
touch the lower part of his ears, at which the
mezzin, or clerk above, cries out, " God is great,"
at the hearing of which they all touch their ears,
faying the fame to themfelves. The iman then
fays a fhort leffon out of the koran, which being
ended, he bows with his hands refting on his knees,
at which the mezzin again makes the fame exclama-
tion, and when the iman recovers himfelf and ftands
upright, it is again repeated.

The iman now placing his hands on his thighs,
gently finks on his knees, then ftretching forth his
hands on the ground, brings his forehead to touch
it, at which he repeats again, " God is great." The
imam then recovers himfelf on his knees, with his
hands on his thighs, and ftretches his hands on the
ground as before, the clerk repeating the fame expreffions. All which poftures and ceremonies the
imam performs a fecond time, and the mezzin ufes
the fame words as the firft : which being done, the
imam fits ftill on his heels about a minute, with his
hands on his thighs, and fixing his eyes on the floor,
fays a fhort prayer, at the conclufion of which he
looks over his right fhoulder, and then over his left,
faying at each, welcome, my angels ; or peace be to
you ; for they hold that every one has two angels
to attend him, efpecially at the time of their worfhip.
It muft be obferved, that all in the fame congregation ufe the fame geftures as the iman, and all at

the fame inftant ; the mezzin fpeaking loud is a fufficient token when to bow or rife ; and they all ftand
with their faces towards Mecca.

At-the conclufion of their worfhip, the iman who
officiates at the upper end of the mofque, kneeling in
an oval place in the wall, and turning his face towards the congregation, who are all upon their
knees imitating him, he takes out his beads, which
are ninety-nine in number, and have a partition between every thirty-three ; thefe they turn over, and
for each of the firft thirty-three they fay, admire
God ; for the fecond thirty-three they cry, thanks
be to God, and for the third thirty-three, God is
great. Which being ended, the iman with the
whole affembly, hold up their hands at a little diftance from their faces, putting up their filent orifons;
and to conclude all, fmooth down their faces with
their hands, take up their flippers, and go their
way.

In this manner they behave in their public worfhip,
which lafts about a quarter of an hour; and is repeated with fome variations five times a day; and on
Friday, which is their fabbath, the iman, with a
ftaff in his hand, mounts fix or feven fteps, and
makes a fhort fermon about a quarter of an hour
long.

My patroon with whom I lived very unhappily,
and whofe cruelty, added to the uneafinefs of my
mind, rendered life a burthen, at length engaged in
a rebellion againft the Dey, with the hopes of obtaining that office; but this at laft coft him his life; for
being taken prifoner he was beheaded.

I was now in hopes that my patroona or miftrefs
would have given me my freedom ; but this fhe
refufed, and fold me in Algiers, where I was led
three days by the cryer about the ftreets, and was
bought on the third by an old batchelor who employed me to drefs his meat, to wafh his clothes, and to
do all thofe things that are looked on as a fervant

maid's work in England. I now wanted for neither
meat, drink, clothes, nor money. After I had lived
with him about a year, he refolved to make his pilgrimage to Mecca, and to take me with him. We
went by fea to Alexandria in Egypt ; but in our
paffage being taken fick, and thinking he fhould die,
he took off a girdle which he wore under his fafh, in
which was much gold, and alfo my letter of freedom,
which he intended to give me when at Mecca, and
bidding me put it on, he took my girdle, and put
it on himfelf; which was a convincing proof of his
regard for me ; but it pleafed God that he recovered.

We ftaid at Alexandria about twenty days, and
then fteered to Rofetta, where we entered the Nile,
and failed up that river to Grand Cairo, where we
furnifhed ourfelves with three or four months provifions, that were to ferve us till our return to Egypt;
and hired camels to carrry us to Suez, a fmall town
fituated at the end of the Red Sea. We there embarked again, and after about a month's fail, came
to a place called Rahbock, about four days fail from
Mecca, where all the pilgrims, except thofe of the
female fex, ftrip off all their clothes, and covering
their bodies with only two wrappers, with their
heads bare, and fandals on their feet, go on fhore
and travel by land to Mecca ; when the fcorching
heat of the fun fometimes burns the fkins off their
backs and arms, and greatly fwells their heads.
However, when any man is in danger of lofing his
health by thefe aufterities, he may lawfully put on
his clothes, on condition that when he comes to
Mecca, he kills a fheep, and gives it to the poor.
But while they wear this mortifying habit, it is held
unlawful for them fo much as to cut their nails or
to kill a loufe or a flea, though they fee them fucking their blood. They are likewife to entertain no
enmity againft any one, to be watchful over their
tempers and paffions, to obferve a ftrict government

of the tongue, and to make continual ufe of a form of devout expreffions. Thefe aufterities laft feven days.

At Grada, the neareft fea port town to Mecca, from which it is not quite a day's journey, we unloaded our fhips, and here were met by perfons who came to inftruct the pilgrims in the ceremonies to be ufed in their worfhip.

On our arrival at Mecca, the above perfons, who were our guides, conducted us into the great ftreet which is in the midft of the town, and to which the temple joins : he then directed us to the fountains where we performed our ablutions, and then he took us to the temple, where leaving our fhoes with one who attends to receive them, we entered at the door called the Gate of Peace. Having proceeded a few paces, our guide held up his hand toward the Beat Allah, and uttered feveral words which the pilgrims repeated after him; burfting into tears at the fight of the building. After which we were led feven times round it, and then were conducted into the ftreet where we were fometimes to run, and fometimes to walk very quick, the pilgrims behaving with the utmoft awe and trembling : performing thefe fuperftitious ceremonies with the appearance of the moft extraordinary devotion. This being over, we returned and fought out for lodgings.

All the pilgrims think it their indifpenfable duty to improve their time while at Mecca, not only in doing their accuftomed duty, and devotion at the temple, but to fpend all their leifure time there, and as far as their ftrength will permit to continue walking round the Beat Allah, at one corner of which is faftened a black ftone, framed in with filver, and every time they come to that corner, they kifs the ftone; and having gone round feven times, they perform two prayers. This ftone they fay was formerly white, but the fins of the people who kifs it have rendered it black.

The temple of Mecca is a fquare building with an area on the infide furrounded with piazzas, much like thofe of the Royal Exchange in London : but the fquare is near ten times bigger, and over the piazzas is, on each fide, a range of domes which cover little rooms or cells, the habitations of fuch as give themfelves up to reading and a devout life ; and at each corner is a minaret or fteeple, from which the criers call the people to prayers. The area on each of the inclofure, is covered with gravel, except fome paths that lead to the Beat Allah. There are forty-two doors in the outer building that open into the fquare.

The Beat-Allah, which ftands in the centre, is a fquare folid ftruĉture near twenty-four paces each way, and about twenty feet high, formed of large ftones perfeĉtly fmooth and plain, without the leaft carved work. It is covered all over from top to bottom with a thick filk, and above the middle part of the covering are letters of gold embroidered all round, the meaning of which I have forgot ; but I think they were fome devout expreffions. Near the lower part of the building is a large brafs ring, through which paffes a great cotton rope to which the lower part of the covering is faftened. The threfhold of the door is as high as a man can reach, and therefore when any perfon enters the Beat, a fet of fteps are brought for him to afcend. The door is plated all over with filver, and a covering hangs over it that reaches to the ground, which is kept turned up all the week except on Thurfday night and Friday, which is their Sabbath. This covering of the door is fo thick embroidered with gold, that it weighs feveral fcore pounds. The top of the building is flat, and covered with lime and fand. It has a long fpout to carry off the water when it rains, at which time the people throng and ftruggle to get under it, that the water which comes off the Beat may fall upon them, which they efteem a great happinefs, and if they can catch fome of it to drink, their joy is exceſſive.

Round the Beat is a pavement of marble about fifty feet in breadth, on the edge of which ſtand pillars of braſs near fifteen feet high, and twenty feet diſtance from each other ; above the middle part of them iron bars are faſtened reaching from one to the other, with glaſs lamps hanging to each, by braſs wires, to give light in the night; for while the pilgrims ſtay at Mecca, they pay their devotions as much by night as by day.

About twelve paces from the Beat is, what they call, the Sepulchre of Abraham, whom they ſay by God's command built the Beat. This ſepulchre is enclofed with iron gates, and has a very handſome embroidered covering. At a ſmall diſtance from it on the left hand is the well Zemzem, the water of which is eſteemed holy. They pretend that it is as fweet as milk, but I could perceive no other taſte in it, but that of common water, except its being ſomewhat brackiſh. The pilgrims on their firſt coming to Mecca drink of it unreafonably, by which means they are not only purged, but their fleſh breaks out in pimples. This they call the purging of their ſpiritual corruptions.

Many of them carry fome of this water home to their refpective countries, in little tin pots, and preſent perhaps a half a ſpoonful of it to each of their friends, which they receive in the hollow of their hands with abundance of thanks, fipping a little of it, and beſtowing the reſt on their faces and naked heads.

Oppofite each ſide of the Beat is a ſmall ſtructure ſupported on pillars, where the iman together with the mezzins perform their devotions and fuperſtitious ceremonies in the fight of all the people. Theſe ſtructures belong to four different forts of Mahometans.

[To give a more perfect idea of this famous building, we have given the reader the following plate, in
which

A is the black ftone already mentioned.

B carpets fpread on the ground to perform their
devotions on.

C the building in which is the well Zemzem, the
water of which is accounted falutary to thofe who
drink it.

D the gate of the Beat Allah confifting of two
folding doors.

E the fleps by which they afcend to them.

F a pulpit from which the iman harangues the
people.

G the places where the four chief fects of the Mahometans meet.]

The Beat Allah is opened but two days in the
fpace of fix weeks, one day for the men, and the next
for the women. As I was at Mecca about four months,
I had an opportunity of entering it twice, an advantage which many thoufands of the hadgees have
not met with. All that they have to do is to hold
up their hands, look over each fhoulder, and fay
welcome my angels, and then offer fome petitions ;
but they are fo devout that they will not fuffer their
eyes to wander. Nay, they fay, that one was ftruck
blind for gazing about. Difregarding this idle ftory,
I now and then caft an obferving eye: but found
nothing worthy of notice ; only two wooden pillars
to fupport the roof, and a bar of iron faftened to
them, on which hang three or four filver lamps,
which I fuppofe are but feldom if ever lighted. The
floor and the walls are of marbler and the latter are
ufually hung with filk, which is pulled off before the
hadgees enter. Thofe who enter the Beat ftay fcarce
half a quater of an hour, becaufe others wait for the
fame privilege, and while fome go in others are going
out.

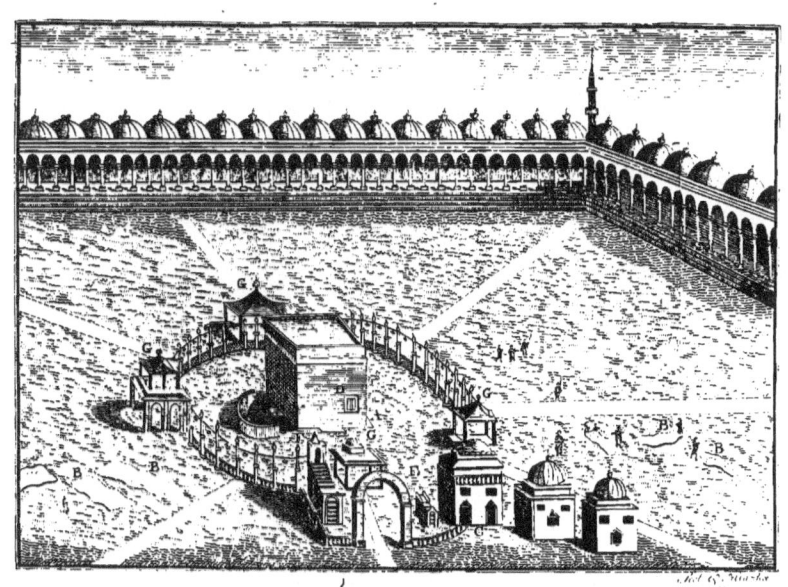

The TEMPLE of MECCA

After all that will, have done this, the fultan of Mecca, who is of the race of Mahomet, does not think himfelf too good to clean the Beat. He and his favourites firft wafh it with the holy water Zemzem, and after that with fweet water. The ftairs which were brought to enter in at the door being removed, the people croud under the door to receive the fweepings of the water on their bodies, and the befoms or brooms, with which the Beat is cleaned are broken to pieces, and thrown out amongft the mob; when he that gets a fmall ftick or twig of it, keeps it as a facred relic.

Every year the covering of the Beat is renewed, and fent from Grand Cairo by order of the grand fegnior; and when the caravan goes with the pilgrims to Mecca, the new covering is carried upon two camels, which do no other work all the year long. It is received with extreme joy, fome kiffing the camels and bidding them welcome. The old covering being pulled down, the new one is put up by the fultan of Mecca; and he cutting the old covering in pieces, fells them at a great price to the hadgees.

At Mecca are thoufands of blue pigeons, which none will affright or abufe, much lefs kill them, whence they are fo very tame that they will pick meat out of one's hand, and I myfelf have fed them. They are called the pigeons of the prophet, and come in great flocks to the temple, where they are ufually fed by the hadgees. I have heard fome fay, that they pay fuch reverence to the Beat Allah, that they will never fly over it; but this is not true, for I have often feen them fly over it.

The pilgrims, before they receive the honourable title of hadgee, again put on their mortifying habit, and go to an hill called Gibbelel Orphat, or the mountain of knowledge, where there are faid to meet no lefs than 70,000 perfons every year, two months and nine days after the faft of ramadam; and it is pretended that if there are fewer than that number,

God will fupply the deficiency by fo many angels. Indeed the number of the hadgees at this mountain is very great, though I cannot think it amounts to fo many. It was however a melancholy fight to behold fo many thoufands in their garments of humility and mortification, with their naked heads, and their cheeks wet with tears: with fighs and fobs earneftly begging in a form of penitential expreffions, the remiffion of their fins ; and promifing newnefs of life, and thus continuing for the fpace of four or five hours. After this they all at once receive the title of hadgee from the iman, which they from thence enjoy till their death.

Immediately upon their receiving this name, the trumpet is founded, and they all leave the hill to return towards Mecca. Having proceeded two or three miles, they reft for that night ; but after their devotions, each perfon gathers 49 fmall ftones about the fize of an hazel nut.

The next morning they move to a place called Mina or Muna, where, they fay, Abraham went to offer up his fon, and there they all pitch their tents, and then every hadgee throws feven of the ftones he had gathered at a fmall pillar, crying, ftone the devil, and them that pleafe him. There are two other of the like pillars fituated near each other, and at each of the three, they, the fecond day, throw feven ftones, and the fame number the day after. It is obfervable, that after they have thrown the feven ftones on the firft day, the country people having brought great flocks of fheep to be fold, each perfon buys one, and facrifices it : fome of the flefh they give to their friends and the poor, then pull off their penitential habits, and fpend the three days in feftivity and rejoicings ; but during this time, there are few who are able, who do not run once at laft, to have a frefh fight of the Beat Allah, which they no fooner behold, than they burft into tears of joy, and having performed their devotions return back to Mina.

The three days being expired they all return to Mecca, where they muſt not ſtay above ten or twelve days, during which a great fair is held, in which are ſold all ſorts of Eaſt India goods. Almoſt every one now buys a ſhrowd of fine linen to be buried in, for the advantage of having it dipped in the holy-water; and this they are ſure to carry with them wherever they go. The evening before they go Mecca, every one takes a ſolemn leaves of the Beat Allah, from which they retire backwards, holding up their hands and offering up their petitions with their eyes fixed on the building till they have loſt ſight of it, and then they burſt into tears.

Mecca is ſituated in a barren ſpot about a day's journey from the red ſea, and is ſurrounded by a great number of little hills. It is without walls, and the buildings very mean. The climate is exceeding hot, whence the inhabitants, eſpecially the men, uſually ſleep on the tops of the houſes or in the ſtreets before their doors. Some lay their bedding on a thin matt on the ground, and others have a ſlight frame, on which they put their bedding ; but before they bring it out they ſweep the ſtreets and water them. I uſually lay on the top of the houſe covered only with a linen cloth dipped in water, and wrung out ; when I awoke I found it dry, and therefore wetted it again, and this I did two or three times in a night.

On our leaving Mecca we proceeded on camels to Medina, where Mahomet lies entombed. This is but a ſmall mean town : but it is walled round, and has a large moſque, in one corner of which is a place built about fourteen or fifteen paces ſquare ; this building has ſpacious windows fenced with braſs grates. On the inſide it has ſome ornaments. It is covered with a dome, and has a number of lamps; ſome relate that there are no leſs than 3000 of them :

but I am fure there are not above a hundred. In the middle of this place is the tomb of Mahomet furrounded by filk curtans like a bed : but none of the hadgees are permitted to enter it ; for the eunuchs alone go in to light the lamps, which burn by night. It is pretended by fome, that Mahomet's coffin is fufpended by the attractive virtue of a loadftone, fixed to the roof; but this is falfe ; for when I looked through the grate of the window, the curtans that covered the tomb were not half fo high as the dome, fo that it is impoffible the coffin fhould hang there ; nor do the Mahometants pretend that it does.

On our leaving Medina, we paffed through Eygpt, and having reached Alexandria, I was walking with an Irifh renegado on the quay, where we faw an Englifh boat with a man in it, whom the renegado earneftly defired me to fpeak to, which I was afraid of doing ; however, I at laft afked him fome queftions, which made him enquire where I learnt Englifh. I told him in England. He then defired to know if I was an Englifhman, and from what part of England I came. I told him from Exeter, and related the manner in which I was taken ; but being afraid of holding a long difcourfe with him, I haftily retired.

The next day, when I was again walking, I obferved the fame man and another perfon with him, who running up to me hugged me in his arms, crying, I am glad to fee thee, with all my heart. At firft I did not know him, till he told me who he was, when I found that when boys, we had been play fellows. I was very defirous of having further talk with him, and he preffed me to drink a glafs of wine; but I refufed. He then invited me to a coffeehoufe ; but I told him I could not go, becaufe it would be full of Mahometans. I however inquired after the health of my father, and my friends, and he told me that he faw my father a little before he left England. At my defire he readily promifed to carry

a letter for me, and I afterwards fent by him a Turkifh pipe to my father, a filk purfe to my mother, and
gave him a fafh for himfelf, telling him that I hoped
God would find out fome way for my efcape ; but my
heart bled at parting with him.

My patroon had however, before this, the generofity to give me, according to his promife, my
liberty at Mecca. I was therefore no longer a flave,
yet the cruel death that would have been inflicted,
had I been found to endeavour to make my efcape,
and the ill confequence of my giving room for fuch
a fufpicion, made me thus cautious.

On my return to Algiers, I entered into the
army, and my generous mafter, who loved me as if
I had been his fon, freely gave me my board, and
let me know that he propofed to leave me fomething
confiderable at his death : but notwithftanding this
pleafing profpect, and all the gratitude I felt for
his kindnefs, the hopes of being retaken, made me
leave him and go to fea ; but my wifhes were not
granted : At length the grand fegnior fending to the
Algerines for fome fhips, I refolved to go into one
of them, flattering myfelf with the hopes of making
my efcape at Smyrna.

I had fome time before been afflicted with a humour
in one of my eyes, on which I applied to an Englifh
flave who underftood phyfic and furgery, and who
lived with Mr. Butler, an Englifh merchant, and he
undertaking the cure, I went twice or thrice a day
to be dreffed, where being in no fear of being feen
by a Mahometan, I frequently took up a bible and
read in it. One day being found thus employed by
Mr. Butler, he feemed to wonder at it ; but all I
dared to tell him was, that I had no hatred to the
bible. In a little time growing better acquainted
with him he invited me to dinner, and among other
things had a piece of bacon ; but I had the precaution to refufe to tafte it. He, however, foon
found the way to remove my referve, and I opened

my whole heart to him, on which he promifed to affift me all in his power to make my efcape, and was fo kind as to propofe it to Mr. Baker, conful of Algiers, the brother of the conful of Tunis, who had generoufly endeavoured to redeem me from my flavery to my fecond patroon.

Mr. Butler introduced me to that gentleman, who kindly wrote me a letter of recommendation to Mr. Raye, conful of Smyrna ; charging me, if I fhould be in danger of death, or a difcovery, to convey it overboard, for his fafety.

With this letter I fet fail with the above fleet, and on our arrival at Smyrna, I prefented it to the con-ful, who having read it, ordered the interpreter to withdraw, and as foon as he was gone, afked me if I was the man mentioned in the letter. I told him I was, then obferving that the defign was very dange-rous, and that if it fhould be known to the Turks that he was any way concerned in it, it would coft him his life and all he was worth ; he added, that however, on Mr. Baker's account, he would do me all the fervice in his power: but cautioned me not to come to his houfe, except on fome extraordinary occafion.

A day or two after this, I found out an Englifh merchant, who had ferved part of his apprenticefhip at Exeter ; I made myfelf known to him, and this gentleman whofe name was Eliot, promifed to affift me, and kindly told me, that I need not run the hazard of going to the conful's houfe ; but if I had any thing of moment to communicate to him, he would do it for me, and I gladly followed this friend-ly advice.

In a month's time it was cried about the city of Smyrna, that all Algerines fhould repair to their fhips. All this time no Englifh or Dutch fhips came to Smyrna ; it was therefore agreed, that to prevent fufpicion, I fhould go to Scio with the Algerines, which I accordingly did, and ftaid there till the

Algerines were gone ; but fome time after returned to Smyrna, where I kept myfelf very private, till a French fhip was ready to fail.

On the evening before her intended departure I went on board, drefled like an Englifhman, with my beard fhaven, a campaign peruke, and a cane in my hand, accompanied by three or four of my friends. The boat that carried us on board was brought juft to the houfe where I lodged ; and as we were going into it, there were fome Turks of Smyrna walking by, but they had happily no fufpicion.

My good friend Mr. Eliot had agreed with the captain of the fhip to pay 4l. for my paffage to Leghorn; but neither the captain nor any of the French-men knew who I was. After they had brought me fafe on board, they took their leave of me, and told me, that if the fhip did not fail the next morning, they would vifit me again, which accordingly they did, bringing wine and provifions aboard, and were very merry, though I could not help being extremely uneafy till the fhip had made fail : nor did I enjoy the leaft peace of mind till we reached Leghorn, where, as foon as I came afhore, in a tranfport of joy, I proftrated myfelf, and kiffed the earth, blefling Almighty God for his undeferved mercy, in fuffering me once more to fet my foot in a Chriftian country.

From thence I fet out by land, and having travelled through Italy and Germany, and at laft arriving at Helvoetfluys, croffed in the Englifh packet to Harwich. I had received many inftances of civility from ftrangers on the road ; but the very firft night I lay afhore in my native country, I was impreffed into the king's fervice, they being at that time at war with France. And though I made known my condition, acquainting them how many years I had been in flavery, and begged for my liberty with tears, yet I was carried to Colchefter prifon, where I lay fome days. While I was there I wrote two

letters, one to my father, and the other to Sir
William Falkener, who was one of the Turkey or
Smyrna company in London, and on whom I had
a fmall bill for a litle money. In a few days I was
put aboard a fmack, that was to carry the impreffed
men to the Dreadnought man of war ; but I had
not been long there before my name was called,
there being a letter for me, when, to my great furprize and joy, I found it came from Sir William
Falkener, who, upon the receipt of mine, notwithftanding my being an abfolute ftranger to him, had
the humanity to go immediately to the admiralty
office, and get a protection for me, which the lieutenant had received. This news was fo fudden and
unexpected, that I could not forbear leaping on the
deck.

My firft bufinefs on my arrival at London, was
to wait on that worthy and honourable gentleman,
to pay him my thanks for fuch a fingular favour,
After which I made what hafte I could to Exeter,
where I at laft arrived to the great joy of my father,
and my other relations and friends, after being
abfent above fixteen years: but I had the grief to
find that my mother had died about a year before
my return.

TRAVELS

THROUGH

BARBARY,

BY

T. SHAW, D. D. and F. R. S.

Containing a defcription of the different kingdoms and provinces,
with their governments, of the manners and cuftoms of the inhabitants; with an account of the climate, beafts, birds, and
reptiles of thofe countries,

THE author, whofe ingenious defcription of
the Holy Land, we have added to Mr. Maundrell's
travels, has, in his account of Barbary, ranged his
obfervations under diftinct heads, without mentioning the time, place, or manner in which they were
made: but as the method of furveying thefe countries;
the diet and reception of the traveller, with the
hardfhips and dangers to which he is expofed, ought
not to be paffed over in filence, he gives the reader
in one view, fuch material circumftances and obfervations, as might have been difperfed through his
travels.

VOL. VI.   Z z

The reader is therefore to be informed, says he, that in the several maritime towns of Barbary where British factories are established, I was entertained with extraordinary marks of generosity and friendship, having the use not only of their houses, but of their horses, their janizaries and servants. In the inland towns and villages there is generally a house set apart for the reception of strangers, with a proper officer to attend it, where persons are lodged and entertained for one night, at the expense of the community, in the best manner the place will afford; but except these, and the places before mentioned, I met with no houses of entertainment, through the whole course of my travels. The furnishing ourselves with tents would not only have been attended with expense and trouble, but would have raised the suspicion of the Arabs; if therefore in the course of our travels, we did not fall in with the hovels of the Kabyles, or the encampments of the Arabs, we had nothing to protect us either from the scorching heat of the sun by day, or the cold of the night, unless we had the happiness to find a grove of trees, the shelf of a rock, or sometimes by good fortune found a cave. When this happened, which was indeed but seldom, our horses were the greatest sufferers: they were however our first care, and we gathered for them the grass, stubble, boughs of trees, and such like provender, before we sat down to examine what fragments of a former meal were reserved for ourselves.

When travelling in Barbary, we were so fortunate as to find an encampment of the Arabs, for we were not fond of visiting the Kabyles, who are not so easily managed, we were entertained for one night at free cost, and furnished with a sufficient quantity of provisions for ourselves and our horses; besides a bowl of milk, and a basket of raisins, dates, figs, or other dried fruit, generously presented to us upon our arrival, the master of the tent where we lodged, fetched us, according to the number of our company either a kid, a goat, a lamb or sheep, half of which was immediately boiled by his wife, and served up with cuscusu ; the rest was usually roasted, and reserved for our dinner or breakfast the next day.

But though the tents of the roving herdsmen may shelter us from the weather, they are not without their inconveniences ; for the cold and the dews to which we were every night exposed in the deserts of Arabia, are much more supportable than the vermin and insects, which constantly molested us here ; for besides fleas and lice, which are here in all their quarters, the apprehensions we were under of being bit or stung by the viper, the scorpion, or the venomous spider, rarely fails, in some parts of these countries, to interrupt the rest so grateful to a weary traveller. Indeed upon sight of one of these venomous creatures, a thaleb or writer, who happened to be one of my spahees, after he had muttered a few words, exhorted us all to take courage, as he had made it tame and harmless, by his charms and incantations ; we are also no less offended by their kids, calves and other young cattle, that are every night tied up in the tents, to prevent their sucking their dams ; for the cords being generally made of loose spun yarn, they were continually breaking loose and trampling over us.

When we were entertained in a courteous manner, which was not always the case ; I used to give the master of the tent a knife, a couple of flints, or a little English gunpowder, which being much stronger than theirs, they highly esteem, and keep it to serve as priming for their fire-arms ; and if his wife was obliging in making our cuscusu savoury and with expedition, she would return a thousand thanks for a pair of scissars, a large needle, or a skean of thread, which are great rarities.

During the excessive heats of summer, and particularly when we were afraid of meeting with a party of the Arab freebooters, we travelled in the night, which according to their proverb, having no eyes, few of them dare to venture abroad, from their not knowing what dangers and ambufcades they may fall into. We had then frequent reafon to call to mind the words of the Pfalmift *, " Thou makeft darknefs " that it may be night; wherein all the beafts of " the forefts do move. The lions roaring after their " prey;" the leopards, hyænas, and a variety of other ravenous beafts calling to and anfwering each other ; the different fexes, by this means, perhaps, finding out, and correfponding with their mates, thefe founds awfully broke in upon the folitude, and deftroyed the ideas of the fafety we fought for by travelling at this feafon.

We did not always take ftages of the fame length, for when under the apprehenfion of danger, we travelled through all the by-paths that were known to our conductors, without refting, fometimes twelve or fifteen hours together; but an ordinary day's journey, exclufive of the time taken up in making obfervations, feldom exceeded eight or nine hours. We conftantly rofe at break of day, and fetting forward with the fun, travelled till the middle of the afternoon, when we began to look out for the encampments of the Arabs ; who, to prevent fuch parties as ours coming to live upon them, chufe fuch places as are leaft confpicuous. And indeed, unlefs we difcovered the fmoke of their tents, heard the barking of their dogs, or obferved fome of their flocks, it was with difficulty, we were able to find them, and all our labour was frequently ineffectual. When we came up with them, we were accommodated, as I have already faid, for one night; and if in travelling the next day,

> ———We chanc'd to find
> A new repaft or an untafted fpring.
> We bleft our ftars, and thought it luxury.
>
> ADDISON.

* Pfal. ciii. 2.

In the Holy Land, and upon the ifthmus between Egypt and the Red Sea, our conductors cannot be too numerous ; but in Barbary, where the Arabs are under great fubjection, I was rarely attended by more than three fpahees and a fervant, all of us well armed : though we were fometimes obliged to augment our numbers, particularly when we travelled among the independant Arabs on the frontiers of the neighbouring kingdoms, or when two contiguous clans were at variance ; thefe and the freebooters make no fcruple of robbing, plundering, and murdering, not only ftrangers, but one another.

The beft method to prevent falling into their hands, is for a traveller to be always dreffed in the habit of the country, or like one of the fpahees. For the Arabs, are jealous and inquifitive, fufpecting every ftranger to be a fpy, and fent to take a furvey of thofe lands, which, at one time or other, they are taught to fear will be reftored to the Chriftians.

I cannot help here obferving, that a traveller can fcarce fail of falling into a ferious train of thought, when he obferves fuch large fcenes of ruin and defolation as are feen in thefe countries. He is ftruck with the folitude of the few domes and porticoes that are left ftanding, which hiftory tells him were once crowded with inhabitants : where Syphax and Mafiniffa, Scipio and Cæfar; where the orthodox Chriftians and the Arians, the Saracens and the Turks have in their turns given laws. Every pile, every heap of ruins points out to him the weaknefs and inftability of all human art and contrivance, reminding him of the many thoufands that lie buried below, now loft in oblivion, and forgotten to the world.

Two of the moft confiderable diftricts of that part of Africa, which latter ages have diftinguifhed by the name of Barbary, are the kingdoms of Algiers, and Tunis. The former is bounded on the north

by the Mediterranean Sea ; on the eaft, by the river
Zaine, the ancient Tufca, which feparates it from
Tunis; on the fouth, by the Sahara, or defert ; on
the weft, by the village of Twunt and the mountains of Trara, which feparate it from Morocco.
According to the exacteft obfervations I could make,
I find, its true length from Twunt to Tabarka, to
be 460 miles, it extending from fixteen minutes weft
longitude from London, to the river Zaine in nine
degrees fixteen minutes eaft.   To the weft it is generally about fixty miles broad ; and the eaftern part is
no where lefs in breadth than 100 miles. This country is at prefent divided into three provinces, that
of Tlemfan to the weft ; the province of Titterie to
the fouth, and of Conftantia to the eaft of Algiers.
Each of thefe provinces is governed by a bey or
viceroy, appointed and removed at pleafure by the
dey of Algiers.   .
    The remarkable chain of hills which geographers
fometimes place between this country and the Sahara,
and at others within the dominions of Algiers, I
take to be a continuation of Mount Atlas, though
they are not fo high as they are reprefented by the
ancients : for thofe parts of them which I have feen,
are rarely equal to fome of the moft lofty mountains
in our ifland ; and I queftion whether they are any
where fo high as the Alps or the Appenines. If
you form the idea of a number of hills, ufually of
the perpendicular height of four, five, or fix hundred yards, with an eafy afcent, adorned with groves
of fruit and foreft trees, rifing fucceffively one behind
another, with here and there a rocky precipice, and
place upon its fide or its fummit, a village of Kabyles,
encompaffed with a mud wall, you will have a juft
and lively idea of one of thefe mountains, and you
will have no occafion to heighten the picture, with
the imaginary nocturnal flames the melodious founds,
or the lafcivious revels of the fictitious beings attributed to them by the ancients.

Twunt and the mountains of Trara, are the weftern confines of the province of Tlemfan, as the river
Ma-faffron, at near 200 miles diftance, bounds it to
the eaft. This province is almoft equally diftributed
into mountains and valleys. Twunt, the frontier
village of the Algerines to the fea, is fituated about
four leagues to the fouth-weft of Cape Hone, and
defended by a fmall fort. This cape is the largeft
and one of the moft confpicuous promontories to
the eaftward of the river Malva or Mellooia.

At fome diftance from the above cape is the river
Tafna, on the weftern bank of which, almoft contiguous to the fea, are the ruins of the ancient Siga,
once a royal city of the Numidian kings.

The firft town on the coaft of any note, is the
city of Warren, commonly called Oran ; which is
about a mile in circumference, and fituated on a declivity near the foot of a mountain, on the fummit
of which are two caftles. Within lefs than half a
furlong of this mountain is another caftle in a fituation fomewhat higher than the former ; but a large
vale lying between them, their refpective ridges are
fo remarkably difunited, as to form a convenient
land mark for mariners. To the fouth and fouth-
eaft are two other caftles erected upon the fame level
with the lower part of the town, but feparated from it
by a deep winding valley, which may be confidered
as a natural trench to the fouth fide of the city. In
the upper part of this valley is a fpring of excellent
water above a foot in diameter, which forming a
rivulet, adapts its courfe to the feveral windings of
the valley, and pafiing under the walls of the city,
plentifully fupplies it with water. At every opening of this valley we fee fuch a confufed view of
precipices, plantations of orange trees, and rills of
water trickling down from the rocks, as appears
extremely delightful : for nature rarely difplays fuch
a variety of profpects and cool retreats. Near this

fine fpring is another caftle, which is alfo an important defence to the city.

Three of thefe caftles are regular polygons : but the other two, that is, the higheft upon the ridge, and the eaftermoft of thofe before the town, are of a different form, and built like the old Englifh caftles, with battlements and loop-holes.

The city of Oran has only two gates, both of which open into the valley. The gate of the fea, the name given to that neareft the port, has a large fquare tower erected over it, which, upon occafion, might be converted into a fort. Adjoining to the upper gate, called the Gate of Tlemfam, is an oblong battery ; and the citadel raifed on the higheft part of the city towards the north-weft, has all its angles mounted with cannon, while the lower and oppofite corner towards the north-eaft is defended by a regular baftion.

The Spaniards on their taking this city, built feveral beautiful churches and other edifices in the Roman ftyle, but of lefs ftrength and folidity, and have alfo imitated them in carving upon the friezes and other convenient places, infcriptions in large characters in their own language.

Three Roman miles from Oran is Arzew, the ancient Arfenaria, behind which the country extends in rich champaign grounds ; but on the other fide we look down upon the fea, from precipices that are a natural fafe-guard to the city. Yet the water at prefent ufed by the inhabitants, is drawn from wells below the precipices, that appear as old as the city ; but this water being beneath the furface of the fea is brackifh ; however, to procure the advantage of frefh water, the city was built on cifterns cut in the rock, in order to collect that which fell in rain. But though thefe ftill fubfift, they are converted into a different ufe, and ferves the inhabitants as caves to dwell in. Among the ruins of the ancient

city are fcattered feveral capitals, bafes and fhafts
of columns ; a well wrought Corinthian capital of
Parian marble fupports a fmith's anvil ; and in the
cadi's houfe I accidentally difcovered a beautiful
Mofaic pavement, through the rents of a ragged carpet fpread over it. There is here alfo a fepulchral
chamber fifteen feet fquare, built plain without niches
or any other ornaments ; though on the walls are
feveral Latin infcriptions in Roman capitals.

Five miles to the fouthward of Arzew is a large
fpace of ground full of pits, from which the neighbouring people are fupplied with falt. This commodity, from the facility of digging it, and the fhort-
nefs of carriage to the adjacent port, would, under
any other government, be an invaluable branch of
trade, the pits being inexhauftible.

Thefe falt pits take up an area of about fix miles
in compafs, furrounded with mountains. In winter
this fpace appears like a lake ; but in fummer the
water is exhaled by the heat of the fun, and the falt
left behind chryftalized.

Five miles to the eaft of Arzew we pafs by two
galley ports, under fome fteep rocky cliffs, one of
which opens towards a place called Muftigannim, and
the other towards Arzew. Both feem to have been
under the protection of a fort fituated above them,
that was formerly fupplied with water from an adjacent mountain, by a conduit that might be eafily
repaired for ufe.

The next town to which we came was Mazagran
or Mazachran, an inconfiderable place, encompaffed
by mud walls, and fituated upon the weftern declivity of a range of hills, within a furlong of the fea.
In travelling between this place and Muftigannim
we were entertained with the profpect of a number of
orchards, gardens and country feats, ranged in a
beautiful variety along the fhore. A chain of hills
bounds them to the fouth and fouth-eaft, which not

only intercepts the noxious winds from thefe plantations ; but every where breaks out in fountains to
cherifh them during the hotter feafons.

Near it is the city of Muftigannim, which was
once an epifcopal fee, when this country was in the
poffeffion of the Chriftians. This laft piace is bigger
than Oran, and built in the form of a theatre, with a
full profpect of the Mediterranean ; but on every
other fide is enclofed up by a circular range of hills
that hang over it. The inhabitants have a tradition
that the prefent city was compofed of feveral contiguous villages, and fome vacant fpaces between the
ftreets feem to confirm this opinion. In the midft of
the city, near one of thefe vacant fpaces, are the
remains of an old Moorifh caftle, which from its
form feems to have been erected before the invention
of fire arms. The north-weft corner of Muftignan-
nim, which overlooks the port, is furrounded by a
ftrong wall of hewn ftone, and has another caftle
built in a more regular manner, with a Turkifh
garrifon for its defence ; but the city being too much
expofed to any body of men that might lodge themfelves on the hills behind it, its principal ftrength
lies in the citadel erected upon one of thofe eminences, which has a full command of the city and
country around it.

The good mafonry and beauty ftill fo obfervable
in fome walls and a caftle to the north-weft, render
it probable, that they formerly belonged to fome
Roman fabric ; but I did not meet with any thing
that had the appearance of the ancient architecture.
However, both Muftigannim and Mazagran are
fo copioufly fupplied with water, fo commodioufly
fituated with regard to the fertile and extenfive
downs behind them, and enjoy fuch a delightful
profpect of the fea and its coaft, that they feem
ftations too valuable to be neglected by the Romans, and it is probable that here was the city of
Cartenna.

Three leagues to the north-eaft is a heap of ruins
enclofing a fountain of excellent water, near which a
bloody battle is faid to have been fought, in which
the weaker party were all put to the fword ; whence
this place is called Kelmeeta, or All dead ; and three
miles to the north-wefl of this, is the mouth of the
Shelliff, the moft confiderable river in the kingdom.

Farther to the eaft-north eaft, at a fmall diftance
from the fea is Tnis or Tennis, which though in a
low dirty fituation, was before the conqueft of the
Barbaroffæ, the metropolis of one of the petty kingdoms of this country. It has now only a few miferа-
ble houfes, with a little brook winding by them ;
but it has been long famous for the great quantity of
corn fhipped off from thence to Chriftendom. The
Moors have a tradition that the Tniffans were formerly in fuch reputation for forcery, that Pharaoh
fent for the wifeft of them to difpute miracles with
Mofes, and they are ftill the greateft cheats of all this
country.

Farther to the eaftward is the city of Sherfhell,
where the inhabitants are famous for making earthern
veffels, fteel, and fuch iron ware as are in demand
among the neighbouring Kabyles and Arabs. It
confifts of low tiled houfes, and is a mile in circuit ,
but was once much larger, and the feat of one of the
petty kings of the country. This town is fituated
amidft the ruins of a city that was not much inferior
to Carthage in extent. Thefe ruins are a proof of
its former magnificence ; for they abound with fine
capitals, columns, capacious cifterns, and beautiful
Mofaic pavements. The water of the river Hefhem,
as it is now called, was conveyed thither through
a large and noble aqueduct, little inferior to that of
Carthage, in the loftinefs and ftrength of its arches,
feveral of the fragments of which fcattered among
the neighbouring mountains and vallies are incontef-
tible proofs of the grandeur and beauty of the work.
There are likewife two other conduits, brought from

the mountains to the fouth and fouth-weft; thefe ftill
fubfift, and as they furnifh Sherfhell with excellent
water, while that of the wells is brackifh, they may
juftly be confidered as two ineftimable legacies left to
this place by the ancients.

The fituation of this place was nobly adapted to
ftrength and beauty. It was fecured from the en-
croachments of the fea by a ftrong wall near forty
feet high, fupported by buttreffes, and winding near
two miles along the feveral creeks of the fea-fhore.
For two furlongs within this wall the city was on a
level, and afterwards rofe gradually for the fpace of a
mile to a confiderable height, extending over a variety of little hills and valleys. One of the principal
gates on the land fide, placed about a furlong below
the fummit of thefe hills, leads to the rugged mountains of the Beni Menalfer ; and of the two others
near the fhore, that to the weftward lies under the
fhade of the high mountains of the Beni Yifrah, while
the eaftern gate opens towards the mountainous diftrict of Shenoah.

This place, from many circumftances, evidently
appears to have been the Julia Cæfaria of the Romans;
which was the fee of a bifhop. The inhabitants have
a tradition that the whole city was deftroyed by an
earthquake, and that the port, which was formerly
large and commodious, was reduced to its prefent
miferable condition, from the arfenal and the other
adjacent buildings being thrown into it by the fhock.
The cothon, which had a communication with the
weftern part of the port, affords a proof of the truth
of this tradition, for when the fea is low and calm,
we difcover all over the area maffy pillars, and pieces
of great walls that can fcarcely be conceived to come
there by any other way, than by fome fuch violent
concuffions. Indeed no place could be better contrived
for the convenience and fafety of their veffels than
this cothon, which was 50 yards fquare, and in every
part fecure from the wind, the fwell and the current

óf the fea, which are troublefome enough in the port.
The founders art and ingenuity in fupplying it with
water cannot be fufficiently admired. For this purpofe feveral floors and pavements of terrafs and mofaic
work were laid upon an eminence, forming the northern mound of the port and the cothon, in which the
rain water was received as it fell, and thence conveyed by means of fome fmall conduits, into an oval
ciftern capable of containing many thoufand tuns of
water. This port is nearly of a circular form, 200
yards in diameter ; but that part of it which was
formerly moft fecure, is now filled up by a fand bank,
that is daily encreafing.

The country about the city is extremely fertile,
and exceedingly well watered by feveral brooks ; on
the banks of one of them is an old ruined town under
a high rocky precipice ; and at fome diftance near
thefe fountains the Algerines have a fortrefs, in which
is a garrifon of Moors and Arabs, to prevent the incurfions of the Bene Menaffer. Certainly nothing
can be more entertaining than the variety of profpects
every where to be met with in this delightful country.

Five miles to the northward of this fortrefs is the
high mountain of Shenoah, which extends above
two leagues along the fhore, and is covered to its
very fummit with a fucceffion of fine plats of arable
land, almoft every where hedged in with fruit-trees.

Having paffed the river Gurmoat, which is formed
by feveral rills of water that fall from this mountain,
we difcover a number of ftone coffins of an oblong
figure, and a little farther to the eaft, under a rifing
ground, are the ruins of Tefeffad or Tfeffad, extending two miles along the fea fhore, but the breadth is
not equal to one third part of the length. Both at
this place, and at Sherfhell, we fee many arches and
walls of brick, of a kind not commonly found in
other parts of Barbary, where we may fuppofe the
work to be Roman. The bricks are of a fine pafte

and colour, only two inches and a half thick, but near a foot fquare.

Tefeffad is fituated thirteen miles from Sherfhell, and appears to have been the ancient Tapfa, which was the fee of a bifhop. The coaft all along from this place to Algiers, in fome parts for the breadth of two or three leagues together, is either woody or mountainous, by which the fine plains of the Mittijiah behind it, are fheltered from the northerly blafts of wind from the fea.

The Kubber, Romifh or Roman fepulchre, or as it may likewife be rendered the fepulchre of the Chriftian women, is fituated on the mountainous part of the fea coaft, feven miles from Tefeffad, and is a foild compact edifice ; it confifts of a very high bafe, on which is formed a kind of pyramid of fteps. This ftructure, which is built of the fineft free-ftone, I computed to be an hundred feet in height, and the diameter of the bafe ninety. The opinion that this ftructure was erected over a large treafure, has caufed feveral parts of it to be broken down ; however, it is ftill of a fufficient height to be a convenient land mark for mariners. This appears to be the monument built by Mela for the royal family of the Numidiam kings.

We fhall now examine the fouthern parts of this province, and fhall begin with the city of Tremefen, or according to the pronunciation of the Moors and Arabs, Tlemfan, or Telemfan. It is fituated upon a rifing ground below a range of rocky precipices, upon the firft ridge of which is a long narrow piece of level ground, watered by many fprings, which uniting their ftreams, fall in a variety of cafcades in their approach to Tlemfan ; the weftermoft of thefe rivulets turning a variety of mills. In the city is a large refervoir of water, conducted thither by a fubterraneous channel, and from thence the ufual demands of the city are fupplied; for which purpofe the water is conducted from thence to the caftle, the mofques, and other places. In the weft part of the city is a fquare bafon of Moorifh workmanfhip 200 yards long, and about half as broad, in which, according to a tradition of the inhabitants, the kings of Tlemfan took the diverfion of failing, while their fubjects were at the fame time taught the are of navigation : but this bafon was probably defigned rather as a refervior in cafe of a fiege, and to preferve at all other times a quantity of water fufficient to refrefh the great number of fine gardens and plantations below it.

Moft of the walls of Tlemfan are compofed of a mortar made of fand, lime and fmall pebbles, which being well tempered and wrought together, form a fubftance that has all the ftrength and folidity of ftone.

Tlemfan was formerly divided into diftinct wards or partitions, in order, perhaps, the better to put a ftop to any inteftine commotion, or to prolong a fiege. There were two of thefe divifions in the time of Edrefi, each of which might be confidered as a diftinct city; it being of a fquare or oblong figure, enclofed by a wall of the fame ftructure with that of the city : but about the year 1670, Haffan, Dey of Algiers, laid moft of the city in ruins, as a punifhment for the difaffection of the inhabitants. The ancient Tlemfan was about four miles round ; but at prefent there is not above one fixth part of it remaining. Among thefe ruins we meet with feveral fhafts of pillars, and other fragments of Roman antiquities ; and in the walls of an old mofque, I faw a number of altars dedicated to the Dii Manes.

In the village of Hubbed, a mile to the eaft-ward of Tlemfan, is the tomb of Sedi Boumaidian, which is vifited by all the neighbouring people with the greateft devotion. At the fame diftance to the weft-ward was the city of Manfourah, which at prefent has neither houfe nor inhabitant, though the greateft part of the wall, which is built in the fame manner

as that of Tlemfan, is ftill remaining, and enclofes
an area of two miles in compafs, above half of it
arable land. Near the centre of this area is a
fountain, and a high beautiful tower; but the
mofque which belonged to it has undergone the fate
of the other buildings.

The plains of Zeidoure begin at the river Iffer,
below Tlemfan, and extend themfelves through a
beautiful interchange of hills and valleys, to the
diftance of thirty miles: this delightful diftrict,
watered by a number of fprings and rivulets, is
cultivated by two numerous clans of Arabs, named
Welled Zeire, and Halfa. About the middle of this
tract, is a high pointed precipice, called the Pinnacle
of the Ravens, with a branch of the Sinan running
below it. This river waters a piece of ground on
which formerly ftood a city of the fame name, 32
miles to the northward of Tlemfan.

Near this river, I was fhewn the place where
Barbaroffa ftrewed about his tréafure; his laft, but
fruitlefs effort to retard the purfuit of his enemies.
Upon an eminence on the other fide of the river is a
Moorifh fanctuary inhabited by feveral religious.

Eight miles to the fouthward of Muftigannim is
El Callah, the beft market of this country for carpets. It is a dirty, ill contrived town, built on an
eminence of a chain of other mountains. Around
it are feveral villages of the fame name, and in a
like fituation, all of them employed in the fame
manufacture. It is defended by a citadel and garrifon, and from fome large ftones and pieces of marble
that are here and there to be met with, we have
fome reafon to believe it was formerly a city of
the Romans, perhaps the Gitlui or the Apfer of
Ptolemy.

In a fine plain, five leagues to the fouthward of
El Callah, is the town of Mafcar, which confifts of
a confiderable number of houfes built with mud walls;
it has feveral leffer villages in its neighbourhood,

and a little fort, to prevent any fudden revolt of the Arabs; but it is not allowed to have a Turkifh garrifon.

Ninety miles to the eaftward of Tlemfan are the ruins of Tagadempt, a large city fituated between the rivers Mina and Archew; but abandoned a few years ago by the Arabs, who have, as ufual, taken care to leave us feveral marks of their own humility and ignorance in architecture, by defacing or pulling down whatever was beautiful or magnificent in the buildings of their anceftors.

Six leagues to the eaft of Tagadempt are the ruins of Meratte, and two leagues farther are thofe of Loho. The fertile country below the parallel of the place where the laft-mentioned city formerly ftood, is cultivated by the Sweede or Swidde, the moft powerful tribe of Arabs in this province. The name fignifies black, and, I am told, was occafioned by a ftandard of that colour formerly difplayed in their marches and battles. They pay no taxes, and ferve the Algerines only as volunteers.

Seven miles farther are the ruins of Mejiddah, formerly a Roman ftation, feated upon a rifing ground with the river Shelliff below it; and at fome dif-tance on the banks of the fame river, are the ruins of Memon and Sinaah, formerly two contiguous cities, and the fee of a bifhop. The latter, which I judged to be three miles in circuit, feems to have been by far the moft confiderable; but the only re-mains now to be feen, are large pieces of walls, and feveral capacious cifterns.

El Khadarah, according to Edrefi, the ancient Ghadra, which was the fee of a bifhop, is the next remarkable place in this fituation. It is likewife feated on a rifing ground on the banks of the Shelliff and is equal to Sinaah in the extent of its ruins. A range of mountains rifing from the oppofite bank of the Shelliff, fhelter it from the north wind, while two other mountains, at a mile's diſtance, fronting it from the fouth, fupply the beautiful little plain they inclofe, with a plentiful rill of water. A few paces to the eaſt of the ruins of Chadra are the remains of a large ſtone bridge, perhaps the only one ever built over the Shelliff, notwithſtanding the inconveniences which travellers are fometimes, in winter, obliged to fuffer, by waiting a month together on its banks, before they can ford it.

On an eminence, three miles from the ruins of Sinaah, is a mud walled village under the Turkiſh yoke, named Merjejah, only remarkable for being under the influence and protection of a family of Marabbuts, the greateſt and moſt powerful of this country, who have fucceeded from father to fon through a number of ages.

Beni Raſhid, the Beni Arax of modern geographers, which is feated eight miles from Merjejah, is in much the fame fituation. It made a confiderable figure in former ages, and had a citadel, 2000 houfes, and a race of brave and warlike inhabitants, that commanded the country as far as El Callah and Mafcar. But at prefent the caſtle is in ruins; the 2000 houfes and its large territories are reduced to a few cottages, and its inhabitants are become cowardly and timorous. The nature of the foil is, however, ſtill the fame, and is famous for producing figs and other fruit, remarkably large and delicate.

Defcending the mountains of Beni Raſhid, we came to El Herba, formerly a Roman city, fomething more than a mile in circuit, fituated two leagues to the eaſtward of the village of Beni Raſhid. Here are feveral columns of a bluiſh coloured marble, of good workmanſhip: but their capitals, which are of the Corinthian order, are much defaced.

Paffing to the eaſtward over a fertile plain, through which the river Shelliff pleafantly winds its ſtream, we come to Maniana or Maliana, built upon a mountain, two leagues from El Herba. This city, which was once the fee of a bifhop, has at a diftance the appearance of antiquities ; but the fatigue of climbing up to it, is poorly recompenfed by the fight of only a fmall village, the houfes of which are covered with tiles inftead of terrace, the ufual covering of buildings in this country. Maliana has, however, many advantages ; it being well watered, furrounded by a number of pleafant gardens and vineyards, and commands a moft delightful and extenfive prolpect. Hither the devotees of Algiers, Bleda, and the neighbouring country repair in the fpring to kifs the tomb of Sede Youfeph, the tutelar faint of the city. There are here feveral fragments of Roman architecture ; and from an infcription, that feems to relate to the family of Pompey the Great, Martial's fine thought on their misfortunes receives an additional beauty ; on our finding that his grandfon, and probably his great grandfon, were buried in fuch an obfcure place, and at fuch a diftance from their anceftors.

Eight miles to the eaft-north-eaft of Maliana, between the Shelliff and the fea, are the baths of Mereega, the Aquæ Cálidæ Colonia of the ancients. The largeft and moft frequented of thefe baths is a bafon twelve feet fquare, and four deep. Here the water bubbles up with a degree of heat juft fupportable, and hence paffes off to another fmaller ciftern ufed by the Jews, who are not allowed to bathe in company with the Mahometans. Both thefe baths were formerly covered with handfome buildings ; but they are now expofed to the weather, and when I faw them, were half full of ftones and rubbifh. A great concourfe of people are ufually here in the fpring, the feafon of thefe waters, which are fuppofed to remove rheumatic pains, to cure the jaundice, and to alleviate moft other inveterate ill habits. Higher up the hill is another bath, the water of which being of too intenfe a heat for bathing, is conveyed through a long pipe into another room, where it is made ufe of in an operation of the fame nature and effect as our pumping.

Between this and the lower baths, are the ruins of a Roman town, equal in fize to that of El Herba, and at a little diftance from them, are feveral tombs and coffins of ftone, fome of which, I was informed, were of an unufual bignefs. The late lieutenant of this province affured me, that he faw a thigh bone belonging to them, near thirty-fix inches in length: but on my being at thefe baths half a year after, I could not receive the leaft information about it; and the graves and coffins that fell under my obfervation, were only of the ufual dimenfions. However, the people of this and other countries are full of ftories and traditions of this nature ; which, provided thefe fhould not be human bones, which may really be the cafe, as the Africans are far from being nice and fkillful obfervers, we may poffibly account for, from a cuftom I have fomewhere read of among the Goths and Vandals, that might pafs over with them into Africa, of interring the horfe with his rider, and the armour of the latter in the fame grave, and this affertion is confirmed by the long fwords with handles fhaped like croffes, often dug up in this country.

Thefe baths are furrounded by a fucceffion of very rugged hills and deep valleys, each of them in their turn very difficult and dangerous to pafs over. But this fatigue and danger is fufficiently recompenfed by our being afterwards conducted through the rich and delightful plains of Mittijiah, lying beyond them to the northward, which are fifty miles long and twenty broad, every where well watered by a number of fprings and rivulets. Here are many country feats of the principal inhabitants of Algiers, and the farms which fupply that city with the greateft part of its provifions ; for here grain of all kinds, roots, fruit, pot-herbs and flax, are produced in the greateſt perfection. However, only a part of this plain properly belongs to this province, the reſt, which is bounded by the rivers Mafaffron and Budwowe, being claimed by the ſouthern province, of which I am now to give a deſcription.

The ſouthern province of Algiers, or the province of Titterie, which is bounded to the eaſtward by the river Booberak, is greatly inferior to the weſtern in extent, it being ſcarce ſixty miles either in length or breadth. The ſea-coaſt, to the breadth of five or ſix leagues, is chiefly made up of rich champaign ground ; behind which is a range of rugged mountains that run almoſt in a direct line through a great part of the province ; but beyond them are extenſive plains, though none of them are equal to thoſe of Mettijiah.

In the province is Algiers the Warlike, as it is termed by the Turks, the capital of the whole kingdom of the ſame name. This place, which has for ſeveral ages braved the reſentment of the greateſt powers of Chriſtendom, is not above a mile and half in circumference, though it is ſaid to contain 100,000 Mahometans, of whom not above thirty are renegadoes, 15,000 Jews, and about 2000 Chriſtian ſlaves. It is ſituated on the declivity of a hill facing the north and north-eaſt ; the houſes riſing ſo gradually above each other, that there is ſcarce one in the whole city that has not a view of the ſea. The walls are however weak, and incapable of defence, except where they are ſtrengthened by aditional fortifications. The citadel, which is built upon the higheſt part of the city, at the weſtern angle, is of an octagonal figure, and each of the ſides in view has port-holes or embraſures. The north angle, near which is the gate of the river, and the ſouth-angle near Bab Azoone, are each guarded with a ſmall baſtion. The new gate between Bab Azoone and the citadel has a ſquare upright battery, and betwixt the citadel and the gate of the river are ſome jettings out of the wall, with port-holes, but with few or no cannon. The ditch, which formerly furrounded the city, is almoft entirely filled up, and is of little confequence. From the gate of the river and Bab Azoon to the citadel, the diftance each way is about three furlongs, in an afcent of fifteen or twenty degrees.

Between the gate of the river and a fandy bay that lies a furlong from it to the north-weft, is the caftle of Sitteet Ako leet, for the moft part built in a regular manner, and very capable of annoying an enemy, both in their landing, and afterwaads lodging themfelves in the adjacent plains and gardens. Half a mile to the weft of Bab Azoone is the Ain Rebat, where there is alfo another fandy bay; between which and Algiers the road is more narrow and rugged than at the gate of the river, though in the narroweft part of it, thirty men may march in front. There is likewife a caftle for the fecurity of this road, but it is inferior in ftrength and extent to that of Sitteet-Ako-leet. Both thefe bays are overlooked by a ridge of hills lying nearly upon a level with the citadel. Two well built caftles are placed here, one of which, from its five acute angles, called The Caftle of the Star, is within a furlong of the citadel, and commands the fandy bay by the gate of the river; the other, called The Emperor's Caftle, at the diftance of half a mile, has a full command of the Caftle of the Star, and the fandy bay towards Ain Rebat.

Beyond the gate of the river, as far as Ras Acconnatter the fhore confifts of rocks and precipices; but to the eaftward, from Ain Rebat, the fhore is in moft places acceffible. The emperor Charles V. in his unfortunate expedition againft this city, in 1545, landed his army at Ain Rebat, where there ftill remains a part of a pier fuppofed to have been erected for that purpofe. The better to fecure a communication with his fleet, and to fuccour his troops in their intended approaches to the city, he poffeffed himfelf of the ridge already mentioned, where he built the

inner part of the caftle that is ftill called by his
name.

Such is the fituation and ftrength of Algiers on
the land fide; but towards the fea it is better fortified,
and capable of a more obftinate defence: for the embrafures here have all brafs guns in good order. The
battery of the Mole gate, upon the eaft angle of the
city is mounted with large pieces of ordnance, one
of which, if I am not miftaken, has feven cylinders,
each three inches in diameter. Half a furlong to
the weft fouth-weft of the harbour is the battery of
Fifher's Gate, or The Gate of the Sea, which confifts
of a double row of cannon, and commands the entrance into the port, and the road before it.

The port is of an oblong figure, 130 fathom, long,
and 80 broad. Its eaftern mound, which was formerly an ifland, is well fecured by feveral fortifications.
The round caftle built by the Spaniards while they
were mafters of the ifland, and the two remote batteries erected within this century, are faid to be
bomb proof, and the embrafures of each of them are
mounted with thirty-fix pounders; but the middle
battery, which appears to be the oldeft, is the leaft
defenfible. However, as none of the fortifications
are affifted with either mines or outworks, and as the
foldiers who are to guard and defend them cannot be
kept up to any regular courfe of duty and attendance,
a few refolute battalions protected by a fmall fquadron
of fhips, might foon make themfelves mafters of the
ftrongeft of them.

There is little within the city that merits the attention of the curious. Upon the tower of the great
mofque are fome imperfect infcriptions; but the letters, though of a fufficient bignefs to be feen at a
diftance, are fo filled up with lime and white-wafh,
that I could not particulary diftinguifh them.

The hills and valleys round the city are every
where beautified with gardens and country feats,
whither the wealthy part of the inhabitants retire

during the fummer. Thefe are little white houfes
fhaded by a variety of fruit trees and ever-greens:
the gardens are well ftocked with pot-herbs, melons,
and other fruit, and what is moft admired in thefe
hot climates, each of them, as well as the city, enjoys a great command of excellent water, from the
many rivulets and fountains that every where prefent
themfelves. From thefe fources the fpring water
ufed at Algiers is brought through a long courfe of
pipes and conduits.

Four miles to the fouth-eaft of Algiers is the river
Haratch, which rifing behind the mountains of the
Beni Moufa, and joining the Fig River, runs through
the richeft part of the Mettijiah. It had formerly
a bridge built over it, at a fmall diftance from the fea.
Some authors obferve, that the ruins of Safa, otherwife called Old Algiers, are to be feen near its banks;
but I could never meet with thefe ruins, nor obtain
the leaft information about them.

Bleeda and Medea, the only inland cities of this
province, are each of them about a mile in circuit;
but their walls being chiefly raifed with mud and full
of holes made by hornets, can contribute but little
to their ftrength. Some of the houfes are flat roofed,
and others tiled; they are plentifully fupplied with
water, and are encompaffed with very fruitful gardens and plantations. At Bleeda a branch of an adjacent rivulet may be conducted through every houfe
and garden; while the feveral conduits and aqueducts that fupply Medea with water, fome of which
appear to be Roman works, are capable of being
made equally commodious. Both of thefe cities lie
oppofite the mouth of the Mafaffran; Bleeda at five
leagues diftance, under the fhade of mount Atlas,
and Medea three leagues beyond it, on the other fide
of that mountain; and there is reafon to believe that
the former was the Bida Colonia, and the other the
Lamida of Ptolemy.

Jurjura, the higheft mountain in Barbary, extends at leaft eight leagues from the north-eaft to the fouth-weft, and from one end to the other, appears a continued range of naked rocks and precipices, fecuring by its rugged fituation a number of Kabyles from becoming tributary to the Algerines. In the midft of winter the ridge of this mountain is covered with fnow; and it is remarkable that the inhabitants of one fide maintain an hereditary and implacable enmity againft thofe of the other ; while by common confent a little fnow puts a ftop to their hoftilities during that feafon.

I now come to the eaftern province of Algiers, diftinguifhed by the name of the province of Conftantina, which is nearly equal in extent to the other two, it being 230 miles in length, and about 100 in breadth. The tribute collected here by the viceroy is even much greater than that of the other two; for the bey of the fouthern province pays annually into the treafury of Algiers only about 12,000 dolls. and the bey of the weftern province 40 or 50,000 ; while the viceroy of Conftantina never delivers in lefs than 80, and fometimes 100,000.

The fea-coaft of this province is rocky almoft through its whole extent. The river Booberack is its weftern boundary, and at a league's diftance upon the fea-coft, the town of Dellys is built at the foot of a high mountain, out of the ruins of a large city, probably the Rufucurim of the ancients. Here a great part of the old wall, with other ruins near the fummit of the mountain, promife at a diftance fome extraordinary antiquities ; and in a wall juft over the harbour is a fmall niche with an image placed in it, in the attitude of a Madona ; but the features and drapery are defaced.

Paffing by fome villages of little confequence, we came to the port of Boujeiah, called by Strabo the port of Sarda. It is much larger than either that of Oran or Arzew, though it is formed in the fame

manner by a narrow neck of land running out into
the fea, a great part of which was formerly faced
with a wall of hewn ftone, and there was likewife an
aqueduct for bringing frefh water to the port; but
at prefent the wall, the aqueduct, and the bafons
into which the water difcharged itfelf, are deftroyed.

The town of Boujeiah, or Bugia, as it is called
by the Europeans, is built upon the ruins of the
ancient city, in the fame manner, and in a like
fituation with Dellys, though of thrice the circuit.
A great part of the old wall is ftill remaining, and
carried up to the top of the mountain. Befides a
caftle, which commands the city, there are two
others at the bottom of the mountain for the fecurity
of the port, and upon the wall of one of them
are ftill remaining the marks of the cannon-balls
fired againft it by Sir William Spragg, in his me-
morable expedition againft this place. This town is
defended by a garrifon, notwithftanding which the
neighbouring Kabyles lay it, in a manner, under
perpetual blocade. The inhabitants, however, carry
on a confiderable trade in plough-fhares, mattocks,
and other utenfils, which they forge out of the iron
dug out of the neighbouring mountains ; and alfo
great quantities of wax and oil are brought there
every market-day by the Kabyles, and fhipped for
the Levant and Europe. Yet thefe laft every market day raife difturbances ; indeed as long as the
market continues, every thing is tranfacted with the
utmoft tranquility ; but it is no fooner over, than
the whole place is in an uproar, and the day is feldom
concluded without fome flagrant inftance of barbarity
and rapine.

A little beyond the cape that forms the eaftern
boundary of the gulph of Boujeiah, is Jijel, the
Igilgili of the ancients, which, though once the fee
of a bifhop, is now reduced to a few miferable houfes,
and a fmall fort, where the Turks keep a garrifon.

Paffing through fome inconfiderable villages, and feveral rivers, we came to the Sebba Rous, or the Seven Capes, which are a clufter of fo many high rugged and barren promontories. Among the eafter-moft of thefe capes the Zhoore, a confiderable river, difcharges itfelf into the fea. The Welled Attyah and the Beni Friganah, two of the principal clans of thefe capes, drink of this river, and do not, like the other Kabyles, live in thatched hovels under the fhelter of fome foreft or mountain ; but in caves of the rocks, which they have either dug themfelves, or found made to their hands. Upon the approach of any veffel, either in the courfe of failing, or by diftrefs of weather thefe inhofpitable Kabyles immedi-ately iffue out of their holes, and covering the cliffs of the fhore with their multitudes, utter a thoufand execrable wifhes, that God would deliver it into their hands.

At a confiderable diftance farther to the eaft is the city of Bona, fituated on the fouth-eaft declivity of a hill, on the fummit of which the Algerines have a caftle and garrifon. Befides the capacious road be-fore it to the eaft, Bona had formerly a convenient little port under its very walls to the fouthward ; but by the conftant difcharge of ballaft into the one, and the negleсt of cleanfing the other, both are daily rendered lefs fafe and commodious. However, a confiderable quantity of corn, hides, wool, and wax, are annually exported from thence. This city, by proper encouragement, might be rendered the moft flourifhing place in Barbary ; and by repairing the old ruins, introducing frefh water, and removing the rubbifh, it would become extremely convenient and delightful.

A mile farther to the fouth are the ruins of the ancient Hippo, called Hippo Regius, from its being one of the royal cities of the Numidian kings. Silius Italicus obferves, that it was formerly one of their favourite feats ; and indeed it has the advantage of

being ftrong and commodioufly fituated, both for
commerce and for hunting ; it enjoys an healthful
air, and affords fo fine a profpe&t, that the eye takes
in at one view the fea, a fpacious harbour, a number
of mountains covered with trees, and plains finely
watered. Of this city St. Auguftine was bifhop,
and the Moors fhew a part of the ruins which they
pretend was his convent.   The ruins of the city take
up about half a league in circuit, and chiefly confift
of large broken walls and cifterns.

A little to the eaft of Cape Rofa, is a baftion on a
fmall creek, and the ruins of a fort, which once
belonged to a fa&tory fettled there by the African
company of France ; but the unwholfomenefs of the
fituation from the neighbouring ponds and marfhes,
obliged them to remove to La Calle.   This is at
another creek three leagues farther to the eaft, where
thofe gentlemen have a magnificent houfe and garden, a company of foldiers, a good quantity of arms,
and fome pieces of ordnance.   They command the
trade of the whole country, and befides the coral
fifhery, in which they conftantly employ 300 men,
monopolize the trade of corn, wool, hides and wax
at Bona and feveral other places ; and for thefe
privileges they annually pay to the government of
Algiers, the kaide of Bona, and the chiefs of the
neighbouring Arabs, about 30,000 dollars.

The whole tra&t of this province from the fea-
coaft to the fouthward up to Setcef and Conftantina,
is almoft a continued chain of very high mountains ;
thofe to the weftward being almoft inacceffible ; but
few of the inhabitants pay any tribute to the viceroy
of Algiers. Among thofe to the eaftward, the Turks
have a flying camp during the fummer, by which
the refpe&tive Kabyles are reduced to give fome
tokens of homage and fubmiffion, though they are
all of them fo tenacious of their liberty, that they
will pay no tribute till they are compelled to it by
fire and fword.   The country near the parallels of

Sctccf and Conftantina is diverfified with a beautiful
interchange of hills and plains, which afterwards
grow lefs fit for tillage, till they end upon the Sahara,
in a long range of mountains, which I fuppofe to be
the Buzara of the ancients.

The richeft and moft numerous Kabyles in this
province are the Zwowah, who poffefs a large tract
of impenetrable mountains, and have feveral mud-
walled villages, among which is the church of the
ciftern, famous for the fepulchre of Sede Hamet ben
Dreefe, and a college for the fupport of 500 thalebs
or men of learning. But their principal village is
Konkou, where their fheik, or fultan, as they call
him, refides.

Among the mountains of the Beni Abbefs, is a
narrow winding defile, which, for near half a mile
extends between precipices that arife on each fide to
a great height. At every winding the rock that
originally went acrofs it, and feparted one valley
from another, is cut in the form of a door cafe fix or
feven feet wide, and thefe are called by the Turks the
gates of iron. Few perfons can pafs them without
horror, and here a handful of men might defend the
pafs againft a great army.

Two leagues to the fouth fouth eaft, is another
dangerous pafs, called the Acaba, or the afcent.
This is the reverfe of the former: for here the road
extends along a narrow ridge, with precipices and
deep vallies on each fide, and the leaft deviation
from the beaten path, expofes the paffenger to the
danger of being dafhed to pieces by falling to the bottom. The common road from Algiers to the eaftward,
lies through the above pafs, and over this ridge.

Seteef, the Sitipha or Sitifi of the ancients, and
the metropolis of this part of Mauritania, was built
upon a rifing ground facing the fouth, and appears
to have been about a league in circuit; but the Arabs
have fo demolifhed all the monuments of antiquity at
this place, that there are fcarce any remains of the

ancient walls, columns, or cifterns : and the few remaining ftructures appear plainly to be the work of
the more modern inhabitants.   There are, however,
fome infcriptions ; but the fountains in the middle of
the city are equally delightful and convenient.

To the north-eaft of Seteef are the ruins of Kaf-
baite or Gaf-baite, an old Roman city, feated upon
a hill in the middle of other eminences.   Among the
feveral fragments of ruins and antiquities is part of
the portico of a fmall Roman temple, which, from a
piece of a broken infcription, appears to have been
dedicated to one of the Roman emprelfes.   Upon the
declivity of the hill are feveral fepulchral monuments
and infcriptions, moft of them beautifully carved
with a variety of figures in baffo relievo, reprefenting
perfons mourning, offering incenfe, or performing
fome office for the dead.

Five leagves to the north-weft of Canftantina is
the city Meelah, the Milevum of the ancients.   It is
furrounded with gardens, and plentifully fupplied
with fprings, one of which bubbiing up in the centre
of the city is received into a large fquare bafon of
Roman workmanfhip.   From this place Conftantina
is chiefly fupplied with herbs and fruit, the laft of
which particularly its pomegranates and applies, are
in great efteem all over Algiers.

Cirta or Conftantina, as it was afterwards called,
is fituated 48 miles from the fea, and was one of the
ftrongeft cities of Numidia.   The greateft parts of it
has been built upon a kind of peninfular promontory,
inacceffiable on all fides, except towards the fouth-
weft.   This I computed to be above a mile in circuit,
ending to the northward in a perpendicular precipice,
at laft a hundred fathoms deep.   On this fide we have
a beautiful landfcape, arifing from a great variety of
mountains, vales, and rivers extending before it to
a great diftance.   To the eaft-wards, the profpect is
bounded by a range of rocks much higher than the
city.   But towards the fouth-eaft the country is more

open, and you have a view of a diftant mountains. On this fide the eminence is feparated from the neighbouring plains by a deep narrow valley, perpendicular on both fides, where the Rummel conveys its ftream, over which was formerly a bridge of excellent workmanfhip. To the fouth-weft is a neck of land about half a furlong broad, near which ftood the principal gate of the city. This is entirely covered with a feries of broken walls, cifterns and other ruins, that are continued quite down to the river, and from thence are extended along a narrow piece of plain ground, running parallel with the deep valley already mentioned. This was the fituation of the ancient Cirta: But the prefent city is entirely confined to the eminence I have termed the Peninfular Promontary.

Befides the general traces of a diverfity of ruins fcattered all over this place, there are ftill remaining, near the centre of the city, a fet of cifterns, which received the water brought thither by an aqueduct; they are about twenty in number, forming an area about fifty yards fquare; but though the aqueduct is in a more ruinous condition than the cifterns, its ruins fufficiently demonftrate the public fpirit of the Cirtefians, in erecting a ftructure that required fuch an immenfe quantity of materials.

On the brink of the precipice to the north, are the remains of a large magnificent edifice, in which the Turkifh garrifon is now lodged. Four bafes, each feven feet in diameter, with the pedeftals, are ftanding, and feem to have belonged to a portico; they are of black ftone little inferior to marble, probably hewn out of that very range of rocky precipices on which they are built. The fide pofts of the principal of the city gates, are of a beautiful reddifh ftone not inferior to marble, and are neatly moulded and pannelled; an altar of white marble alfo makes part of a neighbouring wall.

The gate towards the fouth-eaft is in the fame form as the other, though it is much fmaller. It leads to the bridge, which I have obferved is built over this part of the valley. This bridge was a mafter-piece of its kind, having had the gallery and the piers of the arches adorned with cornices and feftoons, oxen heads and garlands, and the keys of the arches are embel-lifhed with caducei, and other ornaments. Between the two principal arches is the figure of a woman treading upon two elephants, with a large efcallop-fhell for her canopy : this is well executed in a ftrong relief ; the elephants ftanding with their faces turned towards each other, twift their trunks together ; and the woman who is dreffed in her hair, with a clofe-bodied garment, like an Englifh riding habit, raifes up her petticoats with her right hand, looking fcorn-fully at the city. In any other fituation this groupe might be fuppofed to belong to fome fountain ; thefe being fometimes ornamented with fuch wanton de-figns.

Below the bridge, the river Rummel begins to turn to the northward, and continues that courfe through a fubterranean paffage in the rocks, which is in feveral places defignedly laid open, probably for the convenience of drawing up the water. This feems to have been an extraordinary provifion of na-ture for the admiffion of this river, which muft have otherwife formed a prodigious lake, and have laid great part of the neighbouring country under water, before it found a paffage to the fea. This river falls from its fubterranean cavity in a large cataract, a quarter of a mile to the eaftward of a place called Seedy Meemon.

Among the ruins to the fouth-weft of the bridge, on the narrow flip of land already mentioned, is the greateft part of a triumphal arch, called The Caftle of the Giant. All the mouldings and frizes are cu-rioufly embellifhed with the figures of flowers, battle-axes, and other ornaments. Corinthian pilafters are erected on each fide of the grand arch, which is between two fmaller. Thefe pilafters are pannelled like the fide pofts of the city gates, in a gufto that feems peculiar to this city.

At fome leagues diftance to the eaft of Conftantina, are the Silent or Inchanted Baths, fituated on a low ground, furrounded with mountains. There are here feveral fprings of an intenfe heat, and at a fmall diftance, there are others that are comparatively extremely cold, near which are the ruins of a few houfes, built, perhaps, for the convenience of thofe who came here for the benefit of the waters. It is remarkable, that befides the ftrong fulphureous fteams, the heat of the above fprings is fo great, as to boil a large piece of mutton very tender in a quarter of an hour, and that the rocky ground, over which the water runs, is, for the fpace of an hundred feet, in a manner diffolved, or rather calcined by it. Thefe rocks being originally foft and uniform, the water, by making every way equal impreffions, leaves them in the fhape of cones and hemifpheres, which being fix feet high, and nearly of the fame diameter, the Arabs believe to be the tents of their predeceffors turned into ftone. But where thefe rocks, befides their ufual chalky fubftance, alfo contain fome layers of a hard matter, not fo eafily diffolved, you are entertained with a confufion of traces and channels, diftinguifhed by the Arabs into camels, horfes, and fheep, with men, women and children, whom they fuppofe to have undergone the like fate with their habitations. I obferved, that the fprings which afforded this water had been frequently ftopped; or rather, ceafing to run at one place, had broke out in another, which feems not only to account for the number of cones, but for that variety of traces continued from one or other of thefe cones or the fountains, quite down to the river Zenati.

On riding over this place it gives back such a hollow sound that we were every moment apprehensive
of sinking through it. It is therefore probable, that
the ground below us was hollow ; and may not then
the air pent up in thefe caverns, afford that mixture
of shrill, murmuring, and deep sounds, which, according to the direction of the winds, and the motion of the internal air, issue out along with the
water ? These sounds the Arabs affirm to be the
music of the Jenoune, or fairies, who are supposed
in a particular manner to take their abodes at this
place, and to be the grand agents in all these remarkable appearances.

There are likewise other natural curiosities at this
place ; for the chalky stone dissolving into a fine im-
palpable powder, and being carried along with the
stream, lodges itself on the sides of the channel, and
sometimes on the lips of the fountains themselves ;
or else embracing twigs, straws, and other bodies in
its way, immediately hardens and shoots into a bright
fibrous substance like the asbestos, forming itself at
the same time into a variety of glittering figures, and
beautiful chrystalizations.

The mountains of Aurefs, to the southward of
Constantina, are a knot of eminences running into
one another, with several little plains and valleys between them. Both the higher and the lower parts are
generally extremely fertile, and are esteemed the
garden of the kingdom. They are about 130 miles
in circuit, and all over them are spread a number of
ruins. The most remarkable of which are those of
L'erba or Tezzoutte the Lambese of the ancients.
These ruins are nearly three leagues in circumference;
and among others, consist of magnificent remains of
several of the city gates ; these, according to a tradition of the Arabs, were forty in number, and the
city could send 40,000 armed men out of each : there
are still also to be seen the seats and upper part of an

amphitheatre ; the frontifpiece of a beautiful temple of the Ionic order, dedicated to Efculapius ; a fmall but elegant maufoleum eiefted in the form of a dome, fupported by Corinthian columns; and a large oblong chamber, with a great gate on each fide, intended, perhaps, for a triumphal arch. Thefe, and feveral other edifices of the like nature, fufficiently fhew the importance of this city in former times.

It is remarkable, that the inhabitants of the mountains of Aurefs have a quite different mien and complexion from their neighbours: for they are fo far from being fwarthy, that they are fair and ruddy ; and their hair, which, among the other Kabyles, is of a dark colour, is with them of a deep yellow. Thefe circumftances, notwithftanding their being Mahometans, and their fpeaking only the common language of the Kabyles, render it probable that they may be a remnant of the Vandals.

The diftrift of Zaab, the Zebe of the ancients, is a narrow traft of land, that extends under the mountains of Atlas, from the meridian of Meffeelah to that of Conftantina, and confifts of a double row of villages. At Bifcara, the capital of this diftrift, is a garrifon of the Turks, who have here a fmall caftle, lately built by the bey of Conftantina : its chief ftrength lies in fix fmall pieces of ordnance, with a few unwieldly mufkets, likewife mounted on carriages.

The richeft of thefe villages is Lyæna, where the independant Arabs lodge their money and effects. It is under the proteftion of a numerous clan, to whofe bravery it is indebted for the uninterrupted enjoyment of liberty, and for the ill fuccefs that has attended all the attempts of the Turks againft it.

The eating of the flefh of dogs, from whence the Canárii receive their name, and for which the Carthaginians were fomerly remarkable, continues in practife to this day, among the inhabitants of this diftrift.

Leaving Conftantina to the north, we enter into the moft extenfive and fertile diftrict in all Numidia, peopled by a powerful and warlike tribe called Hanneifhah, who have often been of fignal fervice to the Algerines in their wars with Tunis. This whole country is finely watered, and was once interfperfed with cities and villages, of which the only veftiges are heaps of ruins.

The midland boundary of this kingdom is the river Serrat, the waters of which are brackifh, and difcharge themfelves into the Mejerdah. Near its weftern banks is Gellah, a confiderable village built upon a high pointed mountain that can only be afcended by one narrow road. This village, which is not to be conquered but by hunger or furprize, is a fanctuary for the rebels and villains of Algiers and Tunis, where they are hofpitably entertained till their friends have either procured their pardon, or compounded for their crimes.

Tipfa, the Tipafa of the ancients, is alfo at prefent a frontier garrifon of the Algerines. This town enjoys a fine fituation, and has the principal gate of the ancient city, with fome remains of its old walls, and other marks of the figure it formerly made among the cities of Numidia.

The government of the Algerines, which differs little from that of Tunis, confifts of the dey, and a common council, compofed of thirty yiah bafhefe, though the mufty, the cady, and fometimes the whole foldiery are called in to affift. All affairs of moment are fometimes agreed upon by this affembly, before they pafs into laws, and the dey is entrufted with the execution of them. But lately little account has been made of this body, which is only convened to confent to what has been before concerted between the dey and his favourites.

The dey is chofen out of the army, the moft inferior order having an equal right to that dignity

with the higheft. And every bold and afpiring fol-
dier, though taken yefterday from the plough, may
be confidered as heir apparent to the throne. They
are not afhamed to own the meannefs of their extraction. Mahomet Baffa, who was dey when I was at
Algiers, in a difpute he had once with a deputy
conful of a neighbouring nation, freely mentioned
the meannefs of his birth: "My mother, faid he,
" fold fheep's feet, and my father neats tongues ;
" but they would have been afhamed to have ex-
" pofed to fale fo worthlefs a tongue as thine." He
who afpires to this high rank does not wait till ficknefs or age has removed the prefent poffeffor, it is
enough if he be able to protect himfelf with the
fame fcymitar which he boldy fheaths in the bowels
of his predeceffor ; for fcarcely one in ten of them
dies in his bed. However, this factious humour
feems, at prefent, to be fomewhat purged and al-
layed by the many feafonable executions that have
been lately made of thefe afpiring members.

Though the Algerines acknowledge themfelves
the grand fignior's vaffals, they pay him no manner
of obedience.

In the diftribution of juftice, the cady is judge.
He is generally educated in the feminaries at Conftantinople, or Grand Cairo, where it is faid the
Roman codes and pandects, tranflated into the Arabic tongue, are taught and explained ; he is obliged
to attend once or twice a day at the court of juftice,
where he determines the fuits that are brought before
him ; but as he is generally fuppofed guilty of bri-
bery, all affairs of moment are laid before the dey,
or in his abfence, before the treafurer, mafter of the
horfe, and other principal officers of the regency,
who conftantly fit in the gate of the palace for that
purpofe. At thefe tribunals the caufe is foon determined, after which the fentence is executed within
lefs than half an hour. Small offences are punifhed
with the baftinado. For clipping or debafing the

public coin, the old Egyptian punifhment is inflicted, which is cutting off the hands. If a Jew or Chriftian fubject is guilty of murder, or any other capital crime, he is burnt alive without the gates of the city : but for the fame crime the Moors and Arabs are either impaled, hung up by the neck over the battlements of the city, or thrown upon hooks fixed in the walls below ; where they fometimes hang in the moft dreadful agonies thirty or forty hours to-gether, before they expire. The Turks, out of re-fpect to their characters, are fent to the aga's houfe, where, according to the nature of the offence, they are baftinadoed or ftrangled. When the women offend, they are not expofed to the populace ; but fent to a private houfe of correction; or if the crime be capital, they are tied up in a fack, carried out to fea, and drowned. The weftern Moors ftill ufe the barbarous punifhment of fawing the offender afunder; for which purpofe they prepare two boards, of the fame length and breadth with the unfortunate per-fon, and having tied him betwixt them, they proceed to the execution by beginning at the head. It is faid that Kardinafh, a perfon who was formerly am-baffador at the court of Great Britain, lately fuffer-ed in this manner: for with refpect to the punifh-ment of thefe countries, little or no regard is paid to the rank of the offender.

As to the form of government among the Arab tribes, it is to be obferved, that though they have been for many ages under the Turkifh yoke, yet they are feldom interrupted in the enjoyment of their laws ; for if they live peaceably, pay regularly the eight part of the produce of their lands, with a fmall poll-tax, annually demanded by the Turks, they are left in the full poffeffion of all their private privileges and cuftoms. Every camp may be con-fidered as a little principality, over which it is ufual for the family of the greateft reputation and fub-ftance to prefide. This honour does not, however,

always defcend from father to fon ; but as among
their predecellors the Numidians, when the heir is
too young, or fubjeȼt to any infirmity, they make
choice of the uncle, or fome other relation, diftinguifhed by his wifdom and prudence. Yet notwithftanding the defpotic power lodged in this perfon, all
grievances and difputes are accommodated in as
amicable a manner as pollible, by calling to his
alliftance one or two perfons out of each tent ; and
the offender being always confidered as a brother,
the fentence is given on the favourable fide ; and
even in the moft enormous crime, banifhment is
generally the only punifhment inflicȼted.

The kingdom of Tunis is bounded to the north
eaft by the Mediterranean fea ; to the weft by Algiers ; and to the fouth by Tripoly ; extending
from the ifle of Jerba in 33°. 30'. to Cape Serra in
37°. 12'. north latitude ; it being 220 miles in
length, and only 170 in breadth. Shekkah, the
fartheft city to the weft, being fituated in 8. and Cly-
bea, the fartheft to the eaft in 11°. 20'. eaft longitude from London.

Tunis is not like Algiers, divided into provinces ;
but is under the immediare infpeȼtion of the bey,
who goes in perfon to colleȼt the tribute ; for which
purpole he once a year vifits the principal parts
with a flying camp ; in fummer feafon traverfing
the fertile country near Keff and Baijah, and the
diftriȼts between Cairwan and the Jercede ; and in
the winter taking a circuit through the reft of the
country ; therefore under thefe divifions I fhall defcribe this kingdom.

The fummer circuit is much better inhabited,
than any part of the neighbouring kingdoms of
the fame fize, it having a greater number of cities,
towns and villages ; and from there being fewer inftances of oppreflion in the government, there is a
greater appearance of affluence, profperity, and chear-
fulnefs. The country is pretty fruitful ; but its

fertility is interrupted by feveral hills, plains and marfhes difperfed over it, that will admit of no cultivation, nor any manner of improvement.

A fmall ifland oppofite to the mouth of the river Zaine is in the poffeffion of the Genoefe, who pay an annual rent for it to the regency ; but the coral fifhery, which chiefly induced them to make this fettlement, failing confiderably, it is not probable that they will long keep poffeffion of it. They have, however, built a fort for their protection againft any furprize from the neighbouring Arabs on the conti-nent, and from the infults of the cruizing veffels of Algiers and Tripoly.

Cape Negro, which is about five leagues to the north-eaft, is remarkable for a fettlement of the French African company, who pay a confiderable fum of money to the Tunifeens for the fame privi-leges they enjoy at La Calle, and have a fmall forti-fication to protect them from the attacks of the neighbouring Arabs.

Five leagues farther to the north-eaft is Cape Serra, the moft northerly part of Africa ; and four leagues beyond it are three rocky iflands, called The Brothers, lying near the continent, half way to Cape Blanco.

Eight miles beyond this laft cape, at the bottom of a large gulph is the city of Bizerta, pleafantly fituated on a canal between an extenfive lake and the fea. It is about a mile round, and defended by feveral caftles and batteries, the principal of which are towards the fea, from which the lake is continual-ly receiving a brifk ftream, or difcharging one into it, the waters flowing into the lake when the wind is northerly, and returning back into the fea when it blows from the fouth. The channel between the lake and the fea was the port of Hippo, which is ftill capable of receiving fmall veffels ; but it was for-merly the fafeft and moft beautiful haven on this coaft, and there are ftill remaining traces of a large pier, that extend a confiderable way into the fea, to break the force of the north eaft winds; but the want of this, and proper repairs, will foon demolifh a haven which in any other country would be ineftimable.

The gulph of Bizerta, the Sinus Hipponenfis of the ancients, is a beautiful fandy inlet near four leagues in diameter. The ground being low, the eyes is permitted to penetrate through delightful groves of olive trees, a great way into the country, and afterwards the profpect is bounded by a high rocky fhore. Were the Turks to give proper en-couragement to trade and induftry, Bizerta might be rendered a town of great wealth ; for it abounds with all kinds of fifh and fruit, with corn, pulfe, oil, cotton, and a variety of other productions.

On the fide of a fpacious navigable bafon formed by the river Me-jerdah lies Porta Farina, which was fome years ago a confiderable city, but is now under great difcouragements. It is chiefly remarkable for its beautiful cothon, where the Tunifeens have their navy.

The Me jerdah is the Bagrada, fo famous in hiftory for the monftrous ferpent faid to have been killed on its banks by Regulus, which Pliny tells us was 120 feet in length. This river winds through a rich and fertile country, and like the Nile makes en-croachments upon the fea. To this caufe we may attribute the many changes that appear to have been made in its channel, and that an open creek of the fea into which, no longer than a century ago, the Me-jerdah difcharged itfelf is now circumfcribed by the mud, and become a bafon or anti-harbour, as it may be called, to Porta Farina.

Utica certainly lay fomewhere in this direction ; but we fhall not be able to fix its exact fituation, un-lefs we allow that the fea has been driven back three or four miles by the eafterly winds, and the increafe of the mud ; and then we may juftly place that fmall but celebrated city at Boofhater, where are many traces of buildings of great extent and magnificence, as walls, cifterns, and a large aqueduct. Thefe ruins lie about twenty-feven miles from Carthage, and behind them we are entertained with the view of the large fields which the Romans have rendered famous by their military exploits.

Indeed Carthage has not much better fupported itfelf againft the encroachments caufed by the north-eaft winds, and the mud thrown out by the Me-jerdah, which together hath ftopped up the ancient harbour and made it almoft as diftant from the fea as Utica. The greateft part of Carthage was built upon three hills, inferior in elevation to thofe on which Rome was erected. Upon a place which overlooks the fouth-eaft fhore, is the area of a fpacious room, with feveral fmaller near it ; fome of them have teffelated pavements ; but neither the defign nor the execution are very extraordinary. In rowing along the fhore, the common-fewers are feen in feveral places, which being at firft well built and cemented, time has not in the leaft impaired; except thefe, the cifterns have fuffered leaft by the general ruin of the city. Befides thofe belonging to particular houfes, there were two fets for the public ufe ; the largeft, which was the grand refervoir, and received the water of the aqueduct, lay near the weft wall of the city, and confifted of about twenty contiguous cifterns, each about a hundred feet long, and thirty broad. The fmaller is in a higher fituation, near the cothon, it being contrived to collect the rain-water that fell upon the top of it, and on fome adjacent pavements made for that purpofe. This might be repaired with little expence, the fmall earthen pipes through which the water was conveyed wanting only to be cleanfed.

Thefe are the only remains of the grandeur and magnificence of this ancient city, the rival of Rome : We find no triumphal arch, or fuperb piece of architecture ; no columns of porphyry or granite, no

curious entablatures : All the broken walls and ſtructures ſtill remaining, being erected either in the
Zothic manner, or by the later inhabitants.

The ruins of the celebrated aqueduct, that conveyed the water into the greater ciſterns, may be
traced as far as Zow-wan and Zung-gar, to the diftance of at leaſt 50 miles. This was a very extenſive
work, and that part of it which extends along the
Peninſula, was beautifuily faced with ſtone. At
Arriana, a ſmall village two leagues to the northward of Tunis, are ſeveral entire arches, which I
found to be 70 feet high, and the piers that ſupported them were ſixteen feet ſquare ; the water channel
that was above theſe arches was vaulted over, and
plaiſtered with a ſtrong cement. A perſon of the
ordinary ſize may walk upright in it ; and at certain
diſtances are holes left open, as well for the admiſſion
of freſh air, as the convenience of cleanſing it. The
water mark is near three feet high ; but it is impoſſible to determine the quantity daily conveyed to
Carthage by this channel, without knowing the angle
of deſcent that was given to it, which from the many
breaches in it cannot be aſcertained.

A temple was erected at Zow-wan and at Zung-gar
over the fountains by which this adueduct is ſupplied
with water. That at Zung-gar appears to have been
of the Corinthian order, and ends very beautifully in
a dome, that has three nitches, and extends over the
fountain. In theſe nitches were probably ſtatues of
water nymphs, or other deities.

Eight miles to the weſt-ſouth-weſt of Cape Carthage
is the Guletta, a ſmall channel that forms a communication between the lake of Tunis and the ſea,
each ſide of which is defended by a pretty ſtrong caſtle. There is alſo another caſtle upon a ſmall iſland
within the lake, half a league from Tunis, and about
two from the Guletta ; but from the little danger of
any attack that way by ſea, it has been long neglected. The lake was formerly a deep and capacious

port, fufficient to contain a numerous fleet; but from its receiving all the filth of the common fewers of Tunis, the main channel is in fummer reduced to fix or feven feet deep, and for the fpace of a mile or more within the banks, the bottom is dry. This lake is remarkable for the number and largenefs of the mullets caught in it, efteemed the fweeteit of any on the coaft of Barbary ; the roes of them when preffed and dried are called Botargo, and are accounted a great dainty.

Tunis, the Tunes of the ancients and the capital of the kingdom, is three miles round ; but not fo populous as Algiers, nor are the houfes fo handfome and fpecious. It is chiefly fituated on a rifing ground along the weftern banks of the lake, having a full view of Carthage and the Guletta. The lakes and marfhes with which the city is furrounded might probably render its fituation lefs healthy, was not the moifture of the air corrected by the great quantity of maftic, myrtle, rofemary, and other aromatic plants with which their ovens and bagnios are daily heated, and that frequently communicate a fenfible fragrance to the air. The want of fweet water is one of the greateft difadvantages under which the inhabitants labour ; for the brackifhnefs of their well water, and the fcarcity of their cifterns, oblige them to fetch a great part of what they drink from fome places a mile diftant; but except this inconvenience, no place enjoys a greater plenty of all the neceffaries of life.

The Tunifeens have little of that infolence and haughtinefs too common at Algiers, and indeed are the moft civilized nation of Barbary. All affairs with the regency are tranfacted in fuch a friendly complaifant manner, that I had no fmall pleafure in attending the Englifh conful at his audiences. This nation has always had the character of not imitating their neighbours in living at open war, or perpetual difcord with the Chriftian princes, but of cultivating their friendfhip, and readily entering into an alliance with

them : they have therefore for many years been more
intent upon trade, and the improvement of their
manufactures, than upon plunder and fitting out cor-
fairs.

On a rifing ground between the lake of Tunis and
the fea, is the town of Rhades, the ancient Ades,
where Regulus defeated the Carthaginians ; and at a
fmall diftance are the hills where Hanno placed his
elephants to oppofe him.

Near the bottom of the gulph is the fmall town of
Solyman, fituated upon the fkirts of a fine plain. It
is remarkable, that this place is chiefly inhabited by
Andalufian Moors, who retain the Spanifh language,
are more civilized than their brethren, and more
courteous to the Chriftians,

Farther to the north eaft is the fanctuary of Seedy
Doude, which takes its name from David, or as they
pronounce it, Doude, a Moorifh faint, whofe fepulchre is here fhewn five yards long. But this ftructure
appears to be a part of a Roman Prætorium, from
three contiguous Mofaic pavements, all of them
wrought with the greateft fymmetry and exactnefs ;
the figures are horfes, trees, birds, and fifhes, finely
inlaid, in fuch a variety of colours, that they even
appear more gay and lively than many tolerable
paintings. The horfe, the infignia of the Carthaginians, is reprefented in the bold pofture in which
it appears upon the African medals ; the birds are
the hawk and the partridge ; the fifhes, the gilt-head
and the mullet ; and the trees, the palm and the
olive. The defigner, perhaps, intending to point
out the ftrength, the diverfions, the fifhery, and the
plenty of dates and oil, for which this country has
always been remarkable. This place is furrounded
with the ruins of the ancient Nifua, or Mifua.

Two leagues farther is Low-hareah, the Aquilaria
of the ancients, where Curio landed the troops that
were afterwards cut to pieces by Sabura. There are
here feveral fragments of antiquities ; but none of

them very remarkable, except a furprifing cavern. For from the fea-fhore to this village, which is at half a mile's diftance, is a mountain hollowed with great art from the level of the fea to the height of twenty or thirty feet, with large pillars and arches left ftanding at proper diftances to fupport the mountain. Thefe are the quarries mentioned by Strabo, from whence the building of Carthage, Utica, and many other neighbouring cities, might receive their materials. As this mountain is all over fhaded with trees; as the arches below lie open to the fea, with a large cliff on each fide, and the ifland of Ægimurus is placed over againft them, while fprings are perpetually runing down the rocks, and feats are raifed for the weary labourer, we can fcarcely doubt, but that this is the cave which Virgil places fomewhere in this gulph ; notwithftanding fome commentators have thought it fictitious,

Within a long recefs there lies a bay,
An ifland fhades it from the rolling fea,
And forms a port fecure for fhips to ride,
Broke by the jutting land on either fide ;
In double ftreams and briny waters glide.
Betwixt two rows of rocks, a fylvan fcene
Appears above, and groves forever green:
A grott is form'd beneath, with moffy feats,
To reft the Nereids, and exclude the beats,
Down through the crannies of the living walls
The cryftal ftreams defcend in murmuring falls.

DRYDEN'S VIRGIL.

A league to the northward lies Cape Bon, called by the ancients the Promontory of Mercury ; from whence I was well informed, that the mountains of Sicily may fometimes be difcerned in fair weather.

Five leagues to the fouth-by-eaft of Cape Bon, is
the fmall Promontory of Taphitis, on which the
city of Clupea or Clypea was anciently built; but
there are now no remains of it to be found; for the
caftle is a modern ftructure, and what is called Clypea
is a knot of miferable hovels at a mile's diftance.
Mafaniffa was fuppofed to have been drowned in his
flight from Bocchar, in a deep and rapid river a
little to the fouthward.

Seven leagues to the fouth-weft is Gurba, the
Curobis or Curubis of the ancients, which feems to
have been in former times a confiderable place;
but the ruins of a large aqueduct, and of the cifterns
that received the water, are all the antiquities it
now poffeffes. 'Tis faid that the port, and a great
part of the city, together with the neighbouring
city of Nabal, were deftroyed by the fea, and that
in calm weather fome traces of them may be feen.

Nabal is fituated five leagues to the fouth-weft of
Gurba, and is a thriving, induftrious town, famous
for its potteries. It is built in a low fituation, a
mile from the fea fhore, and about a furlong to the
weftward of the ancient Neapolis, which feems to
have been a large city, without including what is
fuppofed to have been gained by the fea. Here are
many infcriptions upon ftones fix feet in length and
three in breadth; but they are fo defaced, and filled
up with rubbifh and mortar, that it required more
time than my guides would allow me to copy them.
On the bank of a little brook that runs through
the old city, is a block of white marble, on which
is curioufly carved a wolf in baffo relievo.

Travelling for the fpace of two leagues through
a rugged road, delightfully fhaded with olive-trees,
we come to Hamam-et, a fmall but opulent city
compactly built upon a low promontory, and well
fortified by nature. Some pillars and blocks of
marble are here to be met with; thefe are ruins
brought from the neighbouring places; and the

city probably takes its name from the number of wild pigeons bred in the cliffs of the adjacent mountains.

Near the fea, at two leagues diſtance, is a Mauſoleum near twenty yards in diameter, erected in the form of a cylindrical pedeſtal, with a vault underneath, and on the cornice are ſeveral ſmall altars, each of them inſcribed with the name of a different perſon. Theſe are ſuppoſed by the Arabs to have been formerly ſo many lamps for the direction of mariners.

Fifty miles from Utica is the city of Bay jah or Beja, the Vacca of Salluſt, a place of great trade, and the chief mart for corn in the whole kingdom. The preſent city is built on the declivity of a hill, and has the convenience of being well watered. Upon the higheſt part of it is a citadel of no great ſtrength; and on the walls, which are raiſed out of the ancient materials, are ſeveral inſcriptions. In the plains that lie before the city on the banks of the Me-jerdah, a public fair is kept every ſummer, to which the moſt diſtant Arabian tribes reſort with their flocks and families.

Six leagues to the weſt of Tunis is ſituated Tuburbo, the Tuburbum Minus of the ancients, a ſmall town on the banks of the Me-jerdah, inhabited by Andaluſian Moors. Mahomet, a late bey of this kingdom, planted a great variety of fruit trees in this neighbourhood, placing each ſpecies in a ſeparate grove; thus the orange-trees are all placed by themſelves, without being mixed with the lime or citron; and where you gather the pear or apple, you are not to expect the peach or apricot. In the adjacent valley, the ſame generous and public ſpirited prince erected, out of the ruins of an ancient amphitheatre, a large maſſy bridge or dam, with fluices and flood gates, to raiſe the Me-jerdah to a proper height, for the refreſhing of his plantations: But this was too laudable a work for it to laſt long in Barbary, and therefore it is entirely broken down and deftroyed.

On the eaft-fide of the Me-jerdah, ten leagues to the fouth-weft of Tunis, is an old triumphal arch, of no extraordinary beauty or workmanfhip; but has been adorned with a variety of niches and feftoons, that are now entirely defaced. It appears, by an infcription, to have been erected on the declenfion of the Roman empire.

At the bottom of a large winding of the Mejerdah, is Slou-geah or Salow-keah, the Municipium Hidibelenefe of the ancients; but now a fmall village remarkable for the infcriptions, the remains of cifterns, the fhafts and capitals of columns, and other monuments of its ancient grandeur.

To the fouth-weft is Dugga, the ancient Thugga, fituated upon the extremity of a fmall chain of hills, where are feveral tombs, maufolea, and the portico of a temple, beautifully adorned with fluted columns, on the pediment of which is the figure of an eagle finely executed, and below it an infcription in honour of the founders. There is alfo an infcription on the frieze, and feveral others upon fquare ftones. At the diftance of about a mile and a half is Beiffons, the Municipium Agbienfium of the ancients, which is built upon a hill, and has the remains of two temples, and of a caftle of later workmanfhip.

Mufti, now called Seedy Abdel-abbufs, from a marabbutt of that name interred there, is fituated in a plain within fight of Dugga and Beiffons, is remarkable for the remains of a beautiful triumphal arch, near which is a ftone that might formerly belong to it, containing an infcription in honour of Auguftus Cæfar.

At a fmall diftance is Keff, the Sicca Veneria of the ancients, which is a frontier city, the third for riches and ftrength in the kingdom; the greateft part of the caftle was about nine years ago blown up in the civil wars. The city is fituated on the

declivity of a hill, with a plentiful fpring rifing
in the middle of it ; but fome ancient Roman infcriptions are the only antiquities to be found there.

Tubernoke, the Oppidum Tuburnicenfe of Pliny,
is feven leagues to the fouth fouth-weft of Tunis,
and built in the form of a crefcent, between two
ridges of a very verdant mountain, that form a
variety of windings and narrow defiles. The only
antiquity to be found there is the gate of a large
edifice, over which is a fpreading pair of ftag's
horns well delineated in baffo relievo. Twelve miles
to the fouth-weft is Jerraado, fituated on the declivity of a hill. There are here the ruins of a fmall
aqueduct with its cifterns, and on the portal of an
ancient temple, in the fame ruinous condition with
the city, is an account of the perfons who contributed
to the building of it.

On the north-eaft extremity of a mountain named
Zow-aan or Zag-wan, is a fmall flourifhing town of
the fame name, famed for the dying of fcarlet caps,
and the bleaching of linen ; great quantities of both
being daily brought thither for that purpofe from
all parts of the kingdom. The ftream ufed for this
purpofe was conveyed to Carthage, and over the
fpring-head was a temple, the ruins of which are
ftill to be feen. On an ancient gate of the city is
carved a ram's head, under which is the word Auxilio,
from which it may be prefumed that the city was
dedicated to Jupiter Ammon.

We fhall now take a view of the moft remarkable
places in the Winter Circuit. Here all the parts I
have feen fall very fhort of that fertility attributed to
them by the ancients ; and particularly thofe near
the fea-ccaft are generally of a dry, fandy nature,
with no great depth of foil.

Herkla, the Heraclea of the lower empire, and
probably the Adrumetum of the earlier ages, is built
upon a promontory, two leagues to the fouth-eaft of
a morafs, fuppofed to have been the boundary be-

tween this province and Zeugitana. It appears to have been little more than a mile in circuit, and if we may be allowed to judge of its former grandeur by the remaining ruins, it will appear a place of importance, rather than of extent. That part of the promontory which formed the port feems to have been walled in to the very brink of the fea, and to the weft and fouth-weft of this promontory were the port and cothon which Cæfar could not enter in his purfuit of Varus.

The next remarkable place upon the coaft is Sufa, fituated on the northern extremity of a long range of eminences, above five leagues to the fouth eaft of Herkla. This is the chief mart of this kingdom for oil ; it has alfo a flourifhing trade in linens, and may be reckoned one of the moft confiderable cities of the Tunifeens. Here are feveral columns of granite, vaults, and other marks of it being formerly a confiderable place. It was walled round, and was probably one of thofe towns that fubmitted to Cæfar in his march to Rufpina.

A league and a half from Sufa we pafs over a valley which has a rivulet of fine water running through it ; and half a league farther, upon a declivity of the fame chain of eminences with Sufa, is Sahaleel, where are likewife fome remains of antiquities. It is now fituated a mile from the fea, and was probably the ancient Rufpina.

On the extremity of a cape five miles from Sahaleel, is Monafteer, a neat thriving city, walled round: but it can lay no claim to any extraordinary antiquity. At fome diftance from this place is Demafs, the ancient Thapfus, fituated on a low neck of land. From the great extent of its ruins, Herkla, Sufa, and Monafteer, have received large contributions in building their walls, caftles, and principal houfes: it muft therefore have been the moft confiderable city on this fide of Carthage. There ftill remains a great part of the cothon, which is formed of a compofition of fmall pebbles and mortar, fo well cemented together, that a folid rock could not be more hard and durable.

El Medea, in the modern geography called Africa, is fituated upon a peninfula five miles to the fouth of Demas, and appears to have been formerly a place of great ftrength. The port was an area near a hundred yards fquare, and lies within the walls of the city ; but is not at prefent capable of receiving the fmalleft veffel. Leo fays, it was founded by Mahdi, the firft patriarch of Kar-wan, and therefore affumed his name ; but though it might have been poffibly rebuilt by him, there is fomething too regular, and elegant in the remaining capitals, entablatures, and other pieces of the ancient mafonry, defaced as they are at prefent, to fufpect the founder to have been an Arabian.

Elalia, which feems to be the Achola or Acilla of the ancients, is fituated on the borders of a fertile plain, that extends from Salecto to within a few miles of She-ah. Befides the ruins common in other places, there are here feveral large cifterns for receiving the rain-water, which from the workmanfhip and contrivance, appear to have been formed fince the invafion of the Saracens.

A little farther is Ca-poudia, the Ammonis Promontorium of Strabo, a low narrow ftrip of land, which ftretching a great way into the fea, has a watch-tower on its extremity, with the traces of feveral ruins that might formerly belong to the city built there by Juftinian.

From this cape to the ifland of Jerba, is a fucceffion of fmall flat iflands, fand-banks, oozy bottoms, or fmall depths of water. Of thefe fhallows the inhabitants make no fmall advantage, by wading a mile or two from the fhore, and fixing in the various windings, as they go along, hurdles of reeds, and by this means enclofing great numbers of fifh.

Asfax, or Sfax, is a neat thriving city walled round, where, by the indulgence of the Cadi, 'the inhabitants enjoy the fruit of their induſtry, carry on a good trade in oil, and linen manufaⅽtures, and know little of that opperſſion which is ſeverely felt in moſt other parts of Barbary. The materials uſed in building it were brought from Thainee, the Thenæ of the ancients, once a famous maritime city ſituated at ten miles diſtance, though the country about it is dry and barren, without either fountain or rivulet.

Four leagues to the ſouth-weſt of Thainee is Maharefs, perhaps the Macodama of the ancients, a ſmall village, where are the ruins of a large caſtle, and ſome ciſterns ſaid to have been built by the Sultan Ben Eglib, whoſe memory the people highly reſpeⅽt, from his having left many public marks of his beneficence. Four leagues farther to the weſt ſouth-weſt are a great number of ſepulchres at a place called Ellamaite, but they have no inſⅽriptions, and very little beauty. At Gabs, a new city which riſes from the remains of an old one bearing the ſame name, are many fine ſquare granite pillars, ſuch as I have no where met with in any part of Africa. The old city, where we ſee theſe ruins, was built upon a riſing ground, at the diſtance of half a mile from the new. It had been formerly waſhed by the ſea, which formed a bay half a mile in diameter: but at preſent the greateſt part of it is filled up and gained from the ſea. There are here ſeveral large plantations of palm-trees, though the dates are in every reſpeⅽt inferior to thoſe of Jireed. But the chief branch of trade for which this city is now famous ariſes from the great number of Alhenna plants cultivated in gardens, the leaves of which dried and pounded are diſpoſed of to good advantage in all the markets of this kingdom. This plant, as well as the palm, requires to be well watered; and for that purpoſe many canals from the river Triton were brought through theſe plantations.

Leaving the fea-coaft, and taking an inland courfe, we foon arrived at Hydrah, which is fituated in a narrow valley with a rivulet running by it, and for extent of ruins appears to have been once of the moft confiderable places in this country. For there are here the walls of feveral houfes, the pavement of a whole ftreet, with a variety of altars and maufolea ftill remaining. Many of the latter are well pre-ferved, and are of various forms, fome being round and others octagonal, fupported by four, fix or eight columns; while others again are fquare compact buildings, with a niche in one of the fronts, or a balcony on the top; but the infcriptions are either defaced by time or the malice of the Arabs: however, upon a triumphal arch more remarkable for its large-nefs than its beauty, is a Latin infcription in letters a foot long: but it does not, as ufual, mention either the name of the city, or the people who erected it.

Eight leagues to the weftward of Sufa is Kair-wan, the Vico Augufti of the ancients. It is a walled city, and the fecond in the kingdom for trade and the number of its inhabitants. It is fituated in a bar-ren plain, and at half a furlong's diftance without the walls is a pond and a capacious ciftern, built to receive the rain water; but the former, which is chiefly for the ufe of the cattle, drying up or putrefying in the heat of fummer, caufes agues and other diftempers. Here are fome fine remains of the ancient architecture, and the great mofque, efteemed both the moft mag-nificent and the moft facred in Barbary, is fupported by an almoft incredible number of granite pillars, which the inhabitants fay amount to 500; but I could not be informed of one fingle infcription: and thofe I found in other places were either filled up with cement or defaced by the chiffel.

Eight leagues to the weftward of Kair-wan are the ruins of Truzza, the Turzo of Ptolemy, where are feveral vaulted chambers perpetually filled up with fulphureous fteams, much frequented by the Arabs for the ufe of fweating. The river Mergaleel waters the neighbouring country, and the Arabs make ufe of it in overflowing the extenfive plains that extend along its banks, which are feldom or never refrefhed with the rain.

At the diftance of a furlong from Spaitla, the an-cient Sufetula, is a magnificent triumphal arch of the Corinthian order, confifting of one large arch, and two fmaller, one on each fide, with the fragment of an infcription upon it. From thence, all along to the city, is a pavement of large black ftones, with a parapet wall on each fide. At the end of this pave-ment, we pafs through a beautiful portico built in the fame manner with the triumphal arch. This leads into a fpacious court, where are the ruins of three contiguous temples; but the roofs, porticos and fronts are broken down, though all the other walls, with their pediments and entablatures, remain en-tire. In each of them is a niche, fronting the por-tico: and behind that in the middle temple is a fmall chamber, which formerly ferved, perhaps, for a veftry.

Upon an eminence fix leagues to the weft-fouth-weft of Spaitla, is Caffareen. The river Derb runs wind-ing below it; and upon a precipice that hangs over that river, is a triumphal arch, more remarkable for the quantity and value of the materials than for the beauty and elegance of the defign. It confifts of one large arch with an Attic ftructure above it, that has fome ornaments refembling the Corinthian upon the entablature, though the pilafters are entirely Gothic; but notwithftanding the rudenefs of the workman-fhip, and the oddnefs of the fituation, it has an in-fcription, in which Manlius Felix, the founder, is gratefully commemorated. In the plains below the city are many maufolea, upon one of which is an elegy in hexameter and pentameter verfes. This place feems to have received its prefent name from the Maufolea, which at a diftance have the appearance of fo many towers or fortreffes.

At Jemme, the Tifdra of Cæfar, are many antiquities, as a variety of columns, altars with defaced infcriptions, and trunks and arms of marble ftatues, one of which is of the Colofs kind in armour, another is of a naked Venus, in the pofture and fize of the Medicean ; both by good mafters ; but their hands are broken off. This place is alfo remarkably diftinguilhed by beautiful remains of a fpacious amphitheatre, that originally confifted of fixty four arches and four orders of columns. The upper order, which is, perhaps, no more than an attic, has fuffered by the Arabs, and in a late revolt of thofe people, who ufed this place as a fortrefs, Mahomet Bey blew up four of the arches from top to bottom ; otherwife nothing could be more entire and beautiful. On the infide the platform of the feats, with the galleries and Vomitoria leaping up to them are ftill remaining. The Arena is nearly circular ; and in the center is a deep well of hewn ftone, where the pillar that fupported the Velum, or awning may be fuppofed to have been fixed. It feems to have been built about the time of the Antonines, and as the elder Gordian was proclaimed emperor at this city, it is probable that in gratitude to the place where he obtained the purple he founded this ftructure.

To the fouthward of Jemme is Rugga, the ancient Caraga, famous for a fpacious ciftern, that formerly fupplied the whole city with water, the roof of which is fupported by feveral rows of mafly pillars.

Ferre-anah, which from its lonely fituation, and other circumftances, was probably the Thala of Salluft, lies in the fame parallel with Rugga, and was once the largeft city of Bizacium, though it has now no other remains of its ancient grandeur but a few granite and other columns, which, by fome extraordinary chance, the Arabs have left ftanding on their pedeftals. It has been extremely well watered, for befides a confiderable brook that runs under the walls, there have been feveral walls in the city, each of them furrounded with a corridore, and vaulted over with a cupola. This, with the goodnefs of the air, are the only benefits this city can urge in favour of its fituation ; for excepting a fmall extent of ground to the fouthward, which the inhabitants cultivate by refrefhing it at proper times with the rivulet, all the reft of the adjacent country is dry, barren, and inhofpitable. The profpect to the weftward, which is the only one it enjoys, is terminated by fome naked precipices ; or where the eye is at liberty to wander through fome narrow cliff or valley, we are enter-tained with no other view than of a defert fcorched up with perpetual draught, and glowing with the fun-beams.

At twelve leagues to the eaftward of Fere-anah, is Gafsa, the ancient Capfa, fituated on a rifing ground almoft enclofed with mountains ; but the landfcape is more gay and verdant than that about Ferre-anah, from the profpect it affords of palm, olive, piftachio, and other fruit trees ; this agreeable fcene is however, of a fmall extent, ferving only to refrefh the eye in the more diftant profpect of an interchange of barren hills and valleys. The water that refrefhes thefe trees is collected from two fountains, one of which arifes within the citadel, and the other in the centre of the city. The latter is probably the fountain mentioned by Salluft, and was formerly covered with a cupola. It is ftill walled round, and difcharges itfelf into a bafon, defigned, perhaps, for a bath. Thefe two fprings, uniting their ftreams before they leave the city, form a pretty large brook, which from the quantity of water and the rapidity of the ftream, might continue its courfe to a great diftance were it not conftantly ufed by the inhabitants in re-frefhing their plantations. In the walls of fome pri-vate houfes, and particularly of the citadel, which is a weak and modern building, is a great confufion of altars, columns of granite, and entablatures, that when entire and in their proper fituation, muft have been great ornaments to the city.

We now enter upon that part of the Sabara which belongs to the Tunifeens, and is called El Jereed, or the Dry Country. The villages in this diftrict are built like thofe in Algiers, with mud walls, and rafters of palms; among them may be found granite pillars, and Roman infcriptions. The inhabitants in general trade in dates, which they exchange for wheat, barley, linen, and other commodities brought from the neighbouring parts. The dates of Tozer, one of thefe villages, being moft efteemed, that is become the principal mart for them; great quantities of them are exported to Æthiopia, where they are exchanged for black flaves, at the rate of two or three quintals for a black. The villages in this neighbourhood are divided from others in the province of Nif-zowah, by the lake of Marks, which is fo called from a number of trunks of palm-trees that are placed at proper diftances, to direct the caravans in their marches over the plain. Were it not for fuch affiftances, travelling would be here both difficult and dangerous, as well from the variety of pits and quickfands that could not be otherwife avoided, as that great miftakes might be made in paffing over a plain of this extent, where the horizon is as proper for aftronomical obfervations as the fea. The like extends near twenty leagues in length; and, where I paffed it, was about fix in breadth: it has many iflands, one of which is large and covered with dates, which, according to a tradition of the Arabs, fprung from the ftones of that fruit, brought thither by an Egyptian army for their food.

Near the eaftern extremity of this lake is an entire mountain of falt, as hard and folid as ftone, and of a reddifh or purple colour. Yet what is wafhed down from thefe precipices by the dews, attains another colour, becoming as white as fnow, and lofing that bitternefs which is in the parent rock.

Leaving Maggs, one of the leffer villages of the neighbouring province of Nif-zowah, we proceed near thirty miles through an uncomfortable defert without either herbage or water, till we arrive within a few miles of El Hammah, one of the frontier towns, where the Tunifeens have a caftle and garrifon. At a fmall diftance, are fome remains of its antiquity. It received its name from the hot baths, which are reforted to from all parts of the kingdom. But thefe are only fheltered from the weather, by having a miferable thatched hovel over them; while their ba-fons, which are about twelve feet fquare and four deep, have ftone benches a little below the furface of the water, for the bathers to fit upon. One of them is called the bath of lepers. The water of thefe fprings forms a rivulet, which, after being conducted in a number of fmall ftreams through the gardens, is again united, and directs its courfe towards the lake of Marks; but at a few miles diftance is loft in the fand.

The roving unfettled life of the Arabs, and the perpetual grievances the Moors fuffer from the Turks, will not permit either them to enjoy that liberty and fecurity which give birth and encouragement to learn-ing: Hence the knowledge of medicine, of philofo-phy and the mathematics, which once flourifhed among the Arabs, is now fo loft, that there are fcarce-ly any traces of them remaining.

The children of the Moors and Turks are fent to fchool at about fix years of age, when they are taught to read and write for the value of about a penny a week: inftead of paper, each boy has a piece of thin fquare board flightly daubed over with whiting; on this he makes his letters, which may be wiped off or renewed at pleafure. Having made fome progrefs in the Koran, he is initiated in the feveral ceremonies and myfteries of religion. When a boy has diftin-

guifhed himfelf in any of thefe branches of learning,
he is richly dreffed, mounted upon a horfe finely
caparifoned, and conducted amidft the huzzas of
his fchool-fellows through the ftreets ; while his
friends and relations affemble to congratulate his
parents, and load him with gifts. After being three
or four years at fchool the boys are put to trades, or
enrolled in the army, where moft of them foon forget
all they have learned.

While I was at Algiers I endeavoured to become
acquainted with thofe perfons who were moft diftinguifhed for their learning ; and though from their
natural fhynefs to ftrangers, and contempt of the
Chriftians, it is difficult to cultivate a real friendfhip
with them, yet I foon found, that their chief aftro-
nomer, who fuperintends and regulates the hours of
prayers, had not the fkill to make a fun-dial : That
the whole art of navigation, as practifed at Algiers
and Tunis, confifted of nothing more, than what is
termed the pricking of a chart, and diftinguifhing
the eight principal points of the compafs ; and that
even chemiftry, formerly the favourite fcience of thefe
people, is at prefent only applied to the diftilling a
little rofe-water. The phyficians chiefly ftudy the
Spanifh edition of Diofcorides ; but the figures of the
plants and animals are more confulted than the defcriptions. Yet thefe people are naturally fubtle and
ingenious ; and nothing but time, application, and
encouragement, are wanting to cultivate and improve
their faculties.

The Mahometans, being for the moft part pre-
deftinarians, pay little regard to phyfic, and generally either leave the diforder to contend with nature,
or make ufe of charms and incantations. They,
however, refort to bagnios in all diftempers, and
there are a few remedies in general ufe . Thus in
pleuretic and rheumatic cafes, they make feveral
punctures on the part affected with a red hot iron,
repeating the operation according to the violence of

the difeafe, and the ftrength of the patient. They
pour frefh butter almoft boiling hot into all fimple
gun-fhot wounds. The prickly pear roafted in the
afhes is applied hot, for the cure of bruifes, fwellings,
and inflammations; and a drachm or two of the root
of the round birth-wort is an eftablifhed remedy for
the cholic; fome of them inoculate for the fmall-pox,
though this practice is not much in repute in this
part of Barbary, and they tell a number of ftories
to difcourage the ufe of it. They have few compound
medicines; however they ufe a mixture of myrrh,
faffron, aloes, and fyrup of myrtle-berries, which
is often found effectual in the cure of the plague.

I have fometimes been favoured with the fight of
the ancient kalendars, in which the fun's place, the
femidiurnal and nocturnal arch, the length of the
twilight, with the feveral hours of prayer for each day
in the month, are calculated to a minute, and beautifully inferted in proper columns; but thefe are as
little confulted as their ancient mathematical inftruments, of which they know not the ufe; thus if the
cloudinefs of the weather will not permit them to ad-
juft their fmall and large hour-glaffes to fome inac-
curate meridian lines they have made for that purpofe, their times of devotion, which fhould be punctual
to a minute, are entirely left to the will and pleafure
of the cryers. For public clocks are not allowed in
this country, which is perhaps owing to the great
averfion the Mahometans have to bells.

Notwithftanding the fkill of their anceftors in
Arithmetic and Algebra, not one in twenty thoufand
appears to be at prefent acquainted with the firft
operations in thefe branches of Mathematics; yet
the merchants are frequently very dextrous in the
addition and fubftraction of large fums by memory;
and have alfo a very fingular method of numeration,
by putting their hands into each others fleeves, and
touching one another, with this or that finger, or a
particular joint, each denoting a determined fum or

number. Thus without moving their lips, they conclude bargains of the greateft value.

Several clans of the Arabs go bare-headed all the year long, as Mafanilla did of old, binding their temples only with a narrow fillet, to prevent their hair being troublefome. But the Moors and Turks in general, with fome of the richer clans of Arabs, wear upon the crowns of their heads a fmall cap of fcarlet woollen cloth, of the manufacture of the country. The turbant is folded round the bottom of thefe caps, and by the fafhion of the folds the feveral orders of foldiers are diftinguifhed, not only from the tradefmen and citizens, but from one another. The Arabs wear a loofe garment, called a Hyke, which is a piece of cloth of their own manufacture, ufually fix yards long, and five or fix feet in breadth ; this, which they wrap round them, and gird up with a fafh, ferves them for a complete drefs in the day, and for a bed and covering by night. Above this they wear a cloak or upper garment called a burnoofe, which is wove in one piece with a kind of hood for the head ; it is alfo tight about the neck, and widens below like a cloak ; but this is only worn in rainy and very cold weather.

Some of them wear under their hykes a clofe-bodied frock, or tunic, with or without fleeves, which, as well as the hykes, is girded about their bodies, efpecially when they are engaged in any labour or exercife, at which time they ufually throw off their hykes and burnoofes, and remain only in their tunics. Of this kind was probably the habit worn by our Saviour, when he is faid, "to lay afide "his garments, and to take a towel and gird him-" felf. *" Their girdles are ufually of worfted, wove into a variety of figures, and made to wrap feveral times round their bodies. One end being doubled and fewed along the edges, ferved for a

* John xiii. 4.

purfe; in this girdle the Turks and Arabs alfo fix their knives and poniards; while the writers diftinguilh themfelves by having an ink-horn, the badge of their office, fufpended in the like fituation.

The Turks and Moors wear linen under their tunics; but the Arabs in general wear nothing but woollen. However, in fome places, it is cuftomary for the Arab bridegroom and bride to wear each a fhirt at the celebration of their nuptials; but then they are not to wafh or pull them off, while any part of them is remaining. The fleeves of thofe worn by the men, are wide and open, without any folds at the wrift, while thofe of the women are made with gauze, and different coloured ribbons, interchangeably fewn together.

The Bedoweens, who live in tents, are not accuftomed to wear drawers; though the citizens of both fexes conftantly appear in them, efpecially when they go abroad or receive vifits. The virgins are diftinguifhed from thofe of the matrons in having theirs made of needle work, ftripped filk, or linen: but when the women are at home, or in private, they lay afide their hykes, and fometimes their tunics, and inftead of drawers, bind only a towel about their loins. It is obfervable, that when the Moorifh women appear in public, they conftantly fold themfelves fo clofe up in their hykes, that very little of their faces can be feen: But in the fummer months, when they retire to their country-feats, they walk abroad with lefs caution and referve, and upon the approach of a ftranger only let fall their veils. They all affect to have their hair hang down to the ground, which they collect into one lock, upon the hinder part of the head, binding and plaiting it with ribbons; but where nature has been lefs liberal, they fupply the defect by adding artificial to the natural locks. The hair being thus adorned, they tie clofe together above the lock, the feveral corners of a triangular piece of linen, wrought with the needle in a variety of figures. Thofe of fuperior fortune wear a farmah, as it is called, which is nearly of the fame fhape as the other head-drefs, but is made of thin flexible plates of gold or filver cut through and engraved in imitation of lace. A handkerchief of filk, gauze, or painted linen bound clofe about the farmah, and negligently falling upon the lock, completes their drefs.

However, none of thefe ladies think themfelves completely adorned, till they have tinged the hair and the edges of the eye-lids with the powder of lead ore. This operation is performed by dipping a wooden bodkin of the thicknefs of a quill into the powder, and then drawing it under the eye-lids, over the ball of the eye, which communicates to the eye a footy colour, that is thought to add a wonderful grace to perfons of all complexions. This practice is of great antiquity; for we find that when Jezebel is faid * to have painted her face, the original words are, fhe adjufted (or fet off) her eyes with the powder of lead ore. Indeed this kind of ornament was not only made ufe of by the eaftern nations, but by the Greeks and Romans.

The Turks and Moors are early rifers, and con-ftantly attend the public devotions at break of day. After which each perfon is employed in his proper trade and occupation till ten in the morning, the ufual time of dining; returning again to bufinefs till the afternoon prayers, when all kind of work ceafes, and the fhops are fhut up. The fupper commonly follows the prayers of fun-fet, and then repeating the fame at the fetting of the watch, when it begins to be dark, they go to bed immediately after. Some of the graver people, who have no conftant employ, fpend the day, either in converfing with one another in the barber's fhops, in the bazar,

* Kings ix. 30.

or at the coffee-houſe; while a great part of the Turkiſh and Mooriſh youth, with many of the unmarried
ſoldiers attend their concubines with wine and muſic
into the fields, or make merry at one of the public
taverns ; which though prohibited by their religion,
theſe governments are obliged from the neceſſity of
the times to difpenſe with.

The lives of the Arabs are one continued round
of idleneſs or diverſion. When they are not called
abroad by any paſtime, they ſpend the day in loitering at home, ſmoaking their pipes, and repoſing
themſelves under ſome neighbouring ſhàde. They
have not the leaſt reliſh for domeſtic pleaſures, and
are ſeldom known to converſe with their wives, or
play with their children. The Arab places his higheſt ſatisfaction in his horſe, and is ſeldom in high
ſpirits, but when riding at full ſpeed, or hunting.
The eaſtern nations in general are very dexterous at
this exerciſe, and upon one of the medallions of
Conſtantine's arch is a beautiful repreſentation of this
ſport, as performed at preſent by the Arabs ; who,
having rouzed the beaſt from his retirement, and
purſued it into ſome adjacent plain, endeavour, by
frequently overtaking and turning it, to tire and
perplex it, and then watching an opportunity, they
fix lances in its ſides.

At the hunting of a lion a whole diſtrict is ſum-
moned to appear, who forming themſelves into a
circle, at firſt encloſe a ſpace of three or four miles
in compaſs, according to the number of the people,
and the nature of the ground. The footmen advance firſt, ruſhing into the thickets with their dogs
and lances to rouze their game, while the horſemen
keeping a little behind are always ready to ſally on
the wild beaſt. They ſtill proceed, contracting the
circle, till at laſt they enter cloſe in together, or
meet with diverſion. The accidental paſtime upon
theſe occaſions is ſometimes extremely diverting ;
for the various animals within the circle being thus

drove together, they feldom fail of having a variety
of agreeable chaces after hares, jackals, leopards,
hyænas, and other wild beafts.   It is a common obfervation in this country, that the moment the lion
is rouzed he will endeavour to feize upon the perfon
neareft him, and fuffer himfelf to be cut to pieces
rather than quit his hold.

Hawking is one of the principal diverfions of the
Arabs and gentry of the kingdom of Tunis, where
the woods afford a beautiful variety of hawks and
falcons.   Thofe who delight in fowling, inftead of
fpringing the game with dogs, fhade themfelves with
a piece of canvafs ftretched upon two reeds, and
painted with the figure of a leopard.   Thus concealed, the fowler walks through the brakes and
avenues, looking through fome holes a little below
the top of the fcreen, to obferve what paffes before
him.   It is remarkable that the partridges, and
fome other birds, on the approach of the canvafs,
covey together, though they were before at a fmall
diftance from each other; and the woodcock, quail,
and other birds that commonly feed in flocks, will,
on feeing it, ftand ftill with a look of aftonifhment.
Thus the fportfman has an opportunity of coming
near them, when refting the fkreen upon the ground,
and directing the muzzle of his piece through one of
the holes, he fhoots a whole covey at once.   The
Arabs have alfo another method of catching partridges; for obferving that after their being haftily
fprung two or three times, they become fatigued and
languid, they then run in upon them, and knock
them down with their zerwatties, which are fhort
fticks bound round with iron, or inlaid with pewter
or brafs.   Thefe ferve thofe Arabs who are not
mafters of a gun for offenfive and defenfive weapons.

With refpect to the manners and cuftoms of the
Bedoweens, they retain many of thofe we read of in
facred and profane hiftory; for excepting their reli-

gion, they are the fame people they were two or three
thoufand years ago. Upon meeting one another, they
ftill ufe the primitive falutation, " Peace be unto
you." The inferiors out of deference and refpect,
kifs the feet, knees, or garments of their fuperiors :
while the children or kinsfolk pay the fame refpect to
the heads of their parents, and aged relations. In
faluting each other they lay their right hand upon
their breaft, while thofe who are more intimately
acquainted, or are of an equal age and dignity, mu-
tually kifs the hand, head or fhoulder of each other.
At the feaft of their Byram and other great folemnities, the wife compliments her hufband by killing his
hand.

Here perfons of the higheft character, like the ancient a ptriarchs, and the heroes of Homer, perform
what we fhould term menial employments. The
greateft prince of thefe countries is not afhamed to
fetch a lamb from his flock and kill it, while the
princefs makes hafte to prepare her fire and kettle,
and then drefles it. The cuftom of walking either
bare-foot or with fandals renders the compliment of
wafhing the firanger's feet ftill neceffary. This is
done by the mafter of the family, who firft prefents
himfelf, and is always the moft officious in this act of
kindnefs. When his entertainment is prepared, he
would think it a fhame to fit down with his guefts;
inftead of which he ftands all the time, and waits
upon them. Yet notwithftanding this refpect, thofe
are fometimes overtaken and pillaged in the morning
by the very perfons who have entertained them with
fuch hofpitality at night.

However, to the honour of the weftern Moors,
they carry on a trade with fome barbarous nations
bordering on the river Niger, without feeing the perfons they trade with, or their having once broke
through that original charter of commerce, which
from time immemorial has been fettled between
them. The method is this ; at a certain time of

the year which, if I am not miftaken, is the winter, they make this journey in a numerous caravan, carrying with them ftrings of coral, glafs beads, bracelets of horn, knives, fciffars, and the like. On their arriving at the place appointed, which is on a certain day of the moon, they find in the evening feveral heaps of gold duft, at a fmall diftance from each other, againft which, the Moors place fo many of their trinkets as they judge will be taken for the value. If the Nigritians the next morning approve of the bargain, they take up the trinkets and leave the gold, or elfe make fome deductions from the gold duft, &c. Thus to their great honour, they tranfact their exchange, without the leaft inftance of perfidioufnefs or difhonefty.

The ancient cuftom of plighting their troth, by drinking out of each other's hand, is at prefent the only ceremony ufed by the Algerines in their marriages. But the contract is to be firft agreed upon between the parents, in which mention is made not only of the fum of money which the bridegroom fettles on the bride, but of the feveral changes of raiment, the quantity of the jewels, and the number of flaves with which the bride is to be att nded, when fhe firft waits upon her hufband. The parties never fee each other till the marriage is to be confummated, when the relations being withdrawn, the bridegroom firft unveils, and then undreffes the bride. The hufband may put away his wife when he pleafes, upon the forfeiture of the fortune he has fettled upon her; but he cannot afterwards take her again, till after fhe is married and bedded by another man.

The civility and refpect paid by the politer nations to the fair, are here confidered as abfurd infringements of the law of nature, which affigns the preeminence to man. For the wives of this country are only confidered as a fuperior clafs of fervants, who are yet to have the greateft fhare of toil and bufinefs, while the lazy hufbands take their repofe under fome neighbouring fhade, and the young men and maidens attend the flock's, the wives are either all day emplowed at their looms, grinding at the mill, or dreffing provifions; and to conclude the day, they ftill take a pitcher, or a goat's fkin, and tying their fucking children to their backs, trudge two or three miles to fetch water. Yet in the midft of all this bufinefs, neither thefe country ladies, nor thofe of better fafhion incities, will lay afide any of their ornaments, neither their nofe-jewels, their bracelets for their arms and legs, or their ear-rings, all of which are very cumberfome; nor will they omit tinging their eyes with lead ore. So prevalent is cuftom, and fo zealous are even the ladies in Barbary to appear in the fafhion.

The greateft part of the moorifh women would be efteemed beauties even in England. Their children have the fineft complexions of any nation whatfoever; but the boys are fo expofed to the fun, that they foon attain the fwarthinefs of the Arabs; however, the girls keeping more at home, preferve their beauty till they are thirty, when they are ufually paft child-bearing. One of thefe girls is fometimes a mother at eleven, and a grandmother at twenty-two, and their lives being ufually as long as thofe of the Europeans, thefe matrons fometimes live to fee their children of many generations.

No nation in the world is fo fuperftitious as the Arabs, or even the Mahometans in general. They hang the figures of an open hand round the necks of their children, and both the Turks and Moors paint it upon their fhips and houfes as a counter-charm to an evil eye. The people who are grown up always carry about with them fome paragraph of the Koran, which they place upon their breaft, or few under their caps, to prevent fafcination and witchcraft, and to fecure themfelves from ficknefs and misfortunes. The virtues of thefe charms are fuppofed to be fo

univerfal, that they alfo hang them to the necks of
their cattle, their horfes and other beafts of burthen.
It is a prevailing opinion all over this country,
that many difeafes proceed from fome offence given
to the Jenoune, a fort of beings placed by the Mahometans between the angies and the devils. Thefe
are fuppofed to frequent fhade and fountains, and to
affume the bodies of worms, toads, and other little
animals; which being always in their way, are
every moment liable to be molefted and hurt. When
any one is therefore maimed or fickly, he fancies hat
he has injured one of thefe beings, and immediately
the women, who are fkilled in thefe ceremonics, go
upon a Wednefday, with frankincenfe and other perfumes, to fome neighbouring fpring, and there
facrifice a cock or a hen, a ram or an ewe, &c. according to the fex and quality of the patient, and
the nature of the difeafe ; a male being facrificed for
the female fex, and a female for the men.

The Mahometans have a great veneration for
their Marabbuts, who are generally perfons of a
riged aufere life, continually employing themfelves,
either in counting over their beads, or in meditation
and prayer. Their chaplet ufually confifts of ninety-nine beads, on touching each of which they either
fay, God be praifed, God is great, or God forgive
me. This faintfhip goes by fucceffion, and the fon,
provided he can behave with equal gravity, is entitled
to the fame reverence and efteem with the father.
Some of them pretend to fee vifions, and converfe
with the Deity, whilft others are fuppofed to work
miracles. Being with Seedy Muftafa, the Caliph of
the weftern province, he told me, in the prefence of
a number of Arabian Shekhs, who vouched for the
fact, that a neighbouring Marabbutt had a folid iron
bar, which upon command, would give the fame
report, and do as much execution as a piece of cannon ; and that once the whole Algerine arrny, on
demanding too exorbitant a tax from the Arabs·

under his protection, were put to flight by the miracle. Yet, notwithstanding the frequency, as they pretended, of the experient, all the merit I urged, of convincing a Christian, and the solicitations of the company, the Marabbutt had too much policy to hazard his reputation by putting it to the proof. At Seteef I saw a Marabbutt famous for vomiting fire ; but though I was at first much surprising at seeing his mouth suddenly in a blaze, and at the violent agonies he counterfeited at the same time, I afterwards plainly perceived that it was all a trick, and that the flames and smoke with which he was surrounded, arose from some tow and sulphur which he contrived to set on fire under his burnoose.

The method of building both in Barbary and the Levant, seems to have continued the same without any alteration, from the most early ages. Their houses are square buildings with flat roofs, surrounding a court, where alone they are ornamented. Indeed, large doors ; spacious chambers, marble pavements, cloystered courts, with fountains sometimes playing in the midst, are well adapted to the heat of the climate.

On quitting the streets, which are usually narrow, with a range of shops on each side, and entering one of their principal houses, we first pass through a porch or gateway, with benches on each side, where the master of the family receives visits, and dispatches his business ; few persons, not even the nearest relations, having admission any farther, except upon extraordinary occasions. From hence you pass into the court, which, lying open to the weather, is, according to the ability of the owner, paved with marble, or such coarser materials as are proper to carry off the water. When a number of people are to be admitted, as upon the celebration of a marriage, the circumcision of a child, or other occasions of the like nature, they are seldom received into any of the chambers, but into this court.

which is then covered with mats and carpets for
their more commodious entertainment ; and to flel-
ter them from the heat of the weather, a kind of
veil, as it may be called, is expanded upon ropes
from one fide of the parapat wall or lattice of the flat
roof to the other.   To this covering, which may be
folded or unfolded at pleafure, the Pfalmift feems to
allude, in that beautiful expreffion, Thou fpreadeft
out the heavens like a curtain.

This court is generally furrounded with as many
cloyfters, one above another, as the houfe is
ftories high, with either baluftrade or lattice-work,
round thofe above, to prevent any one's falling
down.   From the cloyfter and gallery, you are conducted into large fpacious chambers of the fame
length with the court, but feldom or never having
a communication with each other ; and one of thefe
rooms frequently ferves a whole family, particularly
when feveral perfons join in the rent of a houfe ;
whence thefe cities are extremely populous in proportion to their extent.

The mofques are exactly in the form of our
churches, only inftead of feats and benches, the
floor is only covered with mats.   A pulpit is erected
near the middle of them, from whence the mufti, or
one of the imans, every Friday explains a part of
the Koran, and exhorts the people to piety and good
works.

At a fmall diftance from the cities and villages, is
a large fpot of ground allotted for burying the dead.
Each family has a particular part of it walled in
like a garden, where the bones of their anceftors
have remained undifturbed for many generations.   In
thefe enclofures the graves are all diftinct and feparate, having each a ftone placed upright both at
the head and feet, while the intermediate fpace is
either planted with flowers, boarded round with
ftone, and paved all over with tiles.   The graves
of the principal perfons are alfo diftinguifhed by

fquare rooms with cupolas built over them, which being conftantly kept clean, white-wafhed and beautified, they continue to this day an excellent comment upon the expreffion of our Saviour, where he compares the hypocrites to whited fepulchres, which appear outwardly beautiful, but are within full of dead men's bones and all uncleannefs.*

Having thus defcribed the buildings of the cities, we fhall take a view of the habitations of the Bedoweens and Kabyles, the former the inhabitants of the plains, and the latter of the mountains. The tents of the Bedoweens are of an oblong figure refembling the hull of a fhip turned upfide down, and are covered with a coarfe hair-cloth. They differ in fize in proportion to the number of perfons who live in them, and are accordingly fupported, fome with one pole eight or ten feet high, and others with two or three of the fame length, while a curtain or carpet placed upon occafion at each of thefe divifions, feparates the whole into feveral apartments, and thefe poles being covered with hooks, the Arabs hang upon them their clothes, faddles, bafkets, and accoutrements of war. They take their reft, by lying upon a mat or carpet without a bed, mattrafs or pillow, and only wrapped up in their hykes. When we find any number of thefe tents together, (and I have feen from three to three hundred) they are ufually placed in a circle, and in the night the cattle are inclofed in the area in the middle to fecure them from the wild beafts. The defcription Virgil has given of their manner of living and decamping is as juftly drawn, as if his obfervations were but lately made.

From the encampments of the Bedoweens we are to proceed to the villages of the Kabyles, which confift of a number of cottages raifed either with hurdles daubed over with mud, with the materials

* Matth. xxiii. 27.

of fome ancient ruins, or with fquare cakes of clay
baked in the fun ; while the roofs are covered with
ftraw or turf, fupported by reeds, or the branches
of trees. There is feldom more than one room in
the largeft of them, which not only ferves for a
kitchen, dining-room and bed-chamber ; but one
corner of it is referved for their calves, foals and
kids.

In thefe huts the women make their blankets
called hykes, and the goats hair cloth for their
tents, weaving them not with a fhuttle, but con-
ducting every thread of the woof with their fingers.

We fhall now proceed to a defcription of the
trade and manufactures of thefe countries in general ;
one principal branch of which is that of carpets.
Thefe are made of coarfer materials, and are not fo
beautifully defigned as thofe of Turkey ; but being
fofter and cheaper, they are preferred by thefe people
to lie upon. Both at Algiers and Tunis are looms
for velvet, taffeties, and feveral kinds of wrought
filks. Over all thefe kingdoms is made a coarfe fort
of linen ; but that made at Sufa is the fineft. The
greateft part of thefe manufactures is confumed at
home ; but fome of them are fo inconfiderable, particularly the filk and linen, that the deficiences are
frequently made up from Europe. Indeed thofe
parts of Barbary fend very few of their commodities
to market.

The cultivated parts of thefe kingdoms enjoy
a very wholefome air, neither too hot and fultry in
fummer, nor too fharp, and cold in winter. For
during the fpace of twelve years in which I attended
the factory at Algiers, the thermometer funk only
twice to the freezing point, and then the whole
country was covered with fnow. The feafons in-
fenfibly fall into each other ; and the extraordinary
equability in the temperature of the climate appears
from the barometer's fhewing all the revolutions of

the weather in the fpace of an inch and a half. In this climate rain is feldom known to fall in the fummer feafon; and in' moft parts of the Sah ra, particularly thofe of Jereed, there is rarely any rain at all. When I was at Tozer in December 1727, we had a fmall drizzling rain, that lafted two hours, on which feveral of the houfes, which, as ufual, were only built of palm branches, and tiles baked in the fun, fell down by imbibing the moifture, and had the drops been either larger, or the fhower of a longer continuance, the whole city would doutlefs have diffolved and dropt to pieces.

In the other parts, the firft rains fall in September and October, after which the Arabs break up the ground, and begin to fow wheat, and plant beans, &c. If the latter rains fall in the middle of April, as they ufually do, the crop is reckoned fecure; the harveft following in the latter end of May, or the beginning of June.

The country produces feveral kinds of grain befides all thofe of Europe, except oats, particularly rice and a white fort of millet, with fome forts of pulfe unknown in England. The Moors and Arabs ftill continue to follow the primitive cuftom of the Eaft in treading out their corn, which is a quicker but lefs cleanly method than ours: for this being done upon a level piece of ground, only daubed over with cow dung, a great deal of earth and gravel muft unavoidably be gathered up with the grain: befides all the ftraw is broke to pieces. After the grain is trodden out, it is only winnowed, by throwing it into the wind with fhovels; it is then lodged in fubterraneous magazines, two or three hundred of which I have fometimes feen together, and the fmalleft of them would contain four hundred bufhels.

Provifions of all kind, are fold extremely cheap. You may have a large piece of bread, a bundle of turnips, or a fmall bafket of fruit, for the 696th part of a dollar, of 3s. 6d. of our money. Fowls are

frequently bought for three half-pence a piece ; a
fheep for 3s. 6d. and a cow and a calf for a guinea.
It is happy for thefe people, that one year with
another they can have a bufhel of the beft wheat for
fifteen or eighteen pence; for the inhabitants of
thefe countries, as well as the eaftern nations in
general, are great eaters of bread ; thiee perfons in
four living entrely upon it, or upon fuch compofitions
as are made of wheat and barley flour.

In cities and villages, the bread is ufually leavened
and baked in public ovens; but among the Bedoweens, the dough is no fooner kneaded than it is
made into thin cakes, which are either immediately
baked upon the coals, or fryed in a pan with butter.

All the fruits of Europe, befides thofe found in
Egypt, are produced here, except the hazel-nut,
the filbert, the goofeberry and currant tree. But
their gardens are laid out without method or defign,
and are a confufed medley of trees, with beds of cab-
bages, turnips, beans, and fometimes of wheat and
barley difperfed among them. Fine walks and par-
terres they would confider as the lofs of fo much foil ;
and the ftudy of new improvements they would regard as fo many deviations from the practife of their
anceftors, which they follow with the greateft reverence.

Lead and iron are the only metals difcovered in
thefe countries. The latter is white and good, though
in no great quantity ; it being dug and forged
by the Kabyles in the mountainous diftrict of
Boujeiah; and brought in fhort bars to the market of
Algiers. It will not be improper to relate here the
ftory the people tell of the plough-fhares of Mahomet
Bey of Tunis. This perfon had the misfortune to
be dethroned by his fubjects ; but having the reputation of being acquainted with the philofopher's ftone,
Ibrahim Hojiah, dey of Algiers, engaged to reftore
him to his former dignity, upon promife of being let

into the fecret. The affair was accordingly agreed upon, and Mahomet was reftored ; when, to fulfil his promife, he fent the dey of Algiers with great. pomp and ceremony a number of mattocks and plough-fhares; thus emblematically inftructing him, that the wealth of his kingdom was to arife from a diligent attendance upon agriculture and hufbandry; and that the only philofopher's ftone he could acquaint him with was the art of converting a good crop into gold.

The beafts of burthen in this country are camels, a few dromedaries ; horfes, which of late years have much degenerated in this country ; affes, mules, and a creature called the kumrah, a little ferviceable beaft of burthen begot between an afs and a cow. That which I faw was fingle hoofed like the afs, but different from it in every other refpect, having a fleeker fkin, and the tail and head, though without horns, refembling the dam's.

The black cattle are fmall, flender, and afford but little milk. Abdy Baffa the late dey of Algiers, and all his minifters, were greatly furprifed, when admiral Cavendifh a few years ago told him, that he had a Hampfhire cow aboard the Canterbury, then in the road of Algiers, that gave a gallon of milk a day, which is as much as half a dozen of the beft Barbary cows could yield in the fame time ; befides the Barbary cattle always lofe their calves and their milk together.

The fheep and goats alfo help to fupply the dairies, the cheefe being chiefly made of their milk. Inftead of rennet, they in fummer make ufe of the flowers of the great-headed thiftle, or wild artichoak, to turn the milk ; putting the curds thus made into fmall bafkets of rufhes or palmetta, and afterwards binding and preffing them. Their cheefes are ufually of the fhape and fize of a penny loaf. Their butter is neither of fuch fubftance, or of fo rich a tafte as ours : their only method of making it is by putting their cream into a goat fkin, which being fufpended from

one fide of the tent to the other, and preffed to and
fro in one uniform direction, foon occafions the feparation of the butter from the whey.

The fheep here are of two forts; one of them common all over the Levant, as well as in the kingdom of Tunis, is diftinguifhed by its having a large
broad tail; which confifts of hard folid fat, not interior to marrow; but the flefh of this fheep generally
taftes of the wool, and has not the tender fibres of
fmaller tailed fheep. Thofe of the other fpecies are
nearly as tall as our fallow deer, and, excepting
the head, are not much different in fhape; but their
flefh is dry, and their fleeces as courfe and hairy as
the goats.

Several of the Arabian tribes, that can bring into
the fields only three or four hundred horfes, have
more than as many thoufand camels, and triple again
that number of black cattle and fheep. The Arabs
feldom kill any of their flocks ; for they live chiefly
upon the milk and butter, or upon what they get in
exchange for the wool. The number of cattle likewife brought to the neigbouring towns and villages
is alfo very confiderable, when compared with the
yearly breed; fo that the flock of cattle is continually increafing.

Of the cattle not naturally tame, are a kind of wild
cows, which are remarkable for having a rounder
turn of body, a flatter face, with horns bending
more towards each other than the tame kind Thefe
are nearly of the fize and colour of the red deer. The
young calves of this fpecies quickly grow tame, and
herd with other cattle. The Lerwee, the moft timorous
fpecies of the goat kind, is fo fearful, that when per-
fued, it will precipitate itfelf down rocks and precipices. It is of the fize of an heifer ; but the body is
more rounded, with a tuft of fhagged hair on the
knees, and neck ; it is of the colour of the red deer,
but the horns, which are above a foot long, are
wrinkled and turned back like the goats. There

are alfo feveral fpecies of the antelope, and deer kind.

Among the ravenous beafts are the lion and the panther ; but the tyger is not a native of this part of Barbary. Some authors in their defcriptions of this country pretend that the women may be familiar with the lion ; and that upon taking a ftick and calling him tahanne or cuckold, and fuch like names, he will immediately fly from the flocks they are attending ; this may poffibly happen when the lion is fatiated with food ; for the Arabs fay, they lofe their fiercenefs, fo that a woman may then feize their prey, and refcue it out of their jaws. Thefe inftances are however rare, it oftener happening that they devour women as well as men, for want of other food. Fire is what they are moft afraid of, and yet notwithftanding all the precautions of the Arabs in this refpect, together with the barking of their dogs all the night long, thefe ravenous beafts frequently outbraving thefe terrors, will leap into the midft of the circle inclofed by the tents, and bring out alive with them a fheep or a goat. If thefe ravages are repeated, the Arab, obferving where they enter, dig a pit, and covering it over flightly with reeds, or fmall branches of trees, frequently catch them, and feed on their flefh, which is much efteemed, it having the tafte of veal.

After the lion and panther the dubbah is the ficeeft of the wild beafts of Barbary. It is of the fize of a wolf, but has a flatter body ; it naturally limps upon its hinder right leg, yet it is tolerably fwift. Its neck is fo ftiff that in looking behind, or fnatching obliquely at any object, it is obliged to move its whole body. It is of a reddifh buff, or dun colour, with fome tranfverfe ftreaks of a dark brown, it has a mane near a fpan long, and the feet, which are well armed with claws, ferve to dig up the roots of plants, and fometimes the graves of the dead.

The Faadh is fpotted like the leopard ; but the
fkin is coarfer and of a deeper colour, and the animal
is not of fo fierce a nature. The Arabs imagine it
begot by a lion and a leopardefs. There are alfo two
other animals marked like the leopard, but their
fpots are generally of a darker colour, and the fur
fomewhat longer and fofter : one of the cat kind, is
about a third lefs than a full-grown leopard, that
may be taken for a fpecies of the lynx ; the other has
a fmall pointed head, with the teeth, feet, and fome
other parts, refembling thofe of the weefel ; the body
which is only about a foot long, is round and flender,
with a regular fucceffion of black and white ringlets
upon the tail.

The jackall, and an animal called the black-ear'd
cat, and both fuppofed to find out prey for the lion,
and are therefore each called the lion's provider ;
though it may be much doubted, whether there be
any fuch friendly intercourfe between two fuch different animals. In the night-time, indeed, thefe,
with other kinds, are prowling in fearch of prey, and
in the morning they have often been feen gnawing
fuch carcaffes as the lion is fuppofed to have fed upon
the night before. This, and the promifcuous noife I
have frequently heard the jackall at leaft make with
the lion, are the only circumftances I am acquainted
with in favour of this opinion. The lion is fuppofed
to feed chiefly on the wild boar ; but that animal
fometimes defends itfelf with fuch courage, that
the carcaffes of both have been found lying dead
together, covered with blood, and dreadfully mangled.

Befides thefe, and fome other creatures not common
in other places ; there are in Barbary bears, apes,
hares, rabbits, ferrets, weefels, moles, porcupines,
and foxes ; cameleons, and feveral kinds of lizards.

Of the ferpent kind, the moft remarkable is the
thaibanne, fome of which I have been informed are

three or four yards long, and I have feen fome purfes made of their fkins, which were four inches or more in diameter. The zurreike, which, as well as the former, is a ferpent of the Sahara, is about fifteen inches long ; it is flender, and remarkable for dart- ing itfelf along with great fwiftnefs ; but the moft malignant of this tribe is the leffah, which appears to be the burning dipfas of the ancients, and is feldom above a foot long.

Among the birds are eagles and feveral kinds of hawks; the crow of the defert, and the fhagarag, which is of the fize and fhape of the jay, though it has a fmaller bill and fhorter legs; the body is brownifh : the head, neck and belly, are of a light green, and on the wings and tail are rings of a deep blue. The houbara is as large as a capon, and is of a light dun colour, marked all over with little ftreaks of brown. The wings are black, with a white fpot in the middle, and the feathers of the neck are re- markable for their length, and for being erected when it is attacked or provoked ; the bill is flat like the ftarling's, and near an inch and a half long. The rhaad is of two fpecies ; the fmaller is of the fize of an ordinary pullet ; but the larger is almoft as big as a capon, and alfo differs from the leffer, in having a black head, with a tuft of dark blue fea- thers immediately below it. The belly of them both are white ; the back and the wings are of a buff co- lour, fpotted with brown ; but the tail is lighter, and marked all along with black tranfverfe ftreaks. The kitawiah frequents the moft barren, as the rhaad does the moft fertile parts of thefe countries. It re- fembles a dove in its fize and fhape, and has fhort feathered feet ; but the body is of a livid colour, fpotted with black ; the belly is blackifh, and upon the throat is the figure of a half-moon of a beautiful yellow ; the tip of each feather in the tail has a white fpot upon it, and the middle one is long and pointed. The flefh, both of this bird and the rhaad, is of an

agreeable tafte, and eafy of digeftion.   There are
here alfo partridges, quails, woodcocks, and feveral
other wild-fowls.

Among the fmaller birds is the green thrufh, which
is not inferior to the American birds in the richnefs
of its plumage.   The head, neck, and back, are of
a light green : the breaft white and fpotted ; the
wings of a lark colour ; the rump of a beautiful yellow, and the extremity of the tail and wings are tipped with the fame colour.   The bird appears only in
the fummer months.

Among the fmall thick-billed birds, is the Capfa
fparrow, which is of the fize of the common houfe-
fparrow ; it is of a lark colour ; but the breaft is
fomewhat lighter, and fhines like that of a pigeon.
This bird is remarkable for the fweetnefs of its note
which infinitely exceeds that of the Canary-bird, or
nightingale : But it is of fo delicate a nature, as immediately to languifh and pine away on its being removed into a different climate.   Here are alfo feveral
kinds of water-fowl, befides thofe common in England.

The infects are very numerous ; among thefe there
is a curious fpecies of the butterfly, which is near
four inches from the tip of one wing to that of the
other, and all over beautifully ftreaked with murrey
and yellow, except the edges of the lower wings,
which being indented, and ending in a narrow ftrip
or lappet of an inch long, are elegantly bordered
with yellow, and near the tail is a fpot of carnation.
There are here adderbolts three inches and a half in
length, and locufts that are three inches long.

NATURAL HISTORY

OF

NORWAY,

BY

ERICH PONTOPPIDON,

Bifhop of Bergen, and Member of the Royal Academy of Sciences at Copenhagen.

Containing an account of the climate, vegetables, &c. with a defcription of the perfons, drefs, and manners of the inhabitants.

T H E climate of Norway is much more various than in moft other European countries, it extending 300 Norway miles* from Cape Lindefnaes in the fouth, to the north Cape on the borders of Ruffia. In the fummer nights the horizon, when unclouded, is fo clear and luminous, that at midnight one may read, write, and do all kinds of work as in the day, and in the extremity of this country towards the iflands of Finmark, the fun is continually in view in the midft of fummer, and is obferved to

---

* The common miles of Norway are computed to be about one fourth larger than a German mile, or nearly equal to five or fix Englifh miles.

circulate day and night round the north pole, contracting its orbit, and then gradually enlarging it,
till at length it leaves the horizon. On the other
hand, in the depth of winter the sun is invisible for
some weeks ; all the light perceived at noon being a
faint glimmering of about an hour and a half's
continuance ; which, as the sun never appears above
the horizon, chiefly proceeds from the reflection of
the rays on the higheft mountains, whofe summits
are feen more clearly than any other objects ; but
the wife and bountiful Creator has granted the inhabitants all poffible affiftance; for befides the
moon-fhine, which by reflexion from the mountains is exceeding bright in the valleys, the people
receive confiderable relief from the Aurora Borealis,
or northern lights, which afford them all the light
neceffary to their ordinary labours.

On the eaft fide of Norway, the cold of winter
generally fets in about the middle of October, and
lafts till the middle of April.   The waters are congealed to a thick ice, and the mountains and valleys
covered with fnow.   However, this is of fuch importance to the welfare of the country, that in a
mild winter, the peafants who live among the mountains, are confiderable fufferers ; for without this
fevere froft and fnow, they can neither convey the
timber they have felled to the rivers, nor carry their
corn, butter, furs, and other commodities, in their
fledges, to the market towns, and after the fale of
them carry back the neceffaries they are there fupplied with. For the largeft rivers, with their roaring
cataracts, are arrefted in their courfe by the froft,
and the very fpittle is no fooner out of the mouth,
than it is congealed, and rolls along the ground like
hail.   But the wife Creator has given the inhabitants
of this cold climate a greater variety of prefervatives
againft the weather, than moft countries afford.
Extenfive forefts fupply them with plenty of timber
for building, and for fuel : the wool of the fheep,

and the furs and skins of wild beasts, furnish them with warm lining for their clothes, and covering for their beds: innumerable flights of wild fowl supply them with down and feathers: the mountains themselves serve them for fences against the north and east winds, and their caverns affords them shelter.

But while the winter rages thus in the east of Norway, the lakes and bays on the west side are kept open by the warm exhalations of the ocean, though lying in a direct line with these frozen eastern parts ; and the frosts are seldom known to last above a fortnight or three weeks. Even in the centre of Germany which is two hundred leagues nearer the line, the winters are generally more severe, and the frosts sharper than in the diocese of Bergen, for here the inhabitants often wonder to read in the public papers of frost and snow in Poland and Germany, when they feel no such weather. The harbours of Amsterdam, Hamburgh, Copenhagen, and Lubeck are frozen ten times oftener than ours ; for with us this seldom happens above two or three times in a whole century. Thus our winter at Bergen is so moderate that the seas are always open to the fishermen and mariners, and here the north sea continues navigable during the whole winter as far as the 80th or 82d degree.

In the summer months the weather is not only warm but very hot. These violent heats, which are, however, of short duration, may be partly derived from the valleys inclosed within high mountains, where the reverberation of the rays of the sun on all sides heat the air ; and as there is almost no night, neither the atmosphere nor the mountains have time to cool. Indeed there cannot be a more decisive proof of the summer's heat in Norway, than that several vegetables, (and particularly barley) grow up and ripen within six weeks or two months.

The air is pure and falubrious, efpecially in the middle of the country about the mountains, where the inhabitants know little of ficknefs. Phyficians are only to be found in the chief towns, where they are eftablifhed and have a falary paid by the public ; but have generally very little employment. However, Bergen and all the eaftern coaft, is fo fubject to frequent rains, that the women, when they go abroad, in all weathers wear a woollen or filken black veil over their heads, while the men fecure them-felves by wearing rain-hats, made like umbrellas.

Norway contains a vaft number of mountains, fome of which extend themfelves in a long chain from north to fouth, while others are fcattered about and furrounded by a level country. The chain already mentioned is faid to equal at leaft the Alps in height ; and abounds with frightful caverns of an amazing extent. Hearing at the parfonage of Oerf-koug, that from the fide of a neighbouring moun-tain called Limer iffued a ftream, over which was a cavern ; I refolved to take a view of it, and furnifh-ed myfelf with a tinder box, candles, a lanthorn, and a long line to ferve me as a clue to find the way out. The afcent to it being extremely fteep, we were obliged to climb with our hands as well as feet, and fometimes were hard put to it to clear our way through the bufhes. After getting through the thicket which almoft hides the mouth of the cavern, I beheld a vaulted paffage of pure marble without the leaft flaw, but with feveral angles and protube-rances fo bright as to refemble a pafte moulded into fmooth globular forms. The paffage continues about a hundred paces in a ftraight direction ; then winds off to the right with afcents and defcents ; in fome places growing narrower, and in others widening to double its former breadth, which was about four or five ells : thus two perfons might go abreaft, only we were now and then obliged to ftoop and even creep, when we felt a damp vapour like that of a vault for the dead, which prevented my going fo far as I intended. Another thing remarkable was the terrible roaring of the waters under us, the courfe of which was what moft excited my wonder, as over it lies a pavement of fmooth ftone, inclining a little on each fide, but flat in the middle, and not above three fingers thick, with fome crevices through which the water may be feen.

The inhabitants of a mountainous country may be faid to labour under more inconveniencies than others. Thus the arable ground is here but little in comparifon with the waftes and deferts, which obliges the inhabitants to procure half their fubfiftence from the fea: the villages are fmall, and the houfes fcattered among the valleys: but in fome places the peafants houfes ftand fo high, and on the edge of fteep precipices, that ladders are fixed to climb up to them, fo that when a clergyman is fent for, who is unpractifed in the road, he rifks his life in afcending them, efpecially in winter, when the ways are flippery. In fuch places the bodies of the dead muft be let down with ropes, or be brought on men's backs before they are laid in a coffin, and, at fome diftance from Bergen, the mail muft likewife in winter be drawn over the fteepeft mountains.

One of the principal inconveniences, efpecially to travellers, arifes from the roads; for they cannot without terror pafs feveral places, even in the king's road, which extends over the fides of fteep and craggy mountains; on ways that are either fhored up, or fufpended by iron bolts fixed in the mountains, and though not above the breadth of a foot path, have no rails on the fide. If two travellers were to meet there in the night, and not to fee each other foon enough to ftop where the road will fuffer them to pafs, it appears to me, as it does to others whom I have afked, that they muft ftop fhort, without being able to pafs by each other, or to find a turning for their horfes, or even to alight. The only refource I can imagine in this difficuity is, that one muft endeavour to cling to fome cliff of this fteep mountain, or if help be at hand, be drawn up by a rope, and then throw his horfe headlong down a tremendous precipice in order to make room for the other traveller to pafs.

Another evil refulting from the mountains, is the fhelter they afford in their caverns and clefts to the wild beafts, which render it difficult to extirpate them. It is not eafy to defcribe the havock made by the lynxes, foxes, bears, and efpecially wolves, among the cattle, goats, hares, and other ufeful animals.

Another evil is that the cows, fheep, and goats belonging to the peafants often fall down the preci-pices and are deftroyed. Sometimes they make a falfe ftep into a projection called a mountain ham-mer, where they can neither afcend nor defcend: on this occafion a peafant cheerfully ventures his life for a fheep or a goat ; and defcending from the top of a mountain by a rope of fome hundred fathoms in length, he flings his body on a crofs ftick till he can fet his foot on the place where his goat is ; when he faftens it to the rope to be drawn up along with himfelf. But the moft amazing circumftance is, he runs this rifk with the help of only a fingle perfon, who holds the end of the rope, or faftens it to a ftone, if there be one at hand. There are inftances of the affiftant himfelf having been dragged down, and facrificing his life from fidelity to his friend, on which both have perifhed. On thefe melancholy accidents, when man or beaft falls fome hundred fathoms down the precipices, it is obferved that the air preffes with fuch force againft their bodies thus failing, that they are not only deprived of life long before they reach the ground, but their bellies burft, and their entrails gufh out; which is plainly the cafe when they fall into deep water.

. On the other hand, a great chain of thefe mountains ferve as a barrier between Norway and Sweden; and are excellent natural fortreffes for the defence of thofe ftates. Befides, thefe mountains exhibit the moft delightful profpects: nature has here been moft profufely favourable in adding greater beauties to the fituation of cottages and farm houfes, than can be enjoyed by royal palaces in other countries, though affifted with all the varieties of groves, terraces, canals, and cafcades A predeceffor of mine is faid to have given the name of the northern Italy to the diftrict of Waas, which lies fome leagues to the eaftward of Bergen ; and certainly there cannot be a more inchanting profpect. All the buildings in it are the church, the parfonage, and a few farm-houfes fcattered on different eminences. The beauty of the place is much heightened by two uniform mountains gradually rifing to a vaft height, betwixt which runs a valley near half a league in breadth, and a river which fometimes pecipitates itfelf down the rocks in foaming cataracts, and at others fpreads itfelf into fmall lakes. On both fides it is bordered with the fineft meadows intermingled with little thickets, and by the eafy declivities of the mountains covered with fruitful fields and farm houfes ftanding above each other in a fucceffion of natural terraces. Between thefe a ftately foreft prefents itfelf in view, and beyond that, fummits of mountains covered with perpetual fnow, and ftill beyond thefe ten or twelve ftreams iffuing from the fnow mountain, from an agreeeble contraft in their meanders along the blooming fides of the hill, till they lofe themfelves in the river beneath.

From the many fprings flowing from the mountains, and the vaft maffes of fnow accumulated on their fummits,'whence in fummer they gently diffolve, are formed many confiderable rivers, the largeft of which is the Glamen or Glommen. But none of them are navigable far up the country, the paſſage being every where interrupted by rocks and cataracts. The bridges over them are no where, that I remember, walled ; but merely formed of timber cafes filled with ſtones, which ſerve for the piers, on which the timbers are laid. The largeſt bridge of this kind is a thouſand paces in length, and has forty-three ſtone cales. In many places, where the narrowneſs and rapidity of the current will not admit of finking ſtone cales, thick maſts are laid on each ſide on the ſhore, with the thickeſt end faſtened to the rocks; one maſt being thus laid in the water, another is placed upon it, reaching a fathom beyond it, and then a third or fourth, in the like manner, to the middle of the ſtream, where it is joined by other con-nected maſts from the oppoſite ſide. Thus in paſſing over the bridge, eſpecially in the middle, it ſeems to ſwing, which to thoſe who are not uſed to theſe bridges, appears ſo dangerous, that they alight from their horſes, till they imagine themſelves ſafe.

Within the bowls of ſome of the mountains are the moſt beautiful kinds of marble, ſome white, others veined, and others variegated with a variety of colours : there is here alſo blue marble with white veins, green marble with greyiſh veins, and black marble ſpotted with white The mountains alſo contain that ſurprizing ſubſtance called the magnet or loadſtone, in ſuch quantities that ſome tons of it have been exported. They likewiſe yield the am-ianthus or aſbeſtos of which incombuſtible linen or paper have been made.

Having heard of ſome wood petrified by a certain ſpring I wrote for ſome ſamples, and a large parcel of it was ſent. At firſt I thought it reſembled hazel that had lain a long time in the water ; but upon a narrower inſpection, and drawing out ſome of the annually exported, chiefly in bars, and the reſt caſt into cannon, ſtoves, kettles, &c. Here are alſo filaments, I found it to be amianthus, much finer than the Greenland ftone flax, which the Rev. Mr. Egede fays, is ufed there as wicks in the lamps, without being in the leaft wafted, while fupplied with oil or fat. This amianthus, from the foftnefs and finenefs of its fibres, deferves to be called ftone-filk, rather than ftone-flax: I alfo made a wick for a lamp of it, and it was not confumed; but its light being much dimmer than that produced by cotton, I laid it afide. I have alfo in my poffeffion a piece of paper of this afbeftos, which when thrown into a fierce fire is not in the leaft wafted; but what was written on it totally difappears.

The manner of preparing this ftone-filk or ftone-flax, is this: after its being foftened in water, it is beaten with a moderate force, till the fibres, or long threads feparate from each other; afterwards they are carefully and repeatedly wafhed till clear of all terrene particles; then the flax is dried in a fieve: all that remains now is to fpin thefe fine filaments, wherein great care is required; befides which the fingers muft be foftened with oil, that the thread may be the more fupple and pliant.

It is remarkable that though this country thus abounds in ftones, no flints have been yet found there, fo that thofe for fire arms are imported from Denmark or Germany: but though there are no flints, there are amethifts, garnets, chalcedonies, agate, jafper, and cryftals.

This country formerly produced gold; but the expence of working the mines, and feparating the gold from the ore being greater than the profit, they have been neglected. There are, however, filver mines of great value, which give employment to feveral thoufand perfons. Thofe of copper are likewife extremely rich, and employ vaft numbers. Iron is alfo one of the moft profitable products of Norway, feveral hundred thoufand quintals being fome lead mines; but none of either tin or quick-filver.

The country produces wheat, rye, barley, white, grey, and green peas; vetches, ufed as provender for horfes; hops, flax, and hemp; many kinds of roots and greens for the kitchen, with a confiderable number of hardy flowers. In Norway, as well as in Denmark, are feveral kinds of cherries, of which the peafants fell great quantities dried: there are alfo many forts of wholefome and well tafted berries, as red and white currants, fun-berries, rafberries; red and white goofberries, barberries, bilberries, cranberries, ftrawberries, blackberries, and many other kinds. Several forts of plums attain to a tolerable ripenefs, which can very feldom be faid of peaches, apricots, or grapes. However, apples and pears of feveral kinds are found all over the country; but the greateft part of thefe are fummer fruits, which ripen early; for the winter fruit feldom comes to perfection, unlefs the fummer proves hotter, and the winter fets in later than ufual.

But though with refpect to fruit trees Norway muft be acknowledged inferior to moft countries of Europe, yet this deficiency is liberally compenfated by the bleffings of the inexhauftible forefts; fo that in moft provinces immenfe fums are received from foreigners for mafts, beams, planks, boards, &c. not to mention the home confumption for houfes built entirely of beams of wood, fhips, bridges, and an infinite number of foundries, which require an immenfe quantity of charcoal, in the fufion of metals, befides the demands for fuel and other domeftic ufes; to which muft be added, that in many places the woods are felled only to clear the ground and be burnt, the afhes ferving for manure.

Among the animals, we fhall begin with the horfes, which are better for riding than drawing; their walk is eafy, they are full of fpirit, and are

very fure footed ; when they mount or defcend a
fteep cliff, on ftones like fteps, they firft tread gently
with one foot, to try if the ftone they touch be faft,
and in this they muft be left to themfelves, or the
beft rider will run the rifk of his neck ; but when
they are to go down a very fteep and flippery place,
they, in a furprifing manner, draw their hind-legs
together under them, and flide down.   They fhew a
great deal of courage in fighting with the wolves and
bears, which they are often obliged to do, for when
the horfe perceives any of them near him, and has a
mare or gelding with him, he places them behind
him ; attacks his antagonift by ftriking at him with
his fore-legs, and ufually comes of conqueror.

The Norway cows are generally of a yellow
colour, as are alfo the horfes ; they are fmall ; but
their flefh is fine grained, juicy, and well tafted.

The fheep here are fmall, and refemble thofe of
Denmark.   The goats, in many places, run wild,
winter and fummer in the fields, till they are ten or
twelve years old ; and when the peafant who owns
them, is to catch them, he muft either do it by
fome fnare, or fhoot them.   They are fo bold, that
if a wolf approaches them, they ftay to receive him,
and if they have dogs with them, they will refift a
whole herd.   They frequently attack the fnakes, and
when they are bit by them, not only kill their an-
tagonifts but eat them, after which they are never
known to die of the bite, though they are ill for
feveral days.   The owner warms their own milk, and
wafhes the fore with it.

Near Roftad, is a flat and naked field, on which
no vegetable will grow.   The foil is almoft white,
with grey ftripes, and has fomewhat of fo peculiarly
poifonous a nature, that though all other animals may
fafely pafs over it, a goat or a kid no fooner fets its
foot upon it, than it drops down, ftretches out its
legs, its tongue hangs out of its mouth, and it ex-
pires if it has not inftant help.

There are few hogs in Norway ; and not many of the common deer ; but the hares, which in the cold feafon, change from brown or grey to a fnow white, are very cheap in winter. Here are alfo in fome parts of this country elks ; but they are not numerous. The rein-deer, however, run wild in herds, and are fhot for food by the inhabitants. Thefe animals conftitute the greateft, and almoft the only riches of the Finlaplanders, who live upon their milk, the cheefe they make of it, and on their flefh : they make their clothing, tents, and bed covering of their fkins ; and of the tendons they make their fewing thread. In Finmark, there are vaft numbers of them both wild and tame, and many a man has there from fix or eight hundred to a thoufand of thefe ufeful creatures which never come under cover ; they follow him wherever he is pleafed to ramble, and when they are put to a fledge, tranfport his goods, from one place to another. They provide for themfelves, and live chiefly on mofs, and on the buds and leaves of trees. They fupport themfelves on very little nourifhment, and are neat, clean, and entertaining creatures.

It is remarkable, that when the rein-deer fheds his horns, and others rife in their ftead, they appear at firft covered with a fkin ; and till they are of a finger's length, are fo foft, that they may be cut with a knife like a faufage, and are delicate eating even raw ; therefore the huntfmen, when far out in the country, and pinched for want of food, eat them, and find that they fatisfy both their hunger and thirft. When the horn grows bigger, there breeds within the fkin a worm which eats away the root. The rein-deer has over his eye-lids a kind of fkin, through which he peeps, when otherwife, in the hard fnows, he would be obliged to fhut his eyes entirely : a fingular inftance of the omnifcience and benevolence of the great Creator, in providing for the wants of each creature, according to its deftined manner of living.

The hurtful beafts are the bears and wolves already mentioned ; the lynx ; valt numbers of white, red and black foxes ; and the glutton, a creature which few other countries know any otherwife than by report. This animal receives its name from its voracious appetite ; it in fize and fhape has fome refemblance to a long bodied dog, with thick legs, fharp claws and teeth ; his colour is black, variegated with brown and yellowifh ftreaks. He has the boldnefs to attack every beaft he can poffibly conquer, and if he finds a carcafe fix times as big as himfelf, he does not leave off eating as long as there is a mouthful left : when thus gorged he preffes and fqueezes himfelf between two trees that ftand near together ; and thus empties himfelf of what he has not time to digeft. As his fkin fhines like damafk, and is covered with foft hair, it is very precious ; it is therefore well worth the huntfman's while to kill him without wounding the fkin, which is done by fhooting him with a bow, and blunt arrows.

The marten is alfo hunted on account of its fkin, as is likewife the fquirrel and the ermine, both of which are therefore fhot with blunt arrows. I am in doubt whether the ermine be different in kind from the Danifh weafel : its valuable fkin is of a beautiful white, and it has a black fpot on the tail. The ermines run after mice like cats, and drag away what they catch, particularly eggs, which are their nicest delicacy. Here are alfo caftors, badgers, otters and hedgehogs.

Among the mice, fome are thought poifonous, and others are remarkable for their being white, and their having red eyes. But the moft pernicious vermin is a little animal, called the læmus or lemming, which is between the fize of a rat and a moufe ; the tail is fhort, au turned up at the end, and the legs are alfo fhort that they fcarce keep the belly from

the ground. They have very foft hair, and are of
different colours ; particularly black, with yellow
and brown in ftreaks, and fome in fpots. About once
or twice in every twenty years, they affemble from
their fecret abodes in prodigious numbers, like the
meffengers of heaven to punifh their neighbouring
inhabitants. They proceed from Kolens rock, which
divides the Nordland manor from Sweden, and is held
to be their peculiar and native place, marching in
vaft multitudes through Nordland and Finmark to
the weftern ocean ; and other bodies of them through
Swedifh Lapmarck to the Sinus Bothnicus, devour-
ing all the grafs and vegetables in their way. They
do this in a direct line, and going ftraight forwards
proceed into the rivers or the fea. Thus if they
meet with a boat on any frefh water river, they run
in at one end or fide, and out again at the other, in
order to keep their courfe. They carry their young
with them on their backs, or in their mouths ; and
if they meet with peafants who come to oppofe them,
they will ftand undaunted, and bark at them like dogs.
This evil is, however, of no long duration ; for on
entering the fea, they fwim as long as they are able,
and then are drowned. If any are ftopped in their
courfe, fo that they cannot reach the fea, they are
killed by the frofts of winter, and if any efcape,
moft of them die as foon as they eat the new
grafs.

As to the reptiles there are neither land fnakes nor
toads beyond the temperate zone, and even thofe
fnakes on the extremities of the temperate climate,
are lefs poifonous than in more fouthern countries :
lizards are here of various colours, as brown, green,
and ftriped. Thofe that are green are found in the
fields, and the others in the cracks and holes of
rocks.

Among the fowls are moft of thofe feen in the reft
of Europe, and fome that feem peculiar to this country. Of the former are cocks and hens, turkeys,

peacocks, tame and wild geefe, ducks, and pigeons; nightingales, larks, quails, partridges, ftarlings, wrens, magpies, water-wagtails, eagles, faulcons, hawks, ravens, cormorants, ftorks, herons, gulls, owls, bats, and many others: among thofe that are in a manner peculiar to this country is the francolin an excellent land bird, which ferves the Norwegians inftead of the pheafant, its flefh being white, firm, and of a delicious tafte. The black cap is almoft as fmall as the wren; the body is black and yellow, it is white under the belly, and the top of the head is black. Thefe birds keep near the houfes, and are fuch lovers of meat, that the farmers can hardly keep them from it, and therefore catch them like mice in a trap.

In fhort, there are here fuch incredible numbers of fea and land fowl near the rocks on the fea-fhore, that they fometimes obfcure the fight of the heavens for many miles out at fea, fo that one would imagine all the fowl in the univerfe were gathered together in one flock.

Norway is alfo as plentifully fupplied with fifh as any country in the world *.

The Norwegians are generaly tall, well made and lively; yet thofe on the coaft are neither fo tall nor fo robuft as thofe who inhabit the mountains; but are remarkable for being fatter and having rounder faces. The people in general, are brifk, and ingenious; which appears from the peafants not employing any hatters, fhoemakers, taylors, tanners, weavers, carpenters, fmiths, or joiners, for all thefe trades

---

* The learned and pious author mentions two or three aquatic animals, which are of fo extraordinary a nature as to exceed all the bounds of probability. But as he never faw them, and only depends on the credit of thofe who furnifhed him with thefe accounts; we who can have no proofs of their veracity, muft at leaft fufpend our belief; and it feems moft prudent to omit defcribing them till we can have more certain proofs of their exiftence.

are excercifed in every farm-houfe, and they think a boy can never be an ufeful member of fociety, nor a good man, without making himfelf mafter of all thefe arts. Thefe are remarkable for their civility and willingnefs to ferve every one; and a traveller is feldom fuffered to pay for his lodging; for they think it their duty to treat the ftranger as well as it is in their power, and look upon it as an honour done them if he accepts of their civilities. Yet the peafant never gives the upper end of the table to the greateft gueft that ever comes under his roof; for he thinks that place belongs only to himfelf. They keep open houfes for three weeks at Chriftmas, during which their tables are fpread and loaded with the beft provifions they can afford. At Chriftmas-eve their hofpitality extends to the very birds; and, for their ufe, they hang on a pole at the barn door an unthrefhed fheef of corn, which draws thither the fparrows and other fmall birds.

The inhabitants of the trading towns live, with refpect to provifions, much in the fame manner as the Danes; but the peafants keep clofe to the manners of their fore-fathers. Thin oat-cakes are their common bread; but upon particular occafions, as weddings or entertainments, they have rye-bread. If grain be fcarce, which generally happens after a fevere winter; the peafants have recourfe to a difagreeable method of preferving life, by boiling and drying the bark of the fir-tree, mixing it with a little oatmeal, and making it into a kind of bread. Even in times of plenty they eat a little of it, that they make think it lefs difagreeable in a time of fcarcity.

The lakes and rivers furnifh the people with plenty of frefh water fifh, and the mountains with game. For their winter ftock they kill cows, fheep, and goats; part of which they pickle and fmoak, and fome of it they cut in thin flices, fprinkle it with falt, then dry it in the wind, and eat it like hung beef. They are fond of brandy, and of fmoaking and chewing tobacco.

The Norwegians who live in towns have nothing remarkable in their drefs ; but the peafants do not trouble themfelves about fafhions. Thofe called ftrile-farmers have their breeches and ftockings of one piece. They have a wide loofe jacket, made of a coarfe woollen cloth ; as are alfo their waiftcoats, and thofe who would appear fine have the feams covered with cloth of a different colour. The peafants of one parifh are remarkable for wearing black cloaths edged with red ; another for wearing all black ; the drefs of another parifh is white edged with black ; others wear black and yellow ; and thus the inhabitants of almoft every parifh vary in the colour of their clothes. They wear a flapped hat, or a little brown, grey, or black cap made quite round, and the feams ornamented with black ribbons. They have fhoes of a peculiar conftruction without heels, confifting of two pieces ; the upper leather fits clofe to the foot, to which the fole is joined by a great many plaits and folds. When they travel, and in the winter they wear a fort of half boots that reach up to the calf of the leg, and are laced on one fide ; and when they go on the rocks in the fnow they put on fnow fhoes. But as thefe are troublefome when they have a great way to travel, they put on fkaits about as broad as the foot, but fix or eight feet long, and pointed before ; they are covered underneath with feal fkin, fo that the fmooth grain of the hair turns backwards to the heel. With thefe fnow-fkaits they flide about on the fnow as well as they can upon the ice, and fafter than any horfe can gallop.

The peafant never wears a neckcloth, or any thing of that kind, except when he is dreffed ; for his neck and breaft are always open, and he lets the fnow beat into his bofon. On the contrary, he covers his veins, binding a woollen fillet round his wrifts. About their body they wear a broad leather belt, ornamented with convex brafs plates; to this hangs a brafs chain, which holds their large knife, gimblet, and other tackle.

The women at church, and in genteel affembles drefs themfelves in jackets laced clofe, and have leather girdles, with filver ornaments about them. They alfo wear a filver chain three or four times round the neck, and a gilt medal hanging at the end of it. Their handkerchiefs and caps are almoft covered with fmall filver, brafs, and tin-plates, buttons, and large rings, fuch as they wear on their fingers, to which they hang again a parcel of fmall ones, which makes a gingling noife when they move. A maiden-bride has her hair platted, and hung as full as poffible with fuch kind of trinkets, as alfo her clothes: for this purpofe they get all the ornaments they can.

Their houfes are, in general, built of fir and pine-trees, the whole trunks of which are only chopped even to make them lie clofe, and then laid upon one another, and faftened with mortices at the corners. Thefe trunks are left round as they grew, both on the infides and outfides of the houfe, and are frequently boarded over and painted, efpecially in the trading towns, which gives them a genteel appearance.

In the country villages the houfes are built at a diftance from each other, with their fields and grounds about them. The ftore houfe for the provifions is generally at a diftance from the dwelling-houfe, for fear of fire, and placed high upon poles, to keep the provifions dry and preferve them from mice, and all kinds of vermin. The kitchen ftands alfo feparate, as do the barns, hay-loft, cow-houfes, ftables, and the like. A farm has likewife commonly a mill belonging to it, fituated by fome rivulet, befides a fmith's forge; for every farmer as hath been obferved, is his own fmith. Up the country, where timber for building is but of little value, there is many a farm houfe as large as a nobleman's feat; it is frequently two ftories high, and has a railed balcony in the front, and the additional buildings refemble a little village. The common farm-houfes have, however, only the ground floor, and no other window but a fquare hole in the wall, which is left open in fummer ; but in winter or in wet weather is filled up with a wooden frame covered with the inward mem- brane of fome animal, this is very ftrong, and as tranfparent as a bladder. This hole which is as high as it can be placed, alfo anfwers the purpofe of a chimney by ferving to let out the fmoke.

Under the light-hole generally ftands a long thick table, with benehes of the fame wood ; and at the upper end is the high feat which belongs to the mafter only. In towns thefe houfes are covered with tiles ; but in the country the people lay over the boards the fappy bark of birch trees, which will not decay in many years. They cover this again three or four inches thick with turf, on which good grafs always grows.

The peafants are bufied in cutting wood, felling and floating of timber, burning charcoal and ex- tracting of tar. Great numbers are employed in the mines, and at the furnaces and ftamping mills ; and alfo in navigation and fifhing, befides hunting, and fhooting ; for every body is at liberty to purfue the game, efpecially in the mountains, and on the heaths and commons, where every peafant may make ufe of what arms he pleafes.

It has been already obferved, that the catching of birds affords fome of the inhabitants a very good maintenance : but it is impoffible to give a juft idea of the fatigue and danger with which the people fearch for the birds in the high and fteep rocks, many of which are above two hundred fathoms per- pendicular. Thefe people who are called birdmen have two methods of catching them : they either climb up thefe perpendicular rocks, or are let down from the top by a ftrong and thick rope. When they climb up they have a large pole of eleven or twelve ells in length with an iron hook at the end. They who are underneath in a boat, or ftand on a cliff, faften this hook to the waiftband of the man's

breeches who climbs, by which means they help
him up to the higheft projection he can reach, and
fix his feet upon. They then help up another
to the fame place ; and when they are both up, give
each his bird pole, and a long rope which they tie
at each end round their waifts. The one then climbs
up as high as he can, and where it is difficult, the
other by putting his pole under his breech, pufhes
him up, till he gets to a good ftanding place : the
uppermoft of the two then helps the other up to
him with the rope ; and thus they proceed till they
get to the part where the birds build, and there
they fearch for them. As they have many dangerous
places yet to climb, one always feeks a convenient
place to ftand fure, and be able to hold himfelf faft,
while the other is climbing about. If the latter
fhould happen to flip, he is held up by the other.
who ftands firm ; and when he has got fafe by thofe
dangerous places, he fixes himfelf in the fame manner, that he may affift the other to come fafe to
him ; and then they clamber about after birds where
they pleafe. But accidents fometimes happen ; for
if the one does not ftand firm, or is not ftrong
enough to fupport the other when he flips, they
both fall and are killed ; and thus fome perifh.every
year.

When they thus reach the places that are feldom
vifited, they find the birds fo tame that they may
take them with their hands ; for they are loth to
leave their young, but where they are wild, they
either throw a net over them in the rock, or en-
tangle thofe that are flying with a net fixed to the
end of their poles. · Thus they catch vaft numbers
of fowls, and the boat keeping underneath them,
they throw the dead birds into it, and foon fill the
veffel. When the weather is tolerably good, and
there is a great deal of game, the birdmen will
continue eight days together on the rocks ; for there
are here and there holes in which they can fecurely
take their repofe ; they draw up provifions with

lines, and boats are kept coming and going to take away the game.

On the other hand, many rocks being fo fleep and dangerous that they cannot poffibly climb up them, they are then let down from above ; when they have a ftrong rope eighty or a hundred fathoms long, and about three inches in thicknefs. One end of it the birdman faftens about his waift, and then drawing it between his legs fo that he can fit on it, he is let down with his bird-pole in his hand, by fix men at the top, who let the rope fink by degrees, but lay a piece of timber on the edge of a rock, for it to flide on, to prevent its being torn to pieces by the fharp end of the ftones. Another line is faftened round the man's waift, which he pulls to give figns when he would have them pull him up, let him lower, or keep him where he is. He is in great danger of the ftones loofening by the rope, and falling upon him ; he therefore wears a thick furred cap well lined, which fecures him from the blows he may receive from fmall ftones ; but if large ones fall he is in the greateft hazard of lofing his life. Thus do thefe poor men often expofe themfelves to the moft imminent danger, merely to get a fubfiftence for their families. There are fome indeed who fay there is no great hazard in it, after they are accuftomed to it ; but at firft the rope turns round with them, till their heads are giddy, and they can do nothing to fave themfelves. Thofe who have learnt the art make a play of it ; they put their feet againft the rock, throw themfelves feveral fathoms out, and pufh themfelves into what place they pleafe. They even keep themfelves out on the line in the air, and catch with their poles numbers of birds flying out and into their holes. The greateft art is required in throwing themfelves out, fo as to fwing under the projection of a rock where the birds gather together ; here they fix their feet, loofen themfelves from the rope, which they faften to a ftone to prevent its fwinging out of their reach, and then the man climbs about and catches the birds either with his hands, or his pole, and when he has killed as many as he thinks proper, he ties them together, faftens them to the fmall line, and by a pull gives a fign for thofe above to draw them up. In this manner he works all day, and when he wants to go up, he gives a fign to be drawn up, or elfe works himfelf up with his belt full of birds.

When there are not people enough to hold the rope, the birdman fixes a poft in the ground, faftens his rope to it, and flides down without any help, to work as before. There are in fome places fteep cliffs of a prodigious fize, lying under the land, and yet more than 100 fathoms above the water, which are likewife very difficult to be got at. Down thefe cliffs they help one another in the above manner, and taking a ftrong rope with them, faften it here and there in the cliff, where they can, and leave it all the fummer: upon this they will run up and down, and take the birds at pleafure. It is impoffible to defcribe how frightful and dangerous this bird-catching appears to the beholders, from the vaft height, and exceffive fteepnefs of the rocks, many of which hang over the fea: it feems impoffible for men to enter the holes under thefe projections, or to walk 200 yards high on crags of rocks where they can but juft fix their toes.

The birds being brought home, they eat part of them frefh, and part is hung up to dry for the winter feafon. Thefe birds afford the inhabitants a very good maintenance, partly from their feathers, and down, which are gathered and fent to foreign parts, and partly from their flefh and eggs. Some forts of the latter are as good as hen eggs, and though of various colours and fizes are fent to market.

ÉND OF VOLUME VI.

PRINTED BY JOHN THOMPSON.

CONTENTS OF VOLUME VI.

www.ingramcontent.com/pod-product-compliance
Lightning Source LLC
Chambersburg PA
CBHW052344110726
47901CB00005B/1348